The White Gazelle

STONES
OF THE KINGDOM

Falcon Pass
Moonlady Falls
The Island of Labyrinths
The White Gazelle

The White Gazelle

Stones of the Kingdom: Book Four

M. C. Foster

A Leaf It To Me Book

ISBN 978-0-9864581-4-9

© M. C. Foster 2022

Published by Leaf It To Me Publishing

Cover design by Leaf It To Me.

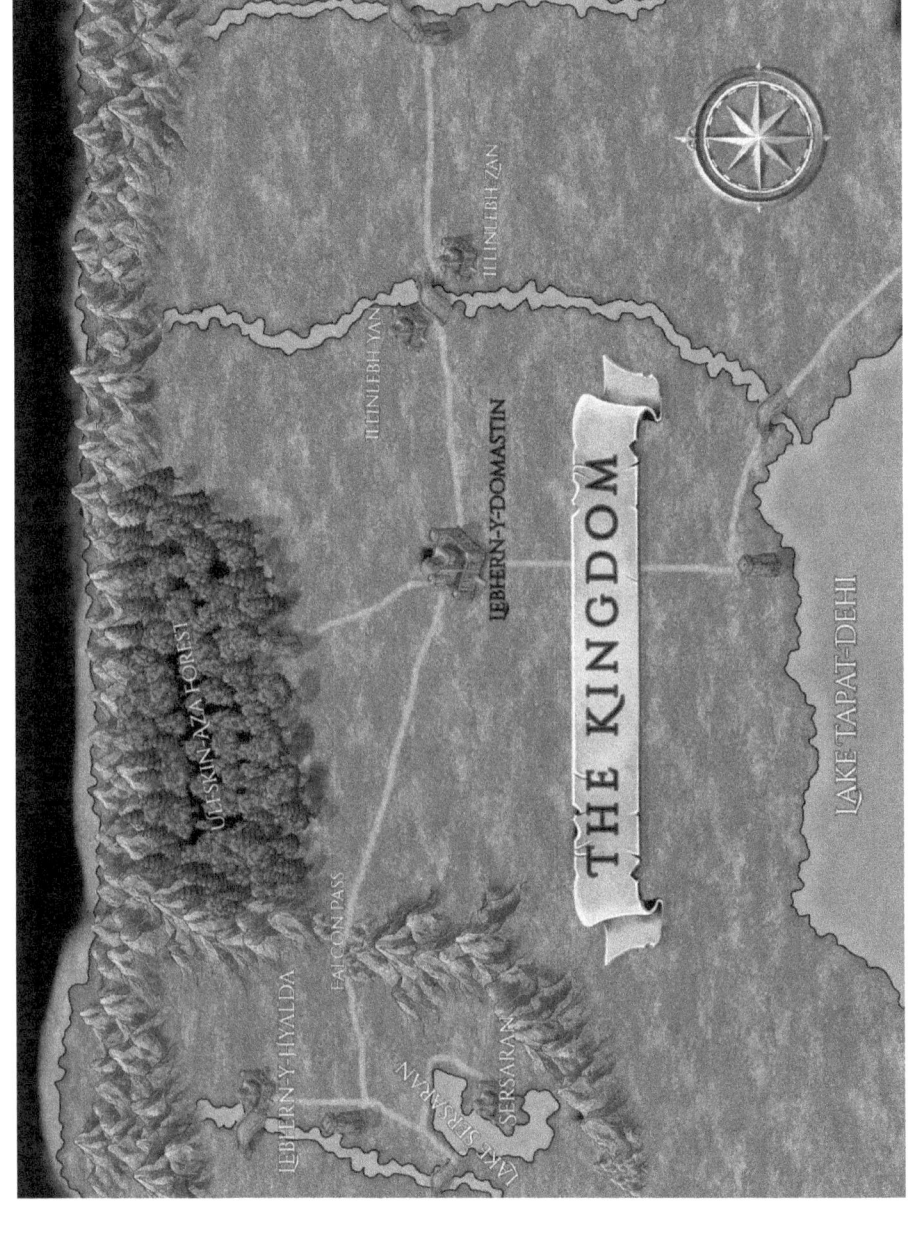

CHAPTER ONE

Azariel Stormwolf straightened and raised her newly sharpened sword, letting the morning sunlight play off the clean blade. Her back and shoulders ached from continual stooping and the roof of her mouth felt dry. A gust of warm northwest wind swirled across the dusty barracks courtyard and swept her long black hair across her face and into her eyes. She brushed her hair back and peered down the length of her sword before feeling along the hard lines of the edge with her thumb. *It needs to be a little sharper at the tip*, she thought. She laid the sword across her knees and continued sharpening it, the whetstone whizzing across the steel. The sunshine beat down on her bent head and the reflected sunlight dazzled her. She tested the point once more, closing her eyes as she felt it. *There. Sharp enough to deal with anything.*

She jumped up off the bench outside the cadets' dormitories and brandished her sword, making gold and white lightnings. She slashed at an invisible opponent, the blade singing through the air. She spun so the sunlight fell from behind and retreated a few paces towards the centre of the barracks yard, watching the play of light and shadow on the steel. "There," she said to the man still sitting on the bench. "That's my sword ready. Shall I do yours, Farren?"

He looked up from the arrow in his hand and his brown eyes met her gaze. A gust of wind ruffled his short red hair and a smile crossed his angular face. "Please do," he said. "I'll be some time getting my arrows checked and ready for this hunt of ours. I only wish the Chief Archer wasn't so picky about keeping his precious sighting tool in the cadets' dorms. The officers' mess would make more sense." He slotted the arrow into the clips in the sighting tool and squinted down its length with one eye, then the other. His forehead creased into a frown and he checked the arrow a second time. "This arrow's badly fletched, anyway." He lowered it, then reached for his sword and handed it to her.

She sat beside him and arched her back, the nagging ache in her right shoulder easing slightly. "Back to the grinding again," she said, taking his sword. The cutting edges of the blade had become slightly rounded here and there, and a deep notch was gouged a handspan from the hilt. She tested the rest of the edges with her thumb. "Hopefully our swords won't be getting too much use this time."

"With a hunting trip? I shouldn't think so." He unclipped the arrow from the sighting tool and neatly slashed the red and black fletchings off with his dagger. "Looking forward to it?"

She smiled. "Out of the city, a good hunt, getting these Stones back, going with you... of course I am." She picked up her whetstone from where she had dropped it on the bench. "I had better start on this."

Beginning near the hilt, she worked the whetstone up and along the blade: five circling rasps with the stone, then feeling the fine razor-edge. A shower of powdered steel fell onto the heavy black cotton of her summer uniform trousers before being whisked away by the breeze. A few scraps of red-dyed feathers blew across from her left as the wind eddied, and she glanced over at Farren as he trimmed and fixed a new cock feather onto an arrow. Somewhere out beyond the barracks walls, a dog barked. She settled back into the rhythm of rasping and testing, and let her thoughts fly free, ignoring the ache in her neck.

"What did you say?" Farren's voice cut across her thoughts.

She looked up. "Was I talking to myself again?"

"Yes. I only caught a word or two, and I thought you were talking to me." He smiled and winked at her. "You said something about hunting."

She laughed and brushed her hair to one side of her face as the wind pulled at it. She shrugged the tension out of her shoulders and lowered his sword. "I was remembering that Vision I was sent." The scene played across her mind's eye again: the dainty white gazelle in the hill country and a sorceress that petted it as she hung a silver-wrapped black gem between its horns. "I hope we're right in thinking that it's literal and not symbolic."

"Well, I never though the sorcerers would chain the Stone of Wind to a gazelle's head. But that's what you said you saw." He clipped the newly fletched arrow into the sighting tool again.

"It didn't have the feel of a symbolic Vision. Besides, you know the Wayasti and their sacred deer. I suppose they view gazelles as being the same. I only hope I understood it clearly when I saw the sorceress die." She reached for his left hand and squeezed it. The smooth surface of his onyx ring had been warmed by the sunshine. "But I'm glad to be off hunting for a change – and I know you are."

He chuckled. "You know me, Stormwolf, and I know you." He stretched his arms and flexed his wrists. "I'm glad that we won't – or shouldn't – have Wayasti gods or sorcerers to face this time – for once."

She smiled grimly. "I hope we're right about that one. But that's why I'm sharpening your sword."

The sound of knocking drifted across the length of the barracks courtyard from the gate. She raised her head, shielding her eyes from the sun. The shrill "Who goes there?" of the sentry rang out and she strained them to catch the words of the reply. She leaned against the sun-warmed wall behind her, watching the sentry creak the large wooden gate open. A horseman trotted through and the gate thudded closed behind him".

The rider crossed the courtyard, the hooves of his dun stallion sending thick clouds of yellow-grey dust billowing into the air. Even over the length of the courtyard, Azariel heard the hard breathing of the horse and saw his nostrils flaring wide with effort. The dun's golden coat was dark with sweat and his muscular withers were flecked with white lather. *That's a horse who's had a hard run in the heat this morning.* She glanced at the rider: a red-haired man in a travel-stained green tunic and trousers. *That's strange; he's a civilian. Wonder what he wants.*

The rider reined in his horse by the doorway halfway along the long grey stone slab of a building that made one side of the courtyard. He dismounted, tied the horse up and hurried through into the depths of the building.

"Wonder why he's in such a hurry," Farren said. "Look at that horse, all over lather and snorting like a blacksmith's bellows. He'd better have some good reason for riding so hard. It's a hot day, too, for early summer." He stood up and clipped his arrows back into the quiver at his belt. "Poor horse. That rider's lucky he hasn't killed it. I'm going to get that stallion a drink. Come on, Stormwolf."

She rose to her feet and handed him his half-sharpened sword. He took and sheathed it before reaching towards her. She twined her fingers through his as they walked through the jumble of buildings to the stables, her long stride easily matching his. The strong wind pushed at her back and her cloak flicked and whirled around her calves.

"I'd like to know what that rider was thinking, leaving a horse that tired and sweaty in this heat," he said as they stepped into the cool shadow of a whitewashed building.

"Probably that his errand was urgent," she replied.

He paused as a red-cloaked soldier led a grey horse past them out of the wide stable doors. "I certainly hope so." Farren opened the door of the barracks stables and she followed him into the long lines of stalls filled with the earthy, tangy smells of straw, leather and horses. "I wish we were coming in here to take Storm and Princess out riding. Tomorrow, though…"

He rummaged around in a locker at one end of the stable and brought out a tin bucket. "A good hunting trip in the hills. I can't wait to be off!"

He straightened up and strolled back past the rows of horses, his red hair ruffled by the wind and a twinkle of enthusiasm in his brown eyes. The diamond in the centre of the betrothal earring through his left ear glittered as a shaft of sunlight caught it. She smiled as she ran her gaze over the breadth of his shoulders, raising one hand to touch her matching earring. *You are a good-looking man, Farren Blackarrow. I'm certainly fortunate to be the one you're going to marry.* "Neither can I, especially after these last few months," she said aloud.

"You never do like sitting around doing nothing, do you? If you can call all those hours put in on our knees in the chapel waiting for instructions sitting around doing nothing." He tweaked a lock of her hair. "Shame on you, arch *minyaster*."

She stepped out of the stables into the strong sunlight and blinked. "You know what I mean," she said, jostling him with one shoulder. A rumble of iron wheels mixed with a bullock's bellow drifted in from beyond the buildings. "I want to get out of the city and back onto the plains. It must be at least two months since I've stood on top of the Watchtower of the West with the clean wind in my face and no noise except the birds and sheep."

"And plenty of wretched Yellow Claws trying to cross the river into Wayast and back or trying to burn the Watchtower down. I haven't been missing those." He stopped by the pump near the stable door and set the bucket under the spout.

She glanced westwards and shook her head. "At least they're the worst we'll have to put up with this time, and only if their sorcerers manage to find out what we're up to. But we can deal with them or avoid them if we're cunning enough. Hurry up and get that horse a drink so we finish getting ready for tomorrow. You're getting slow in the heat."

The water surged from the pump to the bucket, a current of liquid light. The sinews stood out in his arm as he smoothly worked the handle. His eyes were fixed on the stream of water and she grinned. Waiting for the moment when he bent his head as he clanked the handle down, she grabbed the half-filled bucket and quickly emptied it over him.

He spluttered and shook the water from his hair, stirring a laugh out of her. He lunged towards her, a grin lighting up his angular face. "You'll see how slow in the heat I'm getting. I'm going to get you back."

"You'll have to catch me, Farren!" she taunted. She leaped away, but a firm grip on her cloak pulled her up short. She struggled, stomach aching with laughter, as she was hauled backwards. He locked onto her arm and twisted it behind her back. She dropped to her knees, striving to break his hold. Then his other hand clamped around her neck and forced her around and down. The smell of wet earth drifted up from the dirt beneath her. The pump clanked and a bitingly cold cascade gushed over her head, plastering her hair across her face. An icy trickle of water worked its way beneath the high neck of her chainmail tunic and slid down her spine. She writhed, trying to break free of his iron grip on her. He doused her a second time and she gasped, water worming painfully up her nose and into her mouth. She coughed it out and his grip relaxed. His chuckle roused her. *Right, Farren Blackarrow, my beloved, you're for it now.*

She straightened up with a jerk and grabbed the bucket. Swiftly, she yanked the pump down once and caught the water. He danced aside as she hurled it at him, then surged towards her.

His fingers met hers on the edge of the bucket as he tugged and twisted at the rim. The wet metal slipped out of her hands and she leaped backwards two paces as he refilled the bucket. The silvery-white sheet of water flew towards her and she nimbly dodged to one side before darting towards him again. "You've got the bucket," she panted, "but you haven't got this!" She whipped her head around, lashing him across the face with her wet hair.

"Want another bath?" he asked, clutching at her arm and shoulder, and pulling her close. "Because, my sweetheart, you're going to have one."

"Oh really?" She pressed closer to him and embraced him tightly, deliberately rubbing her wet hair against his cheek. The delicate smell of lavender soap rose from his skin.

"Minx." He caught her face in his hands and tilted her chin up so he could kiss her firmly on the mouth. The water on his lips had mixed with his sweat and tasted salty.

She pulled back from him. A groom walked out from the stables, wheeling a barrow full of dirty straw and horse dung, and smiled at them.

"You really are spoiling for some action, aren't you?" he chuckled. He replaced the bucket beneath the pump and refilled it. "Don't you dare empty that bucket again! Just for that, you can carry it back there to that poor tired horse – without throwing it over me again."

He handed the brimming bucket up to her, the muscles and tendons on his left arm standing out with the strain. She glanced at his face, poised on the balls of her feet, expecting him to throw the water over her. His hand shook and she stepped forward to take the load from him. Leaning to one side to counterbalance the heavy bucket, she followed him back through the maze of buildings to the long grey office building where the dun stallion still stood bridled and saddled.

The horse snorted at them as they approached. She set the bucket down beside his dusty hooves and he eagerly plunged his muzzle in. He gulped at the water, rippling it down his gullet. The waterline fell steadily lower and lower.

Farren ran his hand along the horse's dark brown mane, inhaling the sharp smell of its sweat. "I'd like to take your tack off, boy," he murmured to the stallion, "but I don't know if your owner would like me interfering with you." The horse raised its head and nuzzled at his face with its velvety muzzle, snuffling hot breath over him. He patted its smooth, sweat-damp neck and wiped some of the lather off its golden withers. "I wonder why a civilian would be riding here in such a hurry."

"You never do like seeing a horse over-driven, do you?" she said. "By the looks of the dun horse, I'd say he's a Yellow Claw that's turned his coat and joined us. That would certainly explain his urgency."

"Possibly." He scratched the horse behind the ears, feeling a hot, slick band under the leather crown piece. "But you can't always tell a Claw by the colour of the horse. You rode a piebald horse once, remember." He turned to look at her as she leaned against the wall where the horse was tethered to an iron ring. Beads of water dripped from her long dark hair, glittering in the sunlight like the hundreds chainmail links that clung snugly to her long slender body. "And my father has duns as well as other colours on his stud. It always breeds true from the stallions, so it's common enough. Not like palomino, the sorcerers' other favourite."

"Or red hair in humans." She shook her hair back from where it was plastered across her face and winked at him, dark blue eyes sparkling. "And that's a very attractive colour."

He ran his hands through the stallion's dark wiry mane. "I might as well take his saddle off. If I leave it beside him, the rider won't mind too much. He needs to cool off." He fumbled beneath the saddle-skirts and unbuckled the girth strap. He tugged the heavy saddle off the stallion's back, a patch of dark roughened hair showing where it had been. *A nice-looking stallion. Wonder where he's from.* He glanced at the golden hair of the stallion's neck, searching for the brand. It lay beneath the mane, a white curve flanked by two dots. "Look at that," he said, pointing to it.

"It looks like the one on Princess's neck," she said.

"It's the same; it's my father's brand." He combed his fingers through the stallion's mane again. "This is probably one of old Tussock's colts. I didn't know my father was selling horses to civilians as well as keeping the army in horses." He rubbed along the line of the brand. "I probably haven't met you, boy, unless it was on leave," he said to the horse. "But I've ridden your father a couple of times." A drop of filthy sweat beaded on his hand and he wiped it clean on his trouser leg. *Has he finished drinking? I'll have to take the bucket back before we get back to work.* "Tussock must be getting on for eighteen years now."

The door slammed behind him and he swung around as a cadet burst out of the building and nearly crashed into him. "Steady on, youngster," he said, helping the boy regain his balance.

"Thanks," the cadet said and began to run off. Before he had taken a few paces, he turned back and said, panting, "Aren't you Farren Blackarrow?"

"I am. Are you looking for me?"

"Yes. You're to go to Captain Karissa's office straight away. Message come for you. You and... and... Karissa didn't say her name. She just said 'that woman'. Would that be you, madam?"

"That is how Karissa would refer to me," Azariel replied grimly.

He shifted the saddle further away from the stallion and brushed the rest of the dust and grime of the horse off his hands. Azariel stood with her fists clenched at her side and one tooth raking the side of her bottom lip. *And I don't blame her for being upset after what she told me about that Zenifi-hating bully.* "Captain Karissa," he said softly. "What on earth does your old cadet-trainer want you for?"

"Nothing good," she answered in a voice of steel. "I hope it's something to do with the stallion's rider. Last time I met her, I felt like I was a cadet with her riding whip slashing at me again." She bared her teeth and a shudder made the sunlight dance on the chainmail. "But she never broke me then; I won't let her break me now." She spun on her heel, making her black cloak swirl like wind-whipped cloud around her and stalked towards the door.

He caught up with her and held her back with an arm around her shoulder. "She won't dare lay a hand on you now, arch *minyaster*," he said in a low voice by her ear. The sharp scent of rosemary clung to her hair. His other arm slid under her cloak and around her waist, gliding over the smooth leather of her belt. She turned to him, one hand resting on his shoulder, and he pressed a kiss onto her white forehead then another on her mouth. His arms tightened around her. *And anyone who tries to harm my lady will have me to deal with.*

She pressed close to him and laid her head on the folds of his red cloak at the shoulder. Gently, he nuzzled at her damp hair as their armour grated together. "Come on, sweetheart," he said softly. "Let's go and face the old dragon quickly or she will have something to complain about, apart from the two of us being soaked."

He cupped her face in his hands and kissed her one more time before threading his fingers through hers and entering the office block. Their boots rang on the stone floor as they paced along the length of the dark corridor. Azariel rapped briskly on the second door from the end on the right. A woman's voice barked, "Who's that?"

"Azariel Stormwolf and Farren Blackarrow."

"Enter."

Azariel shook her hair and cloak back from her shoulders and marched before him into the small office. They both drew their swords and dropped to one knee in the official salute to the middle-aged woman behind the desk in the centre of the room. A large cupboard stood along one wall and a pair of legs wearing stained green trousers stuck out from the far end with the rest of the body hidden. *So we're going to find out about that civilian after all.*

Captain Karissa gestured for them to rise with a well-manicured hand. Her gaze locked with Azariel's for a few heartbeats in a sharp, frowning stare. The older woman's lips twitched at the corners, then her blue eyes flicked up and down over him. "What have you been doing, Lieutenant?" she asked him crisply. "You look as though you've been trying to give a cat a bath. That's probably exactly what you've been doing by the looks of that girl beside you, and I don't blame you for trying. I hope you give the dirty Zenifi slut the hiding she deserves."

He looked down at his nails uneasily, an ember of irritation beginning to heat and glow inside his chest and stomach. Unbidden, his fingers curled into fists but he forced them to relax. *Keep your temper; keep your temper, Blackarrow. It's only words, and words can't hurt her or you.*

"I apologise for our appearance, Captain," Azariel said, sharply straightening her *minyaster's* armbands and rings. "But, as you know, we have been hastily sent for."

"Well, Lieutenant?" Karissa flicked back her sleek brown hair. "What have you to say for yourself?"

Azariel just apologised for both of us, you cat. "Sorry we're both drenched," he said dully. "You sent for us in a hurry, after all."

"You're excused, Lieutenant," Karissa said. "A message has come for you." She turned towards the end of the cupboard where the civilian waited. "Well, boy, give your message."

A young man stood up and emerged from behind the cupboard, running one hand through his dark red hair. A wide grin crossed his face and his green eyes met Farren's. "Hello, brother," he said.

Farren's jaw dropped and his eyes snapped open. "Yvain!" He reached for his brother's hand and squeezed it firmly. "What are you doing here?"

Yvain's mouth twisted. "There's news from home. And I'm afraid it's bad."

CHAPTER TWO

A jolt of fear kicked Farren in the pit of his stomach. He reached for Azariel's hand and gripped it. "Has... has somebody died?"

"No," said Yvain. "Fortunately not. Bur we've been raided by those damned Yellow Claws. Being the best cavalry stud in the Kingdom does carry some risks."

"What happened?" In his mind's eye, he pictured his childhood home in flames, the people butchered or wounded and the horses maimed. *No! Not that.*

"Our five best stallions were carried off from the herd one night: Tussock, Rainshadow, Firebrand, Phoenix and Warlord. Tina was supposed to be keeping watch, but somehow they slipped past her. And by the time the rest of us at the house knew what was going on, it was too late. They had gone by the time Dad, the grooms, Firalina and me could get our weapons and go."

"And Tina?" He tried to swallow a lump in his throat. *If they've killed her...* "Where was she in all this?"

"We don't know. We haven't seen her, but we think she was taken at the same time as the stallions. I think the others are looking for her, but I rode out to get you as soon as I could."

"What about Anna? When will she get the news?"

"As soon as Firalina can ride to her. She set out this morning when I did." Yvain paced towards the window. "I've made good time, haven't I? Sultan's a good horse."

"Well then, Lieutenant," said Karissa, standing up and leaning her perfect fingertips on the table top. "Your course of action is clear. You must go and get those stallions and your sister back. We cannot have one of our major suppliers of horses harassed in this manner." She paused and drew a deep breath, sliding one hand through her glossy hair. Her gaze flicked away from him and briefly over Azariel. "Take someone with you that you can trust. I wouldn't take that Zenifi bitch. The Claws are mostly Zenifi and blood is thicker than water."

The ember stirred and glowed in his chest again and his hands balled into fists. *Keep your temper and your fists to yourself,* he told himself. *She's a woman, for one thing; for another, she outranks you.* "Are you saying that I can't trust my future wife?" he said through gritted teeth.

"The slut's bewitched you, hasn't she? I knew her long before you did, Lieutenant. You can't trust a werewolf."

"You've at least admitted I've got my shapeshifting Gift, Karissa." Azariel stepped a pace backwards from the desk. "If you won't accept my *minyaster's* oaths of loyalty, then believe this." She drew her sword from the sheath and laid the flat of the blade across her left palm. "I'll give you Oath on Edge that I'll hunt down those Claws." She raised the blade above her head, the fingers of her left hand beginning to curl around it.

"Take care, sweetheart," he said, stepping towards her. "It's hardly half an hour since you sharpened that." He reached for her right elbow, then stopped himself, seeing her glaring at Karissa as if she could set the air on fire, her teeth bared. *I'd better not try to stop her. Nothing can stop her, anyway, when she's in a stubborn mood like this.*

Azariel's lips hardened to a tight line. "I swear, Oath on Edge, that I am a true woman of the Kingdom. I swear that I will take a warband and hunt down the Yellow Claws that stole the horses and kidnapped my... my future sister-in-law or die trying. I and my sword will not rest until the deed is done. If I fail, may this edge I bear be turned against me. This is my Oath on Edge." With a swift slash, she sliced the muscle at the base of her thumb, then lowered the sword and let a small stream of blood trickle down the blade. "Blood Oath on Edge that none may break."

Karissa's tongue ran around the inside of her lips. "Clean your sword, Zenifi," she snapped after a few heartbeats of silence. "Don't you ever learn anything?" Breath hissed rapidly in and out of her as Azariel wiped the blade of her sword on the hem of her cloak and sheathed it. "Now that that nonsense is out of the way, Lieutenant, we can get back to business. You will need a small unit of soldiers – about ten. You, of course, have your own abilities to help you against the Claws. All you need now is enough authority to commandeer the troops you need. So if you will excuse me a moment, I will give you the necessary documentation." She reached down for a drawer in the desk.

"There is no need for that, Captain," Azariel said, scarcely above a whisper but each word hard and clear as diamond. "I don't need it. I am Azariel Stormwolf, arch *minyaster*, and as arch *minyaster*, I outrank you by three degrees, Captain." She spat the title out. "I don't need your authorisation." She slowly bent across the desk and stretched out her left hand, dripping blood onto the table. All warmth had drained from her cheeks and lips, leaving her skin icy and her eyes had narrowed to furious slits. Karissa shrank back. "I could commandeer you, if I could bear more than an hour in your company. And if you disobeyed, it would be my hand that brought the lash across your back."

Azariel broke off and straightened up, clamping her right hand across her left and stanching the blood. "I've said enough. We won't waste any more of our time or yours." She spun on her heel and let her cloak swirl around her in a dark flurry. "Come on Farren, let's go. You too, Yvain." She left the room, leaving the door wide open behind her.

Farren followed her out into the corridor. She was waiting five paces down, pressing hard on her left hand with her eyes closed and her head tilted back. "What did you go and cut yourself for?" he asked. "Oath on Edge is binding enough, isn't it?"

She looked at him, eyes brilliant. A thin line of moisture beaded her lower lashes. "That woman brings out all the worst in me. God Incarnate forgive me, I wanted to hurt her instead of myself." Her lips bit together and she blinked. "I needed to show her I'm not coward or traitor."

Yvain pulled the door closed behind himself. "Oooh my! That was good! I thought Tina and Firalina were bad enough getting catty at each other, but they're nothing to those two. Pity that spat didn't last longer. That Captain woman's an old battle-axe for all her smart turn-out. And as for Azariel – you're a brave man taking her on, big brother."

Azariel glanced at him, then at Yvain and he felt a spasm of laughter rising. Her eyes flashed, one tiny tear pooling in the inner corner of one eye in spite of the ferocity frozen on her face. Another bead of moisture trickled down the side of her face from her hair. The laughter burst from him. "Giving a cat a bath! I'll remember that one next time you throw buckets of water over me, Stormwolf."

A smile broke over her face and she chuckled as well. "I felt more like a puppy under that pump." She wiped the single tear from the corner of her eye, leaving a smear of blood across her cheeks. She drew a deep breath and stepped away from the wall. "And what a time and place to pull rank for the first time." Her tone had grown calmer. "Thanks, Yvain, for making light of it. I wish you could have done it sooner. Never mind. Oath or no oath, we're wasting time." She slipped her right arm through Farren's left. "The gazelle will have to wait. At least we're packed and ready to go. We only need to find some extra sword-hands and saddle up. We won't need many."

He turned his head at Yvain as they walked down the corridor. "Will your horse be ready to ride back, the poor thing? What do you mean by leaving him out in the hot sun like that?" He edged to one side as his brother caught up. "Come on, little brother. We'll show you the stables where you can put him for a rest."

"Little from you is a bit much," chuckled Yvain, digging a finger into the small of his back. "At six foot two inches, I've got three inches' advantage on you, unless you've grown since you last were on leave. But I doubt that, unless it's sideways."

Releasing Azariel's arm, Farren spun around and cuffed playfully at his brother's head as they stepped out into the courtyard. Yvain ducked beyond his reach, then lunged at him. For a few seconds, the brothers grappled, then Farren twisted Yvain's leg from under him and toppled him to the ground. He knelt astride his brother's chest, pushing down on his shoulders. The green cotton of Yvain's tunic felt damp and he stank of old sweat. "Looks like I still win," Farren said. He stood up, hauling Yvain to his feet.

Yvain brushed the dust off his back and turned to his horse. "Someone's taken his saddle off. Who did that, eh, Sultan?"

"I did," Farren answered. He fidgeted with the onyx and diamond betrothal earring through his left ear. "You really must have been in a hurry, or have you forgotten everything you were taught already? It's a wonder Mother and Dad let you out of the house without a nanny." He stooped and picked up the empty tin bucket. "This way to the stables. I'll get your horse – Sultan – something more to drink as well as getting our horses ready."

"I'll go and fetch some soldiers," Azariel said. "My gear's in my room at the foot of the bed in saddlebags." She leaned towards him and pressed a kiss onto his cheek. "I'll tell Kiihaon, too. She needs to know and she might want to come, too." She turned and walked away, still holding her left hand with her right.

He watched her leave, then led Yvain across the barracks courtyard into the maze of buildings. "That's our headquarters," he said, pointing to a whitewashed two-storey building with a slender tower jutting up from it like a unicorn's horn. "Remember where it is, because we'll be in and out of there getting all the gear we've packed. We'll eat our midday meal there, too, as soon as Azariel returns from raising a warband."

He dropped the bucket by the pump, smiling as he saw the dark patches of spilled water across the dust. His black cotton trousers still felt clammy and cool when the wind brushed them. He opened the latch of the stable door and led the way in, breathing in the dusty stable-smell. He turned down one of the long rows of looseboxes and pursed his lips in a shrill whistle. A neigh answered from halfway down the row, and a chestnut mare butted her head through the upper half of the stall door.

"Princess!" he called. He ran down the line of stalls and she nickered to him in greeting. A black gelding pushed in beside her and the two horses nudged and nuzzled at him with warm velvety noses. He scratched the chestnut mare's ears and felt the invisible cords of his animal taming Gift that bound the mare to him tug at his heartstrings. "That's my lady," he crooned. "Are you ready to be off and away again?"

He looked over his shoulder at Yvain, who stood holding Sultan's bridle in the centre of the row. "These are our horses. You might remember Princess. I chose her from home about seven years ago. One of Firebrand's fillies. And this," he said as he pressed his cheek onto the whiskery muzzle of the black gelding and patted his thick glossy neck, "is Azariel's Storm. He's gelded, although you wouldn't tell that from looking just at his neck. You needn't be too worried about him and Sultan fighting." He opened the loosebox and slipped in.

The horses jostled him as he walked to the hooks where their bridles hung. Princess nibbled at the hood of his cloak. He turned and reached for her. "Come on, my lady." The fine-boned chestnut mare raised her head and he slipped the snaffle bit between her teeth while guiding the bridle along her face and over her silky ears. She ground and toyed with the bit as he fastened the buckles under her chin and cheeks. The white coronet on her left foreleg was stained green with dung. *And I gave her a good grooming this morning. She can't help it, but it's a pity Dad won't see her at her best.* "There you go," he said aloud, patting her withers.

He turned to Storm and slid the bridle over him. The black gelding tossed his head as he buckled the straps up. "Steady, Storm," he murmured. "I won't take long." He took the reins of the two horses and led them out of the stall to the tack shed at the end of the stable. "Right. Come and help me saddle them up and stick the saddlebags on."

***

Azariel marched away from the office block towards the dormitories. The warm wind wafted a tang of frying onions towards her, making her stomach clench hungrily. The fleshy pad at the base of her left thumb stung and throbbed. *I should be able to dig up some unposted soldiers over here,* she thought. *But we won't need ten. Five – no, eight – will be enough with two* minyasti *and Kiihaon, too.* She rounded a corner and made her way to the door of the women's rooms. *I'll start here. Hopefully, I'll find somebody I know.* The strong floral scents of perfumes and soaps met her as she walked in, drowning all other smells. She slowed her pace to her normal long, smooth stride along the hallway.

A voice drifted down from the other end of the building and a plumpish brunette strolled out of one of the many doors. "Shadira!" called Azariel. "You're a long way from the Watchtower."

"So are you, Azariel. How's things?" Shadira walked towards her and shook her hand. "You look like you're in a hurry. And what's happened to you? You've got blood everywhere."

"My hand – I'll tell you later. I'm looking for some unposted soldiers – urgently." Azariel shook her hair back from her face and twisted the opal ring on her right hand. "There's been a Yellow Claw raid on Farren's parents' stud and his sister Tina has been kidnapped. We've got to be off this afternoon."

"Hmmm. That's no good." Shadira leaned against the wall and twirled one of her curls around her finger. "Why do you need a warband, anyway?" she said after a pause. "I thought you and Farren could deal with them by yourselves."

"I swore it to Captain Karissa."

Shadira threw back her head and laughed, making her curls dance. "You promised Karissa something?"

"The sleek bitch kept sneering at me," Azariel said softly. Her chest felt tight and her heart began to pump harder. "I swore Blood Oath on Edge to shut her up. It didn't work – I had to pull rank."

"And that's what happened to your hand. Well, say no more. I don't blame you – I know Karissa!" She shuddered. "But let's see... I'm free and so are most of the crew from the Watchtower. Morgan's not – he won't leave his precious window boxes until summer's over – but everyone else is. Let's go and get Kayti and then we'll go and dig up the blokes." Shadira's elbow dug into Azariel's ribs and she winked. "If you want to do Kayti a good turn, then get the fellow from Sersaran called Kenyon along. She's sweet on him."

"Good. I'll need four more. I don't suppose there's anyone you've got a fancy for that I can ask?"

"Well, actually... no, I'm just teasing. Not that I'd mind you bringing along some new fellows." Shadira elbowed Azariel again. "Find me some new talent. I'll come and tell you if they're good-looking enough. We'll see what Kenyon's friends are like."

"I need you to point out Kenyon for me anyway, as I wouldn't know him if I ran into him."

"Let's not wait around then."

Azariel walked in step with the other woman out of the women's dormitory to the men's quarters. Outside the open door, about a dozen soldiers, men and women, were kicking a leather ball around in a circle. "Looks promising," said Shadira. "I like the look of the Zenifi fellow in between the two blonds."

The ball flew just out of reach of one of the soldiers and rolled beside Azariel. She trapped it with her foot, then picked it up. "Please, madam, can we have our ball back?" said one of the men in a mock-childish voice."

Azariel tossed the ball to him. "I need four soldiers who aren't needed for City Watch duty to help me deal with some Yellow Claws. Are any of you free?"

"I am, madam," said a dark-haired man with broad shoulders. "I'm only on cleaning detail."

"Thank you," said Azariel. "We need to leave as soon as possible. Pack for several days. "What's your name? I'll need to let the secretaries know."

"Taniran of Illinlebh-Zan," he replied. He brushed the dust off his trouser legs and vanished into the men's dormitories.

"Anybody else?" Azariel scanned the circle of soldiers.

"I'll come. I'm Kerrhona of Wolf Creek," said a red-haired woman. "I'll get my husband to come as well. His name's Corrhan."

"And I'll be the fourth." A blond man with a narrow face and a hawk nose stepped forward. "I'm Halbor of Longwood Hill."

"Thank you." Azariel nodded to all of them.

"What a pity – one of the men is married already," said Shadira quietly. "Still, the other two look promising."

The other soldiers crowded closer to Azariel as the volunteers headed away. "What's going on?" one of them asked.

"And why do you need four if you're dealing with Yellow Claws?"

Azariel straightened her rings. *How many times am I going to have to explain this?* "There's been a raid on one of the cavalry studs and a woman's been taken captive," she said. "I'm one of two *minyasti* riding out after them, and I already have some others in mind. And I'd best keep going. Don't let me spoil your game further."

"And now to find the others," said Shadira. "We'll try the common room. By the way, I suppose you're going to be bringing the little bastard?"

"Who?" Azariel twisted a lock of her hair briefly, then tossed it back.

"That acolyte of yours – Farren's niece. His sister's lovechild, isn't she?"

"You mean Kiihaon. Don't let her hear you calling her that. Yes, I do have to get her." She paused at the entrance of the men's corridor. The door stood open, letting in a large patch of sunlight. "Could you go and pass my orders to Kayti and the others? Kiihaon could take a bit of finding, depending on what Janna's doing with the acolytes at the moment. Tell them to be ready to ride early this afternoon."

"I'll do that – arch *minyaster*. Meet you at the gate this afternoon, then."

Azariel left the dormitories. I don't suppose I'll be able to stop and get this cut of mine seen to. It's not too bad. I'll have to requisition supplies as well as soldiers. At least I've stopped bleeding everywhere. She made her way back to the minyasti headquarters. I'll start hunting here. She crossed the corridor in two paces and turned the handle of the common room door. Peering inside, she saw Janna Greyhawk seated in the room's only armchair, his staff across his knees. Another grey-haired man sat at the round card-table beside him, sketching something for the two acolytes. The youngsters looked up, first the pale boy who seemed to be all knees and elbows, then the girl with the lustrous dark brown hair. "Kiihaon," Azariel said softly to the girl as the older men looked around. "Sorry to interrupt, Janna, but I've got to call her away."

"No, no, it's not me teaching them anything – Kalmian is," Janna said. "Take her,"

"And return her in one piece when you've finished with her," the boy put in.

"What do you want me for?" Kiihaon got to her feet, dropping a stick of graphite onto the table. "I want to finish the maze he's setting us."

"Get ready to ride. Your aunt Tina's been kidnapped."

***

Azariel ran her eyes over the band waiting for her by the gate: Arturus with the white scar travelling across his furrowed face; Kayti, blonde and deceptively delicate-looking; Shadira with a sword on each ample hip and brown curls dancing across her soldier's cloak; and Kenyon, looking almost too long and tall for his bay warhorse. The other four soldiers milled around on horseback. Storm pranced beneath her, tossing his head and whipping his mane onto her hands. Hot breath brushed over her leg and she turned as Farren edged Princess close beside her, squeezing her leg between the sides of the two horses. "Well, sweetheart," he said. "You're in command this time, so take us off. We should arrive before nightfall."

She cleared her throat. "Soldiers, thank you for coming. I wish I could have given you more time to prepare, and more details about how many Claws we're hunting. We've got an afternoon's ride ahead of us, so we'd best start. Follow me." She tapped Storm's sides with her heels and rode out of the barracks gate. The hoofbeats clattered and rumbled loudly on the cobbled streets as they wound their way across the capital city to the eastern wall.

She led the warband through the eastern gate out of the city. The northwest wind raced across the Kingdom plains, driving the long summer grass near the roadside into waves as it blew unhindered from the arch over the northern mountains. It caught and streamed her hair and cloak out around her, tugging her towards the plains. The sun beat down on the grasslands from an open blue sky, raising a heat-haze between her and the dim line of the mountains. "Good to be out in the open again," she said, patting her horse as she breathed in the smell of dry grass and earth. The gelding tossed his head and snorted. "Ready to run?"

She clapped her heels to Storm's sides and gave him his head. The black horse leaped forwards into a canter. She swung and rocked easily with the rhythm of his strides. Princess neighed beside her and Farren swept alongside her at a fast canter, his red cloak and auburn hair blown by the wind. "Away at last," she said to him, looking across the plains to the eastern horizon.

"Not too fast," he replied. "Don't forget poor old Sultan." He edged Princess closer to Storm so the two horses were running nose and nose.

She checked Storm to a trot and the rest of the warband slowed around her. "Our horses are spoiling for a run."

"They'll get one soon enough, hunting Yellow Claws, then hunting the gazelle." He twitched his cloak to the right of his body. "I hope we're making good enough time to be able to stop the Claws before they get too far away – or do too much to little Tina. Yvain!" he called over his shoulder. "When did the raid happen?"

"The night before last," his brother answered as the dun stallion drew level. "I set out before dawn this morning as soon as we had finished our own searching for Tina. You don't think we're going to be too late, do you?"

"We shouldn't be." She relaxed her grip on the reins and Storm shook his mane. He tugged once or twice at the bit and struggled to run on. "There'll still be a good enough trail to follow. How big was the raiding band?"

"I don't know. It can't have been very big or else we would have heard them sooner than we did." Yvain's stallion trotted ahead a little, then jolted from a trot to a canter to run in front of the band.

Storm jerked at the reins and followed Sultan's lead. The midday sun struck unrelentingly onto her head, and her armour felt like an oven. The insides of her elbows and knees grew damp with sweat. She reined Storm back to an easy pace. "Calm down, old fellow," she said, patting the gelding's neck. "You'll need all your strength for later."

Yvain checked Sultan until Storm and Princess drew alongside them. The stallion snorted. "Now, then," said Yvain. "I overheard something about a gazelle and hunting. What's up? Off on leave without coming to see us, Farren? Shame on you!"

"Not at all," replied Farren. "One of the lost Stones of Protection is chained onto a gazelle near Lebhern-y-Hyalda and we've got to go after it if we want to rebuild the barrier around the Kingdom and keep Wayast from invading us again."

"So you're off hunting by orders?" Yvain whistled. "Lucky you. But what are you going to do about hounds and falcons?"

"What?" Azariel flexed one arm and let the wind work through the links of her armour and cool her.

"You're going to need hounds and falcons if you're off gazelle hunting. That's what I learned when I was in Lebhern-y-Hyalda."

"A big trip for a small boy," laughed Farren. "What were you doing all that way from home?"

"I was taking a string of horses to Duke Milanan, you big idiot. If I wasn't riding, I'd knock you flat for that."

"Don't forget what happened last time," he snorted. "Anyway, you'll have to catch me first." He hissed something to Princess and the mare sprang forwards into a light canter. Yvain thumped Sultan's sides and the dun lurched in pursuit. Azariel felt Storm pull at the reins again and the gelding whinnied.

"Well, if I can get on with my story," said Yvain as he checked his stallion. "Duke Milanan had sent a messenger to select a number of horses for the troops guarding his palace. Wanted a dozen perfectly matching chestnuts. And while I was there, I went hunting."

"With the Duke and Duchess? I don't believe you," said Azariel. "Anyway, the Duchess doesn't hunt."

"Not them! With the messenger and a few others. Nice girl, she was, too. A pretty blonde with a luscious figure. I doubt I'll see her again, but there's some hope. She could come back to the farm again. She's a Nightraven, I think." He sighed and looked westwards over his shoulder. "It was fun."

She shot a look at Farren and his glance met hers. *That sounds like Stessa, and I know you think so, too.*

"Never mind whoever's caught your fancy, Yvain," Farren said. "Where do the falcons come in?"

"Well, you have a falcon that's trained to go at the gazelle and blind it while the hounds bring it down. Stop wincing, Farren; I thought you had a stronger stomach than that! You can also shoot them, but that's risky with the hounds near it. Falcons are best, I hear. Stessa – that's the blonde – didn't have one but the Duke's stable master told us what he does."

"Well, I can provide at least one hound," she said. She glanced away. *We were right. He's fallen for Stessa.*

"No, don't, Stormwolf." Farren reached out and caressed her hand. "I want to hunt by your side, not watch you running in wolf-form. We've got our pay with us; we should be able to buy a hound in Lebhern-y-Hyalda. But not falcons. Too expensive, for one thing, and what will we do with them once the hunt's over? My bow will do," he said, running his right hand over the wooden curve of his bow as it hung in place on the saddle by his knee.

The sun wheeled through the sky, sweeping in a high arch from east to west and slowly sinking behind the Seranyai-y-Taranar that jutted down from the main mountain chain. The northern mountains stood in sharp purple-brown silhouettes rising from the plains. The long leggy shadows of the horses and riders stretched ahead of them on the sea of wind-whipped grass, and their hooves thudded on the dirt of a small track that led away from the main highway. Farren glanced ahead and saw the Illin-Ast river shining in the yellowing sunlight as it ran between two high banks that swelled from the plains. *Almost there. I remember that line of river well.*

A flicker of movement caught his eye in the long grass beside a bush near the track. He turned his head to follow it, reaching for his bow. The small sandy-brown shape of the rabbit stopped beside a cluster of stones half a bowshot away, huddling down to mimic their round shapes. *I had better shoot something if we're expecting to eat dinner tonight. Mother will have enough to feed all of us with the supplies we've brought, but she'll appreciate fresh meat.* He nocked an arrow from the quiver at his belt to the string, flowing in long-practised movements. He pushed his bow arm towards the rabbit and drew the string, feeling it press into the calluses on the insides of his fingers. He let the string slip free, and the arrow flew. The string stung against the inside of his right wrist and the curved bow hummed. The rabbit started up and shrieked as the arrow passed through it, then fell. He rode to take it up and hunt for the arrow.

He remounted Princess, swinging the rabbit across the saddle before him and trotted back to the warband. Azariel was waiting for him, her skin and hair gilded by the rich evening light. "Good shot," she said. He smiled and turned towards the small group of buildings ahead of him.

Princess reared underneath him, neighing. He brought her down and looked ahead. A white-headed man drawing hunting bow stepped into the middle of the trail. After him came three other men, holding bows and pitchforks. The sharp steel points gleamed in the yellow light as they angled towards Farren and the other riders. "Now then," the old man said, bow quivering in his grasp as he turned it towards Azariel. "We're not the only ones here, so don't try any tricks. If you Yellow Claws think you can come back here and take any more horses, you're mistaken!"

Yvain laughed rode forward. "Stephan, you old idiot!" he said. "It's us. Don't you recognise me? I've only been away a day! Put that bow down."

Stephan lowered the bow and his bony hands untwisted as he allowed the bow to relax. "Sun was in my eyes, youngster. Couldn't see the uniforms. But welcome back to you, and to you too, Farren. Glad to have you back – and your lady. Come back to the house. If you're lucky, your mother will be able to find enough to feed you and all your friends."

"I've thought of that." Farren held up the rabbit carcass. "I've shot this and we've brought food. Lead on."

Farren leaned forwards to look ahead to the homestead at the foot of the high banks. A heart-achingly familiar scent of river-water, dry grass and stables eddied on the wind. The whitewashed walls of the homestead caught the light of the setting sun and glowed like candles. A ring of tall poplars encircled the house and the orchard beyond it. Between the poplars, a figure was riding towards them. The sunlight shone on the rider's long hair, dark red mingled with silver. "It's Grandmother!" shouted Kiihaon, her pony galloping past Princess. "It's us!" she called. "We've come!"

Princess neighed as the pony passed her and Farren let her canter towards his mother. Gently, he checked the mare and swung himself off her back, balancing the rabbit on the saddle. "Welcome home, Fox... Farren," his mother said, leaning down and ruffling his hair. "I knew you'd come quickly, you and Azariel." She dismounted and rested both hands on his shoulders.

He smiled and hugged her. *I am so glad she stopped herself calling me my old baby name in front of everyone. Otherwise I'd have Shadira calling me Foxy-cub all the time.* "I'm glad to be here," he said aloud, lowering his arms off her. "I only wish it was in happier circumstances."

Azariel slid off Storm's back beside them. "Here we are, Rose," she said as she clasped the older woman's hand in both of hers. "We'll get Tina back for you, I swear. I won't – we won't rest until we've hunted them down."

"You can rest long enough for dinner, surely, but I like your spirit. Farren couldn't have chosen a better woman. No, there's no need for you to flush like that." Rose bent her head and started. "What happened to your hand?"

"Blood Oath on Edge that I'd get Tina back," Azariel replied, expression turning to a mask as she tossed her black hair aside. "I was trying to impress an officer who hates me. And I'd just sharpened my sword."

"I'll clean that up for you and get you and all of your band some dinner. You'll have to introduce me to them. See to your horses, then come inside."

***

They all sat around the long table in the large dining room. Farren leaned back in his chair and looked around. *Nothing's changed,* he thought, slipping his arm around Azariel. *Every crack in the ceiling, every piece of crockery. The only thing that's different is that Mother and Dad look older. Old Stephan doesn't look different, but then he's looked ancient for as long as I can remember.* He gazed through the windows at the trees and the banks beyond, half-listening to the grooms and soldiers talking. *If I wait long enough, I'll see a rabbit or two. There always used to be rabbits on the lawn at twilight.* A figure passed across the wide tree-ringed lawn outside the window, then a second. "I wonder who that is," he said to Azariel. "I thought all the grooms had come in for their evening meal with the family."

She leaned in front of him slightly, turning towards the window and her soft hair brushing his cheek. He buried his face in her black mane, his lips searching for the smooth skin of her cheek. She hissed sharply through her teeth and he released his hold on her. "Sorry. Shouldn't I have done that?"

"Look out there," she said.

He turned to the window. More figures wandered through the trees and across the lawn. The pallid light of the full rising moon glittered off chainmail. *Anna? Already?* Straining his eyes through the muted twilight colours, he saw that the figures wore the red tabards and yellow cloaks of the Yellow Claw. "The Claws are back," he whispered.

A knock boomed on the door and a voice outside called "Setharan!" The rise and fall of voices broke off and all heads turned.

Farren's father rose to his feet and strode to the door. "Who is that?"

"It's us again, and if you want your daughter back safe and sound, you and all the soldier boys and girls you've got in there with you had better sit quietly and not do anything. We've got the house guarded front and back, so don't think you can sneak out that way."

"What do you want?" Farren's mother glided across the room to stand beside her husband, one hand on her hip.

"All your horses, grain and gear. They're for the Yellow Claw, not Caph Domastin's army. When we've got them all, we'll give your little girl back – unharmed and untouched, pretty little piece that she is. If you keep nice and quiet without trying anything, you and she will be perfectly safe."

CHAPTER THREE

Azariel stood beside the window, breathing in the evening air and watching the Yellow Claws striding to and fro in the moonlight around the surrounding buildings. They rolled a large cart across the lawn and heavy things thudded onto the floorboards. "You'll be beggared by this," she said, turning away from the window to Setharan. "We've got to find a way to stop them. They really do mean to take everything."

"If we tried to cut our way out, they'd leave the stuff alone and come and deal with us," said Arturus. "There are ten of us warriors, eleven if you count the young lass. And the rest of you are fit and strong."

"No good, Arturus," said Kenyon, stopping his pacing to and fro by the fire and coming to sit down. "You know the Claws. As soon as they see we're getting serious, they'll fire the house. The only way I can think of preventing that is if some of us could slip behind them before the ones inside started to make a sortie – keep them busy both ways, if you know what I mean."

"Well, that's no good," said Arturus, shoving his chair back and standing up. "They're guarding the doors and there's no other way out."

"They'd let us out to piss, surely," said Shadira. "A couple of us could go and…"

"I'm going to try." Halbor drained his mug and wandered to the door.

"Stay in there!" snapped the voice of the Yellow Claw outside.

"A man's got to use the outhouse," replied Halbor.

"Very well. None of your tricks, though. Hey, Connor! Dump that sack in the cart and take this lad to the outhouse. Keep a good eye on him."

Halbor slipped through the door. Before it swung shut again, indistinct voices drifted through. Azariel waited, leaning her head against the lintel of the window beside the open shutter, trying to hear what was happening. She breathed deeply, the rich scent of the bread and beef stew from dinner lingering in the air. A few minutes later, Halbor returned. He sank down at the table and buried his head in his hands.

"What happened?" asked Shadira.

"They let me go to the outhouse, all right, but they came right in there with their swords drawn, standing right beside me. You've no idea how humiliating it is to stand there with your trousers down with two men waving blades about."

A mixture of sympathetic murmurs and chuckles greeted his tale, and Shadira patted him on the shoulder.

Farren picked at his fingernails and waited for the voices to subside. "There is a way out if we wait until it's darker," he said. He bowed his head and looked sheepishly up at his father. "I... I've slipped out of here unseen before." A flush spread across his cheeks. "Unless you've cut down that old pear tree by my bedroom window."

"You young scamp, you did too," Setharan laughed. "I haven't forgotten that yet."

"Oh really?" Azariel left the window and strolled over to Farren. She ran her hands over his broad shoulders, feeling the pattern of little bumps made by his chainmail. "Well, beloved, it's not dark yet, so while we wait for that, you can tell the story behind this." She dropped a kiss onto the top of his head.

"I was a young fool," he muttered, the tips of his ears turning rosy. He ran one hand through his hair. "I'm a bit ashamed of it."

"Go on, Farren! Let them hear it," said his father. "We've got a bit of time until it gets dark and it'll let those vultures out there think we're being tame little mice. And your escapade was when the *minyastin* in you came out for the first time."

"You shot a phoenix while you were hunting rabbits, or you told me," Azariel said. "Is there more to it?"

"I wasn't supposed to be out hunting rabbits." He glanced up at her and his eyes flashed. He grabbed her by the wrists and pulled her around to sit beside him. "I'll tell you now." He draped his arms around her and she nestled in close to him, feeling his chest and shoulders rise and fall with his breathing. "It was such a good night for hunting rabbits," he said. "The moon was just right; there was hardly any breeze. So I decided to slip out after curfew and go hunting. I made my way to the tack shed to get Flame's bridle and ran into Stephan."

"And I handed you over to your father and you got a good hiding," the old man said, lowering his mug to the table.

"Fair enough, too." Farren refilled his mug from the pitcher of water on the table. "And that's where it would have ended if you hadn't said that I'd have to try harder than that if I wanted to steal past you. I wanted to be a Nightraven at that stage, which shows you how stupid I was. And I thought that if I was a Nightraven, I would need to be able to steal past guard with the risk of getting more than just a hiding if I failed. So I set myself a challenge.

"After about the fourth night, the groom started setting traps for me. There were tripwires in the tack shed, dogs on guard behind haybales, bells on Flame's bridle and more. And I kept on getting caught."

"I knew you had some game on with the grooms," his father said. "I would have thought it funny if I didn't have to tan your hide every time you got caught. But I couldn't go soft, or I'd have had all five of you running about the place all night long." He shook his head and sighed. "I've got to say I admired your courage and determination – and cheek. And if it's going to help us now, I'm glad you did do it." He laughed. "I never thought I'd catch myself saying that!"

"We were almost laying wagers as to when we would hear a knock on the door and see one of the grooms standing there smirking with a riding crop in one hand and our rascal of a son caught by the collar in the other," said Rose. She picked up a ladle and peered into the stewpot. "I certainly haven't got any appetite left now, but if anyone wants any more.... I can't exactly go out and give it to the hens, and it's not worth making into soup."

Azariel turned her head to look at Farren. *I remember seeing you for the first time when we were both fourteen years old,* she thought. She pictured him as an adolescent, all arms and legs, red hair rumpled and disordered, a dusting of freckles across the bridge of his nose and a sparkle of mischief in his eyes. *He's all man now.* She studied his face and the broad set of his shoulders. A few small lines were beginning to show around the corners of his eyes. She smiled and snuggled closer against his shoulder, their chainmail grating together. A loud neigh startled her and she glanced out of the window. The light from the tall candles on the table turned the whitewashed walls to soft cream, framing the intense cobalt blue outside. "The light's almost faded."

"Well," Farren continued. "The grooms didn't stop at laying traps for me, either." He glared exaggeratedly at Yvain. "They even bribed somebody to betray me to Dad when I slipped out."

"How did you know that?" asked Stephan.

"Having opened his mouth once to Dad, he didn't have the sense to shut it again." Farren paused to sip some water. "Yvain betrayed himself by bragging. I really am sorry about what I did after that." He grinned wryly. "I blacked his eye. Sorry, Yvain."

"No hard feelings, big brother." Yvain hurled a cushion towards his brother but it struck Azariel squashily in the face.

Farren put the cushion on his lap and fidgeted with the fringe around the edge. "It's almost dark enough. To keep a long tale short, I succeeded after a fortnight. I'd planned everything, and it's a pity I won't have everything ready now. We'll still be able to do it, though – don't worry. But that day, I had carefully exhausted Yvain so he fell asleep promptly." Yvain looked indignant and the others laughed. "I had left Flame with muffled hooves and his bridle in the long grass by the trees. I dressed in black as soon as Yvain was asleep and blackened my hands and face with soot like the Nightravens do. And I took my bow, crept out the window and away."

"Plenty of soot on the bottom of the pots," said Yvain, helping himself to the last of the stew. "Want to do that again now?"

"I had quite a good night's shooting, even though there was no moon," Farren continued. He smiled and ran his hand through his hair, rumpling it up from his forehead. Then his smile faded. "But the phoenix came. It came plunging and burning out of the sky and killed Flame. All of a sudden, I didn't feel like the cunning Nightraven and great hunter I'd been playing at. I felt very small, very alone and very guilty with my horse lying dead and me out after curfew. I tell you, Dad, watching that phoenix tearing Flame to pieces hurt me more than your riding crop across the seat of my trousers ever could." He got up from the table and walked across to the window. "I hope I never lose a horse like that again, especially with my Gift fully developed."

"So what did you do?" Azariel followed him to the window and ran her hands along the linen cloth covering the sill. The trees surrounding the lawn were indigo shapes against the blue-grey of the grass. *It's dark enough now. We'd better move soon.*

"Well, I'd heard how to kill a phoenix. Uncle Aahlin was a *minyastin* – Aahlin Rainmaker. He'd told us how he'd killed one once. You need an arrow charged with fire – the Power's fire. And I... I knew I could do it, although I never had tried before. It was like knowing I could walk or ride a horse. So I asked for the fire. I asked Him to forgive me for sneaking out and I asked Him to help me." He closed his eyes and drew a deep breath. "And He answered. It was... It was... I can't describe it. It's one of those things you have to experience to understand. Remember your first time of opening up and being flooded, Stormwolf?"

She nodded, remembering the quickening of her breath and heart, the tingling and trembling racing up her arms and spine. Beside her, Kiihaon fidgeted and nodded violently, twisting her fingers hands together. *She knows, too.*

"And then what happened?" asked Kayti in a baby-voice. "Tell us!"

"I had a favourite arrow," Farren said. "I'd made it myself. I'd stained it black – playing Nightravens again – and I even feathered it with raven's feathers. The Black Arrow, I called it. I never thought when I made it that I would be named for it."

"Just as well you didn't paint it pink then, eh?" said Yvain.

Farren reached down and picked up the cushion from beside the table. He flung it at Yvain, catching him squarely on the ear, then paced up and down the length of the window. "I took my black arrow and held it in my hand, seeing silver and black fire crawl around it." He stared distantly at his hands and raised his arms as if drawing an invisible bow. "I shot the phoenix with the Black Arrow. One shot, straight through the breast as it took to the air and flew at me." He raised a fist triumphantly. "A good shot."

"We came looking for him," Setharan said. "Janna Greyhawk was with us at the time and we were sitting up waiting for the knock at the door. We were about to turn in for the night, thinking that you'd succeeded, Farren, or given up. But then we saw the phoenix descending on the rise. We set out after it. We found him on the hill, holding Flame's dead head in his arms and sobbing his heart out. The phoenix lay dead beside him and I knew what had happened. I've never felt such a muddle of things before or since."

"Well, that's how I did it," said Farren. "And I never thought I'd have to steal out that way again – with your permission this time, Dad. I guess the trees are taller now, but so am I." He leaned on the windowsill and gazed out. "It's dark enough now. I'll take a chance with the moonlight." He pulled the shutters closed across the window. "It's best if they don't see us leaving the room. Come with me, Stormwolf. I'll show you the way out. The two of us should be able to create enough of a disturbance for them to come and get us. Are you ready?"

She felt for the hilt of her sword and twisted the rings straight on her fingers. Candlelight caught the opal on her right hand and the stone glinted with points of red and green fire. Outside, the lawn looked empty, but thuds and whinnies came from the side of the house nearest the stables. At least they're still busy taking gear. "I'm ready," she said. "Let's go."

"The rest of you, start cutting your way out when you hear me whistle." Farren glanced at the door.

"Hey, take care, Farren," said Stephan. "These are Yellow Claws who'll cut your throat, not a bunch of us having a laugh with a fourteen-year-old rascal. They're seasoned warriors."

He stretched out his right arm so that the light from the candles fell fully onto the hair and hard muscle. "See that?" he said, pointing to a long silver scar. "A Claw sword did that last spring. I've got another to match on the other arm and a beauty above my knee. That's just a few of my battle scars. Seasoned warrior? What do you think I've been doing for the last ten years?" He strode across the room and picked up his bow from where it lay on the floor beside the other gearbags and bundles. "I'm not the sort to put a tally mark for each kill on my bow, but I've lost count of how many Claws and Wayasti I've killed. I'm not a fourteen-year-old rascal any more, Stephan. This isn't the first time I've tangled with the Claws and it won't be the last." He slung the bow over his shoulder, pulling an awkward line across his cloak, and marched to the stairs.

She dropped behind him as they climbed the narrow staircase, following him up the creaking steps in the darkness. Something thudded on the roof. "Ouch!" he said from somewhere slightly above her. "I'm a lot taller than I was. The ceiling's a bit low here." His hand touched her head and pressed her down as she reached the landing. His footsteps padded across bare boards and a thin strip of carpet, then the soft light of stars fell through the door he held open. "This way," he said.

His silhouette stood black against the indigo of the night sky with the light of the waning moon glimmering silver through his hair. "This was my old room," he said softly. His arms wrapped around her as she walked in, and he drew her close. His chest rose and fell against her, slowly and softly. "I didn't tell them this downstairs, but I'll tell you. When I was slipping out, I always pretended I was on a mission to rescue a beautiful maiden." One of his hands caressed her cheek and travelled down to the top of her chainmail. "And here you are with me, my dream come true." His lips pressed onto hers, soft and crisp as velvet, and the tips of his fingers trembled in the hollow behind her ear. "I thank the King of Heaven for you."

She shook her hair back from her face and breathed in the smell of woodsmoke, dry grass, horses and sweat that hung about him. "So do I," she replied. "Thank you for choosing me."

He bent his head and kissed her again. "One more before the fighting starts," he said. He released her and slowly eased himself onto the sill. The night breeze stirred the thick summer leaves on the pear tree outside, making them dance and rustle. "It's tree-work here for a while until we get to the end of the home orchard. Follow me, step for step." He slipped out of the window and the leaves quivered again.

Voices drifted across the lawn from the Yellow Claw carts. *God Incarnate, protect us,* she thought, and passed through the window behind him. She followed him from tree to tree, gingerly shifting her handholds and footholds. The sweet watery scent of ripe pears drifted around her, and moonlight gleamed dully on patches of bark and the upper surfaces of the full summer leaves. *I'd be better off stalking in wolf form, than creeping through the trees.* She coiled her grip around the nearest branch and pulled herself from one tree to the next. This one carried the tangy scent of plum. A sharp spike on the branch jabbed at the side of her hand.

The black figure of a Yellow Claw carrying a bulky bundle moved across the starlit lawn, passing through the square of golden candlelight that shone through the window. She froze, her hands quivering uncontrollably in their strained position. The twigs and leaves rustled, and the Claw glanced up. *He's heard me!*

Ahead of her, Farren gave a series of guttural coughs that sounded like a sack of pinecones being jerked across paving slabs. She bit her lip to stop herself laughing. *That's the best possum imitation I've heard. I had no idea he could do it so well.* The Claw shrugged and continued walking across the lawn. She relaxed, easing her hand away from the spike on the branch. *I must be more careful.*

She followed Farren to the far end of the lawn where the orchard trees gave way to tall poplars. He leaned towards her so his shoulder brushed hers. "This is where we drop," he breathed in her ear. "I'll go for the horses. Go ahead and start the fight quietly." The branches rustled and he thudded softly to the ground.

She edged along the branches and leaped. *Now to use my Gift.* As she dropped, she closed her eyes and concentrated. She changed swiftly to wolf form, her face and forearms lengthening, her hips and shoulders folding and her teeth swelling against her lips. Her forepaws caught her as she landed. Wild instincts bubbled and whirled in her brain and she paused as the confusion blurred and blended with the doubling and redoubling of her senses of smell and hearing. The odour of horses drifted on the wind towards her on her right and the mouth-watering smells of meat and bread came from the house. She hesitated, waiting for her human intellect to rule the wolfish brain.

Her head cleared and she listened for the Claws. She cocked her ears towards the stables and caught the sound of horsehooves. *They must be almost ready to leave if they are moving horses.* She slunk through the long grass and around the orchard to the farm outbuildings. Two carts stood between the house and the stables, the scent of leather and grains wafting down from the bundles piled on them. Five yards from them, she paused and crouched in the grass, hackles prickling and one paw quivering as she lifted it.

A Claw lumbered around the carts, burdened with a sack that smelt of potatoes. She leaped, jaws opening and a snarl rising from her throat. Her fangs met in his neck as her forepaws grappled with his arms and shoulders. She shook him as they tumbled to the ground together, crushing down with her jaws and pulling back in a hot salt stink of blood. A shrill whistle split the night air. She changed shape and spat the blood out of her mouth. *King of Heaven, flood me and fight through me!* Her flesh tingled and her rings heated around her fingers. She set her back against the cart and drew her sword, eyes and ears ready for the next Claw to come.

The sound of running footsteps filled her ears and the dark figure of a man rounded the cart. "Hey! Over here, lads!" he yelled. His sword rasped from the sheath and pale light flickered on the steel. Her blade sang through the air, slashing at the Claw. A shock jolted through her right arm as the Claw caught her weapon with his own. She plunged her sword down, shifting and dancing to and fro, and brought it up and across in a backslash. She stepped to one side and blocked the Claw's sword as it whistled towards her left shoulder. From the corner of her eye, she saw more shapes swarming towards her. She clenched her teeth and drove her sword at the Claw, feeling it strike flesh. Above the drumming of her heartbeat, the sounds of feet and shouting came from the house, mixed with the neighs and hoofbeats of many horses. She whirled her blade up and around, parrying the Claw's blow. Her sword caught his and his grip loosened. Another attack flashed at her head and she ducked as she smashed the weapon from the hand of the Claw in front of her.

One quick slash and the Claw lay dying at her feet. She spun to face the small group of men and women around her, their eyes and naked weapons glittering cold and hard in the moonlight. Her rings burned on her fingers and she raised her left hand, lapis lazuli ring facing the Claws. Her arm trembled as fire sparkled and tingled through her and a bolt of dark blue lightning seared out from her ring. A second Claw crashed to the ground, enveloped in cobalt flame. The rest stepped back a few paces, then closed in again.

The shouting from the house grew louder, followed by the clash of sword on sword. Then the yards and lawn were filled by people running and fighting. Horses neighed and one bolted across the lawn in a thunder of hooves.

Farren rode bareback on Princess towards the cluster of carts, Storm galloping beside him. The golden light from the doorway fell on the other soldiers cutting the Claw guards back from the threshold. A blaze of green light shot up and he heard Azariel shouting in the Old Tongue. He wheeled Princess around the carts, guiding her with the light touch of his hands and heels as well as the unseen cords that bound his horse to him with his Gift. Princess reared beneath him and he grabbed her mane to keep his balance as she surged at the small group of Claws, screaming fiercely. He felled the Claw on his left with a slash of his sword and saw another drop in front of Azariel.

The party of Claws scattered as the other soldiers rounded the carts. In the confused half-light, he saw the raiders take horses and ride off towards the northeast, black figures against the silver and blue-grey of the moonlit grass. "After them!" he barked. "We'll chase them to their den."

With a touch on Princess's neck with his right hand, he headed the mare after the Claws. He clapped his heels to her bare sides. "Follow them, my lady," he said softly. The mare tossed her head and snorted in reply. He checked back over his shoulder, watching and listening for the other warriors following him. *Where are they? We'll lose the Claws if they don't hurry up!* He strained his eyes through the darkness ahead, picking out the moving shadows and listening to the rumour of fleeing hooves. *The others behind aren't animal tamers like me and can't ride without saddle or bridle. But I hope they don't lose me and leave me to face the pack by myself.* "Come on, my lady," he said aloud, tapping the mare's sides. "Let's hunt them down."

He crested the swell of the high banks and checked Princess to look back towards the squares of light in the dark bulk of the homestead. Across the western horizon, a thin band of greenish-white twilight lingered. The sound of drumming hoofbeats thundered and a hooded black shadow rose beside him. The dark horse neighed and Princess nickered in welcome. The figure pushed the hood back, revealing Azariel's face. "Good, I've caught you up," she said. "I had to get Storm's gear on. The others are coming as soon as they can find horses and gear, and I've got this for you. Catch."

He heard something jingling and held out his hand. Leather straps slapped around his arm and he felt the smooth metal of a snaffle bit between his fingers. *Princess's bridle.* He hung it over his shoulder, careful not to entangle the reins with his bow. Then he put heels to Princess, and the mare turned and galloped after the group of shadows that raced across the moonlit grass.

"Kiihaon's following the main party with your saddle," Azariel said as Storm swept up beside him. "She's only half trained as a *minyaster* and completely untrained as a fighter, so I told her to hold back." She shook her hair back from her face, and her eyes glittered. "And now it's just you and me hunting in the darkness." She clapped heels to Storm and the big gelding surged ahead of Princess.

They followed the Claws until the moon had climbed almost to the top of its arch and both Storm and Princess were breathing noisily. Then the fleeing riders vanished behind a dark building. A volley of barking rose as the hoofbeats stopped. He wheeled Princess around the building, leaning back and letting her slow to a tired walk. Ahead, a light shone through a single window onto a line of sweat-slick horses. A door slammed, booming across the yammer and yelling of the dogs. "Journey's end," Farren said. "We've got them."

He slipped off Princess's back and dropped her bridle. Behind him, he heard the hoofbeats of the other soldiers' horses rounding the building. "Guard our backs," Azariel said to the newcomers. She took his hand and they walked along the side of the building. He ducked as they passed close under the lighted window and his shadow fell long and black across the dusty yard. "Here's the door," she whispered. She knocked, softly at first, then battering the wood so it boomed. "Open in the name of Caph Domastin, ruler of the Kingdom!" she demanded.

Footsteps shuffled inside, and he slid his sword from the sheath. The handle turned and the door slowly opened. He blinked and stepped backwards as light fell through the doorway around a human shape. The Claw holding the door retreated to one side, letting Farren see into the dim interior of the barn.

In the middle of the barn, Tina sat gagged and roped to a chair. A dark-haired man in the bright saffron robes of the sorcerers stood over her, watching them with a triumphant smile. Yellow lamplight glittered off the blade of the knife he held to Tina's throat. The girl's eyes stared in terror and beads of sweat gleamed on her forehead under her dark red hair. *Tina, you're only twenty! You're too young to die, sister!*

"Well," said the yellow-robed man. "Now we can talk. You, I suppose are her brother, if your copper hair and pointy chin are anything to go by. If you try to attack, I'll cut her throat."

CHAPTER FOUR

Farren stepped back through the doorway and lowered his sword, blade quivering as his hand shook. His pulse hammered at his wrists and temples, and he clenched his jaw. *Tina! What have they done to you? If anything happens to you, they're dead!* Tina's green eyes fixed on his, tears pooling in the corners. His mouth felt dry and his stomach was knotted. He tightened his grip on his sword hilt. "What do you want? What do you want with her anyway?" he growled.

The yellow-robed man's eyes flicked up and down Azariel. "Black cloak over Kingdom uniform..." he muttered. Then his eyes snapped wide and the knife blade trembled in the light. *Fear? Or eagerness?* Farren wondered. The man's tongue slid around his lips and his eyes darted to and fro before locking onto Farren's. "I've got a bargain to drive with you," he said. The hand holding the knife dropped slightly but the point lingered near Tina's throat.

"Let her go and then we'll talk." Farren raised his sword and inched forward, eyes narrowing. "We'll make no bargains with thieves and woman-stealers."

"I think not. If you want your sister to stay alive and whole, then listen to me."

Farren's breathing quickened and his left hand tightened around the hilt, squeezing the blood from his knuckles. "Just give me half a chance and you'll be in little pieces, scorpion!" The large room and the Claws surrounding Tina and the yellow-robed man all blurred to a haze of angry red. He took a single pace forwards.

Azariel clutched at his arm and pulled him back. "Calm down," she said, stepping in front of him. Both her hands rested on his chest. "You'll only make things worse if you lose your temper, beloved," she whispered, leaning forwards and blocking his view of the room.

She turned back towards Tina and her guards, one hand still holding Farren by the right forearm. "What's your bargain?" she asked.

"You want your stallions back, no doubt,' the robed man said. "And we'll surrender them." The circle of Claws stared at him and muttered. "Silence." He raised his bare left hand and glanced at his men. "Well surrender them – if you win them back in trials by combat."

"And if we don't accept the combats?" asked Azariel. "There are other colts in the Kingdom to become stud stallions for the cavalry."

"I think you will," he said. He pressed the knife against Tina's skin and she whimpered through the gag. "Accept it or she dies – slowly. There's only one of her. Shall I tell you what I'll do to your sister? This sandy floor can soak up plenty of blood."

"No, don't!" Farren snarled through gritted teeth. His stomach churned as his imagination threw up grisly pictures. He stepped back, pulling Azariel with him. "We must accept," he said in the Old Tongue. "We can't let them do that to her."

"I think we can fight and win quite easily," she replied in the same language. "Look at his hands – he's got no rings. In spite of those robes, he's no sorcerer. He's a novice at best."

His jaw unclenched and he closed his eyes. "That's something. And we might get a chance to free her without fighting." He opened them again and stared at the yellow-robed man. "We accept," he said in the Common Tongue. "Who are we fighting, where, how and when?"

"It's very simple." The man smiled. "I'll release one stallion for every fight you win, five fights in all. And I'll tell you what they'll be in the morning." He turned his head to the men around him. "Close the door, Lionel. We'll see those two outside tomorrow at dawn."

"One moment." Azariel leaned against the door, holding it open. "I am Azariel Stormwolf, arch *minyaster* of the Kingdom. I won't accept a challenge from a Yellow Claw thief who hasn't the guts to give his name. Who are you?"

"Kadir of Ulfskin-Aza," the Claw replied, grinning. "Close the door, I said, Lionel. You're not afraid of a woman, are you?"

The door slammed shut as Azariel stood aside. Farren strode forwards and raised one fist, ready to batter at it. *I'll smash it down, the cowards!*

Her hand flashed out and grabbed his. "It's no good," she said. "Don't bother rising to his taunts and making a fool of yourself. You'll only make him laugh at you. Save it up for tomorrow when you need it. Let's go away from here, meet the others and camp for the night."

He lowered his hand and sheathed his sword. The fire of anger died inside him, leaving grey anxiety to smoulder. "I don't know how I'm going to sleep," he said, embracing her and drawing her close to him. "I know I've got to, but poor Tina!" He buried his face in her rosemary-scented hair.

"We'll get her back. And I doubt they'll hurt her tonight." Her hand, cool and comforting, rubbed up and down on the back of his head above the high neck of his chainmail. "We'll win all five stallions back and then her." She ruffled his hair gently. "With the Power's help, we can win any fight."

"There speaks the arch *minyaster*, my Stormwolf." He squeezed her tightly and a ripple of calm spread down his spine. "We had better go and tell the others what's going on." He kissed her lightly on the mouth before releasing her.

***

Azariel heaped a small pile of sticks, bark and dead grass together just out from the shelter of a spinney of birch trees and struck sparks from her tinderbox onto it. A small blue and yellow flame danced on the tinder and wavered. It ran along the blade of grass, leaving a trail of glimmering red in its wake. She bent to blow on the flame, holding her hair back behind her head with one hand. Warm white smoke stung her eyes and nose, leaving her coughing and blinking as she sat up again. The grass and frayed bark caught fire and the flame spread to the twigs, crackling and whispering.

Firelight gleamed off the faces and armour of the circle of soldiers gathered under the birches. She laid more sticks on the fire before sitting back from it. "We'd better make sure that doesn't spread to the grass around," she said. "The northwest wind is still running in the skies and the grass around is dry. We don't want to roast ourselves." She looked away from the others and across the grasslands to the dark bulk of the Claw buildings two bowshots away and the lights of a village beyond that.

"That would save the Claws a job, wouldn't it?" grunted Arturus. "Unless we managed to set fire to the barn where they've run to ground." He rubbed his hairy hands together and held them over the fire. "That fellow in there thinks pretty quickly on his feet. Not a bad plan for using a hostage now his first one's fallen to bits, thanks to you, Farren."

"Poor Tina," Farren said. He knelt beside Azariel and idly snapped a twig and tossed it piece by piece into the fire. "At least he didn't just cut her throat when he saw us there."

"Well, a dead hostage is no use as a hostage any more," the old soldier said. "Sorry to be so blunt about your sister and all. But this way, he's got five chances to pick off a Kingdom soldier – or *minyast* – and keep a good stallion, too, if he wins."

"There are more than five of us here," said Kayti, leaning forwards. "You can always let us fight instead of you if you're sure he's not really a sorcerer."

Azariel stared into the flames. *Can I ask them to get killed in my place?* The cut on her hand throbbed dully as her fingers tightened. *I know I can, but should I? I wish I wasn't in this place where I can decide everyone else's fate.* She leaned her head against Farren's shoulder. The links of his chainmail were cool and hard. "We'll wait and see what sort of duels we're actually facing before we decide who'll fight," she said aloud.

"That Kadir hasn't thought them up yet," Farren said. "He'll probably spend all night thinking up something unusual. Heavy axes, for example."

"I've done some axe fighting," said Taniran, one of the new soldiers. "It's rough work but I'm not too bad at it. So if they decide on that, I'm your man."

"Does anyone else have any unusual fighting skills?" Azariel sat up and hugged her knees to her chest. "I know what the ones from the Watchtower of the West can do, but how about the rest of you?"

"Just sword and bow for me," said Kerrhona, twisting a strand of her red hair around her finger.

"Sword and cross bow," said Corrhan, her husband. "Except I haven't got my crossbow with me."

"Sword and bow." Halbor stood up. The shadows cast by the fire made his nose look even more hawk-like. "I'm a good wrestler and I've learned a few unarmed combat moves from a friend who's a Nightraven."

"I wouldn't mind learning some of those," said Shadira. "Pity we won't have time for you to teach me some."

"Kenyon, what about you?" asked Farren.

"Plain, ordinary swordsman, although I can make shift with a pike well enough. I was in the pikes during the battle at Falcon Pass. We all saw what you can do at that battle, ma'am."

"Call me Azariel," she said. "Anyway, we'll decide in the morning once we find out the terms of the combat. We'll need as many as we can to keep an eye out during the trials to make sure that they don't try any dirty tricks." She gazed into the flames and traced one hand along the line of the scar that ran from her left collarbone to her breastbone. *I know all too well that sorcerers don't always honour the terms of single combat.*

He yawned. "I don't know about anyone else, but I'm tired. Let's decide who'll take first watch. Stormwolf, you're our leader; you pick our guards."

She looked around the circle. "We'll draw straws. We're all equally exhausted after tonight's work."

"I'm not," said Kenyon. "I hardly got out of the house before someone pushed my horse at me and told me to ride for it. I'll take first watch. Draw your straws for the second."

Azariel plucked a tall stem of grass and broke it into differing lengths before handing the straws around the circle. "Not you, Kiihaon," she said as the girl reached forward. "Not unless somebody watches with you."

"I'll watch with somebody anyway," she said, pulling her fingers and making her knuckles crack. "I'm only an acolyte but I have been with my mother in the army all my life, after all. I can fight. I'm not scared."

"I don't doubt your courage, just your skill. And you don't need to prove anything to us by acting tough." She opened her hand, glancing at the last straw in the wavering firelight and the red gash beside it. *Which is exactly what I needed to tell myself when that wasp Karissa was stinging. I can't believe it was only this morning that happened.* "You can join second watch if you like, though. Who drew the short straw?"

"I did," said Shadira, spinning her straw into the heart of the fire. "It'll be good to have you to chat to, Kiihaon, if you like. You ought to get someone to talk to as well, Kenyon. Kayti might oblige you." She winked at Azariel and grinned. "And maybe one of you lads can watch with me as well. How about teaching me some of those moves during second watch, Halbor?

"Why not?" the blond replied. "Best to have two of us in case things turn nasty in the middle of the night. And if they don't turn nasty, well, there are worse ways to spend the night."

"I'll wake you when it's our turn, then." Shadira yawned and shook her head, making her curls dance. "And now, goodnight all."

Azariel found a comfortable clump of grass to pillow her head, and wrapped herself in her cloak. The wind stirred her hair as she stretched herself and closed her eyes. A few paces away to her left, Farren breathed deeply and slowly; from beyond him came the rhythmic sound of horses cropping grass. Shadira stepped around her and lay down back to back with her, humming quietly. Azariel ignored the other woman and let her limbs grow heavy and her mind drowsy. The smell of smoke and dry grass wafted over her, the last thing she noticed before she slept.

A distant cockcrow woke her. She opened her eyes and rolled over, seeing the sky covered with high clouds stained salmon. To the northwest, the cloud-blanket arched, showing brilliant blue sky above the jagged line of the Seranyai-Cheli. The wind blew from the mountains, warm, dry and swift. She sat up and dug the sleep out of her eyes with her knuckles. Shadira and Kiihaon were chattering to her right, and other voices rose and fell a little further off. Several people lay bundled in their cloaks in a rough circle around the campfire. Azariel shook the hair back from her face and stretched. "All well?" she called to them as she shook out her cloak and buckled it on.

"Not a sound from them all night," said Shadira. "And our horses haven't strayed either." She waved a hand towards where Arturus and Halbor were grooming their horses.

Kiihaon tossed a twig onto the ashes and embers of the campfire. "Shall I go now? How much shall I get?" she asked Shadira, then turned to Azariel and added, "She's sent me to buy us some breakfast."

"That'll teach you to complain that you're hungry," Shadira said. "Off you go, girlie. Get lots." She opened the pouch at her belt and fished out some silver coins. "Men eat lots, so see if you can be back before they all stop snoring."

"Good idea." Azariel strolled over to them and sat down in the grass, hugging her knees to her chest as Kiihaon caught and saddled her pony. "I don't fancy eating anything the Claws care to give us. Not if I want to stay alive." She yawned and ran her fingers through her hair, combing out knots and dry grass with her fingers. "It's a pity it's too late to do any hunting. I should have thought of that last night."

"Too late now, 'Zariel. You should have gone on watch."

Kiihaon returned shortly after the rest of the soldiers had woken. Azariel lounged in the grass, resting her head on Farren's knee as he leaned against one of the birches. She tore absent-mindedly at the fresh bread, watching the horses as they grazed. Shadira's bay mare raised her head and snorted. Azariel rose to her feet and pulled Farren up after her. "Here they come," she said. Instinctively, her hand strayed to the hilt of her sword.

Kadir rounded the building, flanked by two of the other Claws. Three more came behind him, forcing Tina along. They pulled and pushed the young woman out of the shadow of the western end of the barn-like building and into the sunshine to a cluster of wooden corrals at the eastern end while Kadir turned towards the spinney.

"Damn," whispered Farren. "They're not going to leave Tina for a second. I had half hoped that they would leave her during the combats. One of us could have gone to get her."

"They'd have foreseen that." She walked to meet Kadir, the warm wind sending her cloak and hair flying over her shoulders. The opal ring on her right hand pulsed once with a sudden surge of warmth. *Thank you, Master. I didn't even have to ask you.*

Kadir halted forty paces from her. "Are you ready? Shall I tell you what you're going to do?"

Farren strode to stand beside her and they linked hands. "We're ready," he said.

"Very well," the Claw leader said. "For the return of the dun stallion, one of you will face one of us, mounted and fighting with spears only."

"To the death?" asked Azariel, catching Farren's eye. *I'm reasonably good with a spear and I might be able to win this one. I'll have to see if Kenyon's better than me, but I'm probably the best one out of the rest of us.*

"Only if you want to," Kadir answered. "You can ask for quarter any time, but you will, of course, forfeit the dun stallion. And I might do something to that little red-headed beauty."

"You dare," growled Farren softly. "What about the rest?" he said, more loudly.

"For the grey stallion: a fight on foot with sword and dagger. For the bay stallion: kill a guard-dog using no armour or weapons. For the pair of chestnut stallions: catch and ride a wild stallion we brought in here last week. He's a killer."

"And goaded into a fury as well as being unbroken." Farren slid his arm around her waist. "I think that's a job for me."

"We accept," she said to Kadir. "When will you be ready? And where?"

"Now. Over there." Kadir gestured towards the corrals. More Claws had joined the three with Tina. "Come and be killed."

"What about spears? We haven't got any."

"We'll give you one." Kadir spun on his heel and walked back to the barn, robes fluttering in the northwest wind.

Farren kneaded at her armour just above her belt. "You're our spearwoman, Stormwolf. You'll be the one to win Tussock back. Do you think you can?"

"Of course." She chirruped to Storm and the black horse trotted towards her. "At least I hope my old skill with the spear hasn't faded." She paused, one hand holding the gelding's mane, and looked back at the semicircle of Kingdom soldiers. "You said you had been in the pike squadron, but how good are you with a spear on horseback?"

"Completely hopeless, or at least my horse is." He grinned. "No way out of it, arch *minyaster*. You're the one to do it."

She tugged at Storm's mane and led him to the pile of dumped tack. His bridle was lying near the edge of the heap, easily picked out by the braided leather brow-band. She pulled it up and slipped it onto him. *I'm bound to do something clumsy with everybody watching me like this.* She eased the tongue of the buckle under his neck into place and slid three fingers between the leather and the smooth hairs of his throat. "Did you bring Storm's saddle, Kiihaon?" she asked, staring down at the heap of brown leather and metal.

"Yes." Kiihaon squatted down and picked the saddle up from the bottom of the pile. The stirrups hung awkwardly and she straightened them before handing the saddle to Azariel.

"Thanks." Azariel slung the tack over her horse's back and fastened the girths. Storm turned his head and nudged her in the back with his muzzle. "I haven't got anything for you, I'm afraid, old fellow," she said to him. "Will you still do a good job for me if I don't give you an apple right now?" Something warm and firm pushed her in the back again. "That'll do now, Storm."

"I'm not Storm," said Farren's voice in her ear. His hand travelled up from her waist to her shoulder. "Good luck. May God Incarnate look after you."

"Thanks." She turned around and slid her arms around his neck. "And may he protect you when you tame that stallion."

His strong hands cupped around her face and he bent his head to kiss her on the mouth. The short stubble on his chin rasped her cheek like fine sandpaper. "Don't get yourself killed. And make sure you test the spear they give you."

"I'm not an idiot." She drew back from his embrace and swung herself onto Storm's back. She looked down at him as he smiled up at her, idly twiddling the diamond and onyx betrothal earring through his left ear. His rumpled red hair twitched across his forehead in the wind. "You're a handsome man," she said. "But I'd better go instead of sitting here staring at you."

She rode to the eastern end of the barn and waited, looking eastwards at the Claw rider who was waiting for her on horseback, spear ready. She screwed up her eyes against the strong morning sunlight. *Naturally, I am the one to have the sun in my eyes, but did I expect them to fight fair?* A Claw sauntered over to her and handed her a spear. She ran both hands along the length of the smooth ash-wood shaft, probing for weaknesses. "It'll do," she said when she had finished testing the weapon. *It's been over a year since I last fought seriously with a spear. I hope it'll come back to me fast enough for me to survive and win.* Storm fidgeted and pranced beneath her. "Steady, old fellow." She patted his thick neck and studied the other rider. *Riding the dun stallion Tussock we're fighting for. Well, that will stop me skewering the horse like I would in a real fight.* She tucked the butt of the spear under her arm, fingers tightening around the grey wood. *And fighting with spears alone means I can't shatter his spear with my sword.*

She glanced along the corrals that joined onto the back of the barn. The Claws sat on and around the wooden rails at one end, Tina in the middle of them, still bound. The Kingdom soldiers arranged themselves around a water-pump and trough to the south of the corrals. She caught Farren's eye and smiled at him as he raised his hand to her in salute.

Kadir stood up and placed his hands on his hips. "If you're ready, then start fighting! We haven't got all day."

She clapped her heels to Storm's sides and dropped her spear down into the attack. The black gelding neighed and surged into a canter. She clenched the spear to her side with her elbow and pivoted with his gait, keeping the spear level. Dust billowed behind the heels of the dun stallion swerved as it charged her, hazing the sunlight. The Claw hurtled at her, the shoulders of his armour dazzling in the sunlight. With a quick tug of her left hand on Storm's bridle, she turned him to one side out of the spear's path. "Coward!" yelled one of the Claws by the corral. She ignored the taunts and swung Storm swiftly around, heading him at the side of her opponent, bracing herself and the spear ready for the impact.

Her spear sliced through the air and struck the Claw's shoulder. *Missed! And I won't get a chance to strike from the side again.* The spearhead glanced off the chainmail, grazing the man as Storm flung himself onto the dun stallion. Tussock squealed and reared. His yellow teeth snapped at Storm's neck and muzzle. She turned Storm away, hearing the Claw shouting at the stallion behind her.

She lowered her spear and prepared to charge again. Tussock was rearing and prancing, straining towards Storm with his teeth bared and his ears flattened against his skull. The Claw's spear bobbed up and down like an angler's rod as he tried to rein Tussock in. *Of course! Tussock's a stud stallion, not a trained warhorse.* She laughed and clapped her heels against Storm's flanks. *That stallion doesn't know what to do. He just wants to fight back at Storm.* Her eyes narrowed. *So I'll make him angry.*

She wheeled the gelding out of the path of the Claw's wavering spear, feinting a stab at the man, then spurring Storm at them again, too close to bring the point of her spear back enough to put force behind it. Storm reared, sidestepped and closed with the stallion, whinnying proudly and battering at Tussock with his hooves. She let Storm battle the stallion as the rider fought for control. Her hair whipped around her face and into her eyes as she rocked and pivoted with the violent jerking of her horse. She watched the Claw through the blur of black hair and sunlight, shifting her right hand to grasp the spear from underneath. *We're too close to use the point, but the butt makes a good weapon. As soon as he's vulnerable, I'll strike.*

Tussock reared once more, ears laid back. The stallion screamed angrily and crashed down at her gelding, teeth raking bloody marks onto Storm's muzzle. She edged Storm away as Tussock flailed at him with his front hooves. Again the stallion plunged down, almost pitching his rider over his neck. She dropped the reins and twisted the spear around, holding it in two hands like a quarterstaff. The butt end whirled up and over as she rammed down with her left arm and up with her right. It struck the back of the Claw's head with a solid knock of wood on bone. The two horses closed with each other again and the man swayed from side to side. She swung the butt of the spear around again, aiming at the man, but the heavy shaft cracked into the stallion's shoulder. With as much effort as she could muster, she jerked the spear upwards. The shaft caught the Claw under the chin. The man's eyes glazed as his body toppled forwards over Tussock's neck.

Storm danced backwards as Tussock reared to kick and batter at him. The Claw's body slumped to one side, but his feet were wedged firmly into the stirrups. Baring her teeth, Azariel tucked the spear under her right arm and aimed the point at the Claw's torso. She sent Storm lunging forwards, throwing her weight as well as the gelding's behind her thrust. The resistance against the spear felt like a wall, then the head broke the links of chainmail open. She drove the spear in deeper, making sure of the kill.

She released the spear as the Claw's body wrenched it out of her grip, splinters from the shaft jabbing into the tender, barely-healed cut on her left hand. Tussock reared as his rider fell, eyes wide and white, and blood streaking his golden coat. She gathered up the reins and wheeled Storm to the right. "Enough, old fellow. You can run away now."

The black gelding whirled and galloped past the Kingdom soldiers. The thunder of Tussock's hooves followed close behind. "Catch him, somebody!" she shouted. Storm wove to and fro, eluding the punishing teeth of the angry stallion. She hauled on the reins and leaned back, pushing her weight down hard into saddle and stirrups as she tried to check him. Storm squealed as the stallion nipped at his rump, and kicked and bucked wildly.

She lurched to the side, balance lost. Her feet slid from the stirrups as Storm thrashed and pitched, and she was flung over his shoulder. Her left side crashed agonisingly into the ground as she landed rolling. Dust filled her mouth and eyes. She lay on her side and watched Storm race into the fields, Tussock pursuing him.

She stared after the horses as they ran into the open grassland. *I hope we can get them back before too long.* A smear of blood ran from her elbow, which felt stiff and sore after the fall. She sat up and twisted her arm to look down at the graze.

Footsteps crunched on the ground behind her "Well, you certainly fell into your own trap," said Farren, voice husky with laughter. He offered her his arm and helped her to her feet. His eyes shone as he embraced her roughly, armour grating on armour. "But well done. You've got Tussock back for us – when he finishes putting Storm in his place." He tossed his head and whinnied like a horse. "Fancy a cheeky little black gelding biting and kicking a Stud Stallion Like Me!" He whinnied again and stopped as she laughed. "Good work, Stormwolf. That's one out of the five."

CHAPTER FIVE

Farren slid his arm around her waist and strolled with her to the pump and trough where the other soldiers waited. The wind swept around him, ruffling his hair and raising dust from the dry dirt, making his eyes water. The sunlight hit the small pool of water at the bottom of the trough and reflected into his eyes, dazzling him. He turned away from the glare and perched on the thin stone rim. "Right. Now who's going to face the swordsman?"

"Any of us except Kiihaon could do it, I guess." Arturus plucked a long blade of grass and nibbled at the end of it. "We can draw straws again." He took the grass out of his mouth and flicked it away.

"Before we do that," said Azariel, sitting down on the rim of the trough beside Farren, "does anyone want to volunteer? Who's the best swordsman or swordswoman among us? You're pretty good, Shadira."

"Thanks, 'Zariel. I'm not too bad, I guess. But I don't think those boys will let me use my usual trick of two swords at once." She tugged one of her brown curls out straight then let it bounce back up again. "Kayti?"

"Oh, I'm not the best of us," the blonde soldier laughed. "Not once I'm off a horse. Old Silverbird does most of the work for me, I think." She looked up at her grey mare and smiled.

"We're all well trained," said Halbor. "I know I wouldn't be here today if I didn't know how to hold my own with a sword, and I guess the rest of us could say the same. Just give the order, ma'am. Send one of us in to fight."

Azariel twisted her rings round and around her fingers, brow furrowed. "If I choose someone and they die, it would haunt me forever."

"You've got the right to, 'Zariel." Shadira leaned towards her. "You put your life on the line for us against that sorcerer at Falcon Pass; we can do the same for you."

"I can do it," Kenyon said, breaking in. "I win most of the duels at our border post. I should be able to beat most other swordsmen or women. Unless that Claw's a gammyhander. They're so awkward to fight."

"A what?" Azariel asked.

"A gammyhander." He waved his left hand. "You know – a southpaw, a left-hander. They come at you from the wrong side and really throw you unless you've practised against them. Weird lot, mostly."

"Thank you!" said Farren as the soldiers from the Watchtower laughed.

Kenyon's tanned cheeks flushed. "Sorry. Didn't know you were one of them, Farren." He looked down at his boots and rubbed the dust off one of them on the calf of his other leg. "Hey, Farren," he said, head jerking up again. "I'm not the only person in the world who gets unsettled by—by left-handers. Perhaps you should go up against that Claw."

Farren scanned the open grass that stretched to a distant line of poplars. Storm and Tussock had vanished. "Perhaps you're right. I'll do it."

Azariel rubbed her grazed elbow. "Beloved, we'll need you to do that stallion they talked about. There are other sword fighters among us. I can do it; I'm used to duelling you as well as right-handers. Or Arturus. He's better than me and has sparred against you."

"And lost." Arturus tossed the end of his stalk of grass to one side and picked another. "Hurry up and decide. That lot over there won't wait forever."

Farren stared down at his nails and picked at the dirt beneath them. "I'll do it," he said. "Tina's my sister and it's my father's stallions that we're fighting for." He surged to his feet and a sharp prickle of pins and needles shot through his calf after the pressure of the trough rim. He looked across the pockmarked ground where Azariel had killed the Claw and beyond to the corrals. One of the Claws held the halter of a dapple-grey horse and another was walking towards the middle of the fighting ground. "There's their champion," he said. He unbuckled his cloak and let the heavy weight of hot wool fall to the ground. "I'd better go."

He flexed and stretched his arms as if he were drawing his bow, his muscles warming and filling with blood. He continued limbering up, then stopped as he heard galloping hoofbeats. Storm cantered around the building, Tussock close behind him. He laughed, then whistled to Storm. The black gelding lifted his head and neighed before swerving and running up to him, almost knocking him down. "Take him, Azariel." He lunged forwards and caught Tussock by the bridle. That must be one of their bridles – or one they've stolen off Dad. "Easy now, Tussock," he murmured. "Calm down." He breathed into the wide-flared nostrils of the stallion, pressing his face against the silk-smooth muzzle. The stallion snorted, spraying him with moisture, and the brown ears pricked forwards. "That's the way," Farren crooned. "It's all right." He looked over his shoulder at the other soldiers. "Someone take him from me, please."

Kayti came from behind him and led Tussock away. He looked over at the Claw who stood waiting for him, his armour shining in the sunlight. The man flexed his arms and shrugged his broad shoulders, making the links of chainmail ripple like fish scales over his well-developed muscles. He met Farren's gaze and a smirk crossed his square face. A quicksilver thrill rose from the pit of Farren's stomach, and his wrists and temples pulsed with rising energy. "King of Heaven, help me," he breathed, controlling the surge of fighting instinct. His left hand reached to his side, then he stopped. *I've got an idea.* He grinned and reached for his sword with his right hand. After fumbling for a few moments, he rasped his sword from the sheath. Then he squared his shoulders and tightened his grip on the hilt as he strode to the centre of the beaten dirt by the building. He locked eyes with the Claw champion and waited, heart drumming within his ribs.

"If you're ready, then fight!" came Kadir's voice.

The Claw struck at him. He stepped back, blocking the Claw's blow. The steel blades clashed together, then disengaged. He pivoted and brought his sword up for the backslash. His arm was jarred as the blades met again. *I hope I can pretend to be right-handed long enough to get him guarding that way.* Shouts of encouragement came from the Claws as he danced backwards, swaying out of reach of the Claw's blade.

He circled, keeping his eyes fixed on the Claw. The other man lunged at him, and Farren side-stepped away from the blow, presenting his left side to his opponent. The Claw's blade whistled through the air at his unprotected flank. He dropped and rolled away. *Blackarrow, you idiot!* Roars and whistles rose from the Claw's corner of the corral as their champion spun and towered over him. He scrambled to his feet, dodging the blade as it sliced towards his head, deflecting it with his own. The blades met with a clash that jarred his arm. The shock of the two blades meeting juddered up his arm, and he bounced to his feet.

He rocked to and fro on the balls of his feet, face to face with the Claw. The other man lowered his sword, ready to parry a blow from the right. *Now you're mine.* He stepped forward, inching his left hand towards his right. Farren faked a blow downwards and saw the Claw's arm jerk to the side. Swiftly, he passed his sword from his right hand to his left, the hilt fitting snugly into his practised grip. He struck at the vulnerable side of his opponent and the blade jolted against the Claw's armour.

The Claw took several steps backward. Farren lunged forward, driving the other man's sword aside again and again. He edged around, thrusting and jabbing, searching for a break in the Claw's defences that would give him the chance to disarm or kill. Sweat broke out on his forehead and neck as he feinted and lunged, the sunlight constantly glaring from the other man's armour and blade. The Claw retreated towards the wall of the barn. Pace by pace, Farren followed.

He flashed his sword out and around and dashed the weapon from the Claw's hand. The sword thudded into the dust and he kicked it to one side as Farren raised the point of his blade to the man's chin. "Will you yield?" he panted.

The Claw stepped back from the sword's point into the wall and bowed his head. Farren turned to face the watchers, flourishing his sword triumphantly above his head. He lowered it, then stooped for the Claw's fallen weapon.

"Behind you!" shouted Azariel and several other soldiers.

He started up, then something hard and sharp struck him in the shoulderblade, knocking the breath from him. He swayed and staggered forward, gasping. *But he'd surrendered!* Another blow of red-hot pain stabbed into him, punching through the rings in his chainmail and along his ribs, then another.

He spun around, slashing savagely at the Claw with both swords and howling in pain. He felt one blade rip into the Claw's arm and heard him yell. Grasping the hilt more tightly, he scythed his blade at the Claw's neck with the back-blow. The blow landed and tore on through the resistance, and he turned away. The sharp smell of fresh blood made the back of his mouth and nose ache, and hot stickiness spattered over his hands and face. *I don't want to see the mess I've made of him. It's enough to know I've killed him.* He turned away, the jingle and thump of the Claw's body falling loud in his ears. His shoulder and side throbbed angrily and his stomach rolled with bile.

He marched back to the drinking trough, fighting the pain to make himself walk proudly. *It's hurting like fury, but I'm not going to crawl back in front of those snakes. Or Tina.* He collapsed to his knees in the dust beside the pump and washed the blood off his face, hands and sword.

Azariel pressed in beside him, her soft hair brushing his forearms and the surface of the water. "Are you all right?" she said, squeezing his unwounded shoulder. "You're bleeding everywhere."

"It's not all my blood. I don't think he's hit anything vital," he panted. "It doesn't feel deep. Only hellishly painful. Help me get my armour and shirt off." He unbuckled his belt and fumbled with the lacings at the back of his neck. He wriggled backwards as she pulled the chainmail over his head, then stripped his black cotton shirt off. The sunshine and wind rubbed comforting fingers of air over his bare skin. "How bad do they look?"

She prodded at the gashes in his back and he gritted his teeth. "Your armour stopped the dagger getting too far in," she said. "None of them is deep, but they'll all need stitching. Wait there – I'll get my needle and thread out." She caressed his shoulder then drew back. He heard the small slap and jingle of her pouch opening. "Keep still, beloved," she said softly. Fresh pain dug into him near the line of agony on his shoulder and he stifled a cry as she began to sew.

Footsteps and a woman's voice shouting behind him seized his attention and he started. Three of the Claws had circled the corrals and were charging towards the soldiers from one side. Kayti, Halbor and Arturus met them, swords in hand. The Claw leading the three pulled up and raised his sword defensively, backing away. "I'm not so big a fool as to keep my attention on the fight the whole time," growled Arturus. "If you want to fight, I'm ready."

"We all are," Kayti took another step towards the Claws.

The three in the sortie retreated. "Enough," called Kadir. "Get back here, lads. They won't try anything as long as I've got this little horse-girl nice and safe."

I'm going to kill him. I'm going to kill him. The anger that churned inside Farren's stomach almost blocked the pain of Azariel stitching his ribs. *Cowardly, cheating scorpion! If once we can get Tina away from them…*

"There. Finished." Azariel straightened up. "I hope they won't fester."

"They're clean cuts." He stood up and pulled his shirt back on. "Thank you, sweetheart. I wish I had some willowbark. Do any of you have some?"

Azariel wrapped the remains of the thread around the needle and tucked it into the pouch. *Hopefully we won't need that again. Sewing someone with a bloody needle always seems to make a cut fester.* She shook her hair back from her eyes. "That's the second stallion."

"And I don't suppose I'll hear you offering the job of fighting the guard dog around," said Shadira. "If we've got to do it with our bare hands, you've got what we need, werewolf."

"I'm a shapeshifter, as I've told you dozens of times." Azariel turned the opal ring on her right hand around, gazing at the swirls of green, blue and red that flickered through the milky stone. "But I'll do it. I might not even have to fight."

"You won't." Farren's eyes met hers. A smear of blood remained on the tip of his sharp nose, and his hair had been darkened and flattened across his forehead by water. "I'm going to make sure of that. I can't do much with an animal I haven't touched, but I can do a little bit with my Gift to calm it down."

"And you're the man who never, ever cheats at cards?" Arturus chuckled. "I didn't think I'd ever catch you sneak an ace up your sleeve, so to speak."

"He might just be a very good cheat and not get caught," one of the other men shot at him. "You never thought of that."

"I don't have to play by the strictest rules of honour here," he said. "Look at them – they're threatening to cut my little sister to shreds…" He broke off and swallowed, eyes closed. "Cut her to shreds if we don't fight their guard dog barehanded. Who says we have to be fair?"

"Thanks, beloved." Azariel ruffled the hairs on his forearm. "We've taken enough time already stitching you up." She unbuckled her cloak, then followed it with her sword belt. Her armour hung loosely, feeling shapeless and baggy without the familiar support of the belt. She shook her hair back from her face into the wind and strode into the corral.

"Loose your dog," she called. "I'm ready."

Two of the Claws opened a side-door of the barn and entered it as the rest scrambled over the corral fence, pushing and hauling Tina with them. The pair of Claws reappeared, dragging a chestnut and white dog by two chains. Its square, heavy-jawed head was strapped in a muzzle and a line of hair stood rigid down the length of its back to its whip-like tail that curved between its hind legs. A cold thrill passed down her spine as she recognised its breed. *A bullfighter. More than a match for a wolf in everything except speed.* The memory of another bullfighter, a hunting dog belonging to her brother's friend, passed through her mind, its jaws locked onto the ear of a boar in spite of a gash in its belly where blood and entrails spilled. *They don't give up until they're dead or their strength has gone.* She drew a deep breath. *Master, I'm going to need your help, and so will Farren.*

One of the handlers removed a chain and climbed over the corral fence. Kadir stood on the third rung from the bottom and leaned over, clutching the wooden rail. "You're not ready," he called. "You've still got your armour on."

"You're mad," she replied. "I'm unarmed; the dog has teeth. This isn't a fair fight, and I'm not going to take it off."

"Then I'll start my knife on the girl. Or perhaps I'll let the dog at her, except that will be too quick. Take your armour off, or I'll take bits of her off."

She bared her teeth and bent her head as she reached behind her neck for the laces of her chainmail. A cold hard knot of anger tightened in her stomach. *Forgive me, Master, but I'm starting to think of several painful things I'd like to do to him.* She dropped the jingling links of steel into the dust in a heap and pushed it aside. "Very well then," she said in a voice of ice. "Unleash your dog."

"Not yet," said Kadir. He nodded to one of the other Claws, who unbolted one of the corral gates and led a bay stallion out. "There's what you're fighting for; make sure our dog doesn't kill him instead."

That dog won't touch it. It looks more likely to attack one of them. She tossed her hair back from where it had wandered and twisted her rings straight.

The second handler took hold of the bullfighter's collar and removed the remaining chain. Keeping one hand on the collar, the man wriggled back and through the rails of the corral. Then he slid the muzzle from the dog's square jaws. The bullfighter turned towards him, jaws snapping shut with a sound like a stick cracking. It rushed and retreated several times towards the Claws, then bounced back before whirling towards her, tail still between its legs. It saw her and stiffened, back bristling at the tail rising like a spike. It half barked, half growled at her, then rushed at her, stocky body low to the ground.

She threw herself to one side, dropping to her hands and knees and shifting shape. As her mind whirled, the bullfighter slid to a halt, hind legs scrabbling and skidding on the dusty ground. She tensed, ready for the bullfighter to rear and grab at her with its forelegs. Its hackles stood stiffly above its back, but the tail quivered and wagged tentatively. Its nose twitched violently and it inched around her in a circle. Her own tail twitched behind her, dropping level with her back. *You've never seen or smelled anything like me, have you?*

The bullfighter's nose and whiskers pressed close to hers, tickling and sniffing. It reared half-heartedly, then dropped down, its heavy square head knocking her shoulder. One of the Claws laughed suggestively and a growl built in her throat in response. The bullfighter turned so it stood beside her, facing towards her rear, sniffing again. With both human and wolf instincts, she whirled and nipped at the dog hard, her teeth catching at one of the patches on its shoulder. She leaped backwards and bowed, forepaws spread, head cocked to one side and tail waving.

The bullfighter lolloped around her in a wide circle. She ran after it, overtook it, then bowed and invited it to chase her again. *This is the first time I've ever played with a dog in wolf form.* She checked her rush and let the bullfighter catch her and tumble her to the ground, mock-wrestling. *The wolf part of me must know how to play.* She met the patched dog muzzle to muzzle, both of them rearing and grappling at each other's forequarters. Its tongue slathered over her lips and nose. Instinctively, her own mouth opened. She clenched it shut and let the bullfighter topple her into the dirt again, her mind feeling sick, although her wolf's body welcomed it. *I'd better decide what to do with this dog soon. It's only a matter of time before it tries to mount me.* Again the sensations of nausea passed through her mind but not her body. *I'm only grateful I don't cycle as a shewolf.*

One of the Claws jumped down off the corral fence; her nose recognised him as one of the handlers. "Patch won't fight the bitch without encouragement. I'm going in."

The dog handler strode over towards them, the chain dangling and jingling from his hand. The smell of anger wafted out from him. The bullfighter stood still, tail lowering and hackles rising again as it cowered. "Get in there, Patch," growled the man. He lashed at the bullfighter with the chain, then grabbed the dog by the collar and turned it towards her. Its eyes rolled and its ears were laid flat against its head. "Damn clever, aren't you, bitch?" He struck the dog again. "Kill, Patch! Get in there!"

The dog bristled and growled, trying to turn towards the man. Inspiration flashed through her and she charged. Her teeth closed on the man's arm that held the chain. He yelled and thrashed, breaking out of her grip and throwing both hands up. The bullfighter, all teeth and bristle, turned and leaped, catching the man by the upper arm. She dodged away as the Claw spun around, screaming. The hind legs of the bullfighter flicked up into the air with the Claw's momentum, its jaws relentless. The muscles in its cheeks twitched and she heard the sound of bone beginning to splinter. She bounded in again, clutching the man's leg with her forelegs and sinking her teeth into the thick muscle of his thigh. The hot salt taste and smell of blood flooded her mouth.

The Claw staggered to his knees. The bullfighter dug all four paws into the ground and bent its legs, ready to pull. She released him, a wash of dark blood trailing from her muzzle. The Claw reached to his side and drew a dagger. He slashed at the dog. It whined softly, but the jaws remained clamped. Again and again he stabbed. The dog's eyes glazed over and the jaws went slack. The Claw dropped the dagger and leaned forwards on hands and knees. His bitten arm buckled uselessly beneath him and he lurched forwards.

The blood still tasted strong in her mouth and fire ran in her veins. The back of the man's neck bent upwards as he regained his balance, sunlight catching the close-cropped hair along the spine. She leaped and bit, using bone-crushing pressure. He fell beneath her, twitching, then lying still, her teeth still locked onto his neck. She eased her grip and turned away from the bodies of the dog and the man. *No. Don't change yet. Not with the taste of blood in my mouth and the stallion still there.* She ran hard towards the bay stallion waiting by the corrals and nipped it lightly on the hind leg, making it start forward into a trot. Another snap at the fetlock, and it broke into a canter. Tail held jubilant above her back, she herded the stallion towards the Kingdom soldiers and the water-trough.

The bay stallion passed the pump, then checked its run to a trot and wheeled around to join the other two stallions. Azariel, still in wolf form, raised herself up on the trough to drink, forepaws on the stone rim.

Farren stood up and reached over to clap her on the shoulder. "Well done," he said. "Are you all right?"

Energy prickled beneath Farren's fingertips, and the fur changed to wool, steel and soft hair. She turned her face towards him and smiled, water still moistening the red curve of her lips. "Not a scratch," she said. "Thanks for your help with the dog."

"I didn't do much." He ran his hand along her shoulder and down to her wrist. "I only touched its mind lightly and let it go when you charged the Claw." He pulled her to her feet, the cut along his ribs throbbing. "I had to hold old Warlord, back, though, or else he would have kicked you into the middle of the Claws. Sweetheart, I didn't want them to get hold of you as well as Tina."

She caressed him above his heavy armband. "Thank you," she said.

"I suppose you'll want us to come over to the corrals with you, Farren." Arturus's deep voice came from behind his shoulder, then the older soldier sauntered up beside to rest one foot on the edge of the trough. "Or some of us, at least. I don't trust that lot. We've taken care of three of them now, and they could do something stupid."

"Not while they've got Tina. They won't do anything to risk losing their hostage, and we can't do anything yet either." Farren looked over at the group of remaining Claws; all six had clustered around Tina. The thin shadow of the barn had begun to trail to the south. *The day's half done already.* He searched for the sun, but it had hidden behind the butter and pearl-coloured high cloud that formed an arch above the clear sky to the northwest. The crack of a whip and a horse's fighting scream. He tried to see beyond the Claws to the far corrals. "That's my horse," he said. "Come on, Stormwolf. I want to get to it before they hurt it any more."

"I'm coming, too," said Shadira. "Kayti – how about you and Kenyon staying and guarding the stallions and our horses?" She got to her feet and grinned, her eyes flicking over to meet Azariel's.

Azariel glanced at the Claws, then at the Kingdom soldiers. "Kerrhona and Corrhan, you stay with Kayti and Kenyon by the horses. "The rest of you come with us to the corrals."

Don't tell me Shadira's matchmaking again. He slipped his hand into Azariel's and walked towards the corrals. One of the Claws came to meet him with a bridle. "Your horse is in there," the Claw said, passing him the tack. "Get in there alone and ride him."

He leaned on the fence rails and ran his eyes over the muscular chestnut neck and flanks of the stallion. It reared and pawed the air, snorting and whinnying in warning. His hand tightened around the bridle over his left shoulder. *What a horse!* The stallion bucked and lashed out with its hind hooves, catching the fence and scraping a pale patch in the grey wood. *A killer, but what a beauty!* "He's almost as impressive as that Stallion of the Northwest. It isn't him, is it, Stormwolf?"

She pressed in close beside him, cloak carried over her shoulder and turning her belt into its proper place around her slender waist. "No. Not this one, even though the northwester's running at the moment. This one's smaller. And look at the white star on his forehead." She pointed as the stallion whirled around again. "This could be one of his mortal servants. You remember the two he got to carry us after we found the first of the Stones of Protection."

He watched the stallion rear once more, ears laid flat on its skull and long mane streaming in the wind. "Yes." He closed his eyes and called up the image of the chestnut stallion he had ridden over a year before. "This one looks just like the one I rode. He's certainly tall enough, and I remember that crescent shaped star well enough. Look at the muscle on him! I don't know how they managed to trap him, but he's a horse anybody would love to tame." He winced as Kadir leaned over and slapped a whip over the stallion's broad rump, leaving a weal. "I'm going to keep him, if he doesn't kill me."

"What's up, soldier? Frightened?" Kadir's voice cut across his thoughts. "Get in there and ride the beast or else." Farren turned his gaze away from the stallion and saw the Claw leader holding Tina by the shoulders. "Are you going in or will she? The ropes are good and tight and she won't stand a chance."

The stallion trotted with arched neck and high-lifted hooves to the far side of the pen. Farren shouldered the bridle and vaulted over the fence. *God Incarnate, help me. If this isn't that horse I rode, I haven't got much of a chance, but if it is…*

Gentle warmth cascaded down his arms and hands, and the tendrils of his Gift spread towards the horse. The massive stallion saw him and charged.

He ducked to one side. The stallion's scream rang in his ears, drowning the thunder of its hooves. He lunged through the cloud of yellow dust and touched its neck, then reached for the mind of the horse. It felt harsh, hot and rough around a core of anger and fear. The horse tried to rear as his fingers tightened around the coarse hairs of its mane. He held on grimly, his arm nearly wrenched from the joint. Every wound protested. One of its front hooves struck him on the shin and he stumbled forwards, his face pressing into its forequarters and his lungs filling with the sharp, earthy smell of its sweat.

Its teeth crunched into his wounded shoulder and he stifled a scream. It shook him and he loosened his grip on its mane as his head swam in the waves of agony. He groped for its head and managed to slide one arm around its neck. Eyes streaming with the dust and pain, he clung to the horse in a rough embrace and dragged the horse's head down. He reached for the stallion's upper lip and clasped it firmly and pulling it forward. The tight knot of anger in the horse's mind loosened for one infinitesimal moment then hardened again. "Come on, you wild beauty. Look at me."

He stared into one of the white-rimmed eyes of the stallion and felt invisible cords flowing from his mind into the horse's. The hard knot of anger unravelled as the texture if its mind changed from harsh spikes to coarse sandpaper. Gradually, he eased back and gripped it by the mane, placing his right hand on the crescent-shaped star on its forehead. Wave after wave of warmth poured down his arms and hands until a thread of his will wrapped around the horse's. It rolled its eyes and struggled, lifting him slightly from the ground. He held on. "Veranath," he murmured, saying the name of the horse he had ridden from Moonlady Falls. "Veranath, servant of the Northwest wind, do you remember me?" The white rim vanished from around its dark eye and its ears pricked forwards. It snorted and tried to rear back. "Veranath," he said again, the touch of his Gift flowing down his arm and onto the stallion's star. "You must let me ride you again."

The horse bent its head and neighed. He let go of its mane and stroked the stallion's withers. The horse's skin flinched and twitched a few times under his fingers, then the taut muscles relaxed. The warm breath of the stallion wafted over his face as it snuffed at him. *Thank the Power.* He pressed his head against the stallion's muzzle and breathed into its wide nostrils. He ran his hand over its silky withers, then up the crest of its thick neck. For half a heartbeat, the sandpapery coarseness of the stallion's mind smoothed to the texture of woven wool before turning to sandpaper again. *He's mine. I don't want to ever let him go.*

He took the bridle from his shoulder, still damp from where Veranath had bitten him, and eased the snaffle bit between the stallion's lips. The big chestnut flinched and started back. He slipped the top of the bridle over the horse's ears, catching hold of the horse's upper lip again and squeezing. He pressed the bit into the horse's mouth again as its teeth parted. "That's the way," he crooned, releasing his hold on the lip. The horse champed and ground at the metal as he fastened the buckles. Gently, he took the reins over the stallion's thick neck, then vaulted onto the stallion's back.

Veranath reared and snorted and he grabbed a handful of mane to stop himself sliding backwards. "Steady there, Veranath." He sent another flood of calming energy down into the horse. The stallion tossed his head and pranced from side to side. He ran his hand through the stallion's chestnut mane and patted his neck. "That's the fellow. You'll make a splendid warhorse one day with a bit of training, but not for the Claws. You're mine. Good lad."

He relaxed his hold on the reins and let the stallion wander around. *Thank the Power for that! I've done it.* He slid off Veranath's back and led him out of the corral. The gate swung shut behind him and the Kingdom soldiers cheered. He held up his hand. "Don't scare him; it's only me he's accepted. It'll take a while until anyone else can handle him." Azariel stepped forwards, hand raised to caress the stallion. Veranath lunged at her, teeth bared. "None of that!" He tugged the stallion's head sharply to one side. "Don't you dare hurt her. Come on, Veranath. Come and meet my Princess."

"Hey, you can't take our stallion!" one of the Claws called.

Farren looked back over his shoulder. "You say that after taking five of ours as well as my sister? I'm taking him as a penalty." He gripped the reins tighter and the stallion's ears slanted back. "If you don't like it, then you can come and take him – if he lets you." He turned and led Veranath back towards the trough.

Azariel slid her hand into the crook of his right arm. "Well done," she said. He bent his head towards her, and her lips brushed his cheek. "Are you really going to keep him?"

"I've always wanted to find a stallion good enough to be a mate for Princess and now I've found him. Something like a horse *minyastin*, and that might well be passed along in the blood. I couldn't ask for better."

He whistled, and Princess and Storm whinnied in answer. Both horses trotted up eagerly and pressed into him, pushing him back against Veranath's shoulder. Azariel's arm slipped out of his. One of the horses trod on his boot, just missing his toe. "Steady," he said. "Don't crush me." He nudged Storm and Princess back, then walked with all three horses to the trough.

"They've gone!" Veranath shied and nearly pulled free as Arturus shouted.

Farren spun around. "Who's gone, Arturus?"

"Kadir and Tina. They've made off while we were watching you tame that horse."

He tethered Veranath by the bridle to the pump, trying not to fumble the knot in his haste. "Let's get after them – quickly!"

CHAPTER SIX

Azariel swung herself onto Storm's back. "I hope you've got some speed left in you, old fellow," she said, pulling his head up from the grass. "Which way did they go?"

"Don't know," said Arturus. "We didn't see them leaving."

"They didn't come this way," said Kenyon. "But that's all I know."

Farren grabbed his bow from the jumble of cloaks and gear near the trough and scrambled onto Princess's back. "Stay here with the stallions, the rest of you. I don't want them re-stolen." He nudged Princess with his heels. "Don't go near Veranath, either." His eyes met Azariel's. "Stormwolf? You're the better tracker of us two."

She headed Storm towards the end of the barn. "I can't see anything back towards the spinney where we slept. He must have gone the other way." She trotted past the corrals, rising and falling with Storm's pace. The remaining Claws were lounging on the rails and grinning. "I don't suppose they're going to talk," she said softly to Farren. "But look." She pointed to an open gate swaying and banging in the wind. "Kadir's made off with the last two stallions as well as Tina."

"Once we catch him, he's dead." His mouth tightened into a hard line. "There's an arrow in my quiver waiting for him."

She scanned the dirt and short grass at the eastern end of the building for hoofprints. "It's too confused and the ground is too dry to take many marks." An irritated breath hissed out of her teeth as she raised her head and scanned the wide flat sweep of the plains. The wind whirled her hair around her face as she turned northeast. A small cloud of dust rose from the ground in the near distance. She shaded her eyes and strained them through the haze and glare, and made out a confusion of heads, bodies and legs at the heart of the dust-cloud. "That's them. After him!"

She put heels to Storm and headed towards the fleeing figure. The black gelding neighed and thundered off, Princess a little way behind. She swayed with his rocking gallop, the wind buffeting at her left side. She urged Storm on and he snorted in reply. Air howled in her ears as she leaned forwards, moisture torn from her eyes by speed. Storm hurdled a small stream and galloped on. Ahead, she could make out the shapes of two horses and riders through the yellow-brown dust-cloud. "Keep it up, old fellow; we're gaining on them."

She heard Princess's fast breath beside her as the chestnut mare drew level with Storm. "We'll be up with them in a few minutes if we keep this pace up," Farren said, voice blurred by the rush of the wind and the drumming of the hoofbeats. "Tina must be doing something to slow her stallion down."

"Are we close enough for you to shoot?"

"Almost. But I'm not sure if I should do that with the wind this strong. I could easily hit Tina by mistake." He shielded his eyes with one hand. "We're going to have to be cunning. As soon as we get near enough to attack, he'll only pull the knife out on Tina again. We're going to have to think of something soon." Princess put on a burst of speed and edged ahead of Storm.

She urged Storm level with the mare. The gap between them and Kadir grew smaller, and the rumour of the two stallions' hooves became more distinct. "Will splitting up help? He can't keep an eye on two of us at once."

"Yes. Split up now. Leave Storm and creep behind him in wolf-form and attack. I'll keep him talking and looking my way."

She turned Storm to one side. "Good idea. May the Power protect you!"

She checked the gelding to a canter, but he tossed his head and struggled to chase after Princess. "Not now, old fellow. Wait until I've jumped and then you can race her." She slipped her feet from the stirrups and carefully swung one leg over Storm's neck. Gripping his mane for balance, she dangled side-saddle for a few heartbeats. She looked down at the blur of brown, green and ochre beneath her and Storm's pounding hooves. *I'll have to jump far enough to miss him.* She closed her eyes and launched herself from Storm's back, changing shape as she dropped.

The landing jarred her and sent her sprawling, almost landing on her muzzle. She brought her hind legs under her and began galloping through the grass. Storm shied to one side and headed back towards Princess. Stifling the urge to howl, she sped after the fleeing Claw, the scent of horse and dry grass sharp in her nose.

Tina looked around over her shoulder. The scarf gagging her had slipped from her mouth and dangled around her neck. "Farren!" she screamed, leaning back as far as her arms, which were tied around the stallion's neck, would let her. The chestnut horse jerked his head up and slowed for a few strides to a jolting indignant trot, but Kadir yanked at the reins and tugged him back to a gallop.

Farren saw Storm galloping riderless towards him and smiled. He scanned the long grass and saw a slim shadow loping towards Kadir. *Good on her.* He put heels to Princess and gave her her head, tucking his bow onto his shoulder. The gap between him and Kadir closed. Tina swayed and bounced awkwardly in the saddle, head bowed over her mount's neck. *It's a wonder she doesn't fall and get dragged. But all of us could ride almost as soon as we could walk.*

Kadir glanced over his shoulder and met Farren's' gaze. The Claw rider's mouth moved, but the wind blew the words away in a blur of shouting. *Azariel would have heard that but I don't know if I want to know what he said.* The stolen stallions veered leftwards and slowed to a canter. Farren let go of the reins and clenched the grip of his bow in his right hand, steering Princess with the pressure of his legs. His left hand groped at his side for an arrow.

The pair of stallions reared to a halt and Tina toppled off her horse, landing with her arms and hands wrenched above her head. "Stop!" shouted Kadir. Farren reined Princess in to a walk and turned her side-on so that his right hand with the bow faced the Claw. Kadir dismounted and pulled Tina's head back by her hair. The sheen of metal shone beside her neck. "Keep back and keep your bow slack," Kadir said. "Or else she dies."

Farren tugged Princess to a standstill. "Give us the stallions and let my sister go." He swung off the mare's back and stood beside her head. *Where's Azariel? I've got to keep him talking.* "We've won, fair and square, so keep your bargain."

"What, and lose my chance of escape?" Kadir snorted. His face split into a snarl. "I'll give you one of them; the bitch can ride with me. But not two. I'll turn him loose once you get on the march. Go away! Do it now and I might not take it out on her tonight."

"I'm not going to turn my back on you for one second, you Yellow Claw scorpion. Do you think I trust you that much? Turn the stallion loose now, then I'll think about leaving." He caught a glimpse of grey in the long grass that slunk towards the Claw. "Let her go, or I'll shoot." He nocked his arrow to the string and raised the bow, aiming at Kadir but keeping it undrawn. "There's no way I can miss at this distance."

"Get on the march!" screamed Kadir, shoving Tina in front of him. "I'm not releasing the stallion or her. Take it or leave it. I'll give you a count of twenty to leave, and then your sister dies! Understand?"

Farren waited, fighting the shaking in his hands. Beyond Kadir and Tina, the grass rippled as Azariel glided through it, hidden by the long stalks. "Twenty! Nineteen!" Kadir called.

He locked his gaze on Kadir, forcing himself not to watch the grass behind him. *Good, the horses haven't scented her yet.*

"Sixteen… fifteen…"

"Just back off, Farren, please!" Tina writhed in Kadir's grip.

Come on, Stormwolf. You must be close enough to charge now. Farren's fingers crooked around the string, ready to draw. *What if I shot the horses? It would be a sacrifice, but worth it to save her.*

One of the stallions raised his head and gave a warning neigh. "Ten! Nine! Eight! Seven! Six!" The sun broke from behind the arch of clouds and flashed off the knife in Kadir's hand as he moved it to rest the point under Tina's ear. "Three, two…"

"One!"

Azariel exploded out of the grass. Her teeth smashed into Kadir's arm on his bent elbow, knocking the knife away from Tina. He toppled beneath the impact of her charge but the knife struck towards her. She placed her forepaws on his shoulders and changed shape. Still pinning him down, she seized his right arm and shook the knife loose from his hand.

Farren raced forwards, dropping his bow. Wolf and man rolled over in front of him and he hovered above them, sword in hand ready to strike Kadir when he saw the chance. Tina lurched and staggered out of the way and fell against the stallion's shoulder, crying. He started towards her, then turned back to Kadir. "We're arresting you, Yellow Claw," he said.

"The hell you are." Kadir wrenched one hand up and crooked his fingers. Instinctively, Farren raised his right arm across his body as green lightning leaped and crackled from the other man's fingers.

Farren's fist tightened, ready to punch fire at the other man, and the silver of his rings heated. Azariel grappled at the Claw's arms, trying to hold him down. *I can't strike without hurting her.* He strode two steps closer, then flung himself onto Kadir's arm. Another bolt of lightning sizzled into the air, flying well wide of him. "Surrender or die." He forced the other man's hands into the ground, crushing the grass and releasing the sweetish scent of the broken stems.

The Claw screamed and shouted curses at him and Azariel, and struggled. "Kill me now if you've got the stomach for it."

There's nothing for it. He won't stop fighting and we've got nothing to tie him with. I don't know what other choice I have. "Hold him there," he said. She shifted to kneel on Kadir's chest and one arm. Farren drew his dagger, keeping Kadir's arm still pinned down, and raised it over the other man's bare neck.

He set his teeth, the pit of his stomach feeling cold and sick. *Butchering him like a pig. I wish I could have got him cleanly with an arrow.* He drew the dagger across the Claw's throat, breathing hard. A fountain of bright red gushed over him for the second time that day and he turned away, stomach heaving.

He turned away from where Kadir lay and towards Tina. The stallion snorted and jerked back as he approached. "Easy, boy," he said, surprised at how shaky his voice sounded. He raised his dagger, grimacing at the thick coating of blood on his hands.

Tina stared at him, face white. "You killed him. You really killed him."

He reached around and cut the ropes holding her to the stallion. She clung to him, still crying. "It's all right now, Tina," he said softly as he embraced her. "We've got you."

"I've never been so frightened in my life, Farren," she sobbed into his shoulder.

"I don't blame you," Azariel said as she slipped her arm around Tina's shaking shoulders. "I'm glad to see you alive and well."

Tina sniffed and pulled back from both of them. A weak smile flashed across her sharp features, suddenly reminding him of his own face in a mirror. "Thank you," she said. "Both of you." She looked at them, then down at her hands. "You're all over blood. Are you all right?"

"Mostly," he said. "That's his blood, and the sooner I get it off me, the better." He wrapped one arm around Azariel's shoulders. "What about you, though, Stormwolf? I saw him stab you."

"He grazed my shoulderblade. They usually do when I'm a wolf. I doubt it's any worse than yours." Her hand slid around his waist. "Let's catch the horses and go back to the others." She grimaced. "At least we don't have to drag a prisoner all the way back to the capital with us, but I hate playing executioner."

"So do I." He whistled for Storm and Princess, and the two horses trotted up. "Who will you take, Tina?" He swung himself onto Princess's bare back and gathered up the reins.

"Phoenix," she said, taking the smaller of the two chestnut stallions by the mane and lightly vaulting onto him. "Do you want me to lead Firebrand as well?"

"If you want to. He knows you better than he knows me." He turned Princess away from the mountains and towards the Claw's barn. The northwest wind blew warm and strong onto his right cheek. "Let's go. We've got the rest of the stallions waiting for us back at the house with the others."

When they returned to the corrals, the ground had been stained reddish brown in patches, with signs of something being dragged across the ground. Kayti was sitting on the ground holding her arm and Kenyon was kneeling close beside her. Halbor was bending over the trough with Shadira and Kiihaon pumping water over his head. Arturus and the others stood in a tight circle around two bound and gagged men a few paces from the trough and pump. Arturus left the group and walked towards them. "What happened?" Farren called to him.

"The Claws went after you," he chuckled, drawing his sword and swinging it loosely in a circle through the air. "But we stopped them. Took two of them alive, so we took more prisoners than you. I see you've got your sister, so guess that leader's dead?"

"Yes," he said. "Let's get on the road back to the farm. If we're quick, we'll be in time for a late lunch, and I think we all know it."

****

They rode down the slight incline towards the farm buildings. The grey stallion Azariel led lifted his head and neighed. "You're home, Rainshadow," she said. The horse tugged at the rope in her hands and she dropped it, letting the stallion run whinnying down the slope. She cantered down the hill behind them. Rose ran from the door of the house, then Setharan, Yvain and the grooms came out to meet them. A burst of hoofbeats thundered behind Azariel and Tina galloped past her on Phoenix, red hair flying in the wind. The young woman half tumbled off her horse and ran to her mother.

Azariel edged Storm closer to Farren. "A job well done. She's home." Storm clattered into the yard and she reined him in before dismounting.

Farren led Princess and Veranath towards the stables. "Let's get these horses seen to quickly and our prisoners somewhere secure. I'm all over stinking blood and I can't wait to get it off me."

"Race you."

They quickly unsaddled and rubbed the horses down before returning to where the pair of prisoners lay in the grass, staring up at them with furious eyes. "What's the most secure room or building on the farm?" she asked Farren. "They'll need to sleep somewhere and I'd rather not have to tie them to us.

"I've wriggled out of most of the rooms and outbuildings over the years, and most of them have a loose plank somewhere that could be kicked free." Farren raised his hands to his hair, then lowered them, grimacing. "Dad! Have you got any chains?"

Setharan wandered towards them, his head cocked on one side. "Chains? I might have some stowed away." He strode into a shed with rusted barrel hoops and old horseshoes nailed to the front of it. After a few moments of clanking and clanging, he brought out a pair. "It's a while since I trained a horse to harness, but I thought these might come in handy. I never thought I'd use them to chain up Yellow Claws."

"Thanks, Dad. What about padlocks?"

"One moment." He returned into the shed and more metallic scrapes rang out. "Two padlocks with the keys still in them. If you want a good place to put them, I think we've finished with the washhouse for the day. Or I can find a free stall."

"As long as there's nothing they can use to pick the locks, the washhouse will work," said Azariel.

With the help of the other soldiers, they wrestled the two Claw prisoners into the washhouse and shackled them by the legs to a large wagon that stood outside the door, logs chocking the wheels beyond the reach of the Claws. The curses and threats from the Claws still ringing in her ears, she returned to the stable door, brushing horse hairs from her hand and knocking flakes of dried blood loose. Farren finished shutting Veranath into a small paddock with a sturdy wooden fence beside the stables. He took her hand and walked beside her to the house. Setharan was waiting for them by the door. "Well done!" he said, slapping Farren on the back. "Ouch!" Farren's father shook his reddened hand.

Azariel chuckled. *Never slap Farren's back when he's in armour,* she thought, then bit her lip as Farren's hand tightened painfully around hers. He was leaning on the doorframe with his teeth bared and eyes clenched tight. *His back – that must hurt!*

"What's up, son? I didn't hit you that hard."

"I've been stabbed in the back and you hit me across the wound," Farren groaned.

She slid her finger out of his grip and caressed his arm. "Are you all right?"

"What?" said Rose. "You've been wounded? You silly boy, what have you been doing? Don't stand around talking." Farren's mother grabbed him by the arm and hauled him towards the floury kitchen table. "Get your armour and shirt off while I go and fetch some ointment. I hope you've got it stitched, but I doubt it, seeing all that blood over you."

"I'm all right, mother," he protested, pulling free from her grip. "That's Kadir's – the kidnapper's – blood you see all over me. I've been hurt worse than this before, and Azariel's seen to the wounds."

"Sit down and let me see it." Rose opened a cupboard and produced a large bottle. She opened the stopper and Azariel caught the sharp scents of lavender, garlic and vinegar.

Mothers never change, Azariel thought, helping Farren unlace his armour. "I've been stabbed as well, Rose," she said aloud. "Would you be able to see to me? I will need stitching."

Rose pushed Farren down onto a stool. "Yes, of course, Azariel." She bent over Farren's bare back, shaking the bottle in one floury hand. "You poor lad, those do look nasty." Her other hand brushed the skin beneath the angry red slash. "You've done that well, Azariel. I couldn't have done a better job myself. You were brought up as a weaver and seamstress, weren't you? It shows. Now, this is going to sting, Farren." She dabbed the ointment onto the wound in his shoulder, then onto the two in his side. "The last time I did this was when you were about ten and had opened your arm falling off – what was your pony's name? Flame, that's right. You had fallen onto a jagged rock, poor boy. Do you still have the scar?"

Rose finished dressing his gashes and replaced the strong-smelling bottle on the table. She ran her fingers down Farren's arm, frowning and peering closely at the skin. Azariel leaned closer. *Those are hardly a boy's arms,* she thought. Her heart quickened its beat and she rested her hands on his powerful archer's shoulders, savouring the touch of his skin. *My Farren's a strong man with arms of iron.* A surge of desire flooded her, but she kept her hands from wandering.

"Well, I can't find that one, but your arms are all crisscrossed with white scars," Rose said, straightening up. "You've got more than the one you showed us at dinner last night. And there were a few across your back, too. How on earth did you get all those?"

"I'm a soldier, Mother," he said. "I've seen war and I've hunted and fought Yellow Claws many times, and worse things than Yellow Claws."

"Oh." Rose re-corked the bottle. "I should have thought. I was a Nightraven cadet once myself until I came here to fetch some horses and found a husband instead. I should have realized that you'd have fought and been wounded by now. Silly me. I don't suppose Azariel will have as many scars as you, though."

"No," she said. "I've been wounded more times than he has." She traced a path from her left collarbone and down to between her breasts, the scar left from where Izar Gardweil had stabbed her in their single combat. *I could have been killed then,* she thought, staring blankly at the bottle on the table as she remembered, her other hand still on Farren's shoulder. *Thank the Power I wasn't.* Farren reached up and closed his fingers around hers. His neck muscles moved beneath her touch as he turned his head and kissed the back of her fingers.

"It's been quite hectic over the last few days; I'm not thinking clearly." Rose picked the bottle up again. "I've forgotten that you're hurt too, Azariel. Put your shirt on, Farren – quickly, before you catch a cold. And, Azariel, come round here with me and I'll see to you."

Once the two women had disappeared into the pantry, Farren pulled his tunic over his head and slipped his arms through the sleeves. His wounds still throbbed in his side and shoulder. *That ointment burns like fire. What does she put in it?* He fastened the lacings at his neck. Voices murmured behind the pantry door and he smiled. *If Mother thinks my scars shocking, what will she say to Azariel's? I've never seen more than the tip of that one the sorcerer gave her, but she tells me it's long.* He stood up and fastened his belt around his waist, wrinkling his nose as he felt how the cotton of his tunic had stiffened with blood. *At least Azariel distracted Mother from asking about the whip-scars on my back. I'd prefer not to have to explain to my mother how I've earned a few lashings over the years.*

He sighed and glanced back at the closed door before drifting to the stove and lifting the lid on the large pot of water that steamed almost permanently at one end of it. The water sat at the halfway mark and little bubbles danced on the bottom. *I'm going to heat up some water and take a bath.* He found a bucket and slipped outside to the pump and filled it. Ignoring the protests of his shoulder, he emptied the bucket into the boiler before stoking up the fire and shifting the huge pot to the hotter end of the stove. He stood back to wait, leaning against a bare space of the wall in between strings of onions and dried herbs.

"I suppose you'll be off to Lebhern-y-Hyalda now. Will you be starting out this afternoon or staying a little while longer?" Yvain wandered into the kitchen and began idly searching through the cupboards.

"Tomorrow. We'll need to hand our prisoners over, and carting them around makes the journey." He picked at the dried blood around his armbands. "Where's Tina and how is she?"

"Asleep. Mother gave her a dose of poppy to soothe her. I guess her nerves will be all to pieces for a while now."

"Next time you need to deliver horses to the capital, send her with them and tell her to see one of our healer *minyasti* who can work with wounded minds and hearts – Dakhryan Blackhound. He can help her – I know he's helped me. We might not be at headquarters if we're still hunting but he will be."

"I wish I was coming with you, but what with haymaking and everything, I can't." Yvain pulled out half a loaf of bread from the cupboard and ripped a chunk off.

Farren opened the firebox of the stove to feed more logs of elm in. "You're wishing you were back with that pretty blonde Nightraven, aren't you?"

"Did I tell you she was blonde? That's not the half of it," Yvain's expression softened and he smiled, staring into the distance. "Blue eyes, lovely smile and a gorgeous curvy shape. She's the most beautiful woman I've seen."

"I guessed as much. She's Stessa, isn't she?" He stared into the fire, watching the fresh logs catch fire.

"So you know her too? She's nice, isn't she?" Yvain paced around the room and sighed.

"I've worked with her twice. As for her being nice, she's certainly friendly and good-looking. Too friendly, sometimes." He thumped the stove door closed. "I hope she kept her paws off you." *I wouldn't like to think that having failed to seduce me, she succeeded with my brother.* "Enough about her and back to your original question. I'd like to stay a while longer, Yvain. But we're not on leave now; we've got our duty to do."

"A duty catching a gazelle. Don't forget your hounds and falcons."

"I haven't forgotten, although you've forgotten we won't be using falcons." He yawned. "We'll stay here tonight, anyway. We could do with a good sleep after last night's activity. And tomorrow, we're back to the capital, then we'll be off hunting."

CHAPTER SEVEN

Azariel yawned and stretched as the morning sunlight beat down on her as she lay in the tussocks near of Falcon Pass. The cold links of her chainmail on her exposed arms started warming in the sun's rays. Birds sang and she heard the rippling and rushing of a stream to her left. She stood up and brushed the diamond beads of dew off her cloak and blankets, then swept the hair back from her face and looked around her. *Here's where we fought against Wayast. It's a shame we had to leave the capital so late in the day yesterday.* The wind blew in her face and her hair streamed out behind her. *It's hard to think that just over a year ago, the firewall was burning from one side of the pass to the other.* Young plants and grasses covered the black soil of the slopes. In front of her, the grey cobbled highway ran it down to the shining line of the Illin-y-Hyalda river.

Farren dozed a few paces to her right, his head resting on one of the saddlebags. She smiled down at him as his chest and the blankets over him gently rose and fell with the rhythm of his breath. "Sleep on, beloved," she murmured as she stooped to pick up her sword from where it lay between them beside his. *One day closer to the day we can marry. Somebody ought to change this stupid rule that makes* minyasti *have such long betrothals.* She wiped the dew from her sword and sheathed it. *I'm arch* minyaster; *I could change it. But I'd better wait until after we're married so that I don't have to put up with the sniggers if I tried to change it now. Even if I could change it. It could be seen as abusing my rank.* She sighed. *The rest of summer, autumn and winter left to wait.*

She walked to the stream and splashed the cool water over her face, dashing the last traces of sleep from her mind. The sunlight sparkled off the dancing surface and the rough dappled stones of the stream-bed. *It's a pity this stream's not deep or hidden enough for a proper bathe.* She scooped some more up in her hand and drank, savouring the clean gravelly taste of the mountain water. She dipped her hair in the stream, then shook it back, sending flashing drops flying through the air. *That's better.* The cut on her shoulder twinged with pain as she shrugged her cloak back into place. She grimaced, then looked down at the slash on her palm. *Healing well but still tender. I wish I hadn't lost my gloves last winter.*

She heard hooves behind her and turned, shielding her eyes from the bright morning sunlight. Storm walked over and nuzzled her chest, warm and whinnying. "Good morning, old fellow," she said, patting his neck and withers. "Had a good rest and breakfast?" Princess and Veranath were grazing between the tussocks half a bowshot off. Veranath tugged at the rope tethering him to a pine sapling and stretched his neck further to reach a new clump of grass. "I suppose I'd better light a fire and wake Farren, hadn't I?" Storm tossed his head and butted her in the shoulder. Her wound throbbed again. "If I can find some firewood, that is. If not, then it's a cold breakfast for us."

She patted Storm's neck once more and walked to the small shrubs growing near the road. The young mountainthorns waved in the wind that hissed through them. She knelt down and something sharp jabbed her knee. She straightened and pulled a tendril of blackberry free from her trouser leg, bruising the white cluster of flowers. *Too small for firewood. After all that we used to keep the Wayasti back, I'm not surprised. I won't waste too much time looking for it.* She brushed a few grains of blackened earth from her hands and walked back to where Farren lay. *He looks so handsome and so peaceful lying there. It's a shame to wake him.* She studied the sharp lines of his nose, chin and cheeks, and the curve of his mouth. "You would be using the saddlebag with the bread in it for a pillow, wouldn't you, Farren?" she said aloud.

He stirred as she said his name. Groaning, he rolled onto his back and rubbed his face with his hands. The sunlight reflected off the slits of his eyes between his fingers and off his rings and armbands. She knelt beside him, and he tugged on her arm as he sat up. "Good morning, beloved," she murmured, kissing the prickly skin on his cheek and inhaling the scent of grass, horses, sweat and smoke that clung to him.

"I hope you've slept well," he said. "Are you ready to ride?" He yawned and rolled his head so a tight sinew in his neck crackled. "The sooner we get this hunting dog we need, the better."

"We'd better eat first," she said. "You've been sleeping on our breakfast." She reached around him and picked up the saddlebag. The leather was still warm from where his head had been. "I hope the bread isn't crushed."

"It'll still taste good. I know my mother's cooking."

She opened the bag and felt for the loaf. "We're lucky. It was good of her to give us some." She pulled the loaf free and drew her dagger. "You have crushed it."

She sawed a crescent-shaped slice from the badly dented bread and tossed it to him before cutting herself one and trying to pull it into shape. The crust tore loose. She opened the mouth of the bag wider and searched inside for a round of cheese and some dried fruit. Her fingers met the suede-soft disk of the cheese and she took it out.

"King of Heaven, thank you for our breakfast," Farren said, his mouth half full.

"So be it," she replied, slicing into the cheese with her dagger.

After eating, she walked over to the horses. Farren splashed in the stream behind her. She caught Storm by his rough mane and led him to the bent grass where she had lain and the saddles sat. He stumbled over something in the turf, and she recognised it as a bone. *Another reminder of the war.* She stooped for the bridle and slipped it over the gelding's head. "Be quick, beloved. You'll have to do Veranath." She swung the saddle over Storm's back and fastened the girths. "All you need is the saddlebags and we're ready to ride, old fellow," she said to her horse.

She left Storm to graze fully tacked up and picked up Princess's bridle. "Here, girl," she called, walking towards the other two horses. Veranath stamped and laid his ears back before trotting away as far as his rope would let him, but Princess ambled towards her, huffing hot breath over her hand as she bridled the mare. She finished preparing Princess and began strapping the saddlebags behind the saddles. A footstep crunched behind her, and she looked around to see Farren returning from the stream, his hair damp and a smudge of red on his jaw line. "You've cut yourself," she said.

"I know," he said, fingering the red line. It's hard doing it by touch. Is... Have I missed any?"

She slipped the tongue of the last buckle into the hole of the leather strap on the saddlebags before turning to study him. His arms coiled around her waist as she slid her hands along the sharp angles of his cheeks. His skin was damp, smooth and cool beneath her fingers, and her heartbeat quickened. "Smooth as polished steel," she murmured, tilting her head back and pressing a kiss onto his firm lips. "You're a good-looking man, beloved."

His lips parted in a smile, exposing his even teeth as his arms tightened around her. "I try my best," he said. "As much as I'd like to, we'd better not linger here too long. Lebhern-y-Hyalda and the gazelle wait for us."

She darted in to kiss his cheek. He relaxed his hold on her as she turned towards Storm. She swung herself onto the gelding's back then waited. Farren coaxed Veranath closer and untied the rope tethering the stallion to the pine. He wrapped one end of the rope around his wrist and led Veranath to Princess. He mounted the mare and settled into the saddle. Azariel smiled at him. "Ready now?" she asked. She tugged Storm's head up from the grass and headed westwards down the slope, leaning slightly back for balance.

The road zigzagged down the side of the mountains, dropping into the plains once more. The shadows of the Seranyai-y-Taranar stretched ahead of them, sharp in the strong sunlight. The sun wheeled from behind them to the zenith in the north and the shadow left them. Beyond the heat-shimmer and the water-mirages on the grey road, the tall shape of the Watchtower of the West marked the border between the Kingdom and Wayast. *There's our home,* she thought, longing rising inside her for the familiar smells and sounds of the tower. *It must be near midday if we've got this far already.*

"Here's the crossroads," Farren pointed ahead to a milestone under a small spinney of trees. "We'll halt here for a rest. The horses need it." She followed him into the cool shadows and dismounted.

They let the horses rest, then rode on. By late afternoon, they arrived at the border town. The golden light shone off the glass windows of the castle of Duke Milanan of Lebhern-y-Hyalda. They entered through the southern gate of the city wall. The busy cobbled streets rang with cartwheels, people's voices and animals' cries. The crowded rows of shops and houses blocked the castle in the centre of the town from sight, save the topmost turret, where the red and black Kingdom flag flew.

Farren looked around at the people milling about. "Now to find a hound breeder," he said, leaning closer to Azariel. A small group of children ran out of an alley to his left, shouting to one another. He tightened his grip around Veranath's rope. "Easy, lad," he said to the horse. "Don't you dare hurt them."

"I suppose we could ask that leather-trader we get most of our gear from if she knows any," Azariel said. Storm's hooves clopped on the cobblestones and the black gelding drew level with Princess. "Her shop's in the western end of the town, if I remember correctly."

"Good idea." He swung Princess around a corner to the left, nearly colliding with a tattooed Zenifi fruit trader. "Sorry. I didn't hear you coming," he said to the man before turning back to Azariel. "Now to remember the way to Silk Street."

"Silk Street?" said the fruit-seller. "Go down this road until you get to the baker's; turn right, then it's on your left somewhere."

"*Mna fharya*," said Azariel. The fruit-seller grinned and raised his hand to her before walking away.

Farren stared at the trader. *What was he so pleased about?* Then he shook his head with a rueful chuckle. *Of course! She speaks fluent Zenifi.* He tapped Princess's sides with his heels and the mare walked on, hooves echoing off the stones. Before long, a mouth-watering yeasty smell filled his nostrils. He sniffed and looked around. "There's the baker's," he said, guiding Princess around the corner. "That's a smell to whet your appetite."

"We'll have to wait until later for that." Azariel winked at him. "We'll see what we've got left over after buying dogs."

The townspeople drifted to and fro through the streets around them as he rode on, mostly Kingdom men and women, and a few people wearing the gaudy robes of the Wayasti. *Well, we are in a border town and there'll be traders coming over.* Daubed on a wall ahead of him, a faded white arrow had been marked with black lettering. "Silk Street," Azariel said, turning Storm leftwards. "And the leather-trader not far from here, judging by the smell."

He sniffed again and caught the faint tang of tannin and dog dung blown down the dirty street on the warm wind. He gazed down the line of awnings above the shop doors and picked out sheepskin dyed crimson displayed by a door in a long finger of sunlight. "There it is," he said. He reined Princess to a halt and dismounted. He found a well-worn metal ring in the plastered wall nearest him and passed Veranath's rope through to tether him. "You wait here a bit." He patted the stallion's thick chestnut neck. "We won't be long."

"Can we wait long enough to buy from her?" Azariel's boots struck the cobblestones as she landed. "I'd like to get some gloves; I lost mine last winter."

"I was going to get Veranath a bridle. How much money do we have?" He loosened the pouch at his belt. "I've got my twenty silvers of salary, and so should you. Do you have any of the money Storm won for you in that race still?"

"Some of it but not all,' she said. She glanced at him, scratching at the red line on her left palm. "I think I've got fifteen silvers of it on me, plus my pay. That should be enough, and leave ample for hunting hounds. And I can ask her to send the chitty for the gloves to the army barracks."

He stepped past a pile of dyed skins and opened the door of the shop. The rich smell of leather and wool engulfed him. Inside, a dark-haired woman sat behind a table in one corner, cutting a pattern out of a deerskin. She looked up at him. "Greetings," she said, straightening up and brushing her rippling hair back from her face. "What can I do for you two?" She downed her tools and stood up. "You've been here before, haven't you? You're the *minyasti* from the Watchtower."

"That's right," said Azariel. "How's business?"

"Not too bad. I've just sent a number of lambskins across the border and shoes are always in demand. I've had quite a call for new boots from you soldiers. Seems as though the local sable and scarlets are putting in a few miles in the hills lately." She pushed a few offcuts of leather to one side of her work. "But I suppose you'd know more about that than me."

Farren shot a glance at Azariel. "We don't," he said. "We've been in the capital."

"Well, it's been the main topic of gossip here. That and whether the Duchess is expecting a baby. But it seems as though smugglers have been slipping across the river up in the hills. What they've been smuggling and whether they're crossing from here to Wayast or the other way is anybody's guess. Silk is what I think. Anyway, what can I do for you? You didn't come here just to hear the latest gossip. Or maybe you did, but I can reassure you that what I send across the river, I send honestly."

Farren glanced around the shop at the piled hides and the skins stretched to dry on frames along one wall. "I'm after a bridle for a large horse."

"How big? I've got a good selection of bridles are over here." The shopkeeper waved at a rack hanging in the corner then picked up her knife. "I've got something for every horse, from little ponies up."

"About seventeen hands, but he hasn't got the heavy nose of a carthorse."

"Then you'll want to look in the rack second from bottom." She jabbed her knife towards it. "Pick something you like – the ones with plaited leather reins are popular – then I'll fit the bit in for you."

Farren wandered to the rack of bridles and began looking through them. He lingered over one made of black leather with a plaited brow-band. "Could you tell us where we can buy hounds? We're off gazelle hunting and we'll need one."

"And I need a new pair of gloves," put in Azariel. "You'll need to take my measure." She raised her right hand in a bar of sunlight that shafted through a small window, the opal glittering blue-green in the sunlight. "How much extra will that be?"

He gazed at her long pale hand, with the ring finger as long as her middle finger. *You do have unusual and beautiful hands, my sweetheart. If you're going to wear gloves over them to keep that cut safe, I'm going to miss the sight and touch of them.* He sighed and turned back to the rack of bridles.

"It'll only cost five golds more than the glove would normally," the shopkeeper said. "And hounds … My cousin's place by the northwest gate of town would be best. He breeds some quite good hunting hounds and keeps me supplied with the dung I need for bating hides. You can't smell that from the shop – that sort of work gets done outside the city walls. At least I don't get my workshop out there pestered by restless youths and people finding a place to deal contraband like some others do. It smells too bad." She paused and shook her head. "But if you're going over there, don't go at night. At least, I wouldn't. You get some rough types over there. Now, madam, come over here and I'll take your measure. I don't think I can lay hold of the pattern I used last time for you."

He passed over a black bridle inlaid with pieces of bronze. *It's no wonder she remembers us: Azariel with her shapeshifter's hands and my left-handed gear.* He flicked through several more bridles and came to the end of the row. He paused for a moment then turned back to the black with the braided brow-band and another, one made of reddish-brown, white and black leather with both the reins and the brow-band plaited. He lifted the three-coloured bridle out and looked at it more closely. *The leather's nice and supple to the touch, but it's strong.* "I'll take this one," he said aloud, turning with it in his hand. "How much?"

The shopkeeper looked up from where she was tracking a stick of graphite around Azariel's hand. "That one's five silvers. I said that sort were popular. I sold two of those last week and three the week before. What kind of bit do you want for it? That's included in the price."

"Oh – snaffle, as usual," he said.

"With Veranath?" Azariel's dark eyebrows shot up. "Are you sure?"

"Of course. I haven't worked with him for long. Before long, he won't need a harsh bit to control him, so I don't need to buy one." He ran his fingers up and down the bumpy texture of the braided leather. *I'll put it on him as much as I can so he gets used to the feel of it even when I'm not riding him.*

"Snaffle it is, then," said the shopkeeper. "I could just about fit all of those bridles with the braided leather with snaffles, I get asked for that so often. And, madam, I've got your measure, so how do you want me to make the gloves? We've got some nice suede in different colours handy for a good price. You'd suit dark green nicely."

"Fleece lined please," she replied. "And in black, of course; I'll have to wear them as uniform."

"Very well then. They will be ready midday tomorrow. You can pay then. Unless you want me to send the chitty to the barracks. I don't mind heading over that way, as I can catch up on all the gossip and chatter with the quartermaster and the cooks when I do."

Her tongue must work as hard as her awl. He laid the bridle on the worktable beside the outline of Azariel's hand. "I'll take this when we pay for everything tomorrow, too." The reins slipped off the table under their own weight and he bent to pick them up again. "Thank you. We'll leave you to your work and we'll go for these hounds."

"Thank you for your custom. It's always nice to talk to people I don't see very often. Say hello to my cousin for me and I'll see you noon tomorrow."

He stood back to let Azariel walk first out of the shop. He untied the horses and swung himself onto Princess's back, wrapping Veranath's rope around his arm. "To the northwest gate to find some hounds. And here's hoping we can get what we need for less than thirty-five silvers." He headed Princess along the cobbled street, sidestepping out of the path of a rumbling cart. "And we should be done before it gets too dark to do business, unless the dog-breeder is as talkative as his cousin."

The shadow of the western city wall fell across him as he rode beside it past dark doorways and piles of refuse. He wrinkled his nose in disgust at the stench of rotting vegetation, rancid oil and urine. Nearby, a group of men were milling around outside a garishly lit tavern painted bright red. The music of a drum and fiddle drifted out. A scrawny black cur darted off a rubbish heap and yapped at them. Veranath jerked at his arm, aiming a kick at the dog. "Come on, Veranath," he said. "Leave it alone."

"I hope none of the dogs we'll buy are related to that one," Azariel said.

Ahead of them stretched the grey northern wall of the city. "There's the city gate," he said, pointing to the patch of evening sky that showed through the break in the grimy stone. "Watch out for the dog breeder. He should be near here."

He rode past a doorway where a lone woman stood, and snatches of music and laughter issued from inside. The woman brushed a lank strand of unnaturally blonde hair back from her brightly painted face and looked up at him. He avoided her glance. *I know what trade she plies, poor thing.* He turned to watch Azariel as she sat astride Storm, her face as pale as starlight against her blue-black hair. She met his gaze and smiled at him before cocking her head to the right. "There it is, if the dogs on the wrought iron gate are anything to go by, and the live ones behind it."

He scanned the street where she had indicated and saw a rough mud-brick wall surrounding a whitewashed three-storey house. A weathervane in the shape of a galloping hound perched above a pair of black metal gates, head pointing to the northwest. Some of the bars of the gate had been twisted and beaten into long-legged hounds on their hind legs as if they were leaping up at anyone who tried to enter. He rode over to the gate and dismounted. A tall greyhound yapped at him and thrust its thin muzzle through the bars while two others bounced and pranced behind it, baying loudly. A bronze bell hung by the gate, and he rang it. Behind the gate, the barking grew deafening. "Yes, this is the place we want. We should find hounds to suit us here."

"I'll stay here with the horses," said Azariel. "This is a rough part of town and I don't want the horses stolen. Neither do you. Anyway, you've got a better eye for a hound than I do." She slipped off Storm's back and took Princess's bridle.

"Good idea. I'll tie the big fellow up, though." He knotted Veranath's lead rope around one of the bars in the gate near the hinges. "Now, my lad, behave yourself. I think he's seen enough of you by now to know you're not going to hurt him." He caressed the stallion's muzzle. Hearing footsteps behind the gate, he turned to see a man in a leather apron coming towards him with two shaggy hounds trotting behind him. "I'll be as quick as I can, sweetheart."

The tall thin man in the leather apron shouted at the dogs before opening the gate. The dogs fell silent as Farren stepped through, but they milled around him, noses quivering and prodding at his legs. "What can I do for you, soldier?" the man asked.

"I'm after a hound I can hunt gazelle with," he said. "The leatherworker on Silk Street told us you sold them. What could I get for thirty silvers?" He let a greyhound sniff his hand, then stroked its silky ears.

"Two or three, depending on what you choose. Come out the back and have a look at the lot of them."

Farren followed the light, quick stride of the man along a tiled path around a greyish-white house. The man addressed him over one shoulder. "I've got many different breeds for hunting: wolfhounds, greyhounds, deerhounds, gazellehounds, boarhounds and general lurchers that will fetch down anything except dragons. I've bred a good cross between greyhounds and wolfhounds – quite a popular hunting dog it is too. The boarhounds – they're popular as guard dogs or as fighters, if that's what you're after. Fancy a war dog? You can use the boarhounds for that as well…"

Farren half listened to the constant chatter of the dog-breeder as he ran his eyes over the masses of dogs, some tethered and many running loose. *I wonder what their family gatherings sound like. Do they all talk this much?* More hounds thrust their long heads out from kennels, cages and windows. An enormous rough-coated grey male dog trotted to Farren and snuffled at his waist and hands before turning aside to piss against one of the cages, adding to the strong acrid smell of dog around the enclosed yard. "Your prize stud, I suppose," he said, pointing to the tall shaggy dog as it padded away again.

"Yes. He's a wolfhound; lovely dog, with good paces on him." The breeder swerved to one side as a group of three puppies, all legs and eyes, bustled and scrambled in front of him, tugging at the gnawed remains of a bone and each other. "Got several of his progeny over this way, all ready for working, if you'd like one of those."

"They're a bit large for us," Farren said, shaking his head. "I'd almost need another loosebox to keep one in, and I doubt they'd allow me to do that back at headquarters."

"Well, you could try gazellehounds. They're smaller but so are most dogs." The dog-breeder stooped to rumple the ears of a half-grown pup that jumped up at him. "They were very stylish about a year ago, but now it's greyhounds that are all the fashion. So gazellehounds are cheap at the price. Don't really know why, as they look like greyhounds except with long silky ears on them. Here's one over here."

The breeder gestured towards a slender, medium-high dog with a black and silver coat. Farren stepped towards it. It raised its narrow muzzle and gazed at him with large dark eyes framed by a silver mask and black forehead. "A noble looking hound," he said, studying its lean muscular flanks and rump. He held his hand out and the hound sniffed at him while he stroked the short silky hair on its neck. *I might take this one. It's a handsome dog and it looks swift enough to keep up with a horse.* "How much for this one?" he asked.

"For her? Fourteen silvers. I've got others of the same breed, if you'd like to take a look at others of her type. Have a good look around. I like to make sure that you find the one that suits you best."

He raised his eyes from the black and silver to the corner of the building where the breeder was walking. A pair of hazel eyes met him and a quicksilver shock shot through him. A dog build like a large greyhound but with a rough grey-brown coat was staring at him from a corner of the yard. His hands dropped to his sides and he felt the dog's mind connecting with his. *But I didn't even try to use my Gift on it!* He took a step towards it and dropped to one knee as it came to him. It rubbed its head against his hands and arms then tilted its head back to rest the end of its long nose on his shoulder. He caressed its coat, moving from the coarse hairs on its back to the softer pelt on its withers. A wash of warmth spread through him into the dog and rapport flickered between him and it. Its mind felt like freshly washed woollen blankets and well-worn leather boots. "What sort of dog is this?" he said aloud, surprised to hear his voice almost at a whisper.

The dog-breeder cocked his head to one side. "What's that? You've made friends with Lady? She's a deerhound. Ten silvers for her if you want her. Not a bad breed for people who like to hunt on horseback, but not fashionable at the moment at all."

"I'll take her," he said. He patted the dog's ribcage and its tail whipped to and fro.

The dog-breeder shrugged and spread out his hands. "You certainly look like you've taken to her, and she to you. Very well then. I hope you've got a good horse to keep up with the likes of her. Deerhounds aren't as fast as greys or gazellehounds, but they've got stamina."

Farren smiled, picturing Princess in his mind's eye. "I have. I did most of her training myself."

"I hope you haven't left her along on the street. There's horse thieves and worse around here. The dogs will give the alarm if they come in here but …" The other man turned towards the wall and laid one hand on the head of the wolfhound stud.

"No, I haven't left her. Azariel's with our horses and she'll take care of them."

"She?" The dog-breeder swung around and stared him in the face. "Are you mad, soldier? I wouldn't leave any woman alone on the street either at this time of the evening. Haven't you heard of the Bloody Blades? There's a gang of ruffians who prey on women. Every woman gets off the streets, even the whores, when they're on the loose. The Watch have been after them for weeks without luck."

"Azariel's a seasoned warrior like me," Farren said. *But I still don't want her in any danger.* His heart beat faster and his hands trembled. He listened, hearing the sound of footsteps and voices outside in the street. *Calm down, Blackarrow,* he told himself. *You're imagining things. You know you do when you think she's in danger.* "I might need a second dog, so let me see that other gazellehound you were talking about – quickly."

CHAPTER EIGHT

Azariel leaned back against the dog-breeders wall as the gate clanged shut behind Farren. Barking broke out from the yard inside, swallowing the sound of footsteps and voices. *He'll enjoy himself in there with all the dogs to choose from.* She gazed up at the sky, watching the racing clouds overhead change from white to rich saffron against the blue. A lone hawk circled above the walls of the city, riding on the winds. A series of warbling squawks rang out and two black and white birds flew up. The magpies swooped at the hawk and the raptor plunged out of its serene circle as they stooped on it. More magpies attacked, and as the birds circled and dived closer to her, she caught the sharp clip of beaks and wings as they struck the hawk. *If there was only one magpie, the hawk would win the fight, but then there's more...* The hawk stalled, then fled, a single feather blowing on the wind towards her.

She drew a deep breath and released it as she looked away from the city walls to the tiled and thatched roofs. Her gaze roved over the grimy stone buildings and glanced over the whore standing in the doorway. *Poor woman. I pity her, earning her living like that.*

"What are you staring at, Zenifi?" The blonde planted her hands on her hips. "Looking for work?"

Azariel lowered her head and walked over to Storm. "No, thank you. Not your type of work." The black horse nudged her in the chest and nickered at her. "Good old fellow. Hopefully, we won't have too long to wait. Shall I take off your saddle and give you a rubdown?"

"It's better than holding horses, Zenifi," the other woman said, voice ringing off the stones. "With some of the fellows we get through here, you get all the silver and drink you can handle. I can set you up with several."

Azariel loosened Storm's girths and eased the saddle off his back. "You have worked hard today," she murmured to the horse as she ran her hand over the hot damp patch where the saddle had sat. "I don't want anything to do with that," she called to the whore across Storm's back. "I don't suppose you would, either, if you had the choice. How much of your takings does your madam get?" The smell of horse sweat struck her as she stroked Storm's withers and her hand grew sticky with grime. Alert for swelling, tenderness and heat, she felt down the gelding's legs. "Any stones in your hoof, old fellow? Let me have a look."

"You're damn right. Been in the game before?" The whore's voice sounded bitter. "You're lucky. You've got a man to yourself, a good job and everything."

Azariel straightened up and faced the other woman. Her forehead tingled and an image flashed across her mind of an old woman surrounded by cloth. *A Vision, here and now? Am I to tell her?* The vision-woman picked up a length of cloth in her arthritic hands and began painfully snipping it into shape. More details piled into her mind, her forehead burning with the vision. She swallowed, hesitating. *She's going to think me rude.* "You can get a better job, you know," she said. "Your mother may have drunk herself into her grave, but your grandmother's sitting at home with more work than she can handle. She's a seamstress, isn't she? Why don't you go and work with her like you used to? She'll take you back."

The other woman's eyes snapped open wide and her hand flew to cover her gaping mouth. She blinked, then a sudden trickle of moisture ran down her cheek, washing off some of the bright red paint. "How did you know?" she said, words barely audible. She turned and disappeared inside, slamming the door behind her.

"Well, Storm," Azariel said as the other woman left. "How about that hoof of yours?" She eased his foot up and cradled the smooth warm hoof in her left palm, keeping it away from the cut. "Good fellow." Storm butted her in the back and snorted. The distant sound of voices drifted down the street . She dropped his hoof down. "No stones in that one. How about your hind legs?"

"Get off the street, Zenifi, if you've got any sense!" The whore's shrill voice rang out, followed by the door slamming again. Azariel shrugged and lifted Storm's hind hoof off the cobblestones. *Probably the Watch on their rounds.* She shook her hair back from her face and felt at her right hip for her dagger. "There's a stone or two here. Stand still, old fellow. I'll have to use this to free them and I don't want to cut your foot."

"Hey! Zenifi! Get away from those horses, you little thief."

She lowered Storm's foot to the ground. "He's mine," she replied . "Don't worry."

"Don't worry! We're not worried, are we, lads?" A chorus of agreement and guffaws greeted the remark.

She straightened up. A cluster of men stood in the street a little way from her, glancing at each other and grinning. One of them ran his eyes up and down the length of her body with a greedy, hot gaze that made her skin crawl. She slid the dagger back into its sheath and laid her hand on her sword hilt. *They must have taken me for the whore across the road.* "If you're looking for the … the dancing girl, that's her door." She gestured across the road at the closed red door.

"Aren't all Zenifi women whores?" A tall thin man stepped out from the group towards her. She backed away from Storm towards the wall. "But why pay for what you can take?"

Her heart hammered against her ribs and her stomach turned in revulsion. *Ten of them! No – not this! King of Heaven, help me.* Her hand flew to her side and rasped her sword from its sheath. "Get back," she said in a low voice, baring her teeth and forcing the words out of her dry mouth. "I'm nobody's whore."

"Forget it, Maynard. We've jumped a soldier," one of the men growled.

"Ten to one and she's not the Watch," the tall man said. "Let's get her."

She jumped into her fighting stance, sword raised and ready. *I'll die before I let them take me. And I'll kill.* A wall of men ringed her and she glanced from side to side. *Can I get to the wall to cover my back?* She darted her head around, her hair masking her view. With her left hand, she brushed it back and saw a freckled man between her and the plastered mud brick. Footsteps shuffled and the ring of men tightened around her. Veranath neighed, the white star nearly glowing in the dying sunlight as he bit at one of the men near him. The bitten man swore and cuffed the stallion across the nostrils. Azariel smiled with savage satisfaction. *Good on you, Veranath.* Do it again!

The men closed in all around her. She whirled her blade through the air, striking out at the leader. The reddish sunlight gleamed off her blade and also off a knife that the leader raised to meet her blow. As she drove his knife back with her backslash, she heard a heavy tread behind her. She spun around, lashing out with her sword. A man yelled as she felt her blow land and when she drew her sword back, the blade was stained red. She scythed her sword around, meeting resistance and sending a fountain of blood onto the white plaster of the wall.

A pair of hands grabbed her left wrist as she turned back. *They're all round me! How can I get them all?* She writhed and struggled, trying to break the hold on her. Fingernails scored into her arm. She twisted around, hacking her sword towards the man who held her. The smell of sweat, blood and beery breath filled her nostrils. The blade missed, so she rammed the pommel into his knuckles, making him howl. His grip loosened, but another hand seized her sword arm and jerked and shook the weapon from her hand.

They forced her arms behind her back as she twisted, arched and kicked. They wrenched her arms up, forcing her wrists towards her shoulders. One of them was laughing. "She's a fighter – she'll be good."

A rough prickly rope circled her wrists and burned into her skin. It tightened, squeezing the blood from her fingers. *Now I can't use rings or sword, and if I change shape, I'll be wrenched crippled for life.* She kicked out at the man nearest her, her leg jolting into bone. "Farren!" she shouted, then a rank-smelling hand clamped over her mouth. Her lips drew back and she bit hard, drawing blood. *If I was in my other shape, I'd take his hand off.* She glared at them through a curtain of hair and felt sweat trickling down her face. *I won't stop fighting. Not until they kill me.*

The leader stood over her as several of his henchmen forced her back against the wall. She snarled, struggled and kicked, all the time scratching and scrabbling at the knots that held her wrists. She struck out with her heel and heard her foot crunch into the leader's kneecap. He swore at her, then a jarring explosion of pain crashed into her jaw. Her mouth filled with the taste of blood, her own this time, and her head spun. *Farren, where are you?* Again, the leader's fist smashed into her face, scattering splinters of light through her brain. Too dizzy to resist, she was forced back and down. Hands grabbed at her legs, her clothes, her hair, and she heard herself screaming as if watching and listening from outside her body.

Farren put the last of the silver coins into the dog-breeder's hand. "There," he said. "I'll take Lady and we'll be off." He closed his belt pouch. More voices came from the street, followed by screaming. *Azariel!* He spun around and ran for the gate. "I'll be back in a minute" he shouted over his shoulder. "I've got to get to her!"

He raced down the path, pushing his way through the crowd of dogs. *If they've done anything to her...* He fumbled with the catch of the gate and stared through the iron bars into the street. A knot of men surrounded a dark-haired figure on the ground, and he heard the sound of a fist striking flesh. A red hurricane of anger built inside him. He flung the gate back, knocking Veranath on the rump, and hardened his fists.

He pitched into the circle of ruffians, striking out at the man nearest him. A jolt of pain jarred his arm as his fist smashed into the man's temple and the man dropped to the stones. He wheeled around, lashing out like a furious stallion at the throat and gut of another of the Bloody Blades. "You scum!" he snarled.

Beside the wall, one man dangled Azariel's belt in one hand and two others knelt on the ground, holding her legs pinned. His boot caught the kneeling man closest to him in the back of the head then he grabbed the man with the belt by the shoulders and threw him hard into the other kneeling man. He wrenched the belt from the would-be rapist's hands. Azariel was slumped against the wall in front of him, her hands tied behind her back, her lip swollen and bleeding and her hair hanging across her furious narrowed eyes. He dropped to his knees beside her and drew his dagger to cut the ropes around her wrists. "Are you all right?" he whispered.

"Behind you!" she barked.

He whirled to his feet, dagger still in his hand. The man who had been holding her belt stood over him, a knife in one hand and her sword in the other. He ducked as the large blade sang through the air at his head, hearing it whistle above him. His hand reached for the hilt of his own weapon and drew it. His first slash drove the blade down, then the backslash sent the sword flying from the other man's hand. It clattered on the cobblestones as the man jumped backwards. The other Bloody Blades circled them, several with blood on their faces and arms, and all with knives in their hands.

He flicked Azariel's sword to her with the point of his own, then backed up to the wall, his eyes still on the other men's knives. Azariel scrambled to her feet in a jingle of chainmail and collected her sword. Her back pressed against his as he turned his left side to the circle of ruffians and his right to the wall. "Let's kill them like the worthless dogs they are," she growled in his ear. He nodded and tensed, seeking an opening for attack.

Do not slay them but take them alive and deliver them to justice.

He leaned his head back closer to her. "Did you hear that?" he whispered. The men shuffled nearer, their blades dull in the dying light.

"Yes," she replied, her voice pulsing with menace. "And I've never had an order I've wanted to obey less."

The first of the Bloody Blades stabbed at him, and Farren drove his blade up to meet the blow. Behind him came an echoing ring of steel on steel, then a hoarse voice shouted: "Let's get out of here! Run for it, lads!" He struck up and across, the point of his sword ripping his opponent's arm. Above the man's yell, he heard running footsteps fading away. The knife flew from the man's hand, and he turned to flee.

Farren sheathed his sword and ran after the Bloody Blades. A howl split the air beside him and a grey shadow surged forwards. The shewolf bounded level with the fugitive and her jaws closed around his wounded arm. Farren rushed up to where wolf and man struggled, and smashed his fist into the man's jaw. The man reeled with the blow and staggered backwards. Farren raised his fist to strike again as the shewolf released the man's arm and reared up. A thin band of light passed down her body from nose to tail and Azariel stood beside him in her woman's shape. He struck again and felled the man.

He heaved the half-stunned man up. "What do we have to tie his hands?" he asked, forcing his prisoner's arm behind his back and ignoring the torrent of filthy language pouring from the man's mouth. "We'll take him and the other one back there to the barracks - on Veranath." He pointed with his chin to member of the Bloody Blades lying on the cobblestones, the man he had knocked down in the first heat of his anger.

"You've condemned them to death, then," she said. Her boots clicked across the stones then she pressed the cut ropes that had bound her into his hand.

He knelt on his prisoner's back, pinning him. "Veranath will take them if I've got hold of him." He knotted the ropes into one cord and bound the ruffian's wrists.

"That's not what I meant. You know Brigadier Tariyel is in command of the Lebhern-y-Hyalda troops. Didn't you hear about what she did to a group of cadets who pack-raped one of the kitchen girls? She'll have no mercy on these ones." Her toe kicked the pavement just short of the unconscious man's head. "I wish we could have captured more of the swine."

He finished tying the ruffian's arms and turned to deal with his thrashing legs. "I heard about the rape, but I didn't hear what happened to the boys who did it. What did happen? Lashed, hanged or both?"

"Wish I could hang you, Zenifi hell-bitch, and your fancy-man, too." The ruffian spat, the saliva striking Farren's arm.

She ignored the ruffian "Gelded, then hanged. I heard it from Taramaritan, who was on duty in the detention block when it was done. She said they nearly asked her to carry it out and she was glad she didn't have to."

He whistled, wincing. "Well, I can't say they didn't deserve it." He hoisted the bound ruffian up and over Veranath's back. The stallion bucked and pranced around and Farren struggled to keep his prisoner on the horse's back. "Steady, boy," he ordered, stroking Veranath's thick neck. "There's no need for that. Nobody will hurt you now." He pulled the stallion's head down, then used his Gift to calm him. The wash of calm warmth trickled through his hand, briefly stilling his own fierce pulse.

The man twisted from his grasp and struggled to free his hands. "Let me go or you'll be sorry," he snarled.

"Sorry about what?" Farren drew his sword slowly and held it to the ruffian's throat. "Azariel, could you tie up that other fellow I knocked out and drag him over here?"

"I've got friends who'll deal you what you've got coming to you. You haven't caught all of us." The man spat and Farren dodged.

"So have we." He turned, still keeping the point of his sword near the ruffian's neck. Azariel dragged the limp form of the other man towards Veranath. Farren sheathed his sword and lifted the unconscious man onto the stallion beside the first prisoner. "Do you have any more rope?" he asked.

"In the saddlebags." She bent over Storm's saddle, which still lay on the ground, and rummaged in one of the bags. She tossed him a coil of rope and he tied the two men together. "Now I'll get our deerhound and we'll ride to the barracks."

He looked back to the iron gate. The dog-breeder was standing on the other side of the metalwork holding the shaggy deerhound by a leash. "That was a good piece of work!" the dog-breeder said as he opened the gate and let the dog trot out. "I hope you have as good luck with your hunting. Be a good girl for your new master now, won't you, Lady?" He gave the leash to Farren and stood back from the gate.

The deerhound bounded to Farren and pushed her moist nose into his hand. "Thank you!" he called as the dog-breeder walked away along the path.

He ran his hand over Lady's ears, then reached for Azariel. "Are you sure all right?" he asked softly as he slid an arm around her shoulder. "I'm sorry I didn't check before. Your poor lip's all swollen. I'm sorry I didn't come sooner." He kissed the top of her head lightly.

An icy mask settled over her face. "Thank you, beloved. You came before they managed to rape me." Her shoulders shuddered beneath his hands. "I'm unharmed, apart from the bruises. We had better be off. We're getting stared at, and I'm going to be sick."

He reluctantly let her go and she staggered to the side of the wall, retching. *I don't know whether to follow her of whether that would make her feel ashamed.* He looked up. The figures of several women were silhouetted against a lighted doorway. "Can you come back and do that again some other night, soldier boy?" one asked.

"I wish I could," he said. He checked the bound ruffians one more time, dodging another gob of saliva from the conscious man, then caught Princess and mounted her.

After Azariel had returned, he led the way across the city, with Veranath continually shying and tugging at the lead rope. He ignored the stares of the passers-by and kept his eyes open for the barracks. The eastern wall of the city loomed ahead of him through the twilight. "We can't be far off now," he said. "The barracks should be somewhere over in this north-eastern corner, from what I remember."

Ahead, light fell from a high lantern onto the street. An armed figure passed under it and he caught a glimpse of a scarlet cloak. He nudged Princess to a trot and rode to the tall wooden gate bound with iron that stood near the light. "Who goes there?" called a male voice from the wall above him.

"Farren Blackarrow and Azariel Stormwolf, *minyasti* of the Kingdom," he shouted in reply. The footsteps of the sentry clattered down on the other side of the gate. "We're bringing prisoners with us, too."

The gate creaked open and the sentry peered out. The lantern in his hand case shadows from his chin and cheeks. "Give me your prisoners and I'll have them taken to the lockup," he said. "Come in. Who are your prisoners? Yellow Claws?"

"Two of a gang of ravishers that were prowling in the north-western quarter," Azariel answered. "Tell Brigadier Tariyel."

"You mean the Bloody Blades? I certainly will." The sentry pulled the bound men from Veranath's back. One of the struggled against the ropes and cursed; the other groaned, regaining consciousness. The sentry dragged them to the wall, then turned back to Farren and Azariel. "But welcome to the Lebhern-y-Hyalda barracks. You'll find stabling for your horses – and dog – over to your right and someone there will lead you to where you can report in and where the dorms are."

Farren swung Princess around and rode at a gentle walk until he caught the sweet earthy scent of hay and horses. Azariel's feet thudded down onto the ground then she led Storm to the door. She knocked and stood back. Inside, footsteps scuffed and stopped as the door opened, outlining a figure against the yellow light. "Greetings, strangers," a woman said. "Stabling for three horses, I take it. Give them here and I'll deal with them."

"The stallion's a bit wild," he said, dismounting. "I'll need to take him."

The groom arched one of her thick eyebrows and pursed her lips. "Are you sure? I've got a little gadget that will make any horse behave itself, even a big one like him."

Farren coiled up the slack of the lead rope, the rough hemp prickling his hands. "If you mean a twitch, I don't want one used on him. He's suffered enough at human hands already."

"Really?" The groom took Princess's bridle and led the mare down one of the rows of the stables ahead of them. "Dare I ask for the story?"

"I don't know it all. We took him from the Yellow Claws."

"A good piece of work. Anyway, here's a stall for him and you'll find everything you need on the rack nearby." She turned to Azariel. "You can hand your black beauty over to me, ma'am, and I'll take care of him. You look like you need to take care of yourself."

Farren untied Veranath's rough rope halter, then found a brush to groom him. As he swept the brush along Veranath's back in a slow rhythm, the stallion relaxed, slumping his head forward and letting one ear droop to the side.

Azariel stepped into the stall beside him, her boots scuffing the straw and sawdust on the floor. Veranath raised his head and pricked his ears towards her. Her breathing sounded ragged and she tugged and twisted at a lock of her hair as though she were trying to braid it. He placed the brush on a bracing board and reached for her. Her arms wrapped around his neck and pulled his head down. "I want to say thank you," she whispered, lips tickling his ear. "Sorry I didn't say it earlier. Thank you for coming in time."

"I'm glad you're safe." He slid his arms around her warm slim waist and pulled her against himself, the rings of her chainmail digging into his arms. Her head slumped onto his shoulder. "Sweetheart, I wanted to kill them all ten times over for hurting you." He lifted his right hand and ran it through her hair. She tilted her face up towards him. In the dim yellow light of the stable lantern, he looked at her swollen lip and the dark stains marring the whiteness of her skin. "You poor thing; you're all bruised." He bent his head and lightly brushed his lips over hers. "I'm so glad you weren't hurt worse." He began to cover her cheeks and forehead with kisses, savouring the rosemary scent in her hair and the earthier notes of her sweat. A spark of desire heated his blood, and he drew back. *Don't be a fool, Blackarrow. She doesn't need you acting like a rutting stag after what she's been through. Just hold her.*

He ran his hands through her hair and caressed her scalp as she rested her head on the folds of his cloak over his shoulder. Her breathing slowed, and the tension in her arms and shoulders eased. Veranath bunted his muzzle against them and lipped Azariel's hair. She turned towards the horse and laughed. "Don't tell me he's jealous of the attention you're giving me!"

"If he is, I'm glad. He's made you laugh, anyway." He let out a long, slow breath. "I suppose we'd better go and let the officers know we're here. I've groomed him enough."

"We should." Her fingers threaded through his. "Let's go."

They walked across the courtyard towards the row of lights in the centre of the barracks. People sauntered or bustled in and out of the buildings around them. One slender dark shape stepped out from a doorway as he passed and a soft female voice said "Farren Blackarrow?"

He froze, his hand tightening around Azariel's. *I know that voice only too well.* "Is that you, Stessa?" he said aloud. *As if Azariel and me haven't had enough this evening to deal with.*

Stessa stepped out of the shadow of the building and the moonlight shone on the Nightraven's sleek, cropped blonde hair. "It's me," she said. "I saw you coming in and leaving the stables. I suppose you're off to report in." She fixed him with her wide blue eyes. "Don't bother doing that. I'll send a message that the two of you are here." She reached out and laid a hand on Azariel's arm. "I've got some news for you, Azariel. I was on the point of sending a pigeon to the capital for you. Now I can give you the news myself. Come with me to my rooms, both of you."

Stessa turned and walked back through the dark doorway. He glanced at Azariel. "Shall we go?" he whispered to her. *I hope Stessa will behave herself this time.*

"We had better hear her news," she answered. "Hopefully the Claws aren't after the Stones again."

They walked along the dimly lit corridor behind Stessa. The blonde Nightraven swung around a corner and called "Hey, you! Go to Major Elena and tell her that Farren Blackarrow and Azariel Stormwolf are here. Two *minyasti*. I'm dealing with them." Another set of footsteps rang on the floor, and as Farren and Azariel rounded the corner, a figure slipped through the open door at the far end. Stessa jingled some keys and the lock snicked open as she unlocked it. "Come on in," she said.

Azariel followed Stessa through the door. Footsteps shuffled in the darkness and a drawer thudded, followed by the grating of a tinderbox. The flare of a spark flashed off Stessa's face, then the yellow glow grew as she lit a candle. The light flickered and danced off the walls and furniture as she closed the door. "Sit down here on the bed and I'll get you both something to drink," Stessa said, waving at the rumpled pile of sheets and bearskin. Azariel stepped around a small writing desk and sank shakily on the bed, glad to have her weight off her feet. "Have you eaten yet?"

"What with all we've done this evening, we haven't," said Farren. He sat down close to Azariel and wrapped one arm around her waist to rest his hand on her hip

"I'll arrange that as well," Stessa said. She took some beakers and a flask off a shelf and kicked a wooden chest into the centre of the floor. Bending over, she placed the beakers onto the flat lid of the chest.

Azariel reached out and gripped Farren's knee tightly. *If the light wasn't in the wrong place, she'd be showing him everything she has with that low-cut neckline of hers. And she is so very beautiful.* She glanced at him from the corner of her eye; he was staring into the candle flame on the writing desk on the other side of the room.

The splash and trickle of liquid falling into beakers issued from beneath Stessa's shadow, then stopped. "Here you go," the Nightraven said, holding out a beaker to each of them. A frown furrowed her face as her gaze met Azariel's. "What happened to you? You're all bruised."

"We were in the northwestern corner—" she began.

"Ah ... yes. I understand," said Stessa. The breath whistled softly between her teeth. "You ran into the Bloody Blades. They're a pack of wolves, if ever there was one."

"That's an insult to wolves," Azariel said. "They don't behave like that." She raised the beaker to her lips and tasted the biting smoothness of the wine. *I'm still shaking. I hope this doesn't make me sick again.* She swallowed it, feeling glowing tendrils of warmth spread through her.

"Well, you should know, Stormwolf." Stessa poured out another beaker of wine and sipped at it. "You're … They didn't rape you, did they?"

"No," she replied. "I was spared that – just. Farren came in time." She leaned her head on his shoulder and his arm tightened around her. "We managed to capture two of them and we brought them here."

"Excellent. That's two less." She set her beaker down and stood up. "If you came straight here, you won't have had those bruises seen to." The candlelight winked on the hilts of the pair of daggers at her belt as she strolled to the dresser. After a few moments, she returned with a small jar. She uncorked it, releasing the dryish scents of yarrow and comfrey, mixed with aloe vera. "Close your eyes. This shouldn't sting but it might."

Stessa smoothed the lotion over the aches and stiffness on Azariel's cheekbones and around her eyes. Her skin welcomed the cool moisture. "It won't do any harm to tell you but that's my next mission: catching them." Stessa massaged the salve in small circles along Azariel's eyebrow. "I've just crossed over from Wayast and I was to meet up with The Hawk and set a trap for them. They've been a nuisance long enough and regular Watch hasn't managed to get them. You can open your eyes now; I've finished." She smiled and closed the jar of salve. "I'm glad there's only eight to deal with now. I shall have to tell him, unless good old Hawk-eyes has found out already." She paused and picked up her drink again. "You didn't let them know you were *minyasti*, did you?"

"Azariel changed shape to catch one of them," Farren said. "Why are you worried?"

"That's the news I've got for you. There's a price on your heads in Wayast. All *minyasti* are worth three hundred silvers, more if captured alive." She smoothed the hair that hung over her right eye. "Here, close to the border, there're enough unscrupulous people who love money more than the law and wouldn't hold back from trapping you both and taking you across the border to the College of Fire."

Azariel set her beaker down, her hand shaking and splashing the wine inside it. *Power protect us all from being taken there where they'll do anything to break us into joining them.* She shuddered as a cold thrill crept down her backbone. *If those men had found out what I was, then I might have been on my way there by now.* "How many know this?" she said aloud, forcing her voice to stay calm.

"Not many in the Kingdom yet." The other woman set her beaker down and stretched, making the strangely shaped pendant hanging at her neck glitter in the light. "And the news is fresh in Wayast itself. I've got ways and means of finding things out before others do, that flask of wine being one of them. Some sorcerers are living proof that a secret is something you tell somebody else. Don't worry yet, but be on the lookout for Yellow Claws after this week is out if you're anywhere near the borders." She picked up her beaker again and tilted her head to one side. "What are you doing here, anyway? Buying supplies for the Watchtower of the West?"

Azariel shook her head. "No. We're on the hunt for the third of the Stones. It's chained to a gazelle somewhere in the hills up river, I think."

"That gazelle? I've heard of that one. Good luck!" Her full lips twisted in a worried line. "You will have to keep a watch out for Claws crossing the river. By the way..." Her voice dropped to a whisper. "You can guess what I'll be doing after dealing to the Bloody Blades." She winked and drained the rest of her wine. "I might see you up there. But you be careful. You're worth twice as much silver than all the others, Azariel, did you know? A rich prize for any Yellow Claw."

"They won't take you except over my dead body, sweetheart." Farren squeezed her and his lips brushed the top of her head. "You're a prize, true enough, and I know how to guard you."

She chuckled and prodded him in the ribs. "I know you're teasing," she said. "I am the Stormwolf and the arch *minyaster,* and capable of holding my own." She squirmed as he tweaked a lock of her hair. "But I'll let you have your fill of playing the gallant rescuer after what you did this evening. I'll be guarding your back, too."

"I'd better go and find you something to eat." Stessa's voice cut in across her, deliberately breezy. She blinked several times and nibbled at her lower lip. "You'll need it after the shock of being knocked about."

Azariel toyed with her betrothal earring as the other woman rose to her feet. *Is she still wishing Farren chose her instead of me?* She watched Stessa walk smartly out of the door, boots echoing off the flagstones and hips swaying. *Hopefully, she's the only one to regret that choice.*

CHAPTER NINE

The hot wind blew the long lacing clouds across the afternoon sky. Farren followed Azariel out of the northeastern gate of the city. Veranath tugged at the lead rope lashed to the saddlehorn above Farren's bow, ears pricked towards the gate. "Eager to be off, aren't you?" Farren pulled the stallion back. He looked behind him. Lady padded along behind him, tongue hanging out. *Hopefully, she won't race off after rabbits once we're out in the open. Or sheep.* The wind struck him on the side of his face as he rode out of the shelter of the city walls, rich with the scent of dry grass. Princess's mane whipped back at his hands. "You like it, don't you, my lady?" he said, clapping Princess on the neck.

"I'm glad to leave that city behind." Azariel shook her head so her hair flowed like a blue-black river behind her. "Let's gallop and try out that dog's paces."

He reached down and untied Veranath's lead rope. The stallion put his head down and tore at the nearest clump of grass. "Where shall we race to?"

"That pile of rocks two bowshots away." She pointed north towards the bulk of the Seranyai-Cheli at a pile of grey-white rocks that had once been neatly stacked in a cairn but had now tumbled in disorder.

He shifted his feet on the bars of the stirrups. Princess pricked her ears and shook her mane. He smiled, catching Azariel's eye. "Let's go."

The chestnut mare sprang into a canter almost before his heels tapped her side. She surged into a smooth gallop, mane streaming in the wind. He stood in the stirrups and leaned forwards, blinking as his eyes stung with speed and dust. Storm ran level with Princess, nostrils flared to show the pink lining inside. Azariel met his gaze, then threw back her head and whooped as she urged the gelding ahead. Behind her, Lady galloped, long legs blurring, and tongue and ears blown backwards. A snort and whinny behind him made him turn his head. Veranath, neck arched proudly and tail bannered behind him, swept forwards. He drew level with Princess, then inched ahead to run beside Storm. His big hooves beat triple-time on the hard dirt, kicking up puffs of dust behind him. *He's cantering!* Farren thought, suddenly dropping back into the saddle, gaping open-mouthed. *He's only cantering and he's passing both of us!*

The big stallion's tail streamed behind him as he surged forwards. He cleared a pair of the tumbled boulders near the old cairn and thundered on. Azariel drew Storm to a walk, then stopped, and Princess bounced into a springy trot before halting. Lastly, Lady bounded up and flopped down beside the stones, sides heaving like a bellows and her head resting on her paws. "Did you see him?" he asked, swinging off Princess's back.

"Veranath?" She tossed her cloak behind her and sat down on one of the rocks. "He didn't like running last in the herd, did he? He likes to show us who's the lead horse." She grinned and looked at the stallion, who was cantering back towards them. "He looks impressive, doesn't he?"

He sat down on the grass below her, leaning back against her legs. Lady pulled herself forward on her paws and rested her head on his shins. "He was cantering, Stormwolf," he said softly. "He passed both of us at a canter. I heard the triple-beat."

Her hand ran through his hair. "I'll wager you can't wait for Princess to next come in season so you can get a foal off him."

He looked down at his hands and idly picked at the dirt under his fingernails. "I certainly hope so. *Minyasti* Gifts only sometimes pass on in the blood – look at me with my four siblings."

"And look at your niece and your uncle. Gifts stay in the bloodline even if they don't always breed true. Perhaps they're like red hair." She tugged his hair gently. "When you and I are married, our children would probably all be *minyasti*. It should be the same for horses."

His mind went back to the previous winter and the time he had spent imprisoned by Crajaval behind the waterfall. His stomach grew sick and cold and he shook his head to clear the memories away. *If we can have any children at all, after Crajaval left me damaged.* His stomach and groin almost ached with the memory of pain and he swallowed. *Oh, hellfire. I don't know for certain, but I haven't got much hope.* He shifted to and fro on the grass, chill creeping into him and making him shiver.

Her hand slid down the side of his head and rested on his shoulder. A strand of her hair tickled his nose and forehead. "Don't think about Crajaval, beloved," she murmured. "It's over now, you're here with me and she won't come back."

He looked up at her, squinting against the afternoon sunlight that filtered through her hair. "How did you know I was thinking about that?"

"You always shake those memories out of your head. Those and the ones about Stessa. I'm guessing that it was Crajaval this time."

He raised his hand to touch hers. "You know me, Stormwolf." He turned his head to kiss the back of her fingers lightly, then stood up and faced the foothills and mountains to the north. The grass and tussock lay golden over the curves of the slopes, leopard-spotted with wild rose and mountainthorn. The bleating of sheep and the screech of plovers carried on the warm wind that blew around him and ruffled his hair. His eyes roamed up and down the slopes and picked out a small flock of sheep lying in the shadow of a huge twisted cypress. "Here we are," he said aloud. "We're north of Lebhern-y-Hyalda, searching for one small gazelle with a Stone tied between its horns in the middle of all these huge hills. How much of that Vision of yours can you remember? Do we have any other indication where to look?"

Her boots rustled through the grass as she stepped beside him. "I think I saw that gazelle with a sorceress. They were together in a narrow walkway hedged in by mountainthorns. I think it was a maze or labyrinth. Apart from that, all I can say is that it was in the hills up the river."

"It probably isn't too close to the town, then. No sorceress would be that bold." He looked northwest to the gorge between Seranya-y-Doma and Seranya-y-Wayast, the mountains either side of the border. "We'd better go upstream. And we can look out for farmers or somebody to ask the way. It's rather hard to hide a maze."

"And let's hope it isn't three days march upstream like Moonlady Falls. Our supplies won't last that long, and I miss the taste of bread on long journeys."

"I know what you mean, Stormwolf," he chuckled. "At least it's summer, so fruit and plants won't be hard to find." Lady's wet cold nose thrust into his hand and he felt for the top of the deerhound's head to stroke her. "With any luck, we'll be eating gazelle before long."

He caught Veranath and they remounted. The horses moved at a steady walk, first heading west to the willows lining the bank, then north along the gently curving line of the river. Lady trotted beside them, keeping pace with the three horses. The sun beat down, making the surface of the river flash and gleam, and the strong warm northwester kept blowing in their faces. Gradually, the terrain changed from the even flatness of the Kingdom plains to the hills of the border country. Pines, firs and cypresses studded the gold of the slopes, hissing and roaring in the wind. Farren and Azariel passed the grey rectangular guardpost and continued. Ahead, the land rose in undulating downland.

Storm crested the first small hill and Azariel reined him in. The wind blew in her face, streaming her hair behind her and making the skin on her cheeks feel dry and tight. She blinked a few wind-torn tears away and looked down the slope into the tussock-clad valley. On the opposite side, the hillside sloped up towards the jagged line of the Seranyai-Cheli mountains and their foothills, except for one place where time, wind and rain had carved a cliff about twenty feet high. At the foot of the cliff, a bright green caravan gleamed like an emerald set in gold against the tussocks. About seven horses grazed around the caravan as a cluster of dark-haired people stood in a loose circle at the bottom of the cliff.

She pulled Storm's head up from the grass and headed him down the slope, leaning backwards to balance him as he descended. He reached the flatter valley floor and she lunged forwards as he cantered towards the Zenifi band. A stocky bay horse raised its head and neighed at them. The people turned to look at her and she saw the glint of sunlight on metal in the hands of a few of them. She held up her left hand to them in greeting and a woman with a drawn dagger re-sheathed it. "What do ye soldiers want?" one of the Zenifi said.

"We're searching for a sorceress's abandoned labyrinth," she said in the Zenifi tongue. "Do you know where it is?"

They looked at each other, eyebrows raised. "Where did you learn to speak Zenifi?" one asked.

"My mother is one of the Wolf Clan, though my father was a *dawnin*," she said in the same language. She ran her hand through her hair, dragging it forwards, then letting it loose in the wind. A few knots caught at her fingers. "Do I not look enough like one of you?"

"Welcome, then, Wolf," said a man with a tattoo of a foal on one olive cheek. "We're members of the Horse Clan. And who is your companion?"

"My betrothed, Farren." She shot a glance towards him. *I'd better not say "Blackarrow." I don't know if these people stand with the Kingdom or with Wayast.* "He's *dawnin* but harmless." She smiled as they laughed. "Have you heard of a labyrinth in these hills? Or of the sorceress's gazelle with a jewel in its horns?"

"What's going on?" The hoofbeats behind her stopped as Farren halted Princess and Veranath. "Do they know the place?"

"I've just told them who we are and that you're harmless," she said to him in the Common Tongue. "Let me talk. I think they're a bit wary of strangers."

"We know the place ye are looking for," said a woman with silver streaks in her black hair. "It's an hour's ride further up the river just past a stream that runs into the border river. Why are ye seeking it? The sorceress hasn't been seen for a year and more."

"We're hunting and we want that gazelle as a trophy." Her eyes flicked to and fro over the group. *I won't tell them everything. But it's going to be hard for us if someone else has killed it before we get the chance at it.*

"That one!" The streak-haired woman laughed. "Ye have a hard chase in front of ye. It lives near that labyrinth, right enough. But won't ye hunt easier prey? That gazelle has outrun all the hunters that have tried for it." She looked westwards towards the river. "They say that it's had spells put on it so that it'll never be caught unless the Hounds of Heaven hunt it."

Azariel fidgeted with a strand of her hair and stared at the clear blue sky above the cliff. A hawk or eagle was circling. *That sounds like a fireside tale, but so many of those have a grain of truth.* "Thank you," she said aloud. "We'll run it and try for it and be those Hounds of Heaven ourselves."

"You wouldn't be wanting to buy a falcon for your hunting, would you, Wolf?" One of the men grinned. He ran one hand up and down his other wrist, which was covered by a thick gauntlet. "We've been taking haggards all morning, and we've got out trained ones for the selling."

She pulled Storm's head up from the grass. "We haven't the silver for one of your birds. You Horse Clan always have the best birds. I'd have bought one if we could afford one." She laughed and touched her heels to Storm's sides. "May the four winds blow you good fortune."

"And you. Good hunting!"

She trotted away for about a bowshot, then drew Storm back to a walk as Farren brought Princess level with her. "Well?" he said. "Did they know? I only caught a few words I recognised out of all that."

She smiled at him. "Yes. It's an hour's ride upstream by a little tributary. Let's go. I'm glad it's not far."

"But what were they saying about Heaven? I did pick up that word." An eddy of wind caught his red cloak and swirled it over his arms before he tossed it back.

She repeated what the Zenifi had said about the gazelle as they rode. Veranath plodded between them, head hanging lazily low and his eyes half shut. *He hardly looks like the killer horse he was back in that Claw corral. But if I tried to ride him...* A line of sweat darkened the chestnut hairs on the stallion's withers and chest, and Storm's shoulders had grown damp beneath her bare right hand. Her left hand, shielded by the glove, felt sticky and swollen with heat so that her ring dug slightly into her skin. The veins on the underside of her arm stood out and sweat stuck her shirt to her back. *Who chose pure black for the arch* minyaster? *Who made us keep cloaks on all the time? At least we're not sweltering in our leathers.* She released the reins and yanked the glove off her left hand, then looked down at the wound on her hand. The skin to each side of it had turned pink and tender, but the cut itself showed dark brown with clotted blood. Here and there, the edges of the slash had lightened where the stinging sweat had dampened it. *I'm going to have another scar there now. At least this one is only small.* She tucked her glove into her belt and settled back into the rhythm of riding as the countryside rose and fell beneath them.

"There it is!" Farren stood in the stirrups and pointed as they reached the top of another hillock that the course of the river cut through. In the valley ahead, a broad stream ran around boulders and willows, flowing out from between a long spur covered with a tangle of wild roses, and a tall slope where half the hillside had fallen away to form a high, craggy cliff. At the foot of a cliff lay a clump of mountainthorns, not ragged and randomly spaced, but close together and still showing signs of having once been trimmed smooth. "Either that's our maze, or somebody once had a hedge of mountainthorns around their cottage."

"Both, probably. The sorceress had to live somewhere." She leaned back to stretch her arms, and strained her legs against the stirrups. Storm shook his mane and slanted his ears back at her. "Shall we start looking for tracks now?"

"I'd rather have a drink first," he replied. "Lady needs one, the horses need one and I need one. What about you? Thirsty?"

"Parched." She ran her tongue around the inside of her dry lips. "The river or the stream?"

"The river. Then the horses are less likely to leave the water all muddied for us." He put heels to Princess and headed her down the slope, Veranath trailing behind him.

Princess's hooves crunched on the gravel by the riverbank. He guided her under the dappled shade of a willow tree that grew beside a deep green pool before checking and unsaddling her. A solitary leaf twirled and coursed along the smooth, jewel-like surface before it was caught by the rapids that whirled it away to join the main branch of the wide braided river. Lady raced to the bank and lapped the water while the horses waded to midstream in the rapids and drank. The wind stirred the willow, making it sway and rustle.

Farren knelt beside the river and drank deeply before splashing some of the cool water over his face and neck. The refreshing shock travelled down his back and limbs. He turned and saw Azariel behind him, a gleam in her eye. He stood up and leaped away from the edge of the pool. "No, you don't!" he laughed. "I don't want to take a bath in full armour. Or perhaps you want one?" He lunged at her and seized her by the wrists.

"Let go!" she laughed, shaking her dampened hair so that droplets of water spattered over his face. He pulled her towards the edge of the river, struggling to keep his grip on her arms as she pulled and jerked to free herself. Suddenly, her struggles stopped and he staggered backwards, still holding her. Her foot jerked his leg from under him and he fell. He struck the water and gasped a lungful of air before her weight on top of him pushed him down.

He released her wrists and righted himself, feeling for the river bed with his feet. He grabbed the sedges and weeds on the bank and clambered out of the pool, spluttering and laughing. "We'll both rust our armour and weapons now," he said, when he had recovered enough breath. "Did you have a long enough drink?"

"More than enough," she said as she scrambled out of the river and pulled her boots off. "But the horses and Lady might need more of a rest before we go on. Let them rest while we dry off a bit."

"And where shall we go once we've let them rest? Up to the labyrinth to have a look around?" He tipped a stream of water out of his boots then began wringing out the skirt of his cloak. "Or we could start here by the river. All deer need to drink at some time, so it must come down along here somewhere."

"Or the stream." She turned to look up towards the mountainthorn labyrinth. "If you lived up there, where would you come down for water?"

"It's such a smooth slope, it could be anywhere." He pulled his boots back on. "But we've got all the time we need to search, so…"

"Could you locate it or draw it with your Gift?" She stood up and walked to Storm to open one of the saddlebags. "Let's have something to eat before we do anything. I'm hungry."

"Yes, let's." His stomach tightened in anticipation. "Let's eat, I mean. It's not easy to draw down one single animal that I've never worked with. I definitely can't draw one I've never seen. If we're lucky, though, it might sense me and come." He chuckled and raked his wet hair into place with his fingers. "I'm going to enjoy the challenge of a good hunt. What have we got for lunch?"

****

Azariel knelt in the gravel and studied the crumbly silt by the river for tracks. *Nothing but bird tracks of all shapes and sizes. No deer tracks.* She stood up and took Storm's bridle and began walking slowly, neck aching as she scanned the ground. "I'd do better if I changed shape," she said, rubbing her eyes with the back of her hand. "I'm creeping along like an elderly snail."

"Well, Lady is doing the best she can." Farren rode beside her, the dog criss-crossing to and fro underneath Princess's legs. "She's a sight-hound, not a scent-hound."

Azariel stooped to examine a set of tracks, then straightened with a sigh. "She doesn't know what we're looking for. She could easily go after some farmer's sheep – if one's strayed to the river – or some other animal that we don't want." She surveyed the ground in front of her. "Now there's dry gravel hiding the tracks nearest the river. We'll have to move up onto the grass."

She led Storm to the right and heard the timbre of his hoofbeats change from soft crunching on loose sand and silt to the deep thud of earth. Bending forward again, she strained to see the slightest patch of flattened soil or vegetation. The ground began to rise and she pivoted to keep her balance. Ahead, a trail of crushed grass and bare earth cut through the tussock. "Stop," she said, straightening up. Her lower back ached and her wet trousers had grown muddy at the knee. "This looks more likely."

She squatted to examine the patterns in the dust. "Cattle, I think," she said, recognizing the large cloven hoof prints gouging scars in the grass. "There could be gazelle prints underneath, but it would be impossible to tell now." She inched along the path, looking for places where it widened out. Lady pushed her hairy nose in beside her and sniffed at the trail. The deerhound crossed the cattle-path and left cloverleaf prints in the dust. Something beside one of Lady's prints caught her eye: a shallow teardrop-shaped print. She found one pair, then a second. "Here's something," she said, turning and looking back up at Farren. "Not a cow or a horse, anyway."

She stood up and worked inch by inch along the path. To one side of it lay a little pile of black dung-pellets. "Definitely deer, sheep, goat or gazelle, and it passed this way today." She shooed Lady away from the pellets as the dog tested them with her large tongue. "But which set of horns it's got, I can't tell like this."

"How many animals have passed?" His feet thudded onto the earth and he gave her shoulder a light squeeze. "If it's just one, then it could be our gazelle. If it's more, then it's goats or sheep."

She studied the hoof prints a while longer. "I can't say," she said at last. "The path is old and is covered with tracks. Something must use it every day. But there's one test I can do." She rested both hands on the ground and closed her eyes. As she concentrated, her body shape altered, sinews and bones sliding into new arrangements. Her nocturnal wolf's eyes blinked in the bright sunlight and her head swam for a few heartbeats. Then she ignored the monochrome tones of sky, plains, hills and river, and focussed on the vivid scents of the trail under her nose.

She snuffed at the tracks. *That's goat, unless my memory tricks me.* Taking a few small steps forward, she caught another note mingled with the goat-scent. *I've never smelt anything like that before.* She bent her nose to the trail and smelt a second time. *There were no tracks of any hoofless animal. This must be the gazelle. It's not the scent of deer, goat, sheep or pig, and the prints are too small for cattle and the wrong shape for horses.* Eyes half closed, she lifted her muzzle and tested the air, turning her head to and fro. Then she examined the tracks again. *It's half a day old. It hasn't come to drink this afternoon, or at least not here.*

"What have you found?" he asked her, ruffling the fur on her neck.

She sat back on her haunches and closed her eyes once more, feeling her woman's body return again. His hand brushed against her cloak. She gazed on the blue, green and gold of the landscape before turning and relishing the sight of him with human vision once more. "It's mostly goats around here, but there's a half-day-old trail that is nothing I've encountered before. Going by the prints, it's a gazelle. Whether it's the right gazelle, I can't tell."

"So something's beyond your wolf's nose."

"Not totally!" She rose to her feet. "Let me catch the scent after I've seen the one we want making the prints and I'll track it wherever it goes."

He ran one hand through his hair. "If the trail's half a day old, then we should wait here. It'll come back to the river to drink eventually.

"How?" She shrugged her shoulders and arched her neck to ease out the fatigue.

"I guess it drinks like other creatures," he said, winking. "But I think we'll wait on the horses behind that fallen willow." He pointed to a gnarled trunk that lay on one side parallel to the river, hundreds of thin switches and shoots sprouting from the top of it. "That's enough cover and the wind's right. If I miss that shot, then we'll chase it, and see what Lady and the horses can do."

"What about using your Gift to hold it still? I'm using mine, so you should be able to use yours."

He shook his head. "I can't bond with it if we're going to kill it." He stroked up and down Princess's neck." "I can't kill an animal I'm using my Gift on. I've tried and I know that I get hurt doing that."

"Then I'll make the kill." She flicked her hair back.

"No. It still hurts, even if I cut the connection with it before you shoot it. Full bond is worse. I tried that once when I was going through my training. I was home on leave and Dad was butchering a sheep. It was struggling and bunting, so I helped him by calming it and holding it steady. He killed it and I felt as if the knife had gone across my throat instead of the sheep's." He tugged at the neck of his chainmail. "That horse won't gallop, as Dad used to say."

"Right. We wait for it and if you miss, we run it." She swung herself onto Storm's back and headed the gelding around to the far side of the willow trunk. Farren brought his horses and Lady beside her.

He dismounted to tie Veranath to one of the dead and broken branches still attached to the trunk. The big stallion munched at the young shoots, the ends hanging out the sides of his mouth. Farren returned and she caught his eye as he unclipped an arrow from the quiver at his belt and nocked it to his bowstring.

She waited, watching the wind push back the thick blanket of pastel-pale cloud from the mountains and sky, revealing more of the naked blueness. The warm air was filled with the outdoor aroma of grass and horse-sweat. *A pale shadow of the scents that I could catch in wolf-form, but nice all the same.* She yawned and stretched her arms as she looked over at Farren. His shoulders had relaxed and he had slid his feet free from the stirrups, but his eyes were fixed on the track and he kept his bow in hand with the arrow nocked.

Beyond him, Lady lay in the dappled shade in the long grass beneath the fallen willow. The long purple-grey seed-heads of the grasses blended with her coat, almost camouflaging her. A breeze blew down from the hills, rustling the young willow-wands. Lady's ears pricked and she rose to her feet. Heart thumping, Azariel scanned the track leading to the river. A lone blackbird bobbed across the open ground, pausing to peck for insects. "Is that all the dog's interested in?"

Farren raised one eyebrow and cocked his head to the south. She turned to look where he had pointed. Three goats walked in single file to a bend in the river downstream. The sound of bleating drifted on the wind. "If we can't catch the gazelle, I know what we'll hunt for our supper." She let a long breath ease out of her, then polished the jewels in her rings as she waited. *I should have brought my embroidery to fill in the waiting.*

She continued polishing her rings and her silver armbands of protection, working every trace of grime she could from the patterns engraved into the metal. Dragonflies darted towards the river and bees buzzed in the clover and yarrow blooming nearby. A heron perched for a few moments at the end of the fallen willow where they waited, then flew away with a croaking cry.

After the sun had shifted several degrees through the sky, Lady scrambled to her feet again. Her muzzle turned towards the hill beneath the labyrinth. Azariel's gazed travelled from the dog to Farren. His eyes had narrowed and filled with fire. She turned and looked to the crest of the hill. A white figure stood between two mountainthorn bushes, walking daintily down the slope. Her heart kicked inside her as she saw the graceful head and the curling horns above the slim legs and white body.

It passed through a patch of shadow and light spilled across it from a globe between its horns that looked black but still cast light and left afterimages inside her eyelids. *That's the one.* Her heart drummed in her chest and a hard excited knot tied itself in her throat. The gazelle made its way down the path and came to the water's edge.

It lowered its head to the river thirty paces from the willow that hid them. Lady stiffened, quivering with one paw off the ground and tail held erect. In one smooth motion, Farren raised his bow and drew the string back. The gazelle lifted its head for one instant and stared straight at them as the arrow hissed from the string in a blur of motion. A flash and a puff of dust, and the gazelle vanished in a streak of white. Lady bayed and galloped after it, and they followed.

The two horses thundered up the hill, the deerhound bounding through the grass in front of them. Azariel narrowed her eyes as the wind tore moisture from them. Ahead, the white gazelle darted and jinked from side to side as it fled. It reached the top of the hill and halted for the space of half a heartbeat. Then it turned and raced across the flanks of the hill and along the ridge, swift as an arrow or a stooping falcon. Then it vanished over another crest as Storm, Princess and Lady reached the top of the rise. Only a quivering thornbush showed any signs of its passing.

"I've never seen anything run so fast," Farren said, reining Princess in. "We'll never catch up with that. It outran my arrow." He shook his head and stared towards the place they had seen the gazelle last.

"You didn't miss, did you?" She swept her hair back and wiped a smudge of moisture from the corner of her eye.

"From thirty paces? You know me better than that." He pulled Princess's head up from the grass, then put his fingers to his lips to whistle. "Lady!" he called. The tall deerhound halted in her gallop along the gazelle's path and turned.

She looked sidelong at him. "Anyone can miss in a strong wind like this, and nobody's perfect, beloved, not even you." The deerhound returned at a trot, tongue lolling out between her teeth. "What are we going to do now?"

"I'm going back to get my arrow. I know my aim was right." He fitted his bow back into its place beside the saddlehorn and headed Princess down the hill. "I know it was. That gazelle started running away after I had loosed. It outran my arrow. There's no way I could have missed an easy shot like that. It runs like the wind."

"Literally." She leaned back as Storm plodded down the slope, pressing her feet into the bars of the stirrups. The damp seams of her trousers chafed at her, and she realised that her hands were trembling from excitement. "It's got the Stone of Wind strung between its horns. One of the Stones of Protection. The gazelle is being protected by being able to run like the wind. This is going to be an interesting hunt. We'll need to pick a good campsite to last us a few days."

"Good idea." He reined Princess in beside the willow trunk where they had waited. After dismounting, he began to poke around in the bushes on the other side of the deer-trail.

She watched him for a few moments, then leaned over to untie Veranath from the branch. The stallion snorted and slanted his ears back at her in warning, then bent his head to crop the grass. The river water gurgled and chattered, and the willows stirred and hissed in the warm wind. She gazed across the river to the far bank. *That's Wayast over there. I'd rather not camp right beside the river if I can help it.* She looked back downstream to where the little tributary met the main flow. *That stream might be better.* She ran her fingers through her hair. *Not that it's really any safer, but I don't want to be in plain sight of the place where there's a bounty on my head.*

The bushes rustled and Farren returned, an arrow feathered with red and black in his hand. "Found it at last," he said, holding it up to show her before clipping it back into place in the quiver. "And it was exactly in line with where I shot it and not to one side with wind or whatever. I knew I didn't miss from that distance. That gazelle did outrun the arrow."

"Beloved, I believe you. You don't need to say it again." She tossed him the lead-rope. "Let's camp beside that little tributary."

"Further from the border?" He coiled Veranath's lead-rope around his arm and mounted Princess. "And it's less likely to rise quickly. The Illin-y-Hyalda's fed by northwest rains after all, and I don't think this wind's going to change soon."

She rode silently beside him downstream, the sun uncomfortably hot on her back and right shoulder, and the wind pushing her hair around each side of her face. At the meeting of the waters, they turned left and headed along the slowly climbing fold in the mountains where the stream flowed. Two bowshots from the Illin-y-Hyalda, Farren halted. "Over there," he said. "That looks like a good spot."

She reined Storm in and looked where Farren had pointed. Across the stream stood a massive horse chestnut tree surrounded by four or five smaller ones. Beneath them sprawled some broom bushes, bright yellow flowers decking the tips of the branches. She nodded and nudged Storm towards the trees, his hooves squelching in a patch of boggy ground beside the stream. A blackbird flurried out of the broom bushes as they approached, shrilling in alarm. "Perfect," she said, swinging off the black gelding's back. "Where do you want to put your tent up?"

"I don't mind as long as the ground's soft enough." He dismounted and began stripping the tack off Princess. "And look – there's sorrel here and watercress in the stream if we want greenstuffs."

They unsaddled the horses and left them to graze while they set up their tents. Azariel piled flat stones in a small ring for a fireplace, then both of them hauled, broke and stacked fallen branches in a heap nearby. The sun wheeled from north to west and gradually drifted down towards the horizon beyond the river.

Farren finished driving a forked stick into the ground at the side of the circle of stones, then straightened up, mouth dry and stomach gnawing at him with hunger. *We've finished.* He rested his hands on his hips and surveyed the campsite. On one side of the fireplace, the wood had been piled in a tall stack; on the other, the saddlebags containing the dried food and the salt lay, tightly buckled shut with a battered tin billycan balanced on top of them. The tack sat in two neat piles beside a broom bush. The wet clothes draped over the top of the bushes, his cloak making a bright splash of red against the green.

Azariel walked around from the far side of the broom bushes carrying an armload of dry twigs and grass. The late afternoon sunlight picked out her high cheekbones and struck a rich lustre from her hair. He gazed at her as she stacked the twigs in a pyramid in the stone circle, arranging them around the dried grass. *She's lovely. She looks so right here in the wind and the hills.* He smiled. *She looks right and beautiful anywhere.* He dropped to his knees beside her and added another stick to the pyramid. "We've made a good camp," he said. "But don't light the fire yet. We're going to need plenty of meat to feed us and the dog, so don't scare the game away with the smoke."

"Going to wait for some rabbits?" she asked, looking him.

He shook his head. "I think we'll try for the goats – one rabbit won't go far split among you, me and the dog. There must be plenty of goats around here. I spotted a few on that little ridge due north of here as well as the ones we saw before. Will you come with me?"

"In what shape?"

"Your own for now," he said. "If I can't get close enough for a good shot, then you and Lady can run them up to me or pull one down."

"Let's have a quick bite to eat now before we go. That bread won't keep much longer and we may as well make sure of something inside us this evening."

They ate a meal of bread and dried apricots standing over the unlit fire. When he had finished, he picked up his bow from his pile of tack and bags. Azariel slipped her hand into his and they tramped northeast towards the ridge on the other side of the tributary stream, Lady padding beside them. Princess raised her head and snorted at him as he passed, then bent back to grazing. The evening light fell across the mare, turning the hairs along the line of her back, her mane and her tail to gold. The light played across the ridge ahead, making the pinks and reds of the wildflowers stand out like banners in the ochre and green of the grass. Overhead, the wind-smudged clouds were stained salmon and buttercup yellow, and the sky had taken a more intense shade of blue. At the foot of the ridge, they unclasped hands and began to climb.

The spur jutting down from the ridge was covered with wild rosebushes in full flower. He reached out to brush the trailing branches to one side and thorns raked across the back of his right arm. He bit back a sharp hiss of pain and looked down. Three pale lines lay along the back of his arm, one or two drops of blood oozing from them. "These roses bite," he said aloud, turning to her. "Mind your cut hand."

She laid one finger on her lips, then pointed eastwards. He turned his head and listened. From the far side of the tangle of roses came a tearing, rustling sound, mixed with bleating. Cautiously, he inched closer to where it seemed to come from. *Which way is the wind blowing?* It blew over his back and he gritted his teeth in frustration. *They'll scent me now.* His hand crept to his side for an arrow and he nocked it to the string. Another goat bleated, muffled by the hiss of the wind. He dropped to one knee and tried to peer through the tangle of leaves and pinkish-white flowers. Something white was moving fifty paces away. *Can I stalk them with the wind against me? They're intent on their food.*

Pace by pace, he crept through the thorns. Every two or three steps, he paused, ears alert. *I can't hear Azariel. Either she's stayed back or she's shifted shape.* Forty paces lay between him and the end of the roses where the goats browsed. A thorny branch ran along his back with a series of little clicks across the links of his chainmail. Other thorns jabbed at him, but he ignored them, mind and eyes fixed ahead. He counted five in the herd: a black and white doe-goat, two brown does with white spots, a black kid and a black and tan billy with at a full twist in his spiralling horns. *He's no trophy and he's no good for meat, either. I'll leave him. One of the does for me.*

He crept closer. The goats had stopped feeding and were standing still, looking intently into the roses just beyond the black shadow that crept across the grass. *They've scented me, but they're inquisitive. That might be all I need.* His eyes flicked back and forwards across the ground remaining between him and the nearest doe. *Thirty-five paces, more or less. A little over half a bowshot. I'll try it.* He slowed his breathing as if he were falling asleep as he eased himself to his knees, facing side-on to the herd. A line of needles jabbed into one of his shins. He ignored it and twisted to face the goats. Smoothly, he raised his bow and drew it, training the little sight-notch on the riser of the bow above the arrow on the ribcage of the doe he had chosen, one of the spotted ones.

The sight-notch aligned with a splash of white that spread up from under her foreleg onto her belly and chest. He drew a deep breath and let it out slowly, ready to loose the string that strained at his fingers.

The black and tan billy stamped one fore-hoof, then turned and bolted up along the ridge towards the golden flank of the hill. The does and the kid followed him. As the spotted doe turned away, he loosed, hoping to strike her in the chest or flank as she fled, but the red-fletched shaft flew wide of her and buried itself in the grass, feathers flaming in the dying light. *Hellfire!* he thought. *Missed again.*

Two grey shapes burst from the roses and raced after the goats. The shorter of them howled fiercely. "Go, Stormwolf!" he shouted after them. Azariel and Lady bounded up the ridge, legs eating up the distance. Soon, Lady's swift gait had taken her past Azariel and within ten paces of the herd. Farren fought his way through the rest of the roses, watching the chase as he retrieved his arrow. Lady had reached the spotted doe and was snapping at its flank. It stumbled with a screaming bleat as the deerhound caught it in the thigh. Then the shewolf flung herself at the doe and seized the throat. The wolf, the hunting dog and the doe vanished below the cover of the tussock and long grass for a few moments and the goat bleated once more, an almost human cry that clenched a cold hand around his stomach.

Azariel stood on the hillside above him, the sunlight turning her armour to gold and her drawn dagger to fire. Lady pranced alongside in her shadow, tail wagging. Farren ran up the hill towards her, bow in hand. "Well done!" he panted. He looked down to where the spotted doe lay dead.

"It was Lady who pulled it down. I don't know if I could have done it alone. Now what?" She turned to one side, and spat into the grass. "That was disgusting," she said, tossing her hair back from her face. "I changed back before the taste of blood had gone."

"Let's take it back down to the camp, clean it up and eat what we can. As for the rest, we'll have to find some way of keeping it from spoiling in this warm weather."

"Smoking it, I suppose. There's plenty of fuel around to try that." She bent over the carcass of the goat and took hold of the hind hooves.

He shouldered his bow and grasped the front hooves, then they lifted the carcass together. "We'll try it,' he said. "It's better than trying to bury it or store it in the river."

****

Azariel fed another load of willow wood and leaves into the fire. A fresh cloud billowed up into the improvised smoker of cloaks and blankets above the fire where the thin strips and steaks of goat meat lay on a makeshift grill of twigs. The stars overhead flickered and winked in the indigo sky as the warm northwest continued to blow. *How much longer is this going to take?* She yawned and stretched, trying to dispel the sleepy haze that clouded her mind. She glanced beyond the fire to the broom bushes where Farren had fallen asleep, his breaths slow and even. Lady curled beside him, her head resting on her flank. "Good girl, Lady," she called softly. The dog swished her tail through the short grass in answer. In the darkness beyond the circle of the firelight, the horses cropped steadily at the grass, and the leaves hissed in the wind. An owl hooted, answered twenty heartbeats later by a more distant one. Her eyelids drooped and her head slumped forwards. She jolted awake and slapped at her bare arms. *I can't go to sleep with the fire burning beneath those twigs.*

She clambered to her feet and paced about, breathing the cool night air deep into her lungs to keep herself awake. *We're nearly out of wood to get the fire smoky. I'd better collect some more.* She walked out of the circle of firelight and strained her eyes through the dim navy blues and greys of the night world. She made her way to the willows and found another armload of dead branches before returning to the campfire. Kneeling beside the blanket-tent, she folded back one flap and turned her face away as the smoke rolled out. She peered through the smoke, then reached in to snatch one of the strips of meat off the grill. It felt hard and almost brittle in places. *Is it properly cooked yet?*

She drew her dagger and halved the slice. Turning it to the yellow light of the fire, she inspected the middle of the meat. The bright red rawness seemed to have vanished. She sniffed at it, but the smoke overpowered all other aromas. *I'll have to taste it. At least I can do it safely. Raw meat won't hurt a wolf.* She dropped the steak to the ground and shifted shape. Lady pricked her ears and whined softly. Azariel wagged her wolf's tail in reply, then stooped to eat one half of the meat. It tasted smoky to the centre. Relief sending a pleasant ripple down her spine, she sat back on her haunches and slid back into her own shape. *At last.* She tossed the second half to Lady, who caught it in mid-air with a snap of her jaws. *Now to bank up the fire and then I can sleep.*

CHAPTER TEN

Azariel opened her eyes and rolled over. *Thank goodness I'm off that stone at last.* She breathed in the scent of the dewy grass and listened to the dawn chorus of birds. Her head felt heavy and tight at the temples, and she rubbed the tension away as she yawned. She opened the flap of the green canvas tent and looked out. The sky had turned brilliant red, and the first morning breaths of the northwester made the slender branches of the horse chestnut trees dance and quiver. She crawled out to where the wind tugged and tousled her hair, and drove the sleep from her brain. Farren still slept beside the bush where he had fallen asleep. Lady lay with her shaggy head on his chest, rising and falling with the slow rhythm of his breath. His right hand rested on the dog's neck, strong and golden with his emerald ring sparkling in the first gleams of sunlight. *Lady, you lucky dog, I wish I could sleep that close to him.* She tugged at the betrothal earring in her left ear, freeing it from a strand of hair. *Ah well, come springtime, I will.*

She stretched her stiff arms and shook her head free from the lethargy. A very thin plume of smoke still wound up from the ashes and smuts of the campfire to be whisked away by the wind. She peeled the blankets and cloaks off the smoking tent and inspected the gnarled strips of goat meat. *They still look as ready as they did last night. I'll have to put them into the saddlebags away from the dog.* She shook her black cloak out before folding it over her arm. The felted wool smelt heavy with the tang of smoke. *I won't wear that today with the heat, and I'd wager Farren won't be wearing his bright red one, either.*

She tossed her cloak over one of the broom bushes, then turned and walked between the largest horse chestnut tree and its nearest neighbour, stepping over cracked and broken branches. Lady pricked up her ears and watched her, head still resting on Farren's chest. Azariel picked up a dozen sticks twice the thickness of her fingers as she made her way to the branch where the rest of the goat carcass hung. *Good. Lady hasn't been at it and the carrion birds haven't found it either.* After dropping the bundle of sticks beside her feet, she drew her dagger and slashed a few slices off the shoulder and a rough chunk from the neck. Meat in one hand and firewood in the other, she returned to the tents.

She laid the meat on one of the stones beside the heap of charcoal and built the fire up again with dry grass and leaves. The thread of smoke thickened, and she blew at the base of the ball of tinder. She sat up to draw in fresh air, eyes watering and stinging. A yellow flame grew as the grass stems blackened. She cracked the sticks to fit and added them to the fire, building it up. The dry heat of the flames mixed with the already warm air and made the skin on her face feel taut, although her headache began to ease. She drew back from the fire and looked over at Farren. *When is he going to wake up?* Lady looked back at her with wide eyes. "Go on," she said to the deerhound. "Lick his face and wake him up."

Lady raised her head and gave a small, eager bark before scrambling to her feet. Azariel winced as the hound's forepaws dug into Farren's stomach. He groaned and rolled over. "Get off, you clumsy great giant," he growled. Lady whined and slathered her tongue across his face, then bounded over. Azariel gave the deerhound the chunk of meat from the goat's neck. Farren crawled out from under the bush where he had rolled and came over to the fire, wiping his face with the back of his hand. "That is the last time I want to be woken like that."

She caught his eye and winked. "Good morning, beloved," she said. "Are you thinking better of the barracks bugler now?"

He laughed and wrapped his arms around her. "Good morning. No, don't kiss me; I'm all covered in her spittle." He sniffed and turned to glance at the fire. "You've got the fire going again. Or has it been burning all night? How did the smoked meat work?"

"Excellent. I'm just about to cook some of the fresh stuff for breakfast. We may as well finish off the bread and save the dried peas for later."

He scratched at the short bristle on his chin. "I'm going to the stream to tidy up, and I'll see if I can find some watercress there. It'll be good to have something green again. Then we can plan our hunting while we have breakfast."

She grilled the meat over the embers while he prepared the watercress and the end of the bread. Lady lay beneath the trees and gnawed at her chunk of meat. Beyond the dog, Veranath wandered to and fro, nibbling vaguely at the grass while Storm and Princess groomed each other's necks. Azariel lifted the skewered meat away from the embers and sniffed at the savoury aroma of the cooked meat. Moisture flooded her mouth, and her stomach tightened hungrily in anticipation as she passed one of the thin grilled steaks to Farren.

Farren arranged the meat on the bread and watercress. "Thank the King of Heaven for a nice slice of goat," he said.

She nodded, mouth already full. "We'll be eating gazelle tonight, if all goes well," she said as soon as she could.

"We'll have to stalk it carefully, that's for certain. There's no point in trying to pursue this one. I'll have to know more about its habits."

She tore the crust off her bread and wrapped some watercress around it. "It used to be a tame gazelle, according to my vision. That sorceress seemed to keep it in the labyrinth for something." She looked up the golden-green slope of the hill to the tight walls of mountainthorns around the labyrinth. "Does that help?"

He tilted his head to one side. "It might. We could try looking inside the labyrinth and seeing if it still goes there. It might, even if the sorceress isn't there to feed it. It's a good safe place from predators. Would a wolf follow a trail into a maze?"

"I would," she replied. "But what a real wolf would do, I'm not sure. If it was very hungry or the gazelle was injured, then it might." She bit into her bread and meat.

"We'll start by looking in there, then." He uncrossed his legs and stood up. "When do you want to try?"

"As soon as I've finished eating."

He brushed the crumbs off himself. "Don't hurry. I'll go and say good morning to the horses and check them after yesterday's journey. There's no point taking them on a short walk up the hill and through the labyrinth, so they can have a rest."

"What about Lady?"

"I suppose I had better tie her up so she doesn't get lost chasing goats." He took a step towards the pile of gearbags and began hunting through them while she finished tearing at the bread.

While he was tethering the deerhound, she strolled to the stream. She squatted beside it on the boggy ground, catching the sharp scent of crushed pennyroyal beneath her. The water gurgled musically, and a single rose petal drifted and whirled along the current. Scooping the water up in her hands, she drank deeply, then splashed some over her face. The skin under her eyes still felt heavy with tiredness, but her headache began to melt away. *Good. I'm ready.* She shook a few shining drops off her hair and turned back to meet Farren.

He was waiting for her with his bow in his hand and the northwest wind ruffling his red hair. "Do you know how lovely you look with your damp hair tumbling over your shoulders?" he said, smiling widely. His dark eyes shone. "Come on. Let's go."

The wind blew the tussocks in waves as they climbed the hill. The warm wind carried the scent of dry grass mingled the bittersweet aroma of tea-tree blossom. Insects droned and buzzed through the wildflowers on the slope; far in the distance, a goat bleated. *Probably one from that herd we raided last night. If it's lucky, then we'll be lucky and catch this gazelle today.* Her gaze flicked up to the curving grey, black and green wall of mountainthorns surrounding the labyrinth. "No sign of it yet," she said aloud.

"What about a scent of it?" He let go of her hand and shifted the grip on his bow. "If you change, you might save us a march through the labyrinth by telling us it's not there."

"Very well, then, I will." She ran her eyes over the golds and greens of the hillside then up to the fierce bare blue of the cloudless sky before resting on Farren's auburn hair. *One last look at colour before the black and white of the wolf's world.* Then she drew a deep breath and closed her eyes, concentrating on the shape of her body and feeling it shift. The scents blown on the wind doubled and trebled as her mind whirled with animal instincts and emotions. She dropped to all fours, head still spinning, and waited until her human reason and will dominated the wolf's brain.

Farren's hand ruffled the thick, hot ruff of fur at her shoulder. "Well, Stormwolf? What can your nose tell us?"

She sniffed at the air, catching the rank tang of a rutting male goat. *That's no good. I'll try the ground.* Insects crawled through the grass, beneath her nose as she worked over the soil, several of them carrying a tiny scent of their own. *Nothing here.* She jog-trotted up the hill, hearing Farren rustle and thud through the tussocks behind her. A small cloud of pollen dusted her nose, making her sneeze. She rubbed it off against her foreleg and trotted on.

The opening to the labyrinth and the first few paces of the passage faced the southwest. *It's probably aligned to something. Kalmian would know, but I don't. Perhaps we should have brought him with us.* She padded to the beaten dirt between the walls of mountainthorn and studied it with eyes and nose. Hundreds of twin-crescent hoof marks criss-crossed over each other in the golden-brown soil. The unique tang of the gazelle with the Stone of Wind flooded her senses, making a fierce longing surge within her. Her teeth bared and she ran her tongue over her long fangs, mouth already watering in anticipation of the hunt. Instinctively, she stepped forwards, tail and muzzle held in a rigid erect line and one forepaw raised. Then she stopped and shook herself before changing back to human shape again.

"It's been in here," she said, turning as she picked herself up from the dust. "We were right. It uses this place all the time. So do the goats." She straightened up and brushed the dirt off the knees of her trousers before flicking her hair back from her face. Her nose still prickled from the pollen.

"When was it here last?"

"This morning, I think. By the scent of things, it goes out of here for water and fresh grazing, then returns here to sleep."

He slipped his bow off his shoulder. "We're going in to wait for it," he said. "I just hope the wind can't carry our scent to it."

She fell into step beside him, shortening her long-legged stride to match his as they walked into the labyrinth down the straight passageway. The walls of mountainthorn grew well over their heads, straggly limbs reaching out here and there to form rough archways. The wind hissed through the thorns and made the smaller branches and twigs shake. After five paces, the path turned to the left and began to twist and double back and forth. "This one can't be as long as that one on Kalmian's island," she said. "We'll be through this one quickly."

"It doesn't have all the death-traps and terrors, either," he replied. His fingers coiled around hers and he pulled her closer. "I'm glad of that. I wouldn't want a second journey through a maze like Kalmian's."

"Well, we'll keep our eyes open for anything dangerous. But I doubt this one's got any traps. How would the gazelle have survived these past two years?" Her hair snagged on an unpruned branch and she shook herself free.

"Can you feel anything about this place? You're better than I am at that."

She stopped, closing her eyes. *Master, is there anything here?* She breathed slowly in and out, spirit reaching and sensing. Faintly, a cold uneasiness crept up her arms and over the top of her head, soon to be blown away by the warmth of the northwest wind. "Against the path of the sun," she said aloud. "What did Kalmian say about the way labyrinths run?"

He fidgeted with the onyx and diamond betrothal earring in his left ear. "Sunwise paths are dedicated to Shayim, counter-sun paths to Majalis and the ones dedicated to… to Crajaval go up and down steps or underground. Why?"

"Just a very faint sense of unease. Only to be expected in a sorceress's home." She returned her attention to the physical world and breathed in the dry scent of the mountainthorns. A skylark trilled in the distance. "There's no mists and no odd smell. And we should be able to cope with anything that might turn up."

Her back had become sticky with sweat and the sun was beating down from the zenith by the time they reached the heart of the labyrinth. The hedges around the centre had once been trimmed to make the shape of a seven-petalled flower, but the shaggy branches blurred the once-neat lines. In one of the petal-shaped recesses stood a small turf-walled hut. Old spiderwebs hung in the windows, fluttering in the eddies of wind. "The sorceress's house," she said, pointing. She led the way across the clearing towards it, following the trail in the dirt and the little scattered piles of gazelle droppings. A twisted black beech stood in the exact centre with a roughly conical limestone boulder beneath it. Here and there on the velvety black growth covering the trunk of the beech, little beads of honeydew winked. She turned towards it, mouth watering. "That honeydew looks good," she said. "I'm going to get some."

"You and your sweet tooth," he chuckled. "But I don't blame you – I'm ready for a bit of refreshment after the walk. Leave some for me!"

She ran to the tree, leaping onto the limestone boulder to reach out and sweep the little beads of honeydew off the tree trunk with her forefinger. She licked her fingers, drawing in as much sweetness as she could. Farren stood beneath her, busy collecting honeydew below her reach. She swayed forwards on the narrow top of the boulder and steadied herself with one hand on his shoulder before jumping down. A bead of honeydew had caught on his cheek. She wiped the sticky drop off with one finger and sucked it clean. "Now what, great hunter?" she said, coiling her arms around his waist.

"We wait here until the gazelle decides to come back. By the looks of things, it likes the old hut to shelter in. And, luckily for you, it doesn't like honeydew."

"Good. A slow day of waiting will be good after travelling and everything else." Her mind strayed to the street outside the dog-breeder in Lebhern-y-Hyalda and the Bloody Blades circling her. She squeezed Farren's hand and brought thoughts back, then let go of him and turned to look around the centre of the labyrinth again. A curved line across the top of the limestone caught her eye and she stepped closer to study it. A carved scorpion crawled across the top and sides of the stone, sting and claws raised towards the east. She shuddered. "You were right. This place is – was – dedicated to Majalis," she said quietly.

"He's not likely to turn up again, is he?" Farren's hand rested on her shoulder, then slid around her back. "Surely not – not after that fight back on Kalmian's island."

"I doubt it. What's there here for him, anyway?" She leaned her head against his shoulder, the metal links of his chainmail pressing into her cheekbones. "I'm still tired after last night," she yawned. "I'm going to sit down in the sun while we wait."

She found a patch of sunny grass to one side of the circle and knelt to feel for stones before she lay down on her stomach. The sun and wind kneaded warm fingers over her back and scalp while the sweet smell of the vegetation wafted around her. Heavy drowsiness crept over her and she let her head droop onto her folded arms.

"Are you falling asleep?" Farren sat down beside her. "You should have woken me up and made me take my turn watching the meat last night, Stormwolf." He ran his hand along her hair. "You sleep now," he said softly, bending down to kiss her on the top of her scalp. "I can shoot this gazelle alone."

Farren kept stroking the black silk of her hair until he saw the lift and fall of her shoulders slow into the rhythm of sleeping. Smiling, he kissed again. She stirred but her eyes remained closed. "Sleep well, sweetheart," he murmured. He took his bow off his shoulder and laid it in the grass beside him. A pair of blackbirds landed in the shade of the beech tree and began to peck and scuffle in the dirt. From time to time, his focus flicked over towards the path into the centre, waiting for the sound of movement. The wind blew constantly, rising to great gusts that made the mountainthorn hedges dance and lifted the hair off his forehead, then dying away to warm eddies.

He watched the blackbirds as they sunned themselves, sang and eventually flew away. The sun wheeled from north to west in a huge slow arc. *We've been waiting here for hours,* Farren thought as the shadows inched eastwards. *If that gazelle was coming here to rest, it would have been here by now. I had better wake her up and we'll follow the trail again to find where it goes in the evening.* He shook her gently by the shoulder. "Wake up, sweetheart."

She stirred and moaned. Rolling onto her back, she yawned and half opened her eyes. "What is it, beloved?" she asked.

"I think we'd better move on from here. It's past the heat of the day, so that gazelle probably rested somewhere else." He picked his bow up from the grass and brushed dust and pollen off the wood. "We'll try to find it by the river when it goes to drink."

She sat up and shook her hair back, combing her fingers through it and flicking out little ends of dry grass into the wind. "Are you sure it's not coming? I can test the wind and then if it's on the way, we'll know to stay here. Otherwise, yes, you're right. We'll start the march out of here."

"Could you scent it from here?" A small flicker of irritation grew inside him. *No wonder that gazelle hasn't come. We're upwind of it. The best part of the day wasted.* He breathed out, dispelling the frustration on his breath. He rubbed the smooth wood of his bow again, then slipped it over his shoulder.

"I'll find out where the entrance is exactly then I'll sniff it out." She rubbed her hands together and turned towards the black beech. "This won't take long."

She scrambled up the gnarled trunk. The slick leather of her boots and the faded cotton of her uniform trousers contrasted with the velvety growth on the trunk. She reached up for one branch, then a second, the wind blowing her hair around her face. A long strand of hair caught in a twig that had sprouted from the trunk and she turned her head to yank it free as her left hand stretched for another handhold, both feet anchored on the same branch.

The branch beneath her feet cracked before her right hand had found a new hold. She grabbed at the limb overhead and missed. Involuntarily, he stepped forwards, dropping his bow and readying his muscles to catch her. Her boots scrabbled at the jagged stub of the branch, kicking some of the velvet-mould off the trunk. A gasp of pain broke from her and she dropped.

"Stormwolf!" he cried, darting forwards.

She landed feet first beside the limestone boulder, stirring the dust up. Her head bowed and her eyes closed as her breath hissed in and out between her bared teeth. She reached towards the boulder to steady herself and a drop of blood fell from the heel of her left hand. "That cut," she breathed. "That one I got showing off at Karissa – it's opened up again."

He knelt beside her, a tight knot in his throat and his heart pounding. "Show me." He caressed the back of her bare arm, stirring the fine hairs and skipping over her heavy silver armband.

She lifted her hand off the limestone boulder. A smear of blood trailed over the gouges forming the carved scorpion. The thin line at the base of her thumb had split open and seeped dark red. He cradled her wounded hand and bent to kiss her palm. A mingled taste of salt, honeydew and blood crept between his lips and he drew back. "Neither of us thought you'd need your glove today," he said. "But it doesn't look too bad."

Her breath hissed sharply in and her eyes widened. "Farren..."

"Did I hurt you?"

"Get up – now! Look what's happening."

He scrambled to his feet and turned to scan the centre of the labyrinth. White mist was seeping and oozing out of the ground, covering the grass. A stench of rotten meat filled the air. More mist jetted out of the carving on the limestone like steam from the spout of a boiling kettle. Crajaval surrounded her domain with white mist. A sick cold weight filled his stomach. He stooped for his bow with one hand and reached for her with the other. "Let's get out of here!"

He ran towards the entrance leading back into the twisting paths of the labyrinth, cramped calf muscles stretching loose. She raced ahead and tugged him on. The mist rose and curled around his legs and torso, brushing a clammy chill over his bare arms. Two paces away, the mountainthorns arched over the pathway.

He recoiled as something slammed into his whole body, leaving him stinging and stunned. He tentatively felt at his face, expecting to find blood from his nose. His chest heaved as he gasped and he heard Azariel hissing through her teeth beside him. He examined his hands, seeing the usual smears of dust and grime rather than blood. Ahead of him, the exit looked clear, apart from the coils of mist that shimmered in a thin curtain. He reached forwards into the gap and his fingers met an invisible wall, smooth as glass and prickling with energy. A cold hand of fear tightened around his chest. "Blocking off our escape," he muttered. He bent to pick up his bow and fitted the bow over his neck and shoulder, leaving his hands free. "Now what?"

He turned towards the boulder again, linking hands with her. The evil-smelling mist hid the grass and had almost covered the sky overhead. His heart pounded and the prickling tension of fighting energy built in his arms and legs. *This is what that sorceress would have always done*, he thought. *Pour a little blood onto that altar-stone to Majalis and cut off the escape of whatever she wanted to sacrifice. Or whoever.* Unwanted images of slaughtered men and women rose in his mind and he shook them away. *And now…what?* He scanned the shifting mass of white and forced down the bile that rose as the stench grew. Silence fell like a thick eiderdown, cutting off even the sound of the northwester.

Something moved in the heart of the mist near the boulder. A darker patch of vapour was shifting and bending silently, forming itself into a steady shape. Bit by bit, the shape became clearer as if it were approaching through the fog, although it never grew any larger than the size of a horse. Many-jointed legs stretched out from the long body and the foremost pair wielded massive pincers. A whiplike tail arched up and over the hindquarters, ending in a tear-shaped sting.

His hands clenched into fists and the tingling fire built and burned in the tips of his fingers. "So that's how and why the sorceress killed her victims," he said, eyes narrowing. He stepped to one side of the entrance as the misty scorpion turned its great head to and fro and begin to stalk towards the exit.

Azariel's fighting wolf-howl cut the air and two streams of bright blue fire crackled through the mist. The fire hit the scorpion full in the chest and head and passed completely through it. The creature crawled towards the exit without hesitating. It grew more solid, blocking off the blurs of the beech tree and the boulder, and taking on a pale reddish tinge. He punched his own fire towards it from his rings, black and emerald, but still the scorpion prowled ahead.

He ducked to the left when it reached within ten paces from him. It solidified even more, and a faint clicking and scraping came from its claws. Azariel's footsteps pounded the hard dirt on the other side. He whirled and punched a bolt of fire at it again, rings pulsing with heat. *How many bolts can this thing take? Even Majalis or Crajaval couldn't take this many without damage.* The scorpion turned away from him, heading into the mist towards where Azariel's footsteps had run. His stomach lurched and he gritted his teeth. *It's had a taste of her blood and now it wants the rest. Never!* "Stormwolf!" he shouted. "It's after you!"

He ran forwards, the limbs of his bow knocking his left arm as it bounced. The mist ahead blazed with flash after flash of green, purple and scarlet fire, searing the shape of the scorpion into it. The scales and plates armouring it looked slick and wet as the colours played over it. A second shape, black rather than red, darted through the whiteness towards him and turned into Azariel. He held out his hands to her and steadied her. She was breathing hard and her fingers trembled as they gripped him. "Over here," she said, tugging him away from the scorpion.

They stopped as they reached one of the petal-shaped recesses that led off the main circle of the centre. "It nearly had me," she panted. "I saw its claws around me." She closed her eyes and her pale lips drew back from her teeth. "But I didn't feel it. I don't think it's solid enough yet. But it will be. And see the blood on it!" She held out one arm to him and showed him a smear of brilliant red across it. "That's not mine. It dripped off that thing."

His hands tightened around her forearms and he ached to pull her closer and hide her in the circle of his arms. *Not now. Not with that thing stalking us.* "We'll be able to kill it easily once it's solid, shouldn't we? It's probably too misty to blast now."

"I've hit it with seven bolts already; I don't know if I want to strike so hard I pass out."

"I don't have that problem, sweetheart." He released her and peered around the edge of the petal-recess. "I haven't got the measure of strength to take on so much fire it overwhelms me." A thin sheen of moisture coated the thorns and twigs beside him.

The click and scrape of the scorpion's feet drifted through the mist, growing steadily louder. A soft breeze stirred and shifted, forming the whiteness into coils and spirals. A new stench cut across the rotten-meat stink, poisonous and bitter. The hiss of the breeze shaped itself into barely discernible words: *hunger... hunger... searching... hunger... fresh blood... hunger.* The knot in the pit of his stomach tightened and the back of his neck prickled.

"How are we going to know if it's solid enough to kill yet?" Azariel stood beside him, one hand resting on his shoulder. "Look there – here it comes again."

The deep red scorpion inched through the mists, keeping the same slow, relentless pace. *Searching... hunger... searching... fresh blood...kill...hunger,* came the wind-words, growing louder as the creature dragged itself closer and closer.

"Run again," he said. "I'll meet you over beside the exit."

She squeezed his hand then darted away. Her footsteps faded as he turned and ran. He followed the hedge, and the constant whispering of the scorpion died away. *Searching... searching... hunger... blood...* His heart beat a rapid tattoo in his ears and his breathing sounded oddly loud.

He clenched his fists, the metal of his rings feeling like circles of fire around his fingers. *Master, let us know when to strike at it. Don't let us leave it until too late.* He reached the gap in the thorns and waited, chest heaving and mouth dry.

The slender black shape of Azariel plunged out of the mist and halted, hair whipping around her face. He held out his arms to her. "The King of Heaven knows when that thing will get solid enough," he said. "So I asked him."

"So did I." She shook her hair back over her shoulders.

"Then we trust him, wait and keep running when it gets close. I wish it would shut up that ghastly whispering." He glanced towards the centre of the circle. The whispering was growing louder again as the red shape of the scorpion pushed through the foul-smelling vapours.

Azariel's fingers bit into his forearm just above his armband of protection. "I've just remembered something Kalmian said once."

He turned to her, a smile spreading across his face. "Thank the Power for that. What?"

"All labyrinths have what he called an omphalos – a navel. Until one of those is set up and consecrated, they can't raise power with the labyrinth. It's just a maze. So if we can find the omphalos for this one, then that thing should go away."

"The tree or the altar stone. They're both in the centre." Again his rings and fingertips pulsed with prickling energy. "And if they fail, then we'll look in her house." The bulbous eyes of the scorpion swivelled towards him and it increased its pace. *Blood... hunger... searching... hunger... kill...* He tried to swallow some of the dried spittle in his mouth and steady his breathing. "Run again. I'll meet you in the centre."

He reached the tree and the stone, his heart thumping against his ribs, loud but not loud enough to drown out the constant hissing of the scorpion. As he paused and recovered his breath, he heard the click and scrape of its footfalls, now mixed with a soft thud. *It's heavier. It's grown more solid.* He glanced at the stone. The smear of Azariel's blood had disappeared from the limestone, but the ground all about it was sprinkled with hundreds of fine droplets of bright blood. "Is that your blood?" he asked her, pointing.

She shook her head. "I didn't shed that much blood even when I first cut myself." Bending, she placed both hands on the stone. "I suppose we push this over to destroy it."

He paused. The footsteps of the scorpion drew closer and the hissing words grew louder. *Blood… hunger… hunger… blood…kill… kill…*

"Either that or we blast it," he said. He looked down at his hands. The emerald on his left hand and the onyx on his right glowed like stars, illuminating the coils of mist as the tiny droplets of water swirled around them. More energy prickled in his fingertips.

"Let's do both," she said. Bracing herself against the stone, right palm resting on the carved scorpion, she pushed until the sinews stood out hard on the underside of her arms. He reached around her and added his force to hers. The stone rocked backwards then thudded into the dry grass, revealing a patch of bare dirt where suddenly exposed insects scurried for cover. Nothing else happened.

A second thud answered the noise of the stone falling and he spun around. The scorpion had crawled ten paces closer. "I'll hold it off," he barked. "You strike the stone." Rings flaring with heat, he punched fire at its head, black, scarlet and silver.

The scorpion reared up as the flame struck and splintered into a hundred points of light. Its tail lashed like a whip, scattering drops of blood as the beast advanced. One splashed onto his face, cold, sticky and smelling rotten. *KILL… KILL… KILL…* the creature hissed. One of the huge pincer-claws reached for him as he threw lightning at it again.

A surge of heat flared behind him as the droplets in the mist reflected blue and magenta fire as well as the bolts of green and crimson he threw at the creature. The claw struck at him swiftly and he leaped backwards. The tip of it caught him a bruising blow on the back of the arm, a heavy block of ice. His pulse pounded in his ears as he blasted the scorpion again. Another wash of heat beat on the back of his head, followed by a cracking and splintering noise.

Tail quivering, the scorpion reared up again so far that its pincers could have caught its tail. It hissed wordlessly, flailing its forelegs. A warm wind blew into Farren's face, making the grass and the beech tree rustle. The gust caught the mist and blew it back. The scorpion stood still, looking as shadowy as when it had first appeared. A second billow swept through the centre of the labyrinth. The blood-red colour of the scorpion faded to grey and dissipated like smoke. The wind, sweet with the scent of dry grass, blew it and the remaining traces of mist away.

He let out a long breath as the last traces of energy died away inside his hands and arms leaving only a gentle heat lingering in his rings. His hands quivered as his breathing returned to its regular rhythm. He closed his eyes and breathed in the warm, grass-scented air. With a soft metallic clink of chainmail, Azariel turned towards him and slid her arms around his waist. He gathered her close to him and held her tightly. Her chest rose and fell in time with his, and her breath tickled his neck. "Well," he said after a long pause, "the gazelle won't be anywhere near this place now after all our noise. Let's go back to camp."

Azariel slipped her right hand into his as they walked towards the exit. Sweat dampened her palm and her rings still felt hot, much warmer than his. H squeezed her hand gently. "I'm glad you're safe," he said. "How's your hand?"

She shook her hair free from where it was tangled around an outstretched branch of mountainthorn. "A bit sore. I'll be taking those gloves with me for the next few days, and I'll certainly wear them if I have to climb something, or if we come in here again."

"We don't need to worry about the mist and the scorpion again, do we? You broke the stone." He checked his pace as they rounded a corner, allowing her to wheel around on the outside edge.

"Not quite. When I blasted it the first time, the carved scorpion absorbed the light. The second time, the carving filled up with fire – like it had filled up with water instead – and then all the mist went away. You probably helped by blasting the scorpion." Her hand slid out of his and glided up his forearm to draw him to a halt. Her dark blue eyes fixed him. "I wouldn't want to risk shedding blood in there again. I'd rather not go into there at all"

He bent his head and kissed her lightly on the cheek. "We'll find some other way, then." The corners of his mouth twitched into a grin and he winked at her. "Perhaps if we managed to wound the gazelle over that navel-stone or whatever it's called, the scorpion could finish the job for us."

She shook her head, smiling. "I wouldn't trust it. We'll have to do our own hunting."

"I was joking. I don't want to go back and risk facing that scorpion again either."

They continued walking along the twisting paths until they finally left the labyrinth. A blackbird flew out from a nearby broom bush, shrilling in alarm. The northwest wind, hot and unchecked by the hedge in the midday sun, buffeted him and caught Azariel's hair, sweeping it in a soft black cloud around them both. He rubbed his face in her hair before brushing it down.

Azariel turned into the wind and shook her hair back. She stopped sharply and stiffened. "Look at that!" she said indignantly, pointing up at the cliff above the labyrinth.

He followed the line of her finger. Halfway up the cliff, beyond bowshot, stood the gazelle. It bent its head to pluck at the strip of grass that clung to a narrow ledge where it perched, then raised its head to look at them again. Sunlight winked off the glassy surface of the black Stone between its horns and off the silver chain binding it there. The gazelle shook its horns at them, making the reflections dance again through the shimmers of heat rising from the rocks, and whirled away. In three bounds from rock to rock, it had reached the top of the cliff. It paused to glance down at them once more, then darted away, swift as the northwest wind.

"It could have been watching us all that time we were in there," he said, running his hand up and down the smooth wood of his bow. "Why didn't I think of that?"

"Well, at least we know how we're going to see if the gazelle's inside that labyrinth tomorrow without going in ourselves." She twisted her lapis lazuli ring around her finger. "It'll be worth taking the horses for a ride along the ridge this afternoon, though. Perhaps we'll see where the gazelle has run to."

CHAPTER ELEVEN

The wind caught Azariel's hair and swirled it out on each side of her head as they walked down the slope towards their camp. A strand tickled Farren's face and he breathed in the smell of smoke and grass that clung to it before brushing it down. Ahead, Princess raised her head from the grass and whinnied to them. A deeper whinny came from another part of the broom bushes, followed by a volley of yapping. "They're all pleased to see you, beloved," said Azariel.

"And I don't think they would have liked to come with us up there." He lengthened his stride and jogged down the last few paces of the slope.

"Who will we take with us this time?" She drew level, then overtook him.

The slope flattened out and he jolted to a walk. "All except Veranath and we'll take some lunch inside us. I need something after that scorpion." He looked down at his hands, expecting to see them still trembling after his exertions. "It's a pity we don't have anything sweet."

She turned to look back up at the labyrinth. "Plenty of honeydew back on that beech tree."

"No, thank you. I don't want to go back into that labyrinth again." The chatter of the stream sounded deliciously inviting, and the roof of his mouth felt dry. "A good drink might help."

They ate and drank, sitting back to back by the ashes of the campfire. He leaned forwards slightly, letting her weight rest against him. He took a pinch of salt from a little canister and rubbed it over a strip of smoked meat. Her armour grated against his. "It would be too easy to stay here all afternoon," she said. "We should move."

He leaned back and rested his head on her shoulder so he could look up past the curve of her jawline and ear. "Is that an order from the arch *minyaster?*" he asked.

She tweaked a lock of his hair. "Yes," she said. She stood up, removing the pressure of her body, so he took his weight on one hand as she stood up.

After cramming the salty, smoky meat into his mouth, he got up and walked to the bushes where the tack was bundled up with the blankets and saddlebags. He pulled Princess's saddle and bridle out, and wiped a smear of dust off the skirts. Azariel was kneeling beside her pile of gear, tugging a glove over her left hand. The high horn of the saddle he carried bumped her knee. "Sorry," he said before hauling the gear up and balancing it on his arm.

Lady jumped up at him as he saddled Princess, paws scrabbling at his trousers and chainmail as she strained at her tether. "You're coming too, Lady," he said, scratching her behind the ears then pushing her down. He unpicked the knot tying her to the tree and re-fastened it to the saddlehorn. "And don't you dare tangle Princess up."

He mounted and waited until Azariel had finished saddling Storm. Veranath snorted as he nudged Princess with his heels and headed her across the stream. The mare turned her head to neigh in reply to the stallion then fell into step beside Storm as they headed uphill. They followed the goat-track up past the tangled hedges of the labyrinth and towards the long ridge that led to the top of the cliffs. From time to time, the deerhound raced ahead of the horses and nearly tripped them, but Farren tugged her back. "Heel," he told the dog firmly. Lady looked up at him and rolled her eyes, tail wagging.

They began climbing the ridge. The northwester had risen to a light gale, ruffling and lifting the fine hairs along the back of Farren's arms. *I hope I can judge the wind right for a good shot,* he thought. *And I'll need to get downwind of the gazelle.* The slope fell away sharply on his right towards the labyrinth while the left rolled down in a broad golden curve. The mountains stood to the far north, huge and dusty-blue with distance. The dark speck of a raptor circled in the sky. Beneath it, a trio of plovers darted into the air from one of the far slopes, their shrill cries drifting faintly towards him.

A fly buzzed past his left ear and he raised a hand to bat it away. His gaze flicked up to the scrappy patch of shrubs and spindly trees at the top of the cliff where the gazelle had last vanished. A flicker of white at the top of the patch among the dark green-grey of the scrub caught his eye. *Gazelle or goats?* He reined Princess in and reached out to tap Azariel lightly on the shoulder.

"What?" she whispered, drawing Storm to a halt.

He pointed to the patch of white. "Can you tell me what that is?"

She leaned forward in the saddle, narrowing her eyes so the fine lines at the corners pulled into an arrowhead. "There's only one of it, as far as I can see," she said, scarcely louder than the roar of the wind over the slope. "If only there was some way of seeing further." She shaded her eyes with one hand. "It's pure white, whatever it is. I don't think the goats were that colour. I suppose it's our gazelle. What shall we do this time?" She turned towards him.

He looked up at the animal in the scrub, then back at her. A strand of hair wandered across her forehead. "Sweetheart, could you wait here while I stalk it? One's better than two at that sort of thing. But first, I'm going to use my Gift and try to draw it close." He brushed her forearm with his fingertips. "I'll leave cutting the Stone free to you, whether I draw it or kill it."

"Go, beloved." She smiled at him and flicked back the wandering strand of hair from her face. "I'll watch from here."

He dismounted between the two horses and reached both arms up to her. She bent down to him, her hair tumbling across his face and shoulders. His lips found hers as her bare right hand caressed his cheek. "God Incarnate go with you," she whispered, pulling back.

"Thank you." He let her straighten up then unhooked his bow from its place on the saddle. The string hummed with tension as it bumped against the high pommel. He patted Lady, then Princess, pressing his face against the mare's smooth neck. "Don't let Lady follow me; keep quiet and stay here. If the gazelle runs off, then you can release her."

He crept along the slope towards the area covered in shrubs. Crouching, he worked around towards the edge of the cliff and the lower part of the scrub so that the wind blew his scent away from the white animal. He strained his eyes through the tangled bushes, keeping watch for movement. As the animal took a few steps to one side, a flash of sunlight on metal or glass caught his eye. His heart thumped quickly in his ears. *It is the gazelle.*

He closed his eyes and began to reach out mentally for the gazelle. *Come here, white gazelle,* he willed it. A wave of warm energy poured out of him, then the cords of energy reached the gazelle's mind. He tested the gazelle's mental texture, expecting either the warm spongy velvet of a tame animal or the rock and pinecone roughness of a wild one. The gazelle moved and the tentative connection broke like a cobweb. He slowed his breathing, keeping it quiet but deep, then reached out a second time. His mental touch met a texture like the surface of a well-worn cobblestone, then something as slippery as wet ice and as sharp as a new needle. His eyes widened and he bit back a hiss of breath as the touch of his Gift slid around the gazelle's mind and snapped off. He reached for it a third time and flinched as he touched the slick surface, which sent waves of pain and cold against the warmth golden cords of his Gift. He gritted his teeth. Then his touch was thrust back as if thrown. He shook his head, fighting the urge to run his hands through his hair. *Something's been done to it. Either that Stone is doing it or that sorceress set spells on it to stop people like me taming it.* He stared at the white animal as it stretched up to tear at the higher branches of the tea-tree, making the black glassy Stone sway back and forth. *I'm going to have to kill it after all. I'll need to get closer.*

Willing his breathing and his heartbeat calm, he felt for the quiver at his side. His fingers brushed feathers then found the smooth shaft by the metal clip that held the arrow in place. He drew it out and nocked it to his bow, setting the bright red cock feather perpendicular to the string. His right hand tightened around the grip as he edged through the tussocks, setting his feet down carefully.

He reached the spindly gorse and tea-tree scrub. Gingerly, he stepped forwards. His foot found something springy underneath it and he withdrew, glancing down. The ground was strewn with sticks and twigs fallen from the bushes. He stepped around them, pressing into a gorse bush on one side so that spines jabbed into him just behind the ear. The sharp smell of crushed tea-tree, mixed with the sweet scent of their flowers, drifted around him and he caught the faint tearing sound of the gazelle feeding.

Pace by pace, he stalked the gazelle as it continued browsing on the tea-tree. The gazelle stopped tearing at one bush and walked to a new one, and he paused. As it began ripping and yanking at the foliage again, he crept closer. He ran his gaze over the ground between him and the best, and counted ten paces. He watched, breath quick and silent. The hairs along its back and neck gleamed in the glare cast by the Stone. It turned its head to one side, making the chains jingle. He drew his bow, the string biting into the calluses on his three middle fingers. His left arm stretched back, muscles burning with effort and the stitched wound on his shoulderblade itching and throbbing. His index finger brushed the corner of his mouth, anchoring him as he trained the glittering steel head of the arrow on the hollow behind the gazelle's foreleg. *There's no way I can miss from this close, even if it can run like the wind. Gazelle, you're mine.*

He loosed the arrow. For barely half a heartbeat, the shaft flew straight. Then it began weaving wildly. A roar of wind set the bushes dancing. The arrow soared into the air, spinning and spiralling higher and higher. The sunlight caught the bright cock feather and the head, making them into white and red points against the blue. The arrow arched overhead and backwards on the wind. Then it plummeted beyond the scrub and down towards the cliff. A sick thrill surged through Farren's chest and stomach, and his hands trembled uncontrollably. *I don't believe it. I really don't believe it.* He looked back at the gazelle. It continued browsing as if nothing had happened.

He reached to his left hip for a second arrow, but his hands shook. Gritting his teeth, he tried to will them calm, but nerves and energy made them quiver. *Kill-fever. I haven't had this for years.* His bow scraped along a branch of tea-tree, stirring the bushes. With a gentle tap of hooves and a rustle of leaves, the gazelle vanished. *I was so close I could almost have knifed it.* He kicked at one of the bushes savagely and whistled with the pain as his toe crunched into the tough trunk. *Damn, damn, damn, damn, damn.*

A blur of shaggy grey caught the corner of his eye, and he ducked to one side as Lady hurtled past, ears blown back. He smiled as he watched the deerhound race uphill, long legs straining. *She probably won't be able to catch it, but she may as well try. I'll call her back later. And now for my arrow.*

He made his way to the edge of the cliff nearest to where he had seen his arrow falling. Holding the spindly upright limb of a tea-tree, he looked over the precipice. An angry bee rose from the branch beside his head and buzzed around him a few times before darting away. The labyrinth lay below him, the spiral paths clear and symmetrical. Between him and it, the cliffs stretched down for about two bowshots, broken here and there by little ledges and broken rocks. A tiny point of red about halfway down caught his eye. He fixed more closely on the point of red and saw his arrow jutting out from a small crevice above the larger ledge where the gazelle had stood watching at them as they left the labyrinth. *How am I going to get down to that?'*

He shouldered his bow and walked down the ridge to where Azariel lay waiting in the long tussocks. The two horses pricked their ears towards him and whickered. Azariel rose to her feet and strolled to him after he had pushed the dog down. "What happened?" she asked, wrapping her arms around him.

He leaned his head onto her shoulder. "I got close, but the wind took my arrow. A whirlwind. Up and back and over the cliff."

"Wind?" She ran her hand over the back of his head and ruffled his hair. "It runs like the wind and the wind protects it from arrows. That makes sense; it's carrying one of the Stones of Protection and the Stone of Wind at that."

"I do. That wind that took my arrow was different. And, Stormwolf?" He raised his head and rested both hands on her shoulders. "My arrow's halfway down that cliff. It's going to be a hard climb to get it back."

Azariel bent to kiss the back of his hand, tasting the salt of his sweat. "I'll get it for you. Show me."

Azariel followed him to the brink of the cliff, still nibbling the sweetish end of a stalk of grass. Holding onto one of the tea-tree bushes, she looked over. The wind buffeted the back of her head, streaming her hair around and across her face. She shook it to one side. "Where is it?"

He pointed. "Just above that place where we saw the gazelle coming out of the labyrinth."

Her eyebrows rose. "The gazelle didn't... You mean when we were coming out of the labyrinth." She scanned the face of the cliff and found the tiny speck of red above the thin strip of grass. "It's a pity we left the ropes back down at the camp." Below her, crevices and projections in the browns and greys of the rock caught her attention, and she nodded. *It looks like an easy enough climb without ropes – as long as I protect my wounded hand.* She knelt in the gap between a gorse bush and a tea-tree to test the soil at the edge. It felt dry and stiff, almost rock-hard where the roots of the scrub bound it. "I think I can do this."

She twisted around and wriggled backwards over the edge, gripping a handful of tree roots. *There was a foothold somewhere to my right.* She prodded and felt for it, then eased her toe into the cranny. Taking her weight on her foot, she let herself down until she could just peer over the edge. Farren knelt down above her. "Mind your hand, sweetheart," he said. "Don't fall. I can ride down for ropes."

"I'm all right." She glanced down and saw a firm-looking piece of rock at the level of her knee and planted her left boot onto it. Her hair tumbled around her shoulders as she moved into the shelter of the cliff face. The sun beat down overhead and her armour felt hot and heavy. She shifted down to a new handhold, gingerly grasping at the tree root with her gloved left hand. The opened cut ached as her grip bit down. *I'm going to hold on.*

She reached down, feeling for a handhold in the rock as the roots tapered and twisted back into the ochre soil. Her fingers found a rough projection of sun-warmed rock and she closed her hand around it. Hands secure, she began feeling with her feet again. She wedged her foot onto a crevice, balancing along the edge of her foot. An insect droned behind her head. She glanced down, hunting the next foothold.

Hand, hand, left foot, right foot, she worked down the cliff face. Her muscles ached with the strain and a sweat broke out on her palm inside her glove, making the cut sting. The ledge with the arrow lay half a bowshot beneath her, the solitary broom bush quivering in an eddying breeze. She lowered herself down, searching for a boulder. Her foot found the stone and she leaned onto it, beginning to ease the grip of her left hand. The rock slid out under her foot, sending a sharp thrill up the soles of her feet into the pit of her stomach. Her blood thundered in her ears and the faint earthy smell of disturbed dust rose. The cut on her palm ached as she clung to the crevices, but she ignored the pain as she felt for a new foothold. She drove her fingers into the rock with all her strength, holding herself steady and feeling her fingernails break. A firm ledge met her foot and she moved on.

She eased her fingers out of the crack in the rock around it and let herself onto the shelf of rocks. The shaft of the arrow jutted from a crevice about the height of her head. *That gazelle must be able to almost fly, jumping up and down here as easily as it did.* Relief poured into her arms as she let them drop, feeling light and springy without the strain of her weight. The breeze stirred her hair and made the broom bush hiss. One or two seed pods on the bush snapped. She rubbed the sweat off her forehead and drew off her glove to dry her hand before reaching up and taking the arrow.

She held the glove in her teeth as she twisted the arrow to and fro in her hands. *How am I going to carry that? I should have asked Farren for his quiver.* The salt and bitter taste of the sweaty leather grew unbearable and she let the glove fall onto the short-cropped grass. *I can't carry the arrow in my teeth all the way up, and I need both my hands.* She tested the edge of the head and noticed that the tip had been dented and bent to one side. *If I had my cloak on, then I could have pushed it through like a giant needle at rest, even though that would have torn my cloak. But that's back at camp, and I'm glad of that.* She looked over at the boulder she had disturbed. It was under the broom bush, and several of the branches had been crushed and snapped by its fall. A shudder crept down her back to her feet as she remembered it sliding loose. *I hate to think what would have happened if I had been wearing my cloak to climb in all this heat and wind.*

She sat down on the boulder and stared out to the river below. A blackbird flew beneath her and she watched it swoop down and settle on the mountain beech in the centre of the labyrinth. *Could I find the arrow again easily if I threw it down to the bottom? It should be easy enough to miss the labyrinth's hedges and land it in the grass outside. I would prefer not to hunt for it inside the labyrinth.* She twisted the arrow around again and stroked the red and black fletchings smooth from where she had ruffled them. *I don't think Farren would like that, though. I could lose it too easily.* She turned and looked back up towards the dark line of scrub against the clear sky. Farren's silhouette crouched between two bushes, head tilted down towards her. Beside him, she made out Lady's long nose and ears. *He must have called her back.* She tapped the arrow against the side of her boot and frowned. *I won't throw it down and I can't throw it up. I'm going to have to carry it. Could I take it up in wolf form? I know I can hold on with my teeth for a long time that way.*

She ran her eyes up and down the outcrops and projections jutting out from the rock face. The three ledges the gazelle had used to jump to the top thrust out like giant stairs. She shook her head. *Too far for a wolf to jump. That's no good.* She twirled a lock of her hair between her fingers. *There has to be a way. Belt pouch? Too small. Sheath with my sword or dagger? Not enough room. No pockets in my trousers or my tunic. My belt?* She put the arrow down on the boulder beside her and felt between the thick band of leather and her chainmail. The belt fitted snugly around her waist, but two fingers slid between the metal and the leather. *Too loose. It could slip out too easily from there. It would need something else holding the arrow.*

She smiled as an idea burst into her mind. Fletchings first, she inserted the arrow a short way down her boot along the outside of her leg. *It will fit.* She drew the arrow out again and laid it in the grass before sitting down. Sunlight glinted off the sharp blades of the head. *He keeps his arrows in good order.* She pulled both of her boots off, followed by her socks. After pushing one sock inside the other, she hooded the sharp head with the thick creamy homespun. *That should shield it for long enough without doing too much damage. One day, I'll learn to make my own socks but at least I can darn them.* She drew her boots back on, the leather hard and damp against her bare feet, then wedged the arrow into her boot, tucking the tops of the socks well in to anchor it in place. The shaft pressed against her calf as she stood up and flexed her leg to and fro. *It'll do. I've got it so the blades sit flat. At least it's easier climbing up than down.*

She pulled her glove on snugly into place across the cut. The wound throbbed, but she willed herself to ignore it. She wedged her toe into a crack about the height of her knees, crooked her fingers around the ledges and crannies, and began hauling herself up. The rising eddies of wind lifted her hair as she craned her head back and scanned the rock face for the next handhold. *The gazelle jumped out heading to the right, so that's where I should aim.* Pivoting on her toes, she lunged towards a projection of rock and caught hold of it. *I hope this is as firm as it looks,* she thought, tugging on it to test it. The rock held steady and she put all her weight onto it, inching higher.

Step by step, handhold and foothold, she climbed towards the line of scrub. She reached the first of the ledges where the gazelle had leaped up to on its way up the cliff, then paused, shaking her arms before reaching for the handholds in the rock and pulling herself from crevice to crevice.

Farren looked down at her as she swarmed up the rock face, a lithe black figure against the dusty grey and brown stone. The sunlight picked out a bluish glint in her glossy hair. He fidgeted with his betrothal earring. *She's good, even with one hand wounded. It's a pity she managed to fall from that tree this morning. God Incarnate, keep her from falling now!* He tightened his grip around the tea-tree near the edge of the bluff. The horses cropped the grass behind him, and Lady nudged at his back once or twice before flopping down in the grass beside him, keeping back from the cliff edge. *I should have gone for ropes all the same.*

Azariel climbed to within five bowshots. A sheen of sweat coated on her forehead and a smear of dust spread across one cheek and the bridge of her nose. She tilted her head back to look into his eyes. Holding the slender trunk of the tea-tree, he reached down towards her. The fingers of her right hand clenched like steel around his wrist. He clasped her arm above the band of silver, the sinews in both their arms standing out and his biceps burning with effort. Her free hand clutched at the grass and tree roots before she got one knee onto the firm grass and levered herself up.

She rested on her hands and knees in the grass beside him, teeth bared and hair hanging across her eyes. Her lips tightened into a thin line as she sat back and straightened out one leg. Both her hands clamped around the knee until her knuckles whitened. "Stormwolf," he said. "What's wrong? Did you manage to get the arrow?"

"It's in my boot." She nodded at the leg she was holding. "I felt it cut me, so you're going to have to help me get it out."

He knelt and rested one hand on her bent knee. "Don't tell me that it's gone right into you and the barbs have caught in your leg."

"Nothing as grim as that. I meant that you'll need to help me get it out of my boot."

He stood up and took a step backward, feeling something soft underfoot. Lady yelped and sprang to her feet, showing the whites of her eyes. "Sorry, girl," he said to the deerhound. "Did I stand on your paw?"

The deerhound snuffled at his ear as he knelt beside Azariel and caught hold of her heel. The black leather riding boot eased off her leg and the arrow fell out of it, head wrapped in her socks. He stooped to pick it up, then unwrapped the socks from the head. A red smear stained the white wool. The shaft felt warm and the fletchings ruffled. He smoothed them into place and clipped the arrow back into the quiver. "Thank you," he said. "How badly did you cut yourself?"

"I don't think it's too bad." She flexed her knee and felt the side of her trousers. A small slit in her black trousers showed an inch-long glimpse of white skin tinged red at the edges.

He knelt back down beside her and peered at the cut. A single drop of blood seeped between her fingers, darkening the material. "Let me see." She shifted her hand out of the way, allowing more blood to well up. He shook his head and pressed his hand over the slippery flesh. "Stormwolf, sweetheart, I'm doing the climbing from now on."

She laughed, shaking the snakes of hair back from her face. "It's not much more than a scratch, really. I'm surprised, though. I thought the fall would have blunted it."

He picked at the grime under his fingernails as he watched her stoop to pick up her armour and pull it on. *I hope it is not much more than a scratch and she's not making light of it.* His eyes flicked down to the arrows at his belt. *It can't have cut too far, even when she bent her knee. I should have given her my quiver to climb down with.*

She picked up her socks and shook her head at the red-rimmed slash near the toes of both of them. "Another pair ruined, unless I can find something to darn them with." She stripped off her other boot and wriggled her bare toes.

"Are you ready to go, or do you want to wait until that cut has completely stopped bleeding?"

"Go where?" She pulled her ruined socks back on, and followed it with her boots.

"Back to camp," he said. "We've spent nearly half the afternoon, and we used a lot of wood last night. We'll need to collect more, and it'll be further from camp now."

"You don't want to have one more try stalking the gazelle? Lady and I could track it from where you saw it last."

He shook his head. "It'll be miles away. We'll leave it alone and see what we can do tomorrow. Let it relax." He offered her his hand and pulled her to her feet. "I want to work with Veranath a little, too. He'll have to be broken in and used to people without continually using my Gift on him before we get back to the capital."

"Let me guess – your Gift didn't work on the gazelle?" She shook her hair back from her face. "I didn't really have the chance to ask before."

He shook his head. "It didn't. At least I know it'll work on Veranath."

They remounted the horses and headed back down the ridge at a gentle trot. Storm edged ahead of him, head held high. Azariel's hair swirled behind her, a river of shadow. As they reached the campsite, half a dozen starlings flew out of the trees near the tents. Lady turned aside to the creek and drank.

He began unsaddling Princess. The mare snorted hot breath over him and bunted him in the back with her muzzle. "That's my lady," he said, patting her neck. "Off you go and graze somewhere." She snorted at him again as he turned towards Veranath. "Now it's time to spend some time with you, you big beauty." He reached one hand towards the stallion's muzzle. Veranath's nostrils quivered and the whiskers around his mouth tickled the back of his hand. "Let's see what we can do together this afternoon." His hand brushed the smooth hairs of the stallion's face and he began stroking the horse, letting his Gift work and feeling the texture of the horse's mind warm and soften. "I'll start by grooming you, then we'll go for a ride."

CHAPTER TWELVE

The northwester had eased to a brisk breeze the next morning, although the air still felt dry and warm. Azariel slid her dagger through the soft turf near the stream, cutting out a neat square. *One more sod and I'll have enough to bank the fire up for the day.* Farren splashed in the water upstream from her, sending a drop of water flying to hit her on the cheek. She dug the freshly cut square of turf out then looked across at him. The sharp angles of his jaw were dripping and sunlight gleamed off the razor blade he was rinsing in the stream. *It always amazes me how he can shave himself by touch alone. Good hands, I suppose.*

He glanced back at her and smiled. "How do I look?" he asked.

"As handsome as always," she replied, dropping the turf square onto the pile she had already cut, then walked over to him.

His arms circled around her and drew her close, the links of their armour grating together. "Did I miss any?"

She ran her eyes over his cheeks and chin, studying the contrast between the hard lines of bone and the soft curve of his lips. Her heart danced in her chest. "No," she said. "You've done it again." She slid her hands around his head and drew him down to kiss his mouth. The sweetish smell of waterweed lingered on his skin, mixing with the lavender tang of the soap he always used. Her fingers trembled and her lips began to open. Quickly, she pulled back. *I can't kiss him like that. Not yet.* "What are we going to do about the gazelle today?" she said aloud.

"I don't know," he replied, stroking the back of her head. "At least, I don't know what we're going try to do to it today. I'm going to have to do some hard thinking about how we can hunt it."

She rested her head against his shoulder, the links of his chainmail digging into her cheek. "What about waiting for it by the river again? You should be able to wait for it up a willow tree by one of the game trails and shoot it from there."

"This gazelle can't be shot, Stormwolf." He shook his head and turned to look up at the hills. "I've tried."

"You've only shot at it twice. The wind doesn't seem to be as strong today, so you might..."

He sighed. "I didn't miss because of the normal everyday wind. What took my arrow was something else."

"Are you sure?"

He loosened the embrace and took a step backwards. A frown creased his forehead and his eyes narrowed. "Don't you believe me? I tell you again: I didn't miss because of the wind or because of anything I did wrong. The gazelle itself is protected against that by the Stone of Wind. The best archer in the world couldn't shoot that gazelle."

She glanced away from him towards the labyrinth. "As I said, you've only shot at it twice. Anybody can miss a target twice in a row. I've seen you do that before."

"I do not miss from ten paces!" he growled, spitting each word out. "You wouldn't miss from ten paces. If I hadn't stood there cursing and gazing like a half-witted owl at my arrow yesterday, I could have knifed the beast. I wish I had."

"Or you could have put in a second shot and killed it."

His face flushed. "That would only have given you two arrows to pick up from the cliff. Hellfire, Stormwolf! I can't shoot that gazelle. If it hears the bow, it can outrun the arrow. If it doesn't, then it somehow gets a whirlwind to sweep the arrow away. From ten paces! I don't miss from ten paces!" His hand darted out and seized her by the wrist. His grip tightened almost to the point of pain and the pressure of blood built in her thumbs and fingertips. "You're coming with me and I'll show you what I can do. Then you'll believe me. I don't miss easily and that gazelle can't be shot."

She fell into step beside him as he tugged her back towards the campsite. "What about the fire? I need to cover it over so we don't have to relight it."

"We can relight it. That's not a problem with all the dry grass. But I'm going to make you believe that I'm a damn good shot." He pushed through the broom bushes, snapping twigs. He released her and bent to take his bow out of his tent.

A warm rush of blood filled her right hand with the pressure of his grip gone. Her fingers still clutched her dagger, the blade gritty and grassy. She wiped it clean and sheathed it as Farren slung his bow over his shoulder. A pinkish flush lingered in his cheeks, and his eyes looked hard. "Well?" she said, drawing herself up to her full height and staring back at him. "What are you going to shoot?"

"You can pick the target – any target you like except the scorpion in the labyrinth – and I'll hit it."

She suppressed a chuckle. *Boasting like this always annoys him in other people. He is a good shot, but he's allowed me to ask him for the impossible.* "Do you want to wager?" she said, keeping her voice even.

"Yes. What will you stake?"

She hesitated, reaching out to stroke his forearm. Her mind raced over the few things she owned. *Storm, his tack, my sword and armour, my clothes, a bit of my pay left, a spear back at the Watchtower of the West, my dagger... I'd rather not part with them. And I doubt he'd really want my embroidery stuff or the red silk I'm working on. Soap, scent or lotion, perhaps?* She ruffled the fine hairs on his arm and her fingers glanced over the smooth silver and turquoises of his armband. "Pick something," she said. "Anything except Storm."

His eyes softened and the flush faded from his face. "Sweetheart, I can't take anything of yours. I gave you Storm – and your sword – and I want you to have him." He reached for her hand and squeezed it gently. "There's nothing of yours that I'd take – nothing that you wouldn't share with me anyway."

She smiled and stepped closer to him. "I've heard that you used to stake wagers on target practice when we were cadets. The girls who were archers all came back laughing about it. What did you stake then?"

He laughed and his cheeks flamed scarlet. "If just the lads were practising, then the winner was allowed to give the loser a whack across the seat of his pants with the flat of his sword. If the girls were practising with us, then us lads could wallop each other as usual or else claim a kiss from one of the girls. The girls never walloped each other but they kissed the boys all the time."

"And?" She slid her hands up his forearms to his shoulders.

"My left hand was well respected by all the lads in my unit. As for the girls, well, I wasn't the favourite, but there were a few who chose me."

She tweaked his earlobe. "I'm not surprised, my beloved. You're a very good-looking man. Do you want to wager a kiss now, then?"

"I think I'll shoot to miss then. Being kissed by you is no penalty." He laughed and bent his head to brush her forehead with his lips. "How about the loser saddles up both horses for a week every time we go anywhere?"

"Done. Now do you want to hear what your target is?" She bared her teeth in a fierce smile.

"Tell me." His eyes flashed playfully.

"A bird on the wing."

The smile vanished from his face and he whistled softly. "Stormwolf, you sweet little hellcat! Right." His eyes narrowed again. "You've set me up. But I'm going to do it. I'll show you."

He turned sharply on his heel and walked towards the northeast. Her hair billowed around her face as a gust caught it, blurring her vision with black. She shook it back and strode to catch up with him. They passed into the shadow of a spur covered with wild roses in flower. A few degrees to the south, a cluster of dark green pines hissed and groaned in the wind. Farren headed towards the trees then halted. "This will do," he said. "I've seen birds around that tree before."

"How far from it do you need to be?"

"Well, you ought to set that if we were staking this wager properly like we used to." He winked at her as he unclipped an arrow from the quiver at his belt. "We're twenty paces away from it now, I guess."

"I think that's hard enough for you to do." She sat down in the grass beside him, hugging her knees to her chest as she watched him. He fitted an arrow to the string and stood waiting without drawing the bow, sinewy arms poised with catlike ease. His eyes turned slits of dark fire and his lips pulled into a grim line. She kept her eyes fixed on his face and body, and brushed back the wandering strands of hair. Her breath quickened and her heartbeat increased as a prickle of excitement built inside her.

A clatter of wings cut across the sighing of the pines and a grey pigeon erupted from the trees, flying westward. In one swift, smooth motion, Farren drew the bow and set the arrow free. She gasped and held her breath as the arrow climbed. The pigeon held the line of its flight, wings keeping a constant beat. The bright arrowhead glittered in the sunlight as it passed out of the shadow of the spur. It caught the pigeon squarely in the side. Feathers broke off into the air and were whirled away by the wind as the bird tumbled down. Beyond it, the arrow passed on, trailing blood. It reached the top of its arc then plummeted like a stooping hawk back towards the ground.

"Yes!" Farren shouted. He punched the air and flourished his bow in his other hand. Teeth bared and eyes flashing proudly, he spun towards her and dropped his bow. He scooped her up in his arms, squeezing and kissing her hard on the mouth. Panting and hands trembling, he let her go. "Come on. Let's go and pick it up." He caught her hand and she ran with him.

The dead pigeon lay in a clump of grass, staining the purple-grey seed-heads with bright scarlet blood. "Well done," said Azariel, kneeling beside the bird and picking it up. She turned to him. "You're amazing."

Farren looked down at her and smiled again as her stormcloud blue eyes flashed at him. His heart raced and his veins sang with energy. "Congratulate me properly later; I'm going to get my arrow first." He jogged past her. His eyes flicked to and fro over the grass, searching for the blood-trail. He glanced past the pink of clover flowers and the yellow of dandelions, and picked out the smears of red coating the grass. A blowfly buzzed around one of the splashes of blood, bright metallic blue in the sunlight. He followed the line of drops and found the arrow. Gore stained the wood of the shaft, and the fletchings were rumpled. He stroked the feathers smooth between his finger and thumb, using the sticky residue to hold the little barbs of the feathers in place before clipping the arrow back into the quiver. Rubbing the blood off his hands, he walked back to Azariel.

She stood dangling the dead bird from one hand and was twisting something small between her fingers in the other. "You'll never guess what we've done," she said, looking up as he approached and holding something out to him. "Look at this – it was tied to the pigeon's leg. We've shot a messenger pigeon."

He took the bloodstained parchment from her and straightened it out. *What language is this? I've never seen or heard anything like it.* He scanned the writing once more, knitting his eyebrows in puzzlement. Her hand brushed his arm and lingered, kneading and stroking his skin. "I can't make this out," he said, turning it towards her. "Can you? You know more languages than me." His grip shifted on the crisp parchment and he saw a scribbled lightning bolt that split into three clawlike forks in the bottom corner.

She shook her head, dislodging a small white feather caught in the black strands. "It's in a code or cipher of some kind."

His breath hissed in across his teeth. "Remember how Stessa said she might see us up here? I hope it's not her messenger pigeon we've shot."

"She'll come and spit fire at us if we have," she laughed. "How do you fancy a meal of fresh pigeon, my great archer?

He shouldered his bow and slipped his arm around her waist. "We may as well pluck it while it's still warm. It'll give me a chance to plan our strategy for the gazelle."

He lengthened his stride to match hers as they trudged back to the campsite. He sat down cross-legged beside the remains of the campfire and smoothed the scrap of parchment flat across his knee. She settled onto a boulder that lay in the outer reaches of the shadow cast by the smallest of the horse chestnuts. Lady came up to her and twitched her nose at the dead pigeon before Azariel shooed her away. "I hope you're not thinking of burning that scrap of parchment?" Azariel said.

He shook his head. The pigeon's blood on his hands had dried and was beginning to flake off. "We'll give it to Stessa when we see her, or pass it onto General Alpherastin for the Nightravens. Either it's one of their messages or it's a Claw message. They should have it."

She nodded. "I hadn't thought of the General." She stood up, the pigeon's neck in her hands. Her knuckles whitened as she ripped the head off the carcass. A dribble of blood splashed onto her boot and she jerked her foot back. "Here you go, Lady." She tossed the head to the dog, who caught it with a sharp snap then sat crunching it in the grass, then sat down again.

He stared into the embers of the campfire. A gust of wind stirred them into sluggish life. The random shapes of red, orange and black resolved themselves into images as his thoughts drifted like leaves on the wind. A fly buzzed and whined past him then alighted on his bent knee. He waved it aside and it zigzagged towards Azariel. It settled on the bare patch of skin she had cleared on the pigeon's breast. A flick of her blood- and feather-covered hand sent it back towards him. It spiralled lazily above the campfire before he shooed it back towards her.

She looked up him from behind a lock of her hair and smiled before batting the fly back towards him. "Can't you swat it?" she said. "I don't want a delicious bit of pigeon spoiled before I've even finished plucking it."

He chuckled and shooed it back towards her again. "It'll need to land first."

"Then you can shoot it. Perhaps I ought to have set you that as a challenge." The fly darted away from her hand and droned its way to the campfire.

"It would be easier than shooting the gazelle." He drove the fly back toward her. *Where's something to swat it with?* He flicked his eyes gaze around beside him. The broom bush swayed with the wind just within his reach. He felt for one of the twigs, then bent and twisted a many-tailed switch off it.

Azariel sat frozen. The fly had landed on her armband, perching on the silver like a quivering speck of jet. The sunlight sparkled off its wings in iridescent colours as it ground its forelegs. "Ready?" she asked, then swept it back towards him.

It spiralled above the fire before settling on a spot of blood on the leg of his trousers. He raised the broom switch, then brought it down. The switch stung his leg briefly and smashed the insect into a smudge. He brushed the dead fly off with the twig and tossed both into the fire. "Time to stop our playing and get back to work. I can help you pluck that pigeon if you like."

"There's no point in both of us getting messy." She spread her hands towards him, palms up. Blood smeared her to the wrists and several tufts of down had stuck in the reddish-brown stains. A small cloud of feathers lay at her feet and hundreds were clinging in her hair like grey and white ribbons. A gust of wind caught the pile and stirred it, billowing the plumes out of the heap and making more catch in her hair and clothes. "Anyway, you deserve some reward for such a good shot."

"It wasn't that hard, swatting a fly."

She pulled one of the longer feathers out of her hair. "You know what I mean. Shooting the pigeon. You've certainly convinced me that it wasn't your fault that you couldn't shoot the gazelle."

He picked up his bow from where he had laid it in the grass and traced his forefinger along the grain of the wood before laying it back down again. "It should have been as easy as swatting that fly yesterday when I was only ten paces from it."

She winked at him. "You had me to shoo the fly to you when you needed it. We can't do that with the gazelle."

He stared at his nails and picked at the dirt beneath them. "Can't we? I wonder..." Ideas shot into his mind. He tore at a chipped rag of his thumbnail and smiled grimly. *I think I've got the answer now.*

He continued to fidget with his hands and nails as he puzzled over his idea. A blackbird trilled from one of the branches on the largest horse chestnut, loud without the strong rush of the wind. A black and yellow butterfly danced and hovered past the campsite, then vanished towards the hill. He closed his eyes, relishing the warmth of the sun on his back and shoulders, strong enough to heat the links of his chainmail gently. Other sounds drifted in the soft eddies of the breeze: sheep, the rustle of the leaves and the river, the horses cropping grass and snorting occasionally and the distant rumble of hooves.

He scanned the length of the river as the hoofbeats grew louder. A bay horse was cantering beneath the grey shadows of the willows, heading upstream. His heart kicked inside his chest. *I hope that's not a Yellow Claw – or a shepherd come to complain about our dog.* Sunlight glinted from something on the horse's head, but he saw only a blur where the rider should have been. "Someone's coming," he said aloud.

The horse cantered closer to the campsite. Two bowshots away, it angled away from the river and headed towards them. Farren and Azariel both got to their feet and reached for their swords. The shape of the rider became clear and the white oval of the face beneath a hood pointed in their direction. The triple-beat of the canter slowed to a brisk thudding trot. Veranath raised his head from the grass and stepped towards the newcomer, ears pricked. The rider, a woman covered from head to foot in close-fitting sand-coloured material that had been over-dyed in streaky olive, reined in the bay mare and dismounted. The rider clapped her horse on the neck and ran her hand down the blaze on its face. "Good girl," the rider said. She pulled her hood off her head, revealing her sleek blonde hair. "I thought I'd find you two around here somewhere."

Azariel's heart pulsed cold quicksilver and her shoulders slumped. Every smear of blood on her hands and arms seemed twice as large and sticky. *Stessa. Why did she have to come along when I'm looking like something that's sat on the dunghill with dogs at it?* She laid the half-naked carcass in the grass away from the deerhound and brushed at the tatty pigeon feathers clinging to her cotton trousers. "Hello," she said, forcing herself to sound cheerful. "We were wondering whether we might see you."

Stessa smoothed her hair down. The mottled clothing, though it showed less of her figure than her usual black garb, gave her skin a lively bloom. "Well, we dealt with those marauders in Lebhern-y-Hyalda quickly enough. They were easy to trap. And I did say that I might be coming up this way, so here I am." Her full lips parted in a smile. "Looks like I got here before lunch, too."

"This pigeon wasn't yours, was it?" Farren asked.

"Why should it be mine?"

"It had this tied to its leg." He handed Stessa the scrap of parchment. "I hope it wasn't yours."

She unfolded the paper. She scanned it and her fingers stiffened. "That's not one of ours," she purred. "That's a Claw mark in the bottom corner. A Claw cipher message." Her eyes glittered like chips of ice. "Good shot, Farren. I've wanted to put steel through one of their messenger pigeons for years but I've never been able to do it. I suppose you saw this one sitting in a tree."

"On the wing." Farren glanced at Azariel and winked before stepping closer to her and coiling his arm around her shoulders. "I had a wager to win."

"I see," said Stessa. The smile vanished from her face. "You know what that means, don't you? These pigeons will fly to their home directly and only stop to sleep if they've got a long way to go. If this one was flying, the Claw who loosed it was either based somewhere over by the eastern border – or else they're nearby." She tapped the toe of one grey riding boot on the ground. "You two had better be careful. I found you by the smoke of your campfire, to say nothing of the very obvious military-issue tents. If you don't want to find yourself being dragged across the border to the College of Fire, then you'd better hide them better." She re-folded the parchment and put her hands on her hips. "Make better use of the bushes and hide them as if you were using them as a hunting blind."

"Thanks, Stessa," said Azariel. She rested her head against the smooth warm links of Farren's armour and breathed in the smell of grass, horses, smoke and sweat that clung to his clothing. "I hope you can make use of that cipher, too."

"I will, that's certain. The first thing to do is to crack it." She looked down at the paper again and smiled. "I was planning to move on from here and keep watch on the border after meeting you, but if you don't mind, I'll stop here with you and work on this. Did you have any plans for today?"

"Of course," Farren answered. "We've got a gazelle to hunt."

"Off you go, then. Leave that pigeon to me. I'll improve this campsite of yours, too."

Farren's fingers tightened around Azariel's shoulders, pulling her even closer so that his chin brushed the top of her head. "If you dare go rummaging around inside my saddlebags..."

"What do you take me for? I wouldn't snoop into your things unless I suspected you of being Claws." Her lips curved into a pout. "Off you go and enjoy your hunt."

"Come on, Stormwolf." He clapped Azariel on the shoulder and dropped a quick kiss onto the crown of her head. "You're saddling up for us, seeing as you lost the wager."

She smiled at him and turned to kiss him on the mouth. "Enjoy your winnings."

Breaking out from his embrace, she walked over to the heap of belongings by the campfire to pick up the tack. As she reached Storm and began picking stray scraps of leaf out of his mane, Stessa called after her, "Azariel!"

"Yes?" She glanced back and saw Stessa with the half-plucked pigeon in one hand.

"I swear I won't try to make trouble by putting my bedroll in Farren's tent this time."

"Good," she snapped, a cold hand twisting her inside. She faced Storm again and slipped the bit between his teeth. The gelding champed at the bit, smudges of grassy foam appearing at the corners of his mouth. *Why did she have to say that? What is she thinking of doing?* She finished buckling the tack onto Storm then saddled Princess.

Farren took Princess's bridle from her hand and swung himself onto the mare's back. "The first thing to do is to find where we can drive the gazelle to – as well as finding where it is. We could use that cliff to help us, but there could be a better place in these hills." He whistled to Lady and the shaggy dog stopped scratching herself and bounded over to him. "By the way, Stessa, don't touch Veranath. He'll try to kill anyone except me and Azariel."

"I'll avoid him, then."

Azariel mounted Storm and followed Farren up the tussocky slope. The northwester buffeted the hillside out of the shelter of the valley. The tussocks danced and hissed and the feathers were plucked loose from her skin, hair and clothes. A shadow darted over the gold and vanished. She raised her head to see what had cast the shadow and spotted a hawk gliding on the rivers of wind. A starling took to the air beneath it, shrilling in alarm.

The thorny walls of the labyrinth swayed in the wind. She glanced towards the entrance and fingered the tender skin on her hand. "I hope you're not thinking of trying to drive it into there. I'd rather not risk getting blood on that stone again. If we could trap it in the passage, that would work, but not in the centre."

"I don't want to venture into there again either." he said. "But I'd like to get a better idea of how the land lies. When we went up here before, I don't think either of us was paying much attention to the landscape. We could try to harry the gazelle against the cliff, but there may be somewhere better."

"You're going to have to tell me what your plan is."

"I won't know for certain until I've had a good look around." He reined Princess in. "Take it easy, my lady, at least for now."

He slid his feet from the stirrups and shaded his eyes with his hands. The wind lulled for a few heartbeats, leaving the rushing of the river. Below them, Veranath grazed beside the stream, not far from the fallen willow. *The willow made good cover but the gazelle may be able to jump it, so that won't work to keep it at bay.* He looked northwards, following the line of willows beside the river. *We'll have to stop it running north up the river – we'll never drive it to the cliff if it goes that way.* His gaze travelled along the line of the stream from where it met the river then eastwards below them as the course led back into the hills. "I think we might follow that stream and see where it leads. There might be a place where we can ambush the gazelle and herd it towards the cliff."

"I still don't know what you're planning."

"What we're going to do is this: we'll wait until the gazelle goes to drink – probably around sunset. We could watch for it from up here, or we might find a better spot somewhere along the stream. If it's drinking down there," he said, pointing to the small stream near the campsite, "then we'll herd it towards the cliff. I'll drive it from the south with Lady to help me – Veranath, too, if I can persuade him – while you drive it from the north, either on Storm or in wolf form. Then we'll trap it against the cliff, with the Power's help, and we'll go in with knife and teeth. Well, you can go in with teeth."

She nodded then looked back up towards the sun, shielding her eyes with one hand. "The gazelle usually comes to drink at sunset, but it's not even noon yet. We'll be waiting here a long time."

He ruffled Princess's mane and scratched her withers. "Yes, and it would be a long time to spend around Stessa. I could see you were feeling uncomfortable the moment she rode up."

"Looking like this, all blood and feathers, while she's as pristine and gorgeous as ever, are you surprised?" She spread out her hands. The feathers had blown away, but the pigeon's blood still clung to her in dark crusty patches.

"You don't need to worry, Stormwolf, my sweetheart. A bit of mess doesn't spoil your beauty." He ran his gaze over her tousled black hair and the curve of her cheekbones. "Stessa may be pretty but she'll never be you. And you're the one I love."

Her lips curved into a smile. "Thank you, beloved." She stretched her arms and arched her neck. "Shall we head for the stream and explore it?"

"If we're lucky, we'll find a place where we can swim and cool off in all this heat." He settled himself back into the saddle and nudged Princess back down the hill.

The steep sides of the valley cast a shadow and sheltered the stream from the northwester. Brilliant red, green and blue dragonflies darted above the surface of the water and the reeds that grew along the edge. Lady splashed through the shallows beside Farren and Azariel as they rode upstream, soaking her long fur. Farren scanned the clumps of mountainthorn and the young black beeches that grew in the valley. A subtle perfume rose drifted on the still air and he sniffed. *That must be the mountainthorn.* He sat back in the saddle and studied the bushes. Princess slumped her head forward and let her ears loll to the sides, her gait slowing to a leisurely pace. *Those bushes won't give enough cover for a mounted rider, and we'll need to have the horses with us. Perhaps we'll find something further up the valley.*

The valley grew narrower as they followed the winding course of the stream deeper into the hills. Only a thin strip of rabbit-nibbled grass and a few small bushes grew along the valley floor before giving way to the mosses, lichens and small clumps of coarse grass that grew in tiny ledges amid patches of scree and loose gravel. The steady beat of the horses' hooves echoed off the sides of the valley. Above the steep rock faces, tussocks grew along more gradual slopes. As they rode beneath one of the tussocky slopes, Lady lifted her head and bayed. Bleating came in answer, and Farren made out the blacks and browns of the goats grazing higher up. "No need to chase them today, girl. You can't jump up there anyway."

The sound of the stream changed and the air grew cooler as the valley turned to a deep ravine. Ferns clung to the steep rocky slopes and a breeze blew towards them. They rounded an outcrop of rock, then moisture brushed over his face and hands. Ahead, the steep valley sides closed in and ended in a steep bluff. The stream poured over the head of the bluff in a thin cataract, smashing itself to foam in a small oval pool at the foot of the bluff. Beside the waterfall grew a wild apple tree, its branches bent with unripened green fruit. Swifts swooped above the pool where tiny insects danced in a finger of sunlight.

Lady trotted forward and lapped up the water. "That dog's got the right idea," he said, swinging himself off Princess's back. He landed on a loose stone and staggered, one ankle protesting as the unstable gravel slid away. He righted himself then knelt to drink. The chill of the water and the crisp, moist air sent a wave of refreshment through him, and the grey, greens and golds of the rock and vegetation around him seemed sharper and clearer. He sighed.

Azariel's boots crunched on the gravel beside him. "Is it deep enough to swim in?" She knelt beside him to drink.

"I don't think so. But this will be an excellent place to drive the gazelle, if we can."

"It's going to be tricky getting into the right places to be able to drive it, seeing as it runs so fast." She squeezed a bead of water out of her hair. "Shall we go back down to camp for a meal soon? I'd hate you to miss eating some of that pigeon you shot."

He laughed. "You'd miss it, too. It's not often we get a chance to eat pigeon. Perhaps we ought to start raising them for the pot back at the Watchtower when we go there next." He stood up and waited for Princess to stop drinking before he remounted. "One thing we know for certain: the gazelle's not here. Perhaps we should check if the gazelle's still in the labyrinth – but without going inside."

"That sounds like a task for my wolf's nose." She settled herself into the saddle and looked over at him. "Would you like that pigeon stewed or grilled?"

***

The sun slid lazily along its course and began to sink, turning the afternoon sky to the west dusty yellow. Farren rolled his head from side to side, easing the tense and knotted muscles. The pigeon stew he had eaten for lunch had become a distant memory and his stomach growled. A faint tang of smoke blew on the wind from the campsite, and the horses wandered on the top of the knoll as they grazed. Veranath stood under the spinney of horse chestnuts, a bright splash of brownish-orange against the gold and green of the grass.

"I wish there was some way we could enhance our eyesight so we could scan the hillsides like birds of prey do," Farren said after a long silence. "I've just been watching one over there. He – or she; I can't tell from this distance – was just a speck in the sky before he dived down and grabbed something. I wish we could find the gazelle like that."

"I don't think there's a shapeshifting gift for changing from human to hawk. Wolves, yes. Swans, yes. I've heard a tale about a bear-man and another about a lion-man. But not a hawk. It would be useful, though."

They fell silent again. For what seemed like the thousandth time, he ran his eyes up and down the length of the little stream, then the river. The herd of goats milled about on the river's edge, some rearing up on their hind legs to tear at the trailing branches of the weeping willows that grew among the taller white willows. His gaze passed over the campsite then the pine tree where he had shot the pigeon, then back up the length of the stream that curled in the shadow between the labyrinth's hill and the rose-covered spur. A flash of grey caught his eye. *That looks like my onyx ring before a battle,* he thought.

The point of grey light was suspended above an unmistakable white animal shape. The gazelle meandered towards the stream from the north. He nudged Azariel's leg with his elbow. "There," he said, pointing. "I'll go to the other side of the stream from it and try to drive it up towards the labyrinth. You wait to the west of the labyrinth with Lady and stop it going down to the river."

"What if it turns and runs south?" She clambered to her feet and reached down to him.

"I doubt it," he said, clenching her outstretched hand and letting her haul him up. "That's farmland down there and it would have to go past our campsite to get there. Stessa's there and I think it would stay away." He whistled to the horses and waited for them to trot through the scrub.

"So you want me to wait just over the ridge from the labyrinth and stop it going back up the river. Do you want to tell Stessa to help drive it northwards?"

He shook his head. "She's there; that's all that matters to the gazelle. But before we split up, I've got to give you this." He caught her by the shoulders and slid his hands up the length of her throat and around her face before he pressed his lips onto her mouth. "I'll meet you when we've caught the gazelle by the cliff, if the King of Heaven's willing."

"So be it." She kissed him swiftly on each cheek, then turned to catch Storm.

He headed Princess around the patch of mountainthorn. The gazelle still stood at the water's edge, the Stone of Wind swinging gently between its horns. He spurred Princess to a trot, his shadow spreading out on the grass in front of him, sharp, long and black against the gold and green. He guided the mare to a point several bowshots upstream from the gazelle, circling around it, then let her pick her way down the steep slope. Her hooves rang on some patches of bare rock, and she stumbled. He focused on the white gazelle in the shadows. *Just a few more minutes. Stay there and drink a little longer, gazelle, and you're mine.*

They reached the bottom of the slope and crossed the stream to the rose-covered spur. The gazelle's ears twitched towards him. His breath raced with rising excitement and his hands closed over the reins. With a yell, he stood in the stirrups and punched his heels into Princess's flanks. The mare snorted in answer and tossed her mane as she leaped over a stone then into a gallop.

The gazelle raised its head from the water, trailing a stream of liquid from its muzzle. It whirled and bounded away, heading downstream. "Yes!" he shouted. "Run that way!" It raced out of the shadow between the spurs to where the late afternoon sun turned its white coat to gold and the Stone of Wind glittered between its horns. It rushed within half a bowshot of their campsite, then swerved sharply to the right, heading up the slope towards the labyrinth.

He kept Princess at a gallop, feeling her sides heave for breath beneath him. The gazelle had become a blur of white against the grass, heading up the slope towards the labyrinth. Azariel and Storm rose at the top of the ridge, wind streaming out hair, mane and tail. Storm reared then cantered down towards the gazelle.

The gazelle checked itself in mid-leap and swerved again. The long-legged shape of Lady burst out of the tussock at it, baying. The slim white figure doubled back, jinking north of him and racing back into the shadow of the spurs where the stream flowed out from the hills. He turned Princess with a light touch on the reins, swinging east of the gazelle. His heart pounded and his lungs filled with the sweet scents of grass and tea tree in rapid breaths.

The gazelle swung between the arms of the hills, following the course of the stream. The Stone swayed and bobbed above its head as it ran, ears tilted back. Princess's hooves clattered on the gravel as she headed upstream after the gazelle, followed by the heavier pounding of Storm. *This is where I hope she doesn't lose a shoe and batter her hooves to bits.* The gazelle bounded over a clump of mountainthorn and almost vanished behind it, only the lyre-shaped horns and the Stone showing through the dense foliage. He spurred Princess towards the bush and swayed with her as she launched herself over it.

She landed with a clatter, half stumbling on the loose gravel and boulders on the other side. *Don't lose your footing, my lady*, he willed the mare. *I don't want to lose the gazelle or see you fall onto rocks.* Storm crunched into the stones and surged ahead. Princess tottered for a few moments, regaining her balance then galloped on. The steep slopes hid the valley in shadow, and the gazelle turned to a vague white shape amid the muted shades of ochre and grey. Still it ran, holding the course of the stream.

The stream bent around a large outcrop of rocks, and the gazelle jinked neatly around the corner. He tried to swallow the stickiness in his dry mouth. *This valley didn't seem so long this morning.* The rushing of the stream swelled to the roar of the waterfall, drifting towards them on a moist breeze. Storm and Azariel rounded the bend ahead of him then Princess bounded over the scattered boulders at the foot of the outcrop and turned the corner.

The gazelle reached the rocks tumbled at the foot of the cliff below the waterfall as Azariel and Storm arrived. It leaped, dainty hooves scrabbling for a foothold then slipped. Again it tried, angling itself leap at the valley sides rather than the cliff. Facing them, it stood on all fours as if it was about to jump again, flanks heaving. Farren braced himself on Princess's back. *Don't tell me it's going to try to jump out over our heads.* His hand went to his left side behind his quiver to draw his dagger. The gazelle lowered its horns as if ready to charge. Lady bounded up the tussocks from behind them, red tongue lolling. She paused and bayed, waking echoes from the sides of the gully. "Go in," he urged the dog. The dagger slid from its sheath, and Azariel scrambled down from Storm's back.

The gazelle swept its head from one side to the other in a wide arc. Golden light spiralled out from its horns, wreathing around the dog and felling her. A honey-like smell filled the air. The spirals spun out towards him. One coiled around him, hot and dazzling but not painful. He tried to raise his right arm to block the energy with his armband of protection, but the limb felt as heavy and unresponsive as stone. The dagger fell from his hand and Princess buckled under him. Numb and unable to move, he saw the golden lightning wrapping around Azariel. Then blackness overtook him as he fell.

CHAPTER THIRTEEN

Azariel stirred and opened her eyes. Her shoulders and back were chilled and she was shivering. To the right, the moon had risen above the hilltops, silvering the thin clouds drifting across the thin strip of sky. The wind had dropped and the night breeze sighed through the tussocks, mixed with the constant splash and gurgle of the waterfall and stream. The ground beside her felt damp with dew, and as she hugged warmth to herself, she found a sheen of moisture on her trousers and boots. *What am I doing here?* she thought, looking around and stretching her stiffened muscles. The large black shape of Storm lay near her, moonlight gleaming dully off his saddle. She rubbed her eyes, mind still foggy. Peering into the shadow cast by the bulk of the hill, she made out Lady, sprawled sleeping on the grass.

Memory flooded back to her and she saw the gazelle again in her mind's eye, honey-scented lightning flashing from its horns. *It shot us all. So why aren't we dead?* She stood up and rubbed her hands up and down her arms and legs, trying to warm them. The light wind stirred her hair. *It can't be strong enough in itself to kill, even though it carries the Stone. I didn't think an animal could be used by the spirit world like that, Stone or no Stone.*

She looked around and saw Farren lying beside Princess, his dagger looking like a moonbeam near his hand. *He's so still,* she thought as she bent over him. *I hope I'm right in thinking the gazelle can't kill with that fire from its horns.* The moonlight spread long blue shadows across his face and struck a spark from the diamond in his betrothal earring. *My love, my beloved, I hope you're all right.*

His chest rose and fell with the soft rhythm of his breath. *Thank the Power for that.* He twitched in his sleep as she bent over him, strands of her hair brushing his face. She gazed at the lines of his mouth, nose and chin. *He's so beautiful.* She straightened up, holding back the desire to caress him. *King of Heaven, how did I come to be chosen by him?* She rested her hand on his shoulder and shook him gently. "Wake up, beloved," she whispered. "We've got to get back to camp." She bent down once more and kissed his chilled lips.

She drew back as his eyes opened, glittering slits in the moonlight. "Azariel?" he murmured. "Are you all right?"

"Yes," she said. "Get up. We'll take a chill if we stay sleeping up here. The gazelle's gone. Let's get back to camp."

He held out one hand to her and she helped him sit up. "Where's my dagger?" he said, turning his head to and fro. "I had it just before the gazelle shot us. I'm lucky I didn't fall on it." He felt around in the grass beside him and picked it up. "Where's Lady? I hope she's sleeping too, rather than dead."

"By the cliff. Do you want me to wake her or the horses first?" She stood up and hauled him to his feet after her.

"Wake the horses. I'm only just awake myself."

She walked to Princess and crouched by her side. "Up you get, Princess,' she said, stroking and patting the mare's smooth coat. "It can't be too comfortable sleeping in the saddle."

Princess stirred. Azariel stood back as the mare clambered to her feet and shook herself. Princess whinnied and bent her head to the grass and began eating. Azariel watched the mare grazing, then woke Storm. The gelding got to his feet and pushed her in the chest with his nose, nickering to her. She wrapped her arms around his thick neck and absorbed some of the gelding's warmth into her chilled body, breathing in his nutty-horse smell. She scratched him behind the ears and hummed softly. Behind her, she heard Farren's footsteps returning from the cliff, then a dog's nose pressed against the back of her thigh. "Hello, Lady," she said, turning and looking down at the deerhound. She patted the dog's chest and rumpled her ears. "Good to see you safe and sound. Time for us to head back." She put her toe into the stirrup and mounted Storm. The saddle felt damp.

Tack squeaked, then Princess's hooves tapped lightly beside her, mingled with the padding of Lady's paws. "Ready?" asked Farren. She nodded and nudged Storm into a walk.

They rode silently beside the stream. The moonlight played in ribbons of silver on the stream, dancing in and out of rocks, reeds and tussocks. "How much of the night has passed, do you think?" asked Farren after they had ridden to where the valley shut out less of the sky.

She looked at the waning moon gliding across a star-studded field of indigo, draped in a scarf of cloud. It hung slightly west of north. "I'm not sure; I haven't been watching the moon lately. But I think there's about four or five hours until dawn. Enough time for a good sleep."

"I'm glad to hear that." He yawned. "I just hope we can find where Stessa's hidden our tents."

The eight hooves clopped over the gravel beside the stream as it wound down between the hills until it reached the place where the landscape broadened out and the stream curled away to join the wide shimmer of the Illin-y-Hyalda. The dark shapes of the horse chestnut trees waved against the night sky. Azariel's eyes flicked down to the jumbled shades of grey among the tree trunks. *Where's Veranath? Everything looks like a sleeping horse now that I'm looking for one.* A shadow in the middle of the willows moved and she made out the long neck and head of a horse. Veranath's ears pricked as they came closer and he whinnied to them.

"We're back." Farren slid off Princess's back. "I'll see to the horses, Stormwolf. You go and find where we're sleeping."

She swung herself off Storm and landed heavily. *I must be more tired than I realized,* she thought as her mind clouded. She leaned her forehead against Storm's warm hairy neck. She shook her head clear and patted the gelding before turning towards a nearby clump of broom bushes. *I may be sleepy but I know there are more bushes here than there were this morning. Some must be the tents – but which one is mine?*

She pushed the scraggly branches to one side and looked deeper into the bush, but saw only the tangle of branches, leaves and twigs, hazy in the dim. *This one is a real bush.* She let the branches glide back into place and gave her attention to a neighbouring clump of what looked like mountainthorn. She nudged one of the branches and the whole shrub moved, scratching and scraping against something. Her nose caught the earthy, slightly acrid scent of canvas. Still holding the branches bent, she waited and listened. The constant rush of wind and water sounded loud, but she just made out the sound of breathing. *This must be Stessa's tent. She's hidden them all well.*

The broom branches slid back into place, scratching against the canvas. Azariel peered around the campsite. What seemed to be another large thicket of broom or mountainthorn stood beneath the horse chestnut tree. *That has to be another tent.* She reached for the foliage and jabbed her finger on a thorn. *She must have had a hard job cutting and working so much mountainthorn.* After sucking her finger to soothe it, she reached for the branches again, stopping as soon as she brushed the dense tangle of twigs. *She must have left a way in. She won't have made us crawl through thorns in the dark – would she?* She dropped to her hands and knees, then crawled around the bush until she found a patch where the branches spaced out, revealing the canvas beneath. She felt for the flap; it opened as she tugged it, then she eased herself inside.

Gradually, her eyes adjusted to the din light inside the tent. A long dark oblong lay on the ground, a strip of light dirt showing around it. She touched it and felt the prickly-soft thickness of wool. *That's somebody's blankets and cloaks, but are they mine?* She inched forwards on her knees onto the pile of blankets. She groped around and her hands met a two cold points of metal almost the size of her palm. *Cloak buckle. But whose? I can't tell red from black in the dark.* She raised the material and sniffed at it. The sharp tang of rosemary mixed with the usual scents of horses and woodsmoke. *That's mine.*

She turned and crawled quietly out, hooking the flap open on a twig. "Farren?" she called softly.

He came out from between the trees, moonlight glinting off his chainmail. "Yes, sweetheart?"

"Have you found your tent yet?"

He strode towards her. "I found one but I wasn't sure if it was mine. I suppose it must be." He wrapped his arms around her with a grate of metal on metal and ran his fingers through her hair at the nape of her neck. "I need to give you this before I say goodnight." Very gently, he tilted her head backwards and his lips, ringed by a rough burr of stubble, pressed onto hers. "Goodnight, Stormwolf. Sleep well, and here's hoping we have better luck in the morning."

"Goodnight, beloved." She quickly returned his kiss before wriggling out of his embrace and returning to her tent. She rolled herself up in her pile of cloak and blankets, then shifted around once or twice, finding a comfortable place for her hips and shoulders. The scent of crushed grass and canvas filled her lungs, then the sleepy haze in her mind took over.

***

Farren stirred, sunlight filtering through the green canvas of the tent. Drowsily, he buried his head in the folds of his cloak. A stiff muscle in his neck nagged at him. He drew a deep breath, inhaling the sweetish scent of cut broom. A twig snapped outside his tent. "Beloved?" Azariel's voice asked.

He rolled onto his back and opened his eyes. Bars of sunlight fell through the network of little twigs and branches covering the tent. "One moment." He pushed back the blankets, then crawled outside into the sunshine. Azariel was waiting for him, a single ray catching the crown of her hair and making it gleam with a bluish sheen. He reached towards her and felt for her hand. "Good morning, Stormwolf," he said. "You've woken before me again." The warm wind blew the scent of smoke towards him, along with the tang of garlic and meat. "You've been busy cooking."

She shook her head. "Not me; that was Stessa's doing. She woke me up about half an hour ago."

He yawned and scratched at the stubble on his chin. "I'm so tired, in spite of that sleep the gazelle put on us. At least we know that it can do that now and be on our guard against it next time."

"Do you think our armbands could block that sort of fire?" She cocked her head to one side and one of her eyebrows arched up. "I suppose we can. It's less deadly than sorcerer's killing fire and we can block that."

He loosened the lacings at the back of his chainmail and let the high neck collapse forwards onto his chest. *My shirt feels all clammy. I'm going to have to wash it and myself soon.* "We'll try what we did last night again, I think. We both got close to it until it struck. Harrying and driving it works. Nothing else I can think of will."

"Those books we had to read back at the capital – and there were enough of them – had stories of hunts and so forth. But I don't think they'd be helpful for a gazelle." She ran her fingers through her hair, untangling it. A small white feather drifted free and she grimaced.

"Unicorn hunting, wasn't it?" He laughed, remembering the dusty library back at the monastery. "Well, if being virgin is all that was required to catch this gazelle, then we'd both have caught it ten times over by now. So those stories aren't any good."

She stooped to pick up one of the sticks that had fallen away from the side of his tent. "Whoever wrote that tale never met a real unicorn. Anyway, I'd expect the reverse from a sorceress's gazelle. Perhaps that's the problem."

He snorted. "Taking Stessa with us would work then, if that was the case. But I doubt it."

"Do you want to ask her to come along? With an extra rider, we could drive it wherever we want it to go."

Stessa sauntered around the camouflaged tent. "Did I hear my name?"

"We were wondering if you would like to come with us next time we chase the gazelle," Azariel said.

Stessa shook her head. "Not yet. Not unless I get completely frustrated with this cipher I'm working on. It's a real beast. Good to see you back and awake, Farren. I heard what happened from Azariel this morning. Hard luck. And that's another reason why I won't come along unless I have to. You've got ways of protecting yourselves against that sort of thing; I haven't. And that scorpion in the labyrinth sounded even worse. I don't blame you for not wanting to go in there again." She adjusted the lattice-work of brush. "How do you like my handiwork? Breakfast is ready, if you want some."

"Thanks, Stessa," he said. "We'll come soon. Don't wait for us, though." He looked down at his hands and armband. Sunlight caught the turquoises set in the silver, dazzling him. He rubbed at a tarnished smear on the silver with his thumb, then stared at the river. "I wonder how far that gazelle can leap."

Azariel glanced towards the labyrinth. "It couldn't leap any higher than a horse when it was on the cliff, although it's more agile. Why?"

"If we drove the gazelle towards the river, then perhaps it won't be able to leap or wade the central arm of the river."

Her eyes flashed as she smiled, baring her teeth. "Let's can try it. I hope you're right that it can't leap the river. I don't want to cross the border to hunt it down, given what Stessa said about the bounty on *minyasti*."

He picked at the dirt under his fingernails. "You could cross it in wolf-form," he said after a few moments. "If you did, then we could find out whether it has gone over before."

"What do you mean?"

He reached out and touched her forearm. "I mean that you could cross the river, shift shape then cast up and down the river bank on that side to see if its scent is over there."

"That river's at least chest depth in places, even at this time of the year. And it's fast. Do you think we can cross it?"

"I don't know. Perhaps we should go and have a look." He quickly kissed her cheek, then pulled back, a few strands of her hair following him as the short stubble on his chin caught them. "I'll get myself tidied up for the day over there, too."

"So will I," she said. "I still haven't got that pigeon blood off me."

They ate breakfast sitting around the small campfire on the thick squares of turf that Stessa had used to hide the fire overnight. The fire had reduced to a heap of orange-red embers. The heat beat on Farren's face from a space away, and the air shimmered above them. Farren stretched his legs and yawned again. The warm northwest wind swayed the branches overhead, and the sky to the west was filled with clouds that looked like water-smoothed stones. *Father won't like this long spell of dry weather. Much more of this and the streams will start drying up.* He glanced down at the creek near the campsite. An inch-thick band of dry pale yellow scum ran along the grass at the edge of the water. *That wasn't there when we first came here. King of Heaven, the Kingdom will need some rain soon.*

"I said, are you ready to go?" Azariel's voice cut across his thoughts.

"Sorry," he said. "I was just noticing how the creek had fallen since we've been here. I hope we won't have a drought."

"Then we'd better go and make use of the river while we can," she said, getting to her feet.

Stessa shuffled forwards and picked up the turf square Azariel had been sitting on. She laid some fresh wood on the fire, waited until it caught, then carefully covered it with turf. The embers glowed dull red in the shadow. A few sticks of charcoal had fallen out of the fire and she swept them up in one hand. "These will do to scratch notes with today," she said, winking. "Off you go, and I'll see you later."

Farren rose to his feet and walked over to the horse chestnut trees and found the branches where he had hung the tack. "Here you go, Stormwolf," he said, passing the bridles to her. "Time for you to pay your debt. But I don't think you need to bother about the saddles. We're not going far."

He leaned back against the tallest horse chestnut and watched her catch the horses one by one and fit the bridles over their heads. Eventually, she led Princess and Storm out of the shadow of the trees into the sunlight. "You'll need to help me onto his back, beloved," she said as she tossed Princess's reins to him.

He let the reins swing free from Princess's head as he pressed in close to Storm's neck in front of Azariel. Cupping his hands, he waited for her to slide her knee onto them, then boosted her upwards. Her hair swirled round his face as she swung herself onto the gelding's back. He smiled up at her then vaulted smoothly onto Princess.

The mare trotted towards the river, ears pricked. She tugged at the bit and tried to break into a canter. "Steady, my lady," he said, patting her neck. "We're only going to the river." He tugged lightly on the reins and turned her towards the long line of willows edging the Illin-y-Hyalda river. They passed under the swaying shadows, and he steered her rightwards, heading upstream.

"Well, we know that the gazelle comes to drink here," Azariel said as they reached the fallen willow with the shoots growing from it where they had first seen the gazelle. "I don't suppose you want me to check to see how often it comes here."

"You may as well." He guided Princess towards Storm and swung her in beside the gelding, so close his knee brushed against Azariel's. "Give me his reins."

She tossed the loop of leather to him and it slapped into his hand as he caught it. Storm twitched and shook his mane. She slipped off Storm's back and tumbled to all fours, shifting shape as she fell. Her nose quivered over the stones and beaten dirt leading down past the tree trunk to the water's edge. She took a few steps towards the river, then wove in tight zigzags. After making three passes over the trail, she sat back on her haunches and changed shape again. "It's been here once since that time we tried to shoot it here," she said, brushing a strand of hair back from her face.

"Has it gone further over?"

She shrugged. "How could I know? You know as well as I do that a dog or wolf can't follow a scent trail through water."

Storm pulled at the reins in his hand and tried to stretch down to a clump of thick grass by the river. Farren leaned to one side, letting the gelding graze. "Sorry. I wasn't thinking. Shall we try further up the river for a new trail?"

"We may as well." She stood up and took Storm back from him. After heading the black gelding towards the fallen willow, she climbed onto the tree trunk then mounted. "Shall we race to the next one?"

He shook his head. "Once the horses start racing, it'll be hard to see the trails and stop in time." He winked at her. "And I would rather ride beside you than behind you. I know that Storm's faster than Princess."

The horses plodded around the fallen willow then upstream, weaving in and out of the other trees. The long trailing strands of the weeping willows brushed over Farren's face and bare forearms, leaves caressing him. The wind strengthened, making the treetops hiss and blend with the rush of the river. Ahead, he spotted a streak of yellow dirt in the green. "Isn't that one?" he shouted above the roar of wind and water, pointing.

Azariel tapped Storm's sides and trotted him towards the trail, her hair shaking and rippling as she rose and fell with his gait. Princess pulled at the reins and sprang after them. He reined her in as Azariel slid off Storm's back. She tossed the reins to him again and slipped into wolf-shape to work over the narrow trail. Storm slanted his ears back and back-stepped as the shewolf snuffled round his hooves, a rim of white encircling his eyes. "It's all right, Storm." He sent a wave of calm towards him with his Gift. "Don't you know what she looks like in wolf-shape yet?"

A thin band of light passed across the wolf's body as she changed shape again. "The gazelle has used this trail," she said, shaking her hair back as the wind blew it around her face. "But not very often. Shall we try another?"

"We may as well," he said, leaning forward and handing the reins to her. "I'd like to know how far north this gazelle's range is. Can you get up onto him without help?"

She placed her hands on the gelding's withers. "I don't think so," she said, looking at him over Storm's back.

Smiling, he dismounted and ducked under Storm's neck to stand beside her. "I'll help you with pleasure," he said, curling one arm around her waist and leaning over to brush her forehead with his lips. Her hair tickled his face as he stooped to cup her knee in his hands and propel her up.

He remounted Princess and continued riding upstream. A dragonfly flew like a glittering winged spear past him to a small pool beside the river. He glanced at it, dropping behind Storm as the horses worked through a very dense stand of willows between a bluff and the bank where the Illin-y-Hyalda ran deep and green, tugging at the long strands of weeping willow. A dead branch bent as he pushed past it, then snapped.

On the far side of the narrow spinney, a dry creek bed trailed down a steep-sided valley to the Illin-y-Hyalda. The smooth stones still bore a coating of water-weed, now shrivelled and light brown. "Stop," said Azariel. "I can see hooves in the dust."

She dismounted and checked over the trail in wolf form. "The gazelle's been here quite often and very recently," she said after shifting back again. "I think that – look!" She pointed up the length of the valley. He shaded his eyes to scan the place she had indicated and saw a flash of white disappearing over the top of the ridge towards the labyrinth.

"We'll come here next time," he said as she climbed back onto Storm's back using a large boulder as a mounting block. "This valley's perfect for a pincer movement driving it towards the river. He ran his gaze up and down the steep slopes and nodded. "The slope will give us an extra bit of speed coming down, too."

They rode upstream, checking game trails until, many twists and bends of the river later, Azariel could no longer scent the gazelle's unique aroma. "Well, we've learnt something," she said, standing beside Storm and idly stroking his withers as he drank. "This is as far north as we need to come. I'm glad. If the gazelle roamed any further north, it would be worth making a second campsite."

"We've been riding for less than half the morning," he said.

"But if we wanted to get up early to watch it go for water, then we'd have to get up well before the sun with our camp where it is now." Storm raised his head from the water and she led him to a boulder where she scrambled onto his back. "We'd only manage to do that if one of us kept watch." She pulled the gelding's head up from the grass. "Come on. I've still got blood on my arms and I want to wash it off. Where shall we go swimming?"

"There was a deep pool just downstream from that very narrow valley," he said, turning Princess around. "That'll be good for a swim, anyway."

Azariel rode behind Farren, the wind blowing her hair around the sides of her face like curtains. She flicked it over her left shoulder with one hand. One small strand caught in her mouth. "Do you want me to cast for a scent on the other side of the river?" she called.

"What?" He looked over his shoulder at her. "I can't hear you above the noise of the river."

"Do you want me to sniff it out across the river?"

"If you can cross it," he shouted back before turning and riding on.

She slid off Storm beside the lozenge-shaped pool of green. Her shirt clung to her back with sweat, and her armour had grown hot in the strong sunlight. The water lapped at the gravelly bank with a delicious gurgle. Smiling with anticipation, she unbuckled Storm's bridle and tossed it over a rock. The gelding snorted, then bent his head to the grass beside the river and began cropping it rhythmically. She undid the big buckle of her belt then hesitated. *It's going to take me ages to dry out if I swim fully clothed. Perhaps I should go upstream by myself.* She ran her gaze to and fro over the willows and boulders. *Do I have enough cover?* Shaking her head, she let her belt, sword and dagger clatter down. *My clothes need a wash as badly as I do, if not more. At least the other set's dry, so I'll swim in my clothes and change back at camp.*

"Are you coming?" Farren stood looking at her, barefoot and with his arms folded across his bare chest. The midday sun winked off his rings and armbands, and picked out shadows that highlighted the lean hard muscle on his torso. Her heart kicked and she ran her tongue around the inside of her mouth as half-formed ideas played on the edges of her imagination. *Later. Later. I've only got until next spring to wait. I am certainly going to change this stupid rule about long betrothal times as soon as I can do it without the rest of the* minyasti *laughing. It just isn't fair.* Swallowing, she unlaced her armour and dropped it beside her belt before following it with her boots.

He laughed, and his shadow fell between her and the sun. She darted to one side, but his hand closed over her arm. "Ready to take a dip?"

"Rascal," she gasped. His grip tightened and pulled her closer to himself. She struggled, recognizing the mischievous flash in his eyes. His arms wrapped around her and lifted her. "I'm going to get you for this," she laughed. The muscles of his chest heaved beneath her then she felt herself falling. Hastily, she drew a breath before hitting the water with a stinging smack.

She opened her eyes under the surface as she began swimming. Shafts of light penetrated to the bottom, picking out the smooth stones and mud. She brought her feet under her and stood up, still tingling all over from the shock of the cool water. Her hair clung to her face and she shook it back. "I really am going to get you," she said, arms working to keep herself steady in the chest-deep water.

"You'll have to catch me first." His eyes darted back and forth before he jumped in, sending a sheet of water over her.

She waited until he had surfaced, then splashed wave after wave at him. The water flashed in the sunlight and broke in bubbles under her hands. He sent a wave back at her with his powerful arms, and she closed her eyes as. Again and again, she dashed the water at him until she grew breathless with laughter, then relaxed. The river buoyed her up and floated her downstream, rocking gently.

The river carried her to the end of the lozenge-shaped pool where it narrowed and picked up speed. She righted herself and braced her body against the current before diving forwards and digging her arms into the water. Fighting the current, she swam upstream to the other end of the pool where another set of rapids fed into the pool. Panting and muscles aching from exertion, she let the eddies carry her back again.

She repeated the pattern of swimming upstream and floating back down several times before wading to the river's edge. Farren had climbed out of the water and was kneeling on the bank with his shaving kit open beside him and his face covered with lather. A few blobs of soap and bristle fell from the razor in his hand and were swirled away. She watched, fascinated, as he worked fingers and blade over the sharp angles of his chin and cheeks, around the curve of his lips and down the soft skin of his throat. Finally, he rinsed the razor in the stream and splashed several handfuls of water over his face. "You look gorgeous," she said.

"Thank you," he replied. "What about you? You're beautiful, of course, but have you finished getting all that blood off you?"

She looked down at her arms. The water rippled around them as she rested them on the surface. The diamonds in her armband glittered silver fire and her skin carried some traces of dried blood and soot, as well as a few small scratches and bruises. Shaking her head, she raked her fingers through her hair. "Not quite," she said. "Lend me your soap."

"Don't drop my last bit in the river." He tossed it to her. "Otherwise, you'll have to put up with me going unshaven."

"You mean you'll have to put up with yourself." She rubbed the lavender-scented soap over her arms and scrubbed the last traces off her arms, trousers and tunic. "Now I'm ready." She passed the cake of soap back to him. "Are you going to swim some more with me?"

"You're just itching to throw me in the water in revenge, aren't you?" He folded up his shaving kit and stowed it in his belt-pouch. "I think I will. We've got to see if the gazelle can cross the river. And there's one good thing about swimming across the river: we aren't in uniform."

She turned her head and looked westwards at the line of willows along the opposite bank. "Still, we'd better stay alert for the Wayasti border guards like we do." She twisted a lock of her hair in her fingers, squeezing a trail of droplets out of it. "If we're caught, you hide and I'll play up my Zenifi blood as much as I can."

He slid into the water beside her and took her hand as they climbed out on the far side of the pool. Rough gravel lay between the arms of the river, and she staggered across it, wincing as a pointed stone jabbed her foot. *I should have brought my boots,* she thought, stepping from one flat stone to another. A sigh of relief escaped her lips as they reached a thin strip of grass. After ten more painful paces over the gravel, she and Farren stopped at the brink of the main arm of the river. The water sounded deeper, and the heavy stones ground and rolled audibly below the note of the river. Here and there, slick wet rocks punctuated the cloudy water. The river streamed over and around the boulders in spearhead-shaped ripples, churning itself to foam. She stooped for a stick of willow and hurled it into the current. For a few heartbeats, the stick bobbed and danced on the surface before spinning downstream and out of sight. "I'm not going to try to swim across that in any shape," she said quietly. "How far across do you think it is?"

He released her hand and shaded his eyes. "Just under half a bowshot – forty paces or so."

"Do you think the gazelle could jump over that?"

He dabbed at a small spot of blood on his chin. "I don't think so. I've never heard of any animal that could jump that far without wings." His mouth twisted into a wry grin. "But then, I can't say for certain what this gazelle can and can't do. Let's go back and lie somewhere in the sun to dry off. We can't cross that safely."

They found the horses grazing beneath a willow, then Azariel bridled them both. Farren pulled his tunic over his head and watched her as he wrestled his wet arms into the sleeves. Her damp hair hung down, trailing beads of bright water. His gaze ran down the length of her back and legs, lingering where the damp black cotton clung to her curves. His blood heated and quickened, and he glanced away. *She's so beautiful. I hardly ever see her without her armour and it's a delight to see her in just her tunic and trousers.* He stooped for his belt and armour, then buckled the belt over his tunic. It hung low without his armour, so he cinched the belt tighter. *It's lovely to see how that wet cotton shows off that narrow waist of hers and her... Blackarrow, you stop those thoughts right there and don't make life and other things hard for yourself. She is definitely worth the wait.*

She handed him Princess's reins. "Can you help me up onto his back?" she asked.

"Of course, Stormwolf. Give me your armour; you won't be able to mount holding that." He took the metal shirt from her and cupped his hands. Her hair dripped a stain of water on his tunic shoulder as he heaved her onto Storm's back.

"Thanks," she said, reaching down for her armour. "Shall we go back to camp?"

He slung his armour over Princess's withers, then vaulted onto her back behind it. "Not yet," he said. "Let's go somewhere and lie in the sun to dry off. We can get Lady first, if you like."

"Knowing her, she'll come if you whistle. Where shall we go?"

He looked at the huge yellow-ochre bulk of the hills. "That spur where we shot the goat," he said. "The ground there will have had the sun all day, and there are some large enough tea-trees for shade if I need it."

He led the way back downstream, past the cluster of horse chestnuts and to the top of the spur. Lady lolloped up to them as they passed the camp, and trotted behind them. The wind stirred the tea-trees, making the white blossoms dance and fill the air with the sweet-sharp scent. He swung off Princess's back then slipped on the tussock as he landed. After steadying himself, he removed the mare's bridle. "Off you go, my lady," he said, patting the silky hair on her neck. "Enjoy an easy day." He laid his armour and the bridle down in the grass. The mare bunted him in the shoulder, her breath hot on his neck. He scratched around the base of her ears then watched as she wandered off among the tussocks down the northwestern side of the spur. Storm walked beside her to a clear space on the top before dropping to the ground and rolling. His long legs pawed at the air as he puffed and wriggled, staining his black coat with greyish dust.

"That looks like a good idea," he said as Storm brought himself upright once more and scrambled to his feet. Farren reached for the hem of his tunic and stripped it off. "How are the wounds on my back, Stormwolf? I should have asked before." He laid the shirt flat on the ground, then lay down on his front on top of it in the sunshine.

Her cool fingers slid over his shoulder-blades, then pain pulsed in one place. "It's healing well." Her hands brushed down his back then lifted off. "And the one in your side is the same." The black silk curtain of her hair fell around his face as she leaned over and pressed a kiss onto the top of his scalp. She drew back, taking the shelter of her shadow away from him. He closed his eyes and relaxed in the hot sunshine. *It's so long since I've lain in the grass like this.* He caught the faint scent of wild thyme and garlic blown on the wind, mingled with the tea-tree and the other smells of earth and grass. Broom pods cracked in the heat. He inhaled deeply and sighed with pleasure.

The grass rustled nearby, and he opened one eye to see her seated beside him, her arms coiled around her bent knees and the wind lightly stirring a few dry strands of her hair. Her stormcloud-blue eyes met his with a sparkle and she smiled. "You look comfortable there, handsome," she said. "You rest there, but I don't think I will. My clothes are still too wet and I'd get them dirty again in that dust."

He raised himself up on his elbows and gazed at the sky. High above him, two dark shapes circled and glided on rivers of air. "I wish I could see through their eyes at the moment," he said. "Those falcons would be able to see the gazelle from up there. Which is why wealthy people train the large ones to hunt small gazelle, I suppose." He watched the pair of falcons circle up then veer off to one side as the northwest wind caught them. Behind them, the mountains stood out against a narrow band of slate-coloured cloud to the north of them. *I wonder if the clouds will reach this side of the ranges and give us some rain.* An insect tickled its way across his bare back, and he twitched and shrugged it off. He closed his eyes and let his head drop back down to rest on his forearms.

Azariel smiled as she looked down at his prone body. The scars marked his pale skin, dark angry red with black stitching against ivory. She waved a buzzing fly away from the healing wounds. She reclasped her arms around her knees and looked down the slope to the carpet of grass and golden-grey tussock slashed by the braided bed of the Illin-y-Hyalda. The pines beneath them roared in the strong wind and the willows on the river bank danced. A gust blew her hair around and she brushed it back as she watched a small flock of birds fly screeching from the willows.

Another bird, the blackbird, took to the air from the horse chestnuts. She stared at the trees for a heartbeat and saw a rider beneath them. *Who's that? That's not Stessa!* The Nightraven's words came back to her. *Claws? Somebody released a pigeon yesterday.* Her eyes darted to the open ground between the pines and the horse chestnuts. *They're passing our campsite. Stessa's good. How did she manage to hide Veranath?* Four other riders joined the first, all wearing red cloaks. The wind billowed the cloak of one of them out like a flag, exposing the rider's yellow tabard. She flung herself down flat in the grass.

"What's up?" Farren rolled onto his side and looked over at her. "You threw yourself down quickly. I thought you didn't want to lie down."

"Go to the north side of the hill and get your armour on," she whispered furiously. "And keep down below the skyline. Claws!"

Farren rustled away through the tussock, Lady behind him. "Some of these mountain plants are sharp," he whispered.

She inched backwards, making her way to the northernmost face of the spur. Coarse grass and small scrubby plants rasped at her arms. The five Claw horsemen halted at the foot of the hill under the pines, and more joined them. *How many are there? They don't know we're here – or Stessa, by the look of things – but if they spot Veranath, I'd rather not let him be stolen. Farren likes that horse.*

She reached Farren and began pulling on her armour over the top of her damp shirt. "How many are there and where are they?" he asked.

"I don't know how many exactly. They're under the pines, so shut up and keep Lady back." She buckled her belt around her waist, then laced up the neck of her chainmail.

A tree branch cracked, followed by a thump. She started and her hand flew to her sword hilt as her heart leaped. *Don't be a fool,* she told herself. *With this strong wind, it's nothing unusual for branches to break loose.* Voices drifted up from the foot of the hill, muffled by the wind and the roaring of the pines. "That's them," she whispered. "I hope it's not Veranath they're talking about."

She slithered to the top of the spur on her belly, armour and sword clicking over the small twigs and stones. Crouching beneath the rosebushes, she listened to the voices as they rose and fell. Her breath raced, filling her lungs with the sweet fragrance of the flowers, and she fought to slow her breaths. A shout came from the pines below, followed by the clash of metal.

She glanced downhill. In the shadow of the pines stood a single black figure surrounded by mounted Claws. Sunlight flashed from a drawn blade in the lone fighter's hand. "It's Stessa," Azariel said over her shoulder to Farren. "She's been caught and she's going to die very soon unless she's lucky. Oh!" She gasped as Stessa's lithe black shape swung up into the branches of the nearest pine.

"What? They haven't…"

"She's bought herself some time by going up the trees. We'd better do something for her."

He twisted his rings straight. "And no way of getting the horses properly saddled. How many Claws?"

"About ten and all mounted. She – she's a superb fighter!" She paused as one of the Claw horses reared and plunged wildly, throwing its rider before collapsing. The other Claws encircled the tree as Stessa vanished up into the thick green branches. "But not invincible. She's under siege."

"We'd better go and rescue her. I never thought we'd have to do this for her." He rose to his feet and whistled for the horses.

Storm and Princess thundered up the northern slope of the hill. Farren caught Princess by the mane and vaulted onto her back. "There's no time to bridle him," he said over his shoulder as he put heels to the mare and drew his sword. "You'll have to guide him as best you can. Follow me!"

Her fingers knotted through Storm's dusty mane and she scrambled onto his back, using the slope to help her up. The gelding leaped away after Princess, jerking her backwards. She regained her balance and slid her sword from the sheath. *King of Heaven, help us help her.* She clenched her teeth as her rings began to heat around her fingers.

She leaned back and raised her sword ready as Storm rushed down the hill. Throwing back her head, she vented her usual wolf-howl battle cry. The Claws' faces turned towards her, and the circle around Stessa's tree broke up. One by one, the Claw horses swung around and cantered to meet her and Farren. She locked eyes with the foremost as Storm reared ready to fight, making her slip slightly.

Storm's teeth scored a gash down the Claw horse's neck, then she ducked as in the corner of her eye, she glimpsed a sword whistling towards her. The blade slashed over her head, whining in the air and she struck up with her own blade. To her left, Princess squealed with fury, followed by a clash of metal. Her sword was knocked back by the Claw but she scythed it up in a backslash. Storm pitched forwards, then sidestepped. The palomino Claw horse reared again, sunlight gleaming dully off the odd-shaped horseshoes on the flailing hooves near her shoulder. *It's sharp-shod, like all Claw horses.* One hoof smashed white-hot agony into her knee. She slipped on Storm's back as she thrust her sword through the palomino's throat. The falling, thrashing horse almost wrenched the weapon from her hand, but she clung to the hilt and tightened her grip around Storm's slippery sides as two Claws charged her.

Another horse screamed and fell to its knees, drowning the cry of its rider with a crash. Bright blood spattered across the tawny carpet of pine needles, the two smells sharp and jarring as they mingled.

Farren hacked aside the sword that whistled at him, striking a notch in the Claw's blade. With light touches on the side of her neck, withers and flank, he turned Princess in a quarter-circle and brought his weapon up in a backslash across the gullet of the Claw horse. The blue roan gelding rolled its eyes and shied, screaming as the blade ripped through its hide. *Deep enough to kill, but not instantly,* he thought as he raised his stained sword to parry the Claw's chop at him. *I'd finish it off if I could.* "Back," he said to his mare, tugging lightly on her mane.

Princess danced backwards, the Claw horse following her. With his hands and heels, Farren wheeled her around so his sword arm could swing freely at the Claw. *Now we're not nearly cutting our horses' heads off and I've got you on the unarmed side.* Princess surged forwards, snorting as he put heels to her. He struck down, felling the Claw then putting the blue roan out of its pain with the return stroke. To the right, another set of hooves drummed, and he glimpsed a brilliant flash of scarlet light. Then another Claw, a woman, attacked him and he dodged leftwards as her sword struck at him. It glanced off his mail-clad shoulder with a bruising clang as he spun Princess around, teeth clenched. He eyed his new opponent. *Now she's got me on my weaker sword arm. Power, protect me!* His rings heated and he punched fire at the newcomer

Several large pinecones hurtled down from Stessa's tree. One caught the hindmost Claw in the temple. The man fell from his horse, stunned. The riderless chestnut horse shied backwards away from the fighting. Stessa slithered down the pine tree and onto the chestnut's back.

Azariel noticed Stessa charging from the corner of her eye as she raised her sword to beat back a Claw's blade. Another sword sliced at her from the right. She ducked as it swung at her, trying at the same time to angle Storm around without bridle or saddle, and raise her fist to punch fire at her new attacker. The bolt of flame flew past the Claw's shoulder. The man's eyes widened and the blood drained from his face. *I wish I had a bridle to guide Storm with!* The black gelding wheeled around of his own accord, turning his back on the first Claw. "Not like that, Storm!" she shouted, yanking on his mane and throwing a second burst of scarlet over her shoulder. She glimpsed red fire burning a yellow tabard and heard a yell as she pressed the gelding's flank with her left heel, still trying to steer him. Storm kicked out at the Claw, throwing her forwards. Her next firebolt sizzled through the air and struck the trunk of a horse chestnut. *It's hard to predict what he's going to do as well as what the Claws are doing.* She tightened her grip on Storm's sides and leaned forwards to meet the blow of the Claw in front of her.

The blades clashed down, jarring her arm, then she slashed up, back, across and down, seeking for a weakness in her enemy's defence. Below her aching knee, her trouser leg felt wet with blood, and Storm's back was growing slippery with sweat. Storm reared and sidestepped, squealing as he lashed out at the Claw horse and rider. The Claw reeled back in the saddle as Storm bore down on him and she drove her sword at the man's yellow tabard. The tip raked his armour. She whipped the blade up in a backslash, catching him on the arm. Another brutal hack and his weapon rammed into her chest, knocking the breath from her as her chainmail dug into her. She stabbed his chest in return. A few links fell from the Claw's armour, and her blade thrust home. The Claw slumped sideways and toppled off his horse. The riderless horse bolted as Storm trampled the fallen Claw.

She put heels to Storm and looked around for the Claws. Farren was fighting vigorously against one, Princess wheeling and leaping back and forwards beneath him. *He's got fantastic control of her, bridled or not.* Storm cantered to the mare's right side and lunged at the bay horse that was bearing down on Farren. Azariel whirled her sword around, hearing it hiss in the air before she struck the Claw in the base of the skull above the neck of the armour as he passed her. She turned her head away as hot blood fountained over her hands, stomach clenching. *I will never get used to this type of kill.*

Stessa rode the chestnut horse under the pines, battling the last Claw. The Nightraven's sword flew from her hand and a streak of red sprayed across her bobbed blonde hair as she stooped beneath the Claw's sword. She straightened with a jerk. The man yelled, dropping his sword as the Nightraven pulled something from her sleeve. Azariel saw the flash of sunlight on metal whirling through the air and the Claw howled, clutching at his face. Stessa spurred her horse toward him, then drew a third dagger and stabbed to kill. "Well done, Stessa!" she shouted

The Nightraven dismounted and stooped over the fallen man. She retrieved her daggers from his face and neck. "Well, that's saved me several days' work," she said as she and tucked the knives into her sleeves. "Thank you for coming when you did."

"Are you all right?" Azariel panted as she slid off Storm's back and landed with a thud.

She fingered the streak of red in her hair and grimaced. "I think so. I probably have a few bruises, and I've taken some skin off my elbow. "How about you?"

Farren dismounted and wiped his sword blade clean on the pine needles. "How did they manage to catch you anyway? I saw them go straight past our camp." He sheathed his sword and began to rub Princess down, his hands caressing and kneading the mare's chestnut coat. The fire died in his hands and arms, leaving them shaking. The rhythm of stroking Princess steadied him, and he grew acutely aware of the gore spattering his arms and face. She fixed his attention on his horse, checking for cuts. "Not hurt; that's good, my lady."

"I was up one of those pine trees and a branch broke on me, curse it." She looked back at the pines. "Didn't you hear it from where you were up on that spur? At least it wasn't the only tree that I could climb."

"What were you doing up there?" Azariel sat down in the grass and examined the gash in her knee. A red stain streamed down from a rip in her trousers above the knee, making Farren's heart kick in his chest.

"It was a nice place to sit for working at that cipher. Whoever made that one up was good at his or her job." She rested her hands on her ample hips and stared at the trampled grass around the campsite, and the corpses of horses and people. "We had better get all this mess cleaned up. I still haven't found out what they were about, either."

He unbuckled Princess's bridle and patted the mare on her shoulder again, fighting the urge to let his shoulders slump. *This is the worst part of any battle. The price we have to pay for the kill.* He drew a deep breath and steeled himself. "We don't have a spade. Do you?"

Stessa shook her head. "We'll have to drag the bodies somewhere away from the river to keep the water clean – and so you don't scare away that gazelle you're hunting. I suppose we could put them in the labyrinth."

"No," he said, hearing Azariel echo him. "It would be all too easy to get blood onto the stone and wake that scorpion spirit."

"What about the wild roses?" Azariel stood up and flexed her wounded leg, grimacing. "I know it's uphill, but we can use the horses to drag them."

"We're never going to get the bodies of the horses up there." He shook his head and glanced at the body of the blue roan. "We'll take the people to the roses, but all we can do with the horses is drag them further from the camp – and the gazelle."

"Get any armour and weapons off them first, and strip the tack off the horses." Stessa drummed her fingertips on the hilt of the dagger at her side. "And check their pockets and purses in case they were carrying messages. There are no Claw enclaves within at least two days' ride up the river, so this lot must have been on the move."

"We'll need ropes." Azariel began walking towards the tents, then stopped. "Where's Lady?"

Farren scanned the grass and scrub for the shaggy dog, then reached for her with the touch of his Gift. "Lady!" he called. A squeaking whimper answered him from his tent. He strode to the opening and pulled the flap aside, dislodging a few of the camouflaging brush. Lady's golden eyes stared at him, rimmed with white, from the middle of his bedroll. Her long legs and tail were coiled beneath her, and she was shaking. "You poor thing," he said, kneeling down and stroking her. "Did the fight scare you? It's all right, girl." He poured a wave of calm towards the dog along his bond with her. Her ears pricked, and she sniffed at his hand and arms before licking him. "You're a hunting dog, not a war dog, that's for certain. You can stay here while we clean everything up."

Azariel's shadow fell across him. "Give her some horsemeat. After all, there's plenty of it."

For the next hour, they stripped weapons and armour from the bodies, then hauled them up the hill to the clump of wild roses. Sweat clung to Farren's back and beaded on his arms, mingling with the dried blood. *And to think we went swimming to clean up!* When the last body had been placed in the tangled wild roses, he trudged downhill, mouth dry and nostrils filled with the acrid scent of blood. The sword belt, slightly rusted chainmail and dagger he had taken from the last Claw jingled with every step he took.

At the foot of the hill, Stessa stood beside a pile of gear, several strips of parchment in her hands. She smiled and nodded as Azariel passed her a scrap of ink-stained white cloth. "That's three more messages. Hopefully, they all use the same cipher. If I don't crack it in a few days, I'm going to go back to the capital and get some more of us working on it. With this many messages, we should be able to break it." Her large eyes flicked from him to Azariel then back again. "If Trapper and Blade can't do it, I'll turn it over to the monks."

"The monks?" He dropped the salvaged armour and weapons into the pile. "I didn't think they'd let you through the door of a house full of men dedicated to celibacy."

She sniffed and folded her arms across her chest. "I do have the decency to know when a man's off-limits, Farren."

"Really? I didn't think you did, after what you did to me."

"That'll do," Azariel stepped between them, stumbling on her wounded leg. "I don't want to drag the past back in front of us now. We all know how that ended. Unless..." She stopped and stared at the ground before continuing in a voice of cold iron. "Unless someone's changed their mind."

Farren gazed at Azariel, heart pounding as hard as it had during the fight. *Sweetheart? Do you still fear that I might prefer Stessa to you? Never, never, never!* He strode to her and threw an arm around her shoulders. "I haven't," he said.

"I have," said Stessa. "I know when I'm beaten and when a chase is hopeless. Good for you, Azariel. Incidentally, you'd better learn when to give up on a chase, too."

"What are you talking about?" His grip tightened around Azariel's shoulders.

Stessa waved a hand at the hills. "The gazelle, of course. The Claws tried to get that for about a year and failed. They've given up. If you're wise, you'd give up too." She stooped to pick up one of the Claws' weapons.

"We can't," Azariel said. "We've been told to hunt it by the King of Heaven. And I'm not going to turn back from carrying out my orders."

Stessa shrugged. "Up to you, of course. I'm no *minyaster* to know these things. But I'm hungry after all that, even if you aren't. Who wants some lunch? There's the end of the stew from breakfast, if that dog of yours hasn't been at it, and some bread in my saddlebags that needs eating up before it goes stale."

"Thanks, Stessa." Azariel slid free from Farren's embrace. "We'd better go and pick up our bridles from the top of the hill."

"See you soon, then." Stessa turned towards the campsite.

Farren curled both arms around Azariel again as the other woman walked away. As he felt her arms around his waist, he gently raised his hands to her face and brushed the hair back. "About what you said earlier: never ask if I've changed my mind about you and Stessa again, sweetheart," he said. "I love you and only you, and I always will. Never forget that." He bent to kiss her, first on the forehead, then the bridge of her nose and lastly on her mouth, tasting the salt of her sweat each time. "How's your leg after all that hauling? Are you able to walk back up to get the bridles or would you like to rest?"

"It's just a slash and a bad bruise. One of those sharp-shod Claw horses got me. At least Storm's all right." She glanced over her shoulder. "Where have all those horses gone, anyway?"

"Run off, tack, saddlebags and all. There'll be a few lucky farmers in the next few days."

She arched her neck and stretched her arms above her head. "Good. And we'd better get our bridles or the next lot of hunters will be lucky, too." She leaned forward and pressed her soft lips into his chin. "Come on."

CHAPTER FOURTEEN

Farren lay on his back, staring up at the clouds, satisfied and clean. To one side of him, the two women talked as they finished their late lunch. Now and again, he caught a flicker of black and metal as Azariel's hair or arms entered his field of vision. He flicked a few stray crumbs off his front. The clouds above him pushed across the blue, the ones to the northwest darker than usual and whipped to a shapeless mass by the gale. *It might rain later by the looks of that cloud. About time, too, even if it is northwest rain. I hope the tents are secure. I'll have to take my cloak when we go out after the gazelle this evening.* Lady rested her head against him and wagged her tail.

"What do you think about that, beloved?" Azariel's voice cut across his thoughts.

"What are you talking about? I wasn't listening. Sorry." He rolled over onto his stomach and looked at the two women. The hilt of his sword dug into his hip and he pushed it aside. Stessa was sitting beside Azariel, their knees touching and the piece of bloodstained parchment they had found on the pigeon spread out beside the other coded messages taken from the Claws.

"I was asking if you'd like to help me crack this." Stessa tapped the pile of parchment and cloth. "One more try before I head back to have some of our experts onto it. It will be easier now we've got more messages – assuming they use the same cipher for all of them – but I'd like to break one of them, anyway."

"If you've got experts, why do you need us?" He sat up and shuffled closer to Azariel to nestle in beside her, leaning his head onto her shoulder to look at the ciphers. Her hair brushed his cheek, smelling of woodsmoke and waterweed, as well as a trace of his lavender soap.

"They might not be in the Common Tongue," Azariel said. "For all we know, the cipher could be in the Old Tongue or in Zenifi." She ran a finger along the parchment. The jumble of runes still formed a string of gibberish, smeared here and there with charcoal.

Lady pushed against his knees from the other side of him, and he scratched the deerhound behind the ears. "What do you want us to do, Stessa? I haven't had much to do with ciphers since I was a kid playing at being a Nightraven."

Stessa flashed her summer-blue eyes at him, chuckling. "You wanted to be a Nightraven once? Why?"

"The Hawk used to come to collect horses from my father's stud and I thought he was wonderful."

Stessa's smile faded and she stared into the distance for a moment. "He doesn't go to collect consignments of horses any more. I do, though. The last lot I collected was from the Illin-Ast stud. Have you heard of them? You must have; your mare's got the Illin-Ast brand." The smile reappeared on her face and she ran her fingers through the sleek hair that fell across her forehead. "The stable boy there was an absolute honey, too. He helped me take the horses over to Lebhern-y-Hyalda. I went hunting with him and I'd like to do it again. He's nice."

Farren glanced at Azariel and their eyes met before he erupted in laughter. "The stable boy..." he spluttered. "Wait till I tell Yvain that one." Another spasm of laughter shook him. "Illin-Ast is my father's stud and the man you thought was the stable boy is my brother, Yvain."

"Your brother? I thought he looked a bit like you but I didn't think hard enough. He's better-looking, though." Stessa winked.

He lowered his eyes to the parchment again, reading far too many Bs in the script to make it any language he recognized. *Yvain liked her, too. Well, why not? If she fancies him, at least it gets her interest off me. But I won't say anything yet. I don't want her ripping the clothes off my brother like she tried to do with me.* Uncomfortable memories stirred in his mind and he shook them away. "Anyway, going back to the code or cipher or whatever it is, what can we do?"

Stessa drummed her fingers on the parchment. "I've tried most of the things that you can normally do with the Common Tongue. It's not a take-every-fifth-letter type or any jumbled letter message. You could try doing that with the Old Tongue or with Zenifi. I've tried a few basic substitution ciphers, too, and it's not that, either."

"You take Old Tongue, Farren," Azariel said, raising one hand and ruffling her fingers through his hair. "I'll do Zenifi."

He shook his head. "Well, it's not a jumbled-letter one in the Old Tongue. I can see that much."

"Right, what you can do is look for repeated patterns. If there's a pattern of letters and the pattern fits a common pattern of letters in a real language, then we can try it out." Stessa smoothed the fall of hair across her forehead. "What I really want to know is what language the Claws use and how they encrypt their messages."

"Well, I don't suppose you need to know what that lot we dealt with before were planning." Azariel looked back at the cluster of pines, where drag marks trailed through the carpet of needles and a few bloodstains lingered in the dust.

He snuggled against Azariel's warm body to study the letters as words and phrases in the Old Tongue ran through is mind. *There seems to be some sort of pattern here – all those Bs and Qs. But exactly what, I can't tell. I wish I had my pen and ink with me.*

"You don't have anything we could write with, do you?" asked Azariel, echoing his thoughts.

"No. I've been making do with bits of bark and charcoal." Stessa glanced at him. "What about you, Farren? Can you see anything?"

"A lot of Bs and Qs. And a couple of double Ms."

"Well, that's obvious." Stessa rolled her eyes.

"If the cipher is in Old Tongue, those Ms could be Rs, Ls, Ns or Is. But apart from that, I can't tell. Sorry, Stessa." He straightened up and patted the dog again. "I can't do more without pen and ink."

Azariel picked up the piece of parchment and folded it along the well-worn crease lines. "I don't think there's much I can help you with, either. It's not jumbled Zenifi letters and I don't think its Old Wayasti. Do any of your experts know Old Wayasti?"

"That's what the monks are for." Stessa took the folded parchment from Azariel and stood up. "Well, thank you anyway for trying. I'd probably better take it back and have a go at it with proper writing materials. If I leave now, I'll make it to Lebhern-y-Hyalda before nightfall." She tucked the coded messages into a pocket of her grey hooded shirt. "I'll leave you to try catching this gazelle. I hope I do see you back at the capital one day. If you ask me, this gazelle will never be caught and you'll have to wait until it's dead from old age before you can get the Stone back from it. But if you're that stubborn, I'll know where to look for you if I need you."

"I doubt it'll be that long, Stessa," Azariel said, rising to her feet. "The King of Heaven sent us, so there'll be some way we can catch or kill it. We trust him."

"Good for you. And goodbye." She stepped backwards towards the tents. "Thanks, Farren, for intercepting this message for me and for saving my neck from the Claws. You've done us Nightravens a big favour. I'll return the favour to the *minyasti* one day." She smiled. "Maybe I'll hunt down one of those Stones for you, shall I?"

"If you can, you'll have more than repaid us the favour," Azariel said. "But even knowing where the last of them is would be useful."

"Well, we'll see." Stessa ducked into the camouflaged tent, snapping twigs then rustling around inside.

Farren stood up and wrapped his arm around Azariel's waist. *I'm glad that she is going now,* he thought. *She's been splendid hiding our campsite, but I don't like what she does to my Stormwolf.* He pulled Azariel closer and rubbed his cheek against her soft hair. *Not that it's Stessa's fault, really. It's up to me to show my sweetheart how desirable she is.*

Stessa lurched from the tent, dragging a pair of bulging saddlebags and her horse's tack, as well as some of the Claws' gear tied up in a burlap sack. Swiftly, she took down the ropes, canvas and tent poles, leaving only several piles of brushwood scattered across the grass. "Well, I'm out of here. Have a good hunt." She caught her bay mare under one of the horse chestnuts, saddled her and rode away.

Farren stood holding Azariel's hand as the mare's hoofbeats faded away down the river and the golden curves of the hill country hid the horse and rider. "Just us again, sweetheart." He turned her to face him and slid his hand under the warm canopy of her hair to the back of her head. He kneaded his fingers into the nape of her neck above her armour.

"It's a pity she couldn't stay to help us hunt the gazelle down," she replied. "But we'll make do on our own."

He kissed her on the tip of her nose, stifling the hunger for her that surged inside him. "Of course we can. We'll see what we can do in that steep valley driving it towards the river this evening." A fierce gust of wind tugged at his cloak, and a shadow crossed the sun. The dark clouds that had hung over the distant peaks had crawled closer, cutting off the sunlight, although the air still felt warm against his skin.

"Northwest rain coming," she said. "I hope that won't make the slope too slippery to gallop down." She wrapped her hands over his and squeezed them. "I'll go and saddle the horses and we can spend what's left of the day waiting up there. Can you get my cloak for me? I'll need it."

***

He waited on Princess, looking down into the steep valley. Lady lay in the grass beside him, paws tucked underneath her and pink tongue protruding slightly from her half-open mouth. On the opposite side of the valley, Azariel kept watch, her hair and cloak whirled around her by the wind, mirroring the clouds overhead.

A light pattering began in the dust beside him and a bead of moisture struck him on the cheek. "The rain's come, my lady," he said, rubbing Princess's silky neck. More drops fell, making dark spots on the dry ground. The heady smell of hot wet earth rose from the hillside as the rain drove down. He smiled. *Azariel will be enjoying this rain. It's much more pleasant than drizzle. If only all rain could be like this.* A trickle of water plastered his hair to his forehead and ran down his face. He reached for the hood of his cloak and drew it over his head, feeling his uniform scrape across his back and his skin flaring with heat. *I must have lain in the sun too long.* He grimaced, flexing his shoulder muscles. *Now I'll have trouble holding steady to aim my bow – if I need to aim it.*

He clenched his teeth, focussing on the cool rain rather than the fire on his back and stared up the valley. His fingers chilled and he buried them in Princess's mane. "You're nice and warm, my lady. I'm sorry there's no shelter for us here." He screwed up his eyes against the stinging drops and looked over to the black shapes of Azariel and Storm against the ochre tussock.

He waited, gaze running from the slope opposite him to the brown game trail running along the dry river bed. Princess shifted beneath him and mud squelched as she tapped her forehoof on the ground. Rivulets of rain ran through the tussocks down the steep sides of the valley. *This is a heavy downpour for this time of year.* He wiped the water off his forehead with the back of his hand, the settings of the stones in his armband catching at his hair. *I hope the tents hold out.*

The clouds overhead dragged their way across the sky, driven by the northwester. They emptied themselves of rain, soaking his cloak, then broke up and began to disperse. A ray of red-orange sunlight blazed from the west through a rift in the clouds to the valley floor, illuminating a solitary white figure that pranced along the trail with the Stone of Wind glittering on its head.

He tensed and gathered up the reins, pulse beginning to race. The gazelle passed beneath him, striding smoothly along the game trail. Lady leaped to her feet with a sharp bark. He punched Princess's sides with his heels and the mare leaped down the slope. Across the valley, Azariel and Storm raced across the tussocks. Lady bayed and loped ahead of him. The gazelle looked up and darted like an arrow towards the river.

He leaned back, the wind snatching moisture from his eyes with the speed of Princess's rush. "Go, Princess!" he shouted. The mare tossed her head and snorted, and her stride widened as she hurtled down the slope. The gazelle swung towards him; for a heartbeat, he gazed into its large, dark eyes. "Come on, my lady! It's ours." He reached for his bow, swaying in the stirrups to balance himself. *If it's busy running, it might not be able to deflect an arrow. And if I get the angle right, then I might be able to hit it moving.*

The gazelle bounded away from him, heading diagonally towards the floor of the steep valley. He angled Princess after it. His hand darted down to his left hip to unclip an arrow, then he nocked the arrow into place. He lurched to one side as the mare slowed to balance herself on the slope. Pressing down with his downhill foot in the stirrup, he righted himself, but Princess stumbled beneath him in a clatter of stones and gravel. For half a heartbeat, he saw the gazelle at the foot of the slope, heading for the river. Then Princess fell to one side, toppling him over her shoulder as she collapsed.

He pitched into the tussock and heard something crack sharply as his bow slid under him, bruising his hip. *Damn, that's my bow breaking.* To his relief, the arrow tumbled to the ground, sharp head facing away from his body. Wet grasses slapped and sprayed him as he rolled down the slope, stinging his hands and face. Princess screamed, the shrill sound mixing with the grating of the gravel beneath her. *I hope she doesn't land on me.* He tried to check his fall with his left arm, but the gritty mud under his hand slipped away and his momentum carried further him down the steep incline. Again and again, he jolted onto his sword hilt, adding more bruises. Gravel and tussock whipped into his mouth and he tasted blood along with the dirt. He screwed his eyes shut and raised his arms as best he could to cover his head, his bow still in his right hand.

The spinning and battering stopped. He lay on his back and opened his eyes, head whirling and clammy trousers clinging to his legs. Gold stained the edges of the broken, bruise-grey clouds above him. He staggered to his feet. *If I can get back onto Princess and she can still gallop, we won't lose the gazelle again.* He spat dirt and bloody saliva into the creamy-brown trickle that coursed along the once-dry stream bed at the foot of the valley. *Where is she? I hope she's not as bruised all over as I am. It's a pity about my bow.* He stared down at the weapon in his hand. Apart from the smears of mud, it had stayed perfect. *Then what did I hear breaking?*

Princess squealed as he turned his head up the slope to look for her. The mare lay on her belly, raising her foreleg to lift herself up. She leaned on her leg and collapsed, shuddering and squealing. Again she tried and fell once more. "Oh, no..." His bow dropped from his grasp and his whole body shuddered. He stared wide-eyed at her, a hideous cold hand gripping his stomach. "No!" He covered his face, hot sparks springing behind his eyelids.

He ran to the fallen mare, heart racing and mouth dry. *Perhaps it's just a sprain, not a break. If so, then given time and what little Gift I have as a Healer, she'll run again.* He knelt beside her and caressed her silky wet neck, sending a warm wave of calm down into her. He concentrated on the bond between him and the mare and used his Gift to soothe her. His arm throbbed, and he gritted his teeth against the pain. Princess stopped shivering, and he stroked down her withers towards her weakened limb. "My lady, what's happened to you?"

Gently, he felt her leg. She squealed, making his ears ring, and flinched at his touch. His hands found a hot swelling part way down her cannon bone; below it, the bone bent to one side. He wrapped his arms around the mare's neck. "Oh, Princess," he sobbed, burying his face in her warm wet mane. "I never thought I'd farewell you so soon."

He heard horsehooves and looked up. Azariel looked down at him, her face whiter than usual and her lips pale. "What happened?" she said, voice sharp and frightened. "I saw you fall. Are you all right?"

"I'm all right, I think." He swallowed and tried to fight the wave of grief that broke in him. Choking, he stroked Princess's neck. "But she's... she's broken her leg."

Azariel swung off Storm and strode to him. Her arms wrapped around his shoulders and her wet hair clung to his cheeks. "I am so sorry for you," she murmured in his ear. Her hand rubbed over the back of his scalp. "Is there anything we can do for her, or is there nothing left except putting her out of her pain?"

He leaned his head against the thick prickly wool of her cloak, hot tears running down his cheeks. "There's nothing else we can do. I suppose I'd better do what I must."

He felt at his belt for his dagger as Azariel drew back from him. "Well, my lady, we've gone a few miles together," he said softly, fondling the mare's head and neck. "You were my first warhorse and you're a splendid one. You know me and know how to carry me in a fight, a hunt or a race. Poor girl, you showed me that today when we fought the Claws and you did what I asked without bridle or saddle. You've never let me down and you've been my friend for a long time." He scratched Princess behind the ears, then slid his hand down her fine-boned head to her velvety nose. Memories of the horse played in his mind from the time when he was a newly fledged soldier and *minyastin,* before being posted to the Watchtower of the West, before Azariel. The handle of the dagger fitted into his palm, steel and leather damp and chilly. "I was hoping to breed some good foals off you, but that will never be, now. I hope I've been a good master to you." Princess whinnied and pushed him in the shoulder with her muzzle as he bent closer to her. He drew a deep breath and felt on her neck for the groove of the great vessel where her lifeblood flowed.

His hand trembled as he raised the knife. *I've got to hold still. I don't want to fumble and cause her more pain.* He forced himself steady and lifted the blade to her neck a second time. Then he shook his head and rested the dagger on his muddy knee again. "I can't do this," he said. "I can't cut my friend's throat. She's been bonded to me for years." He handed it to Azariel, hilt first. "Will you do it for me?" She nodded and took it from him, tears pooling in her eyes.

He cradled Princess's head in his lap as Azariel crouched over the mare's neck. "Quiet now, my lady," he whispered, staring into her dark eye and away from the pulsing veins in her neck. "You'll gallop through the stars tonight." He poured calm into her, trying to ignore the soft sound of the knife slashing skin. The mare twitched, and a hot line of agony ran around his own neck under his armour. He gasped and moaned with pain, points of light dancing in his vision. A rush of warmth drenched his leg and the bitter smell of fresh blood rose. A great sighing breath gushed out of the mare and the dark fire in her eyes faded to a glassy mist. Then black warmth surrounded him as Azariel embraced him. He flung his arms around her and held her tightly as he wept.

Finally, eyes burning and hands trembling, he raised his head from her shoulder, conscious of the metal rings of her chainmail pressing into his cheek. He released a ragged breath and lifted one hand to smear away the salt water around his eyes. His throat still ached. "Sorry," he said. "I'm a mess again and I must look a fool crying over a horse like this. I am a fool, feeling barely anything after killing a man but bawling over an animal."

"You're not a fool and don't be sorry." Her arms tightened around his chest and he slumped against her once more. "You've known her long and you loved her. Those Claws were trying to kill you, her, me and Stessa, and you didn't even know their names. But Princess was your friend. I understand."

He leaned hard against her then drew back with a grunt of pain. The blood on his clothes stuck the cotton to his skin. He rubbed at his throat, trying to soothe the ache through the double mail of his armour.

"What's wrong? Did you hit your neck against something on the way down? You're lucky you didn't break that as well."

He shook his head. "No need to worry. It's my Gift. There's – there was - a tie between me and Princess. The bond strengthens with time and I've had Princess for eight years. I was in full bond with her when you cut her throat. That's what's hurting me." He cupped her face with his hands. Her cheeks felt wet and tears clung to her eyelashes. "Do you know the sort of man you're marrying, Stormwolf? She wasn't as close to me as you are, and definitely not as intimate as we will be, but she was closer to me than many people. She was a part of me. Do you mind that a large part of my heart will always belong to animals?"

She drew him close and kissed him on the mouth. He clasped her, hungry for comfort. "I thought so," she whispered as she eased her lips back. "I know you've got a great heart. It was what first drew me to you. And I know my place in it. Thank you."

He kept his arms wrapped around her and looked over at Princess's body. "She was a good horse." Storm nuzzled at the dead mare, whickering. "Does he realise she's dead?" he said, chest tightening as another sob built up in him. "I'm finding it hard to grasp, myself."

****

Azariel scraped her flint over the steel from her tinderbox, striking spark after spark into the nest of soft dry grass and leaves. One caught, making a shrivelled seed-head glow vermilion edged with black. She curled her hands around the fire-nest and breathed on it, coaxing a yellow flame and white smoke to life. The flames spread across the dry grass, twigs and sticks, crackling and snapping as they grew, bright against the twilight. She slid the tinderbox back into her belt-pouch and stepped back from the pile of brushwood and gorse ringing Princess's body and watched the fire grow. Her muscles trembled after the exertion of heaving the dead horse onto the pyre, and the scratches from the gorse on the backs of her hands and arms stung with the salt of sweat and tears.

Farren sat in the grass on the slope nearby, hood over his head. His hand rested on Lady's head, fondling the dog's ears and neck. Azariel strode two paces up the slope and dropped beside him. Wordlessly, she slid one arm around his shoulder, kneading at the links of metal under the thick wool of his cloak. He shook the hood back from his head and rubbed his soft hair against her cheek. "I've saved this from her," he said, passing her a handful of long thick chestnut hairs. "Can you make a keepsake from it?"

"Of course I can." She coiled the hairs into a neat skein and tucked them into her pouch. "Do you want me to do it now?"

He shook his head. "Later. I'd like to watch you do it properly." The fire crackled and roared greedily, and black smoke billowed up, mixed with the bitter tang of burnt flesh, hair and fat. "Hellfire, I can't stand watching this. I've seen horses burnt to death before, and it's horrible. I know she's dead already, but to see her like that... Hold me tight, Stormwolf."

His weight pressed onto her as his arms wrapped around her and he buried his face in the folds of her cloak on her chest and shoulder. She leaned backwards against the springy resistance of a tussock and gathered him into her embrace. *If we didn't have armour on, I'd be better able to comfort him,* she thought. Her wounded knee protested as she made way for his full weight, their armour grating together. A sharp, hot pang of desire surged in her stomach and thighs, making her heart pound and her breath quicken. "Farren," she whispered in his ear. "Please – get off me."

He raised his head and looked down at her with bloodshot eyes. A smile broke across his face, then his eyes lit up as he rolled off her. "Sorry," he said. "Here I am all over you like I'm trying to make love to you. I shouldn't be so selfish." He slid into the tussock and half a pace down the hillside towards the fire. "I didn't think. I'm no better than any other of the soldiers, turning to a woman's body for comfort after a death. I've seen that happen before."

"You're upset about Princess; you aren't expected to think carefully." She sat up and brushed rainwater off her arms and legs.

"I should think. She was a horse and you're worth more than her, Stormwolf." He hitched himself up onto his hands and knees. "Still, I'll miss her. I'll miss her a lot."

***

The shrilling of a blackbird, mingled with the liquid squawks of magpies, filled Azariel's ears at dawn. She rolled over as a raven's hoarse croak mixed with the dawn chorus. Opening her eyes, she pushed back the thick prickly folds of cloak and blanket. The shadows of the broom bushes shimmered and danced in the wind on the pale green canvas walls of the tent. She rubbed her gritty eyelids, mind still drenched and heavy with sleep, then sat up. The saddlebag lay beyond her reach, so she lunged for it and hunted inside for a change of underclothes. After changing, she crawled out of the tent.

Outside, the campfire was still covered by thick squares of turf with only a thread of smoke rising from the cracks between them. A fresh pile of firewood sat beside it, neatly stacked. *Farren's been busy, but I can't see him.* Storm and Veranath grazed beneath the horse chestnuts, meandering between the trunks. She stared at them for a moment. *Something's missing.* Then she shook her head and sighed. *It's Princess I'm missing. I won't be seeing her again.* She glanced upstream towards the steep bulk of the hills. In her mind's eye, she pictured the fire where they had burned the mare's body the night before. *I hope Farren hasn't walked all the way back there to that valley without me.*

Storm raised his head and whinnied to her. She walked over to him, her knee stiff and sore. "Hello, old fellow," she said, clapping him on the neck. "Had a good rest?" She stood stroking his sleek coat and scanned the campsite. Lady had vanished too. *He must have taken her hunting.* She strolled down to the stream and knelt down to splash her hair and face. The cold water washed the sleep from her mind as it shivered down from her scalp to the base of her spine. *That's better. I wonder if Farren's off washing after getting all that blood from Princess over him yesterday.* She looked down at her trouser legs, bloodstained from where he had leaned on her. *Perhaps I should as well. But not yet. Not where he could come and catch me at it.*

The blackbird shrilled an alarm call, and she jolted alert, one hand reaching for her sword hilt. She spotted Farren and Lady under the willows near the main river. He reached for the trailing strands and pulled them to bend a branch down. Sunlight glinted off metal as he slashed at the bark with his dagger. In the grass beside him, Lady lay gnawing the foreleg from the goat carcass. Seeing her, the deerhound scrambled to her feet and whined.

Farren looked around, and Azariel strode to meet him. Shadows lay beneath his eyes, and water darkened his hair. She slid her arms around his neck and kissed his damp cheeks, catching the scent of his lavender soap. "What have you been doing?" she asked when she dew back from him. "You look exhausted."

"I couldn't sleep. My back was on fire from sunburn and I couldn't stop thinking about Princess." He ben and picked up the billycan from the grass beside him. "I got up as soon as it was light and went swimming in the river to quench the fire on my skin." His lips parted in a broad smile and his eyes flashed, in spite of the tired dark circles. "I was looking around me the whole time in case you came and caught me in nothing but my skin. I tried to get the blood and mud off my trousers, but the river's so high and full of silt after the rain I nearly dirtied them more." His nose wrinkled in distaste and she laughed. "I was getting willowbark to make tea. I've got a headache and I imagine your knee is sore."

She flexed her leg; the wound on her knee throbbed. "It's not too bad, but I'll be glad of some willowbark anyway." She glanced over to the place where they had dragged the bodies of the Yellow Claw horses. "Did you find a saddle for Veranath in the gear we took from the Claws?"

"Well, he'll hardly fit Princess's gear, will he?" He cut another strip of bark from the willow. "I haven't worked with him long enough to ride him long without a saddle. I think one was the right size – I'm glad Stessa didn't take that with her but left us some of the spoils to deal with."

"You'd have trouble mounting him in a hurry anyway." She fell into step beside him and they strolled back to the campsite. "He'll make a fine warhorse with his size and strength. You expect to see the broad nose and feathered legs of a carthorse on him, he's so tall."

"I'll be glad of that. You never know, he might have the speed we need to catch the gazelle." He halted and gazed at the tall chestnut stallion, fidgeting with his betrothal earring. "If he's something of a horse *minyastin*, he may have strange abilities. You saw him canter past us the other day."

"We'll find out before the day's out." She bent over the fire and pulled the turf covering off the embers. Feeding more fuel to it, she brought the fire back to full crackling life. "Mind you, that might not be everything we need. We're *minyasti* and we're not tireless. But let's go up to the top of the cliff and watch for the gazelle, and we'll try."

They ate a quick breakfast of stale bread and cheese while the tea came to a boil. "The creek's not too silty to drink from," she said. "What's the river like?"

"I said it was still muddy. It must have rained very heavily in the mountains last night. I just hope it's not too silty for the gazelle. But where else can it go apart from this creek here? I don't think these hills are the right shape for tarns and the ground's too dry to let yesterday's rain pool for long. I can't remember if there was a pool inside the labyrinth but I don't want to go in there again to find out." He stood up and whistled.

The two horses and the deerhound trotted over to the campfire. Storm nuzzled at Farren but Veranath stood back a few paces. "Come on, lad," he said to the stallion. "Time for you to learn to take a saddle. The one from the blue roan should fit you."

Azariel got to her feet. "You'll have to hold him while I saddle up. We had a bet, you know."

He shook his head. "Don't. I'd better do this. But you can fetch the bridle out from my gear for me."

She crawled into his tent and opened his saddlebags. After rummaging through the collection of white cotton underclothes, the old calico wrappings from cheeses, another coil of rope, a small bag of salt and a whetstone, she found the bridle. She drew it out and studied the neat pattern of coloured and braided leather in the browband and reins. *It looks even better out here in the open daylight than it did in the shop.* She slipped it over her shoulder, then closed the saddlebags before leaving the tent.

She passed Farren the bridle, then fetched Storm's gear and threw the soft saddlecloth over the gelding's back. As she fumbled with the girth, Farren caught Veranath by the mane. In his other hand, he held out a crust left from breakfast, keeping his hand low. Veranath bent his head to nibble the bread, and Farren slipped the reins over his neck. The stallion flinched and his ears twitched back. "It won't hurt you, my lad," Farren crooned. He eased the bit between the stallion's lips. Veranath's teeth crunched and ground on the metal.

"You make that look so simple," Azariel said as she bridled Storm. "Are you sure you don't want me to hold him while you saddle him?"

"I'd rather you didn't. He's nervous and probably annoyed, and I don't want him to hurt you." He half-turned towards her, still holding the braided bridle under the horse's chin. "But please pass me the saddle."

She lifted the heavy saddle and balanced it on his outstretched arm. The underside was padded with thick sheepskin, peppered all over by grey hairs. "Are you sure it will fit him?"

"It will." He cast the saddle over Veranath's back and adjusted the straps as the stallion pranced around. "It does. It fits you well, my lad." He pulled the girths tight around the stallion's middle. The big horse danced to one side as Farren tested and lengthened the stirrup leathers. "There you go, Veranath. You'll find that more comfortable after a long day of carrying me. Right. I'm ready. Let's go up to the top of the cliff and have a look around for that gazelle. I've been up since dawn and it hasn't come down to the river to drink yet."

She put her toe in the stirrup and swung herself onto Storm's back, then shook her hair back from her face. "The sooner, the better." She nudged Storm to a trot and leaned over his neck as he worked up the ridge. After a few moments, Veranath's heavy hoofbeats drummed behind her. As the big stallion drew level with Storm, Farren glanced over at her, his face flushed and his eyes brilliant. She smiled. *It's good to see him happy again.*

She reined her horse in and let him graze among the shrubs and coarse grasses at the top of the cliff. The labyrinth lay below them in a neat spiral about the beech tree. She shuddered. *I'm glad the gazelle isn't in there.* After dismounting, she sat down and leaned against a thick clump of tussock that hissed in the wind. Her eyes roved over the hills, the river and the plains. *Maybe I should go down to the trails and change shape to track it,* she thought. *It may have drunk already.* Shrugging, she relaxed and let the warm air caress her face. *Farren's probably right, but if it went to that steep valley, he won't have seen it.* She continued to watch the landscape. Overhead, the clouds fled southwards, driven by the strong northwester. She stared at the patterns in the sky clouds for several hundred heartbeats then turned her gaze back to the goat-trails leading down to the stream and river. Even the goats had disappeared from view. *I hope we haven't scared everything away with yesterday's fight and the fire.* She nibbled at the soft part of a blade of grass, then tossed it aside.

A flash of white caught her eye. The gazelle was picking its way down the goat-track from the rose-covered spur towards the stream, the Stone of Wind swinging between its horns. *I'm surprised it doesn't keep well away from where we put the bodies.* "There it is," she whispered.

"We'll have to go around it and drive it towards the river. Then we'll have it trapped." He rose to his feet and vaulted onto the stallion's back.

The white figure reached the stream and waded until it stood with all four legs in the water. It faced downstream towards the river as it drank, inching forwards a few hesitant paces.

Farren pulled Veranath's head up from the grass and nudged the stallion's flanks with his heels. Veranath tugged on the reins and tossed his mane as Farren leaned backwards to balance the stallion's descent. Lady pricked her long ears and began trotting down the hill towards the gazelle. "No, girl," he called softly. "This way. Got to go round it." The deerhound bounded up to him, tail wagging. "Good girl." The northwest wind blew on his back and the rush of the river behind him seemed quieter than usual. As he reached a point to the east of the gazelle, he turned Veranath straight downhill.

The gazelle neared the river. It still stood midstream in the little tributary, shaking its ears from time to time as if bothered by insects, making the Stone of Wind between its horns dance and glimmer. One of its large leaf-shaped ears cocked backwards. Farren looked over his shoulder at Azariel and nodded. "You stay north of it, Stormwolf," he said. "Stop it running into the hills and we should have it trapped against the river."

The gazelle raised its head from the stream and swung to the left, heading down the course of the Illin-y-Hyalda away from the hills and the mountain chain. "Come on!" he shouted, thumping his heels into Veranath's sides. The white shape of the gazelle flickered between the grey-green trunks of the willows. Storm shot ahead of the stallion and crashed through the trees behind the gazelle. Snorting, Veranath plunged through the line of willows, following the trampled broom and hemlock as he raced downstream. Farren ducked beneath a low branch that skimmed across his back, and kept his eyes fixed on the gazelle's rump.

The dust and hot wind blowing from the strands of gravel in the river tore moisture from his eyes and he blinked it away. Azariel rode beside him, her hair flying around her face like a river of night, fire in her eyes and her slender body in smooth, taut control of the gelding. The deerhound loped beside Storm, ears streaming like flags around her face. The gazelle veered towards the river. It plunged through the lines of willow lining the river bank and kept running south. "We can't lose it now if it keeps following the river," Azariel called from behind him, followed by Storm snorting.

Veranath tossed his head and neighed in answer. Farren punched his heels into Veranath's sides and let him gallop unchecked. The veins on the chestnut stallion's neck bulged as he lengthened his stride on the flatter ground bordering the river. "Go, Veranath! Go like the northwest wind!" Farren shouted. The stallion tugged at the reins and held his head high. *Follow the gazelle,* he willed, sending the command down the fragile bond between him and the horse. *Follow it wherever it goes.*

Bowshot after bowshot vanished under Veranath's hooves as they headed along the course of the river. Ahead, the white rump of the gazelle flickered through the greens and greys of willows, hemlock, broom and gorse, the Stone of Wind continually dancing above its head. The river roared in his ears, almost drowning the thunder of hoofbeats and the rapid pounding of his heartbeat. His eyes stung with speed and beneath his hands, Veranath's neck grew damp with sweat.

The plains opened up before them as he galloped out of the shadows of the hills. Still the gazelle ran on, swifter than the wind and untiring. Sweat dampened Veranath's neck and withers, the earthy smell strong in Farren's nose, and the big horse's sides began to heave, although he carried his head high with his ears pricked forwards.

The gazelle ran on without checking its speed. Farren's thighs and hips ached. *Why are they sore? I ride all the time.* A tight clump of young broom bushes lay in front of them. Veranath gathered himself and soared over them. *Of course – he's wider than Princess.*

Storm's hooves drummed faintly behind him. He glanced back over his shoulder. Storm was lathered in white foam that dripped off him. Lady had vanished. He shook his head. "Stop," he called, reining Veranath down to a canter. "Don't push him so hard."

"You ride on," she called. "Don't wait for me and Storm. We'll stop and I'll catch up once he's rested." The scream of wind in her ears almost drowned her last few words.

He raised his hand to her, then faced ahead again. Veranath galloped on, snorting with each step, for several more bowshots. A trio of plovers took to the air, shrieking, as the gazelle darted past them. Ahead, a mob of black and white cattle grazed on the richer grass of the flatter land. Behind it lay a farmhouse and the scent of newly mown hay drifted towards Farren. The gazelle veered to the right then bounded down the river bank. Another leap took it across the first braided arm of the river and into one of the islands of gravel and wildflowers. Farren turned Veranath to follow it. *No – don't cross the river into Wayast. Not now.* The stallion half slid down the bank, splashing as he landed and staining the water brown with loosened earth. Veranath waded to the strip of gravel, hooves crunching on the coarse sand as he heaved himself out of the water. The gazelle glanced back at them, the Stone of Wind flashing, then hurdled a second strand of the river. *If I keep pushing it, it will reach the main channel soon – but then what will it do?*

The gazelle skidded to a halt, stopping just short of the widest stretch of water, hooves scoring pale lines through the gravel. It hesitated, then swung back to the north, heading upstream. Farren's heart leaped. *Perhaps we'll have it trapped after all.*

The gazelle ran without checking its speed, bounding over thinner braids of the river and hooves clattering on the gravel. Veranath followed, the dull thud of his hooves almost drowned by the rush of the river. Azariel's voice called out to him, but wind, water and hooves blurred the words. Still the gazelle ran on. The back of Farren's throat burned with thirst and his eyes stung with the dust kicked up by the gazelle's hooves. His shirt clung to his back with sweat and his chainmail felt hot as a griddle.

Ahead, the pines and the horse chestnuts of the campsite came into view behind the willows. The gazelle swung to the right again, hurdling a deeper pool that ran beside the river bank. It ran past the campsite, up the hill and into the labyrinth. Farren let the reins fall from his hands and stared, mouth open. *I don't believe it. It could have run anywhere – anywhere at all – but it chose to return to the labyrinth. That's unnatural.*

He leaned back and Veranath checked his pace to a canter, then a smooth trot. The stallion halted by the pool of water and plunged his muzzle into the water. Farren let the stallion drink deeply, then hauled his head up. "You need to cool down properly," Farren told his stallion. "I don't want you to lame yourself. Let's have a nice walk down to meet Azariel and Storm." *And I'll wager she'll be as surprised as I am by the gazelle's actions.*

He wheeled Veranath around and headed back downstream, keeping Veranath moving at a steady walk. The stallion slumped his head forward and plodded on. Farren looked down at his trousers. Dust clung to them where water had soaked the material. *Don't tell me I'm going to have to wash another set of clothes. If I'd know I was going to get filthy this often, I would have packed more – and more soap. At least I haven't worn my cloak today.* He let the reins fall slack and shrugged his shoulders, easing the tension out of them. The thirst sanding the back of his throat nagged at him. *I should have joined Veranath drinking back at the river.*

The afternoon sun beat down strongly, and he eased Veranath into the shade of the willows lining the willow bank as they rounded another bend south of the campsite. Veranath paused to tear at some of the trailing strands, then plodded on, munching. Farren reached out and plucked a few leaves, then ate them without letting the bittersweet taste linger on his palate. *Not as good as the bark but it should help soothe a few aches.*

"Farren!" Azariel's shout caught his attention. She was walking towards him, leading Storm on foot. The black gelding stumbled as he walked, his eyes half closed. A few patches of white foam still clung to his coat. On her other side, Lady trotted through the long grass, tail held low and panting hard. "So how did it get away from you this time?" she asked as soon as she came within ten paces.

He reined Veranath in, then dismounted. "You won't believe it," he said, then turned to pat his horse. "Well done, my lad. You took the saddle well."

Azariel's eyebrows arched. "I can believe that Veranath behaved himself. I know what your Gift can do."

"That's not what I meant." He fell into step beside her and explained. "I don't know what else we can do, Stormwolf. There aren't enough of us to trap it properly, unless we try again to head it up against the cliff like last time. I'm almost starting to wonder if it's a real, live gazelle at all. Any other beast would have gone to find new grazing grounds by now."

"It smells like a live animal, and it eats, drinks and makes dung like a real animal. Perhaps the Stone of Wind has something to do with it – or something in the labyrinth itself." She paused as Lady swung in front of her, sniffing at something on the lower leaves of a mullein plant. "Not that knowing that gets us any closer to finding a way to trap it. It's a pity Stessa left – she could have helped us drive it."

He stared at the grass and trees, turning over ideas in his mind. "We could try laying traps along the game trails, but we didn't bring equipment for that," he said after riding silently for a while. "Not enough rope for a net and no spades to dig a pit, unless we improvise."

"That won't work. It's been tried."

"How do you know?" He ran his hand through his hair and tugged it lightly.

"Yesterday as we were chasing the gazelle down that steep valley, I saw a pit in the middle of the game trail. Storm only just managed to hurdle it, or we could have both been riding Veranath now." She clapped Storm on the neck. "Remember what Stessa said about the Claws having tried to catch the gazelle for years? They must have tried trapping it, too."

"And somehow it got out or away. That's what comes of having a Stone of Protection tied to your head."

He walked silently beside her, his boots swishing through the grass in time with hers. "I can't think what to do. The only thing that has come close to working has been to drive it and trap it against the cliff. But we can't always get it to go where we want it to go, and we can't run the horses ragged trying. Storm won't be able to handle a hard run like today's day after day; I don't know what Veranath can do."

She bowed her head, the curtain of her hair covering her face. "There's only one place we know we can find and trap the gazelle where it can't get away," she said slowly.

A cold knot tied itself in her stomach. "I think I know what you mean."

"Yes. We're going to have to go back into the labyrinth."

CHAPTER FIFTEEN

They returned to the campsite and he stripped the tack off Veranath. Lady wandered to the stream and lapped up water noisily. "Leave Storm to me," he said as Azariel finished unsaddling Storm. "I'll rub him down properly." Veranath huffed hot breath at him, shaking his mane before heading to drink several paces upstream from Lady.

He ran his hand along Storm's withers, wiping off a line of earthy smelling sweat and black hair. "You've had a hard run, haven't you, boy?" He kneaded and massaged at the horse's damp skin, pressing into the muscles underneath. A gust of wind buffeted him on the back. *At least he's had a chance to cool off after that hard run. Poor fellow. I should have never expected him – or Veranath – to keep up with that gazelle with its Stone. It's just too fast for horse, dog or bow to catch.* He sighed. "You'll have a chance to rest while we go into the labyrinth again." *And, King of Heaven, may he not be resting forever, waiting for us to come back out if we get killed.*

He finished rubbing the gelding down, then washed the hair and sweat off his hands and arms at the stream. When he had finished, he knelt down and scooped water up in his hands to drink. The water tasted weedy.

Azariel looked down at him, twisting her opal ring around her finger. "I've put together something to eat. It's cold, but we'll need something before we go in."

He scrambled to his feet. "I don't really feel like eating when I think about going in, but you're right." He fell into step beside her as they walked towards the turf-covered campfire. Several slices of cold meat, watercress and some dried fruit lay on a flat stone. *We're lucky Lady didn't try eating that.* He glanced at the deerhound, who lay in the grass gnawing a bone. "Shall we take her in with us?" He waved a hand at the dog before bending down to pick up one of the pieces of cold meat.

"If things go wrong and that scorpion reappears, it will be hard to protect her. Perhaps she shouldn't."

He swallowed his mouthful of cold smoked goat and bitter watercress. "She might be useful, but I think you're right. The fight with the Claws scared her badly enough, and even a trained warhorse like Storm balks at the uncanny." He glanced at the dog again, who looked up at him with the whites showing in the corner of her hazel eyes. Lady wagged her tail and pricked her ears, then returned to worrying the bone. "One day, we'll have to take her on a hunt for less uncanny quarry."

Azariel flicked her hair back from her face. "Yes – when we've recovered this Stone of Protection." She stared somewhere over his shoulder, holding her slice of meat rolled around the dried fruit. "Beloved," she said slowly. "I hate admitting this, but I'm afraid about going in there again."

A deep breath escaped him and tension he had only been half aware of holding eased. "So am I. I've been trying to tell myself that it's been wisdom or prudence or practicality that's stopped me from going back in there, but yes, I'm afraid. I'm afraid of that scorpion. It turned me inside out last time, seeing it attack you and not being able to kill it." He ran his hand through his hair. "Strange to say, but it's a relief to admit it."

She smiled at him. "I feel the same. I think I was almost as afraid of admitting I was afraid as I was of going back in and facing that scorpion."

"I suppose that makes us both cowards." His chest tightened again.

She shook her head. "Do you remember the first battle you faced – the first time you knew it was a case of kill or be killed?"

He nodded. "I can still remember the face of that thief. My unit had cornered his gang of ruffians behind a tavern. I felt sick before the fight began, and I threw up afterwards."

Her mouth tightened into a grim line. "We all do after our first battle. I remember trying to stop myself shaking so the point of my sword kept still. But I fought anyway, and you fought, even though we were afraid. Fear isn't what makes us cowards. It's giving into the fear that does that."

He downed the end of his meat and watercress. "Well, Stormwolf, we'll both face this battle together, even though we're afraid." He picked up his bow. "Besides, we may not have to fight the scorpion. If we can make this kill without shedding blood, or at least without shedding blood on that omphalos stone, we may not face the scorpion at all."

"And may the Power be with us if we do." She tossed a scrap of gristle to the deerhound and swept her hair behind her face.

Azariel reached out for Farren's free hand as they walked uphill to the labyrinth, relishing the familiar pattern of calluses on his palm and fingers. Her heart beat loud and steady in her ears, a little faster than the steady thud of her boots on the dry earth. *Fear is not my master; I am master of my fear,* she told herself as she looked up at the dense tangle of dark mountainthorns that made the walls of the maze. *We've faced that scorpion once before and we can do it again – if we have to face it at all.* "I suppose that gazelle is still inside the labyrinth," she said aloud.

"I haven't seen it leave, but it may have crept out while I met you on the way back to camp." His hand tightened around hers and he adjusted the bow on his shoulder.

She looked up at the tight hedge of thorns. The wind buffeted them and made them sway as if alive. "I'll use my nose."

"Don't shift now, Stormwolf," he said. "I like walking beside you in your proper shape." He squeezed her hand again.

The scent of clover and the subtler earthy note of mountainthorn drifted towards her, and the wind tugged at her hair. The blackbird in the beech tree in the centre of the labyrinth shrilled an alarm and flew away as they drew nearer to the entrance. At the gap in the hedge of thorns, they stopped, and she freed her hand from his. "I won't have to go far to scent it. I may not have to go in at all."

She shifted shape and dropped to all fours to wait for her head to clear. Among all the other smells, the scent of the gazelle stood out sharply. *It's been in and out of here so many times that I can hardly tell the older trails from the new. If I'd come here before and smelt how often it comes here, I'd have realised how strange its behaviour is a long time ago.* She snuffed at the dust and sparse grass growing near the stems of the mountainthorn, but the separate trails overlaid each other in a confused blend. She sneezed and shook her head as dust stung her nose, then raised her head to test the air. This time, the tang of the gazelle met her senses sharply. She pricked her ears, angling them towards the beech tree in the centre of the labyrinth. The click of light hooves on stones and dry ground mixed with the steady rustle of an animal grazing. She sat back on her haunches and shifted shape again. "It's in there."

She clambered to her feet, shook back her hair and twisted the rings straight on her fingers. Farren slid his bow off his shoulder. The mountainthorns forming the entrance arched overhead, the younger green leaves dwarfed by the long bone-coloured thorns. Her mouth felt dry. *I wish I could have brought some water with us. At least I'm not wearing my cloak.* "Here we go," she said. "In the name of God Incarnate."

"Yes indeed."

She stepped beneath the arch of the mountainthorns and into the shelter of the hedges. Farren drew level with her, and she edged to one side to make room for him. The reaching branches raked at her armour, each thorn clicking across the links of her chainmail. She clenched her teeth. *There's no need to be afraid*, she told herself. *It's not as though that scorpion is waiting in there for us; we'll only find the gazelle. And we worked out how to make that scorpion go away last time, so we can do it again if we need to.*

She continued walking in step beside him around the bends of the labyrinth, left, right, around tight turns and along gently curving stretches. The hedges held back the wind, which hissed and stirred the topmost branches, and cast cool shadows in front of them. Azariel and Farren rounded one last turn, then the shadow gave way to the sunlit clearing in the centre. She shaded her eyes with her hands in the sudden brightness, and Farren stumbled over a rock.

At the far side of the clearing, the gazelle leaped up from where it had been lying in the grass. The Stone of Wind danced on the silver chains binding it to the curving horns. It bleated and backed up a few paces, eyes wide and nostrils flared. Its rump brushed the thorns behind it, then it swung around and tried to run, but halted after a few paces.

Azariel raised her hands, keeping her eyes fixed on the tips of the horns. *I'll be ready for you when you strike.* She kept her fists clenched and her arms half-crossed in front of her chest. The gazelle turned to face them, then bowed with a flourish of its horns. Golden light spiralled out from the tips. Triumph surging inside her, she blocked the stream of light with her armbands, scattering the light to the side and making the emeralds set in the silver glow. *You won't put us to sleep so easily this time, gazelle.* Another golden spiral spun out at her; again she caught it. The metal of her armbands warmed but the heat soon faded. "Time to fight fire with fire," she said aloud. "Farren, would you like to strike first?"

"You're the stronger of us two, Stormwolf."

Heat flooded down her arms into her hands, making the opal ring glitter with red, green and cobalt fire. Clenching her fist, she punched lightning at the gazelle. The green energy from her ring burned out, turning the motes of dust in the air to faint-smelling smoke. It wrapped around the gazelle, outlining each limb and horn in coils of emerald. Then the Stone of Wind flared and her fire vanished.

She lowered her hands, though the fire still burned in her ring. The gazelle stood at bay at the far side of the inner circle, shifting from side to side and flourishing its horns. It bleated, then rushed towards them. Its hooves scraped on the hard dry ground as it soared into the air, high enough to bound over their heads. Without thinking, she sent a bolt of towards it as it leaped. Her bolt of red fire caught it in the belly, and a network of red enmeshed the gazelle and flung it backwards. The gazelle staggered as it landed, sides heaving.

Farren edged forward. "We've got no other choice. I'll have to kill with fire and steel like I did with the phoenix when I was younger." His eyes hardened as he fitted an arrow to the string.

"Take care the arrow doesn't trail blood over the omphalos stone." She glanced at the small pillar of limestone, then back at the gazelle, where it stood at bay.

He whispered as he raised the bow and drew it. The afternoon sunlight glinted off the sharp arrowhead before magenta and violet flame burst from Farren's hand and shimmered up the shaft, wrapping around the head of the arrow. The sinews of his arms stood out as he held the bow steady at full draw. The coloured light flickered off his skin as his fingers brushed his cheek.

He released the string. The arrow flew, trailing streams of coloured fire behind it. The Stone of Wind flared between the gazelle's horns and a strong gust swept her hair backwards. The arrow held its course, fire fading as the light inside the Stone died. It took the gazelle at the base of the neck and plunged through and out of the gazelle's shoulder, streaming with bright scarlet blood instead of flame. The gazelle reared on its hind legs, scattering a fountain of crimson. It screamed, sounding almost human, then staggered forwards and to one side, tottering to and fro. After staggering to the side, it lurched forwards, heading for the centre of the circle.

Dread lanced through her and she rushed forwards. *Not that! Perhaps I can turn it aside.* Every muscle strained as she ran, each movement feeling too slow. Farren's footsteps pounded beside hers. The gazelle staggered from side to side, then forwards, trailing blood from the arrow wound in its throat. It reached the centre and collapsed across the limestone pillar of the omphalos. Blood gushed across the pale stone and trickled to the grass below. The gazelle twitched a few times then lay still, the Stone of Wind still glowing between its horns.

Mouth dry and heart pounding, she covered the last few steps between her and the gazelle. *Perhaps we can take the Stone and leave before the scorpion manifests.* Farren pushed ahead of her and flung the dead gazelle off the stone. The sharp smell of blood rose. On top of the omphalos, the carved lines forming the scorpion stood out sharply in the middle of the redness, as if it had absorbed the liquid. Steam rose from the carving, first in a thin trail, then in a large cloud. "Oh no!" she whispered.

Farren lunged towards the omphalos. As he touched the rising cloud, he jerked backwards with a yelp of pain. Hissing through his teeth, he shook his hand. "It feels like hellfire and I can't touch the stone to overturn it."

"Let's retreat. Perhaps the scorpion won't attack us this time, as it's the gazelle's blood on the stone this time, not mine."

He grimaced. "I'd rather put some distance between us and it. At least we know how to drive it away."

In several quick paces, they retreated to the hedge wall about three paces from the entrance. *I won't even try leaving, whether the way out is sealed or not.* She spun around, the links of her armour and her hair catching on the thorns behind her. *We can't abandon the Stone.* The centre of the labyrinth had completely filled with mist, cutting off the warmth of the sun. Her pulse pounded in her ears, and the hiss of the wind seemed muted. Above the omphalos, the mist darkened, hiding the body of the gazelle and the limestone boulder beside it. She set her teeth. *Hopefully, it won't start that ghastly whispering if it can be satisfied with the blood of the gazelle.* She glanced down at her hands. Her opal ring had twisted sideways, so she nudged it straight. The silver warmed around her fingers and the threads of colour inside the gem gleamed.

The darker patch of fog twisted and formed into the shape of a scorpion the size of a cow, tail and bulbous stinger held high above its head. The mist forming it grew even blacker as if eating the light. She readied her rings. *As soon as I can see that omphalos, I'll strike at it.* The scorpion raised itself up and clicked its pincers together, the sound faint as if it came from a distance. Its tail twitched and it shuffled forwards. Her breath came quick and shallow, and she forced herself to breathe evenly. *What is it doing?*

She clenched her fists and punched a bolt of silver lighting at the small corner of the omphalos just visible beside the scorpion's legs. The scorpion scuttled back and hissed, then lashed its tail forwards as if striking. "How dare you!" it said in a woman's voice. "You!" It took several paces forwards. "You killed my gazelle."

Azariel shot a glance at Farren. *Is it going to hunt him now? But how did it know that he was the one to loose the arrow?* She inched closer to him. *If it concentrates on him, then I can strike at the omphalos.*

"How did that shadow beast become so intelligent?" Farren muttered. "What have we done?"

The scorpion stalked forwards another pace. *"Minyasti.* You must be *minyasti.* Nobody else could have killed my gazelle. I thought I would never be troubled by your like again." The giant claws clicked over the omphalos and on some of the other small rocks lying nearby. "You never thought, did you, that I would bind myself so closely to Majalis that I could live forever as the Shadow Scorpion?" It hissed again and wove from side to side. "Soon I shall see you. You cannot escape. Foolish, foolish *minyasti* to kill my gazelle, the living bearer of the black jewel bound to the labyrinth."

Azariel froze. *If we move, will it see us? But if we stay here, will it come too close for us to escape it?*

The scorpion turned to one side, facing the entrance to her left. The scent of rotting blood rolled out from it, making Azariel gag. She fought back the nausea. "How foolish of you to kill my gazelle here where I could drink its blood and become strong," the scorpion said. "Now I shall drink yours and become stronger. Or perhaps I shall bind you so that you can become the new bearer of the black stone that gives me the power to take this new form of mine."

The nausea rolled in Azariel's stomach again as the metal heated around her rings. *This scorpion – was it once the sorceress who lived here? I don't understand how she's done it or why, but I will not allow this foul thing to remain in the Kingdom.* She clenched her fists and bared her teeth. *King of Heaven, help me know how to fight it.* Slowly, she lifted her hands. "Strike now before it gets too close," she hissed to Farren.

She let fire leap from her rings, the energy prickling and burning down her wrists. To her left, light blazed out from Farren. Their four bolts, green, scarlet, black and silver, blended in a single stream as they struck the omphalos near the base, blackening the grass. The stone held firm. The scorpion hissed, blood dripping from its sting and from its claws. With a clatter of claws, it rushed at them.

Azariel stepped forward and slashed her arm in front of her, summoning up a shield of energy that shimmered in the air between her and the scorpion. *I don't know if this will work but, by the Power, I will try!* The sting of the scorpion lashed forwards, quivering. The point and the bloated poison-gland struck the surface of the shield and stopped. More blood oozed from it and trickled down her shield like raindrops on glass, the stench burning inside her nose. She held herself motionless to avoid breaking the shield, stifling the urge to gag and shrink back.

"Good thinking, Stormwolf," said Farren behind her in a low voice. "I don't know why two bolts of the Power's fire on the omphalos hasn't worked this time, but at least you're holding it off for now."

Again the scorpion flailed at her shield with its sting. More foul-smelling blood spattered across the wall of energy. She gritted her teeth and forced herself not to flinch. The shield held. "I think the scorpion's drunk too much blood for that to work this time." One of the huge claws reached towards them and clashed together, smashing into the shield and recoiling.

"Perhaps it's solid enough for us to strike it directly." He stepped beside her, hands raised, keeping behind the shimmering wall of her shield. "Hold your shield, Stormwolf."

"I can hold this for a while, but not forever." The effort of maintaining the shield of energy pulsed at her temples as her strength slowly leached into it.

The scorpion stalked back and forth five paces away from them, flexing its pincers open and shut. The mandibles beneath its eyes gnashed together. The strange light from the Stone of Wind lit up the segments of the tail, making them glow a sickly yellow-green. Farren dropped to his knees beside Azariel, his hands splayed wide. Lightning crackled out from his fingers and palm, its heat warming her thighs as it burned through the air. The twin bolts of white lighting struck the scorpion near one of its many eyes. The pincers clashed together again and it staggered backwards.

"It felt that." Farren stood up again, the emerald ring on his right hand glowing like a green star.

Azariel's arms started to ache with the tension of remaining motionless and the drain on her strength from the shield. *At least I remembered to keep my arms low.* Her head throbbed, and a sinew in her neck flared with pain as it cramped. "Strike again," she said. "It might have felt it, but you haven't harmed it."

Again he dropped to his knees behind the shelter of her shield and punched bolt after bolt of fire at the scorpion. Each crackling streak of coloured flame wrapped around the scorpion, outlining every joint in its carapace. His elbow bumped into her knee, making her fight to hold her stance. She tensed her hip muscle and stood firm. The shield wavered between her and the scorpion, shimmering like a heat haze and distorting the outline of the scorpion. The beast battered at her shield a few more times, then retreated several steps.

She blinked and drew a deep breath, trying to keep the movement of her chest as shallow as possible. Small points of light danced in her vision and her head throbbed in pain with every beat of her pulse. "I can't hold this... the shield much longer," she said, slurring her words. "We'll have to try something else."

He stood and leaned close to her so his lips brushed her hair a handspan from her ear. "Have you got enough strength to run to the other side of the circle? I don't think it can see us well unless we're moving, and I've got an idea."

"I'm not sure." She fought back the urge to shake some of the tiredness out of her head. "I'm getting light-headed."

"Then I'll carry you. On my count, drop the shield and jump onto my back." He paused as the scorpion scuttled forwards, lashed its sting at the quivering wall of energy then retreated once more. "Stormwolf, are you ready? One, two, three."

She let her hands fall slack to her sides and spun around, dizzy as if she had just shifted shape. Farren had his back turned to her, so she put her hands on his shoulders and leaped, wrapping her legs around his waist. He ran around the perimeter of the centre, keeping close to the mountainthorn hedge. One of the straggling branches caught her hair and snagged it, but she shook herself free. Her fingers started sliding from his shoulders, her nails clicking one by one over the links of metal in his chainmail. He gripped her more tightly. Behind them, the scorpion's legs thudded and scraped across the ground.

Farren reached the abandoned hut at the side of the clearing and lumbered behind it. Her knee bumped against the corner, sending a wave of pain up and down her legs. "Sorry," he said. "Just a few more steps." He reached the next corner of the hut, then stopped.

She slid off his back and leaned one hand against the stone walls to steady herself. Her legs felt as weak as string. "I hope your idea isn't to go round and round the hut trying to avoid it."

"No. Get up on top of the hut if you can. I don't think it can see you unless you move."

She shook her head. "I haven't got the strength. That shield exhausted me. I can barely walk."

He glanced up at the roof of the hut and shook his head. "Then I'll run and catch its attention. While it's hunting me, you make your way to the gazelle and take the Stone. Surely that will have the strength to help us defeat this scorpion."

"Can you outrun it?"

"I think so. I can use a shield as well if I have to – but I'd rather not. If we both get exhausted, we're doomed."

She nodded. "May the Power protect you."

He turned to her and kissed her quickly on the mouth, then ran several strides away from the hut before turning and looking beyond it. He sent a bolt of blue-white lightning searing through the air, then ran again. The scraping and scuttling of the scorpion's legs and body grew louder. Azariel held her breath and tensed. *I hope we're right about it not being able to see things that aren't moving.* She leaned against the sun-warmed stone wall of the hut and reached inside herself for the last dregs of her strength. *If it sees me, I might be able to call up a shield again – but not for long. Perhaps I should try going around the hut after all.*

The steps of the scorpion drew nearer, coming from the wall of the hut that faced towards the middle of the clearing. She took a few slow steps back towards the mountainthorn hedge, heading for the corner. Points of light danced in her vision, and her tongue felt like leather. The huge pincers inched into view, streaking blood across the ground, followed by the mandibles. She darted around the far side of the hut, then peered around the corner as the head, body and whip-like tail appeared. The scorpion stalked forward another pace, then two more, inching past the hut and moving beyond it. Relief poured down her back and her knees wavered. *It didn't see me.*

From the other side of the clearing, Farren threw more bolts of fire, one at the scorpion and the other at the omphalos. Green lightning hit the scorpion and wrapped around its body, running along every joint in the exoskeleton like water. The scorpion hissed and its tail quivered as it stalked towards him.

She waited until the scorpion had moved ten paces away from the hut before she inched out from between the stone wall and the hedge. With her gazed fixed on the scorpion, she crept along the wall, keeping one hand on the stone for support. Her head continued to pound and every muscle in her back, hips and legs ached. She drew a deep breath, then gagged on the rancid smell pouring from the scorpion. *I have to do this. That shield may have sapped nearly all my strength, but I have to do this.*

Footsteps pounded as Farren ran to another part of the circle. The scorpion halted, then turned from side to side. Azariel froze at the side of the hut, fingers digging into a patch of crumbling lichen. *King of Heaven, may it not see me!* Blue lightning crackled through the air and struck the sting of the scorpion, making the liquid oozing from it sizzle and steam. The scorpion swung to the left, facing away from her.

With her eyes fixed on the scorpion and keeping her breath steady and silent, she took several steps towards where the gazelle lay. The Stone of Wind made the silver chains and the white coat of the gazelle gleam, although the glassy surface remained dark. Another bolt of lightning struck the scorpion and shimmered around it. Gathering the strength she had left, she ran to the centre, then dropped to her knees beside the gazelle. *At least now that I'm here, I can stay still and that scorpion won't see me – I hope.*

She reached for the Stone. *How can I take this off the horns?* She felt for the link wrapped around the horn closest to her. The circle of silver had become lodged in the ridges of the horns. She gripped the chain beside the Stone and tugged it up, but it would not budge. *I suppose if it were that easy to pull off, the gazelle would have shaken the Stone loose long ago.* She glanced up at the scorpion. It still had its back turned towards her. *I had better work quickly. Farren won't be able to keep it over there forever. Could I saw the horns off? It would be a shame to spoil the head – Farren would probably like it – and my sword's no good as a saw, but if that's the only way to do it, I will. But not yet.*

She peered at the chains binding the Stone to the gazelle's horns, testing the metal with her fingers. Scratches and dents marked the silver, but only on the surface. *These chains were well forged.* She drew her dagger, her hands shaking with fatigue and making the point quiver. After fumbling a few times, she slid the point of the dagger through the link of the chain nearest to the stone. Placing both hands on the blue stone in the pommel, she thrust the dagger through. The blade slid through the gap a short distance, then caught on the silver. She pushed harder, gritting her teeth. *This must work. It must. Steel is stronger than silver.* The pommel dug into her, and the cut on her left hand flared with pain as it re-opened. "King of Heaven, give me strength," she groaned, putting her weight behind the thrust.

Heat flared in her hands, mingling with the sting of her wound. Cobalt light wreathed around her hands and spread along the hilt, then the blade of her dagger. The rich blue reflected off the surface of the Stone and the silver chains. The link gave way to the dagger, and she staggered forwards. The black jewel sagged down, held by the last chain. With the light still wrapping her dagger, she drove the point into a new link and prised it open. The chains swung loose, jingling, then the Stone fell and rolled down the gazelle's head into the grass.

She caught the Stone of Wind up in her right hand. "Thank the Power," she breathed. "It's done. We've got another one back." She raised it, her fingers glowing red and showing the course of the fine veins inside them as they cut off the strange light. Images of wolves and arches of cloud worked in the silver showed in between, and the glassy surface of the gem pulsed gently like a beating heart.

A screech came from the scorpion, and its claws scraped and thudded on the dry ground. It spun towards her, sting quivering and pincers clashing. She clasped the Stone in both hands, fire racing through her blood. *Perhaps my rings can't carry the energy needed to defeat the scorpion, but this Stone certainly will have.* She held the black silver-wrapped jewel in front of her and opened herself up to the Power's fire. Her fingers burned and tingled, and every vein in her arms prickled with energy. Then she focussed on the jewel to send the lightning inside her out at the scorpion.

The energy left her, dulling the fire in her fingertips, but no lightning blazed at the rapidly approaching scorpion. A strong wind bent the tips of the short grass and made the top of the beech tree hiss above her. Dust billowed up from the ground and mingled with the mist filling the centre. The air between her and the scorpion cleared in a wide circle. The scorpion hesitated, then surged forwards again.

She held still, clutching the Stone of Wind in front of her. Again, she tried to throw fire through the gem at the scorpion. This time, golden spirals curled out from it and wrapped around the scorpion. The tail dropped and the great body sagged lower between the three pairs of legs behind the pincers. Stars danced in her vision and her hands. Her arms buckled and strained as if the Stone had suddenly turned to lead. *If I channel much more fire, I'll pass out. Not here; not now. At least the Stone seems to have slowed the scorpion.*

Footsteps pounded beside her, startling a small surge of energy inside her. "Well done, Stormwolf! Now we can use the Stone to fight it."

"I've tried that." Her words slurred. "It doesn't work."

He shook his head. "Perhaps you're too tired. Let me try." He reached out and she dropped the Stone of Wind into his hand. She collapsed to her knees and sagged against the omphalos, the limestone warm from the touch of the sun.

Farren raised the jewel as the scorpion stirred and inched towards them. A glittering golden wave spread out from his hands like a bubble, pushing the scorpion backwards. He held the Stone in one as if about to throw it and the muscles in his arms twitched. Another dome of shimmering light spread out and flung the scorpion back. The beast hissed and its tail jerked from side to side.

"It's not working for me either." He held the Stone in front of his chest with both hands. "Perhaps it won't work the way our rings do for fighting. It's the Stone of Protection, after all. Perhaps all it does is protect us."

She pushed a strand of hair back from her eyes. "Good. We won't exhaust ourselves holding shields. I don't think I can just now."

"Now all we need to do is to get out of here." He glanced down at the body of the gazelle on the far side of the omphalos from her. "It's a pity I can't take that head as a trophy."

"You shall not leave," hissed the scorpion. "You shall not leave. You cannot leave. You will stay here and become the new bearers and anchors so that I will be the Shadow Scorpion still."

I don't know whether to believe that beast or not. She stared at the scorpion's cluster of eyes.

Farren sent out another golden barrier that pushed the scorpion back again. "If this Stone only works to protect, then it won't help us pass that barrier at the exit. We'll have to find a way to defeat the scorpion. At least we'll be safe while we do."

She smiled wryly. "The question is how to defeat it. We've already tried blasting the omphalos." She glanced at the low pillar of limestone. The blood staining the top had almost completely vanished, leaving only a few traces around the base on the grass. *That carving really has swallowed all the blood. I wonder...* She placed her palms over the carving, flinching at the chill that rose from the lines. "Keep that scorpion back. I'm going to try something."

She closed her eyes and opened herself up to the touch of Power. The chill of the carving fought against the natural warmth of the stone, and the edge of one line jabbed at the cut on her left hand. Energy prickled along her arms, into her wrists and through her fingertips. A flash rose from her hands, shining through her eyelids. Eyes watering, she looked down at the carving. It remained unchanged, though the chill had abated. Again she sent lightning into the rock, green light pulsing around her hands. *Two bolts should be enough. It was before.*

The scorpion hissed wordlessly again. "Fools! Fools! You cannot destroy me," it said. Its pincers clashed and as Azariel looked towards it, it lashed its sting against the bubble of light Farren sent out from the Stone. Foul-smelling ichor dribbled from the point. The scorpion staggered back a few paces, then lunged forwards again.

She bowed her head. *King of Heaven, give me wisdom. Even with the Stone of Wind, we can't keep that scorpion away forever. We'll have to sleep some time, even if the Stone won't put the scorpion to sleep. There must be a way to defeat it. There must be. Show me what it is.* She gritted her teeth and pressed against the carving a third time. *Perhaps if I try again.* Red light flickered from her hands, then the carving absorbed it. Her shoulders slumped and a cold weight settled into her stomach. *Still nothing.*

Thoughts swarmed through her mind. We're never going to defeat it. It's going to kill us or turn us into slaves. I can't think of a single way to defeat it and I'm so exhausted I can barely stand. Farren won't be able to stand there keeping it back without a rest. I don't know what to do. Nothing seems to work on the scorpion or on the omphalos. There must be a way, but I don't know what it is. Growling through her clenched teeth in frustration, she picked up a small lump of grey rock from the grass beside her knee and ground it against the carving.

Behind her, the scorpion shrieked. Fresh energy surging through her, she glanced back, hair whipping into her mouth. The scorpion's legs flailed and danced, and it clicked its mandibles and pincers. "What did you do?" she asked.

"Nothing that I haven't done a dozen times already. What did you do?"

She gasped and clutched the grey rock in her hand. "The carving! The carving drank the blood – a lot of blood, rather than a small smear – and that's somehow made the scorpion stronger. The carving is where the mist came from that formed the scorpion. The scorpion needs the carving in the omphalos. I'm going to destroy it." She pushed all her weight onto the stone and twisted, crushing the edges of the lines forming the stylised scorpion. The limestone crumbled and broke beneath the rock. She raised the rock and pounded the limestone carving again. Behind her, the shrieks of the scorpion grew louder, ringing in her ears. The cut on her hand flared with pain as she bore down on it, and the broken limestone scraped and grazed her fingers. She kept grinding at the carving until the muscles in her arms shook and burned.

The rock trembled in her hands as she lifted it once more. I'm spent. I can't do any more." She stared at the sting and the pincers, all that remained of the carving, then back at the scorpion itself as it staggered blindly to and fro in the centre. It blundered into the hedge and thrashed about, tail lashing.

"Let me do it." He lowered the Stone of Wind and pressed it into her left hand. The smooth surface of the gem eased the sting of her cut. Reaching around her, he took the grey rock. He pummelled the limestone, sending chips of rock and gravel flying. One struck her on the cheek, and she raised her hand to shield her face, fingers trembling.

The scorpion flailed legs, pincers and tail erratically, then shuddered. For half a heartbeat, it wavered before it collapsed. The impact of its fall trembled through the ground beneath her. The long black bulk of the scorpion lay motionless, then dissolved into black mist that thinned to grey, then white, and vanished. The sun's warmth struck down from the clear blue sky, and the northwest wind carried the fresh, clean scents of dry grass, clover and broom.

She slumped into the grass and lay on her back with the Stone of Wind resting between her breasts, a wave of relief washing over her. Her arms and legs felt heavy as bags of wet sand. Beside her, Farren knelt beside the omphalos, his head bowed and sweat beading his forehead. His chest and shoulders heaved with his breath. She closed her eyes and clasped her hands over the Stone, caressing the smooth surface and the network of silver. *It's over. We've done it. We've got the Stone. Thank the Power!*

The sun warmed the links of her chainmail and the black cotton of her trousers as she lay in the short grass. The wind hissed through the thorn hedges, and a skylark trilled in the distance. Closer, Farren breathed steadily and evenly. The acrid tang of what remained of the gazelle's blood made her nostrils twitch. Sleep hovered at the edges of her mind.

"Stormwolf? Are you all right?"

Her eyes opened a crack and she smiled at him. "Just exhausted. Once I've recovered my strength, we can leave the labyrinth."

He stood up and turned towards the carcass of the gazelle. "If you've got enough strength to shift shape, you can eat your fill."

She chuckled. "I think even that's beyond me at the moment." She shifted the Stone on her chest. "Are you going to take the head as a trophy?"

"I certainly will." He drew his sword. "Thank you for sparing the horns."

As he bent over the carcass, sword in hand, she let her eyelids fall closed again, mind drifting. A shadow fell across her and she jolted awake to see him leaning over her, holding the severed head by one horn. A smile twitched the corners of his mouth. "Wake up, sweetheart. We've got the Stone, we've got my trophy and it's time for us to go."

She sat up, clutching the Stone of Wind in one hand. "We've got to get your arrow back, too."

He wiped his sword clean on a longer patch of grass, then sheathed it. "No," he said, half laughing. "We can let one arrow go. I can't remember where it flew after I shot the gazelle, anyway. It would be a long search and I've had enough of that. Come on." He held out his free hand to her. "Let's go back to camp. It'll take us a full day tomorrow to reach the Watchtower of the North and put this where it belongs, and you're not the only one who needs a good rest."

"Then the sooner we start back, the better." She caught hold of his hand and clambered to her feet. Together, they made their way back along the path of the labyrinth, each step an effort. Finally, she stepped out of the shadow of the labyrinth into the sunshine. The wind caught her hair and blew it across her face. Below them, the Illin-y-Hyalda gleamed as the sunlight struck it, marking the border between the Kingdom and Wayast. She looked at the river, then down at the Stone of Wind in her hand. "Then the river won't guard the border alone." She held the jewel up and the silver glinted. "Three found and only one more to go. And thank the King of Heaven for that."

ABOUT THE AUTHOR

M.C. Foster spent a childhood reading Tolkien, mythology and folktales when she wasn't riding horses and climbing trees. She earned a B.A. (Hons) in Linguistics in 1996 from the University of Canterbury. She now lives in Southland, New Zealand, with her husband, a rescue dog, several chickens and a cat who is a terror to the local mice. When she's not writing, she enjoys growing organic vegetables, trying out local walking tracks and doing things with yarn... discovering in the process that it is very difficult to prick one's finger on a spinning wheel.